# In Her Own Footsteps

Flora Ross and Her Struggle for Identity
and Independence in the Colonial West

# In Her Own Footsteps

## Flora Ross and Her Struggle for Identity and Independence in the Colonial West

*A novel based on a true story*

D. J. Richardson

Butterwort
Books

Published by Butterwort Books, Los Angeles, California
www.butterwortbooks.com
www.djrichardson.ca
www.floraross.com

Library of Congress Cataloging-in-Publication Data:
Richardson, David John, [date]
In her own footsteps: Flora Ross and her struggle for
identity and independence in the colonial west / a
novel based on a true story / D.J. Richardson
ISBN 978-1-7352979-0-3 (hardcover)
ISBN 978-1-7352979-1-0 (softcover)
ISBN 978-1-7352979-2-7 (eBook)
1. LCSH Ross, Flora Amelia—Fiction. 2. British
Columbia—History—Fiction. 3. Pig War, Wash., 1859—
Fiction. 4. San Juan Islands (Wash.)—History—19th
century—Fiction. 5. Northwest boundary of the United
States—Fiction. 6. Métis—Fiction. 7. Women—Fiction. 8.
Historical fiction. 9. BISAC FICTION / Historical /
Canadian 10. FICTION / Historical / Civil War Era 11.
FICTION / Native American & Aboriginal
PS3618 .I534459 I64 2020
DDC 813.6--dc23
2020912501

Cover design by Britt Low, Covet Design
Illustrations of medicinal plants licensed from Vectorstock
Maps drafted by the author

Every character portrayed in this book was a real person. This book reflects an effort to tell their stories as accurately as surviving documents permit.

Documents, journals, and newspapers are quoted verbatim.

This book uses terms that are offensive by today's standards, but were commonly used in the era in which these events take place. These terms are used here as they were used then to help illustrate the culture in which Flora Ross lived, as demonstrated by some of the records that are quoted in this book. Their use is not intended to perpetuate offensive terminology in modern culture.

# Contents

# Introduction

This book uses the common label "based on a true story," but a more accurate (and longer) label might be "a true story to the extent surviving documents permit, after more than three decades of research." Every character with a name exists in this book because they existed in real life, and this book tells their stories as accurately as surviving records permit. The only invented name—Anna—is for a person whose name hasn't survived in the records. The vast majority of scenes in this book are based on evidence that such an event happened. In some cases the evidence is substantial, from multiple primary sources, such as newspapers, court records, letters, journals, and other such documents. In some cases the evidence is a single document to establish the likelihood of such an event, or the simple fact of a courtship or failing marriage that suggests certain domestic moments. If Flora is portrayed traveling on a boat from one town to another, with another character, it is because their names appear on a passenger list. If a character is in court or in jail, is ill or dies, it is because this is a documented event. This book is an effort to describe those events as they appear to have happened, to the best of my research abilities, because I find them to be so interesting that they don't need to be varied by imagination. That being said, I have had to invent ordinary domestic scenes that do not tend to be recorded in the historical record, and nearly all dialogue, but have used some dialogue recorded in newspapers or court documents. Of course I can't really know what any character was thinking, or most of what was said. But that is what makes this historical fiction rather than narrative non-fiction.

*D.J. Richardson*

# Disputed Boundary Region, 1859

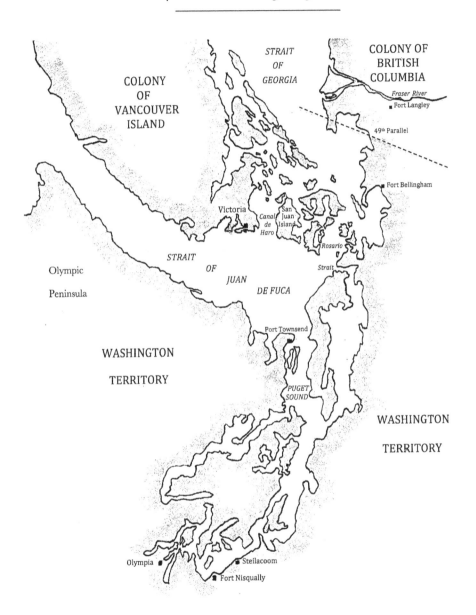

# Victoria, Colony of Vancouver Island, 1859

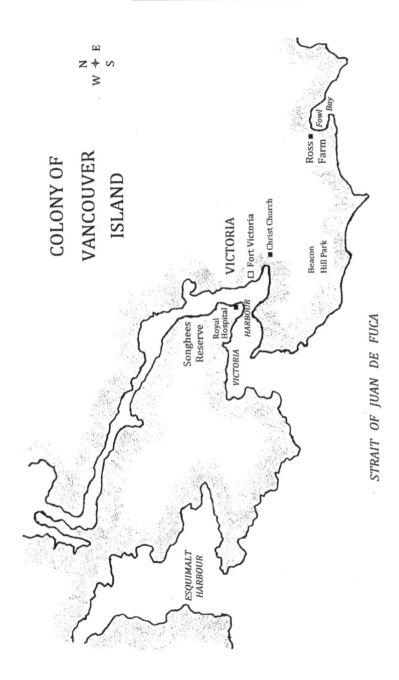

# Part One: Victoria

---

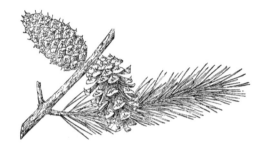

# Chapter 1

<u>Victoria, the British Colony of Vancouver Island,</u>
<u>December 31, 1858:</u>

Flora barely noticed the strong odor of whiskey on the breath of Capt. Jemmy Jones. Though only sixteen, Flora Amelia Ross had learned that there was nothing particularly out of the ordinary if a man's breath was laced with the scent of whiskey. A sip or two could keep the wintry chill at bay whenever cold winds swept in off the Pacific. And as it was mid-afternoon on New Year's Eve, 1858, and a winter storm was soaking the coastal region in a heavy, icy rain, there was little reason to question the foul scent on Jones' breath as he helped Flora, her sister, and her mother, aboard the small schooner, the *Wild Pigeon*.

Flora descended into the narrow passenger compartment and settled on a hard bench at the back, certain that the schooner's simple furnishings would soon become uncomfortable during their long journey, especially in such foul weather. A small, cast-iron stove against the starboard side appeared more useful at filling the boat with smoke rather than warmth, while a rusty lantern cast a pale light across the compartment. But it was the inch of seawater sloshing across the floor that she found especially troublesome. She would spend most of the journey watching the level of the water, though she had no idea how many inches would indicate that it was time to express her concerns. And even if the water wasn't the result of a leak in the hull, it was at the very least an annoyance, as she'd have to keep her heavy skirt and petticoats off the floor throughout the voyage.

The journey between Victoria and Nisqually, at the southern end of Puget Sound in Washington Territory, was a journey that Flora had traveled countless times, whether by schooner, steamer or canoe. But it had never been a journey undertaken under such anxious circumstances. Only a few hours earlier, the family had received word that eldest daughter, Elizabeth, who lived with her husband a few miles from the Company trading post at Nisqually, was gravely ill. Jones had delivered the letter in person to Flora's mother, Isabella Mainville Ross, after carrying it from Nisqually on one of his regular passenger and freight runs along the sound. Flora, her mother, and Mary, Flora's elder sister by two years, had frantically packed their belongings, abandoned the family farm in the care of the three youngest Ross brothers, and rushed to Victoria harbor.

Mary and Isabella settled in beside Flora. Neither of them spoke. Flora assumed it was because anything they might say other than concern for Elizabeth's health would seem trite. She glanced at the two men who were the only other occupants of the compartment, careful not to stare. They appeared to be in their late twenties and seemed well lubricated with whiskey. One was tall and blond, while the other was short and dark, reminding Flora of a pair of mismatched salt and peppershakers that sat on the family table. She surveyed their clothing and concluded that the men were most likely gold miners who had come to the colonies earlier that year to make their fortunes along the gravel banks of the Fraser River on the mainland. And, even more likely, they were now disappointed gold miners returning to the United States for the winter, as were nearly all of the thousands of men passing through Victoria in the winter of 1858. Flora wanted to tell the shorter miner that the legs of his canvas pants were resting in the water, soaking toward his knees. But it wasn't her place to offer such a comment. She knew it wouldn't be received as helpful advice.

"We be off now. All'a'ya comfy?" Jemmy Jones didn't bother to wait for a response before turning away. Flora presumed it was because he'd never been pleased with the answers of prior passengers. Jones was the owner of the *Wild Pigeon*, and an experienced sea captain who had plied the waters off the colony of Vancouver Island and the adjacent Washington Territory since the outset of the gold rush. He was the kind of man who caused just enough trouble to be a regular topic of whimsical conversation about town, while somehow avoiding any major crisis that might turn the whimsy into reprobation; though Flora had long ago concluded that the growing town of Victoria had far more entertaining characters of his type than it needed.

"You never said we'd be sharin' the cabin with a bunch of squaws," the shorter miner blurted at Jones. "Ain't there some boat haulin' cattle that can take 'em?"

Flora barely flinched. She had almost expected such an outburst. At least it had been delivered to Jones rather than at her mother, though the refusal to speak to the women directly was as much an intended insult as the words had been. Flora's mother was three-quarters Ojibway and one-quarter French-Canadian, while Flora's father had been Scottish. She could truthfully have insisted to the miners that most of the blood running through her veins was European in origin, if she thought the distinction mattered to them. But such a comment would have been pointless. For in the eyes of most white men in the small British colony, all three women were "Indians" or "squaws."

Jones paused by the cabin entrance.

"Mrs. Ross is one'a the matriarchs o' this colony. If you wanna git to Nisqually, you'll treat her and the young ladies like me own," Jones replied sternly in a thick Welsh accent before exiting the cabin.

The two miners tossed unpleasant looks in the direction of the Ross women. The taller miner's look was brief and determined, but the eyes of the shorter miner lingered, first on Flora, and then for a much longer time on Mary. When he had first cast his eyes on the women, his mouth had expressed disdain. But the longer he gazed on the two girls, the more his mouth slightly curled upward at the sides. It was almost a smile by the time he looked away, but there was nothing pleasant about it. She decided that she most definitely wouldn't mention the seawater that continued up the man's pant leg.

Flora had been told many times in recent years that she'd grown into an attractive young woman, and there were occasions when she'd been able to convince herself that it might be true. Her body had filled out in all the proper places, and her hourglass figure could compete with any girl's in town. But she also knew that the more eligible bachelors instantly dismissed her as a potential bride because of her features. Her Ojibway background was most prominent in her looks, or at least, apparent enough for many Englishmen or Americans to declare it her most prominent trait. Her thick dark hair, high cheekbones and dark eyes were far more like the features of her Ojibway ancestors than those of her Scottish ancestors. No man ever yelled "Scot" or "Sawney" in her direction. And if any man were to do so, it wouldn't have been delivered with the same derisive tone that accompanied "Indian" or "squaw."

A strong jolt shook the hull as the storm threw the boat against the dock without warning, instantly changing the topic in each passenger's mind. To escape the harbor and reach the Strait of Juan de Fuca, the schooner would need to sail west, into the strong winds, tacking from northwest to southwest, and back again across the small harbor. Flora pressed her face against one of the tiny, smoke-stained windows along the top of the passenger compartment and caught a glimpse of the dock slowly fading from view. The schooner leaned to the port side as it slowly advanced into the harbor, angled against the wind as if hoping to slip past the storm unnoticed. Isabella reached out to take her daughters' hands and recited a short Catholic prayer in French, a language that had been commonly used in the small community of Fort Victoria before the deluge of American gold miners had transformed the colony's culture. French and Ojibway had been the primary languages of her youth, while Chinook was her third, learned during her years at trading posts along the coast. She spoke only the basics of English, burdened by both a heavy accent and a measure of uncertainty. The prayer she recited was from her youth in the Great Lakes region far to the east. It sought safety for travelers, and Flora had heard it many times before. The young miners, however, had not. They exchanged a grimace that told Flora they couldn't differentiate between a Catholic prayer in French and whatever Indian ceremony the men assumed they were witnessing. But it appeared to provide the two miners with a temporary distraction from the fear that was still visible in their eyes; a fear that deepened as the schooner pitched to the starboard side, sending seawater spilling across the passenger compartment.

Flora grabbed a rail along the wall for support, letting go of her skirt and petticoats. A coldness quickly moved up her legs as the material absorbed the seawater. They were only minutes into their journey, yet traveling in the schooner's small passenger compartment was already proving to be a miserable experience. She told herself that at least the experience below deck was far better than that of Jones and his crewman, battling the winds above deck.

The hull of the *Wild Pigeon* slowly righted itself and then veered to the port side once again, as they returned to a southwesterly direction in search of an angle that would drive the vessel into the wind by using the brute force of the storm against itself. But it took only an instant for Flora, and each passenger in the compartment, to realize that something was wrong. The angle of the pitch quickly became far steeper than each prior tack, as the hull continued to lean farther to the port side, sending the sloshing seawater and passengers' belongings across the compartment. Flora held her breath and waited for the crew to adjust the sails so that the hull would ease its steep angle, but instead the hull careened to horizontal as the *Wild Pigeon* capsized.

Passengers. Belongings. Everything and everyone flew across the cabin, falling against the portside as it became the floor of the capsized cabin. The rusty lantern shattered one of the small windows as it fell. Its flame was instantly doused by seawater that bubbled up through the broken window, and by the deluge of water that poured in through the doorway that now lay horizontal to the surface of the bay. The wood stove creaked ominously as it hung above the passengers, and then broke free from its base, falling into the rising waters and striking Isabella on her right leg. She screamed in pain as the hot iron seared her skin through the material of her dress.

"Mama!"

It was the only word anyone spoke.

Seawater sputtered against the blistering iron of the hot stove, quickly smothering the last vestige of light from inside the stove and leaving the watery compartment in darkness. Flora and Mary pulled Isabella free from the hot iron of the stove, burning their hands, while the miners scrambled through the water to escape through the doorway.

Flora and Mary lifted Isabella toward the entryway, only to have their mother pull free from their grasp and push them ahead of her. Flora grasped the edges of the doorway and struggled to pull herself through the stream of water that continued to pour inside. A push from Mary propelled her into the open ocean where she found herself momentarily disoriented. There was no deck beneath her feet. Instead, the portion of the deck that wasn't submerged rose vertically beside her. Rigging swirled around her in the waves, while heavy rain pelted from above and the wind howled from the west.

A shout caught her attention. Jemmy Jones and his crewman reached down from their perch on the starboard side of the hull, above the waves, and hauled Flora out of the water. She grabbed the gunwale for support and crawled behind the two miners to leave room for Mary and her mother to follow.

Flora searched through the dim light and driving rain in an attempt to understand their circumstances. The *Wild Pigeon* was resting on its side just beyond the middle of the small harbor. The dim outline of Victoria was visible to the east, while the Songhees reserve was a few hundred feet to the west. No other vessels were in sight.

Isabella winced as she crawled along the hull and reached Flora, followed by Mary.

"Mama, let me see your leg," Flora insisted.

"*Ça va.*" Isabella waved her hand, dismissing her pain.

Flora ignored her mother's response and pulled Isabella's skirt high enough to reveal a large cut on her calf. The skin was red and burned by the stove, and blood poured steadily from the gash.

"You are not fine."

Flora reached down under her own skirt, grabbed the edges of her petticoats, and ripped off two strips of material. She folded one into a small bundle, squeezed out as much water as she could, and then placed it against her mother's cut. Mary placed her hand on the bandage to hold it in place as Flora used the second strip of her petticoats to tightly secure the bandage.

"Are we sinking? I think we're sinking."

It was one of the miners. Flora had forgotten about them.

"She winna g'down," Jones shouted over the wind, with less reassurance in his voice than Flora would have liked. "But someone needs to swim ashore. We canna sit here. Not in this storm."

Flora understood his meaning. They were all soaking wet, shivering, clinging to the exposed hull of the schooner in the middle of a winter storm. The boat might not sink, at least not immediately, but they would all perish if help didn't arrive soon. The shivering would escalate until the body could fight no more, and then, one by one, each of them would slide from the hull to be swallowed by the dark waters.

She glanced from the miners to Jones and his crewman, waiting for one of the men to rise to the challenge, but there was only silence.

"Surely you know how to swim?" she asked Jones.

He shook his head and grimaced, acknowledging the embarrassment of having spent his entire adult life piloting boats, yet never having learned how to swim. Flora turned to the miners. They lacked the energy to even shake their heads, and responded with only meek expressions of apology, either for being unable to swim, or for being too terrified to attempt to swim across the frigid harbor.

Flora glanced at Mary. They had grown up next to the ocean and were both accomplished swimmers, at least in warmer summer temperatures. But it was the middle of winter and they were already shivering. The likelihood that a cramp would set in before either of them could reach the shore was high, if not a certainty. Others had drowned in local waters in far warmer weather in recent years. No one would dare attempt a swim across the harbor in the middle of winter. Not if they had a choice. But the only choice she and Mary faced was which of them would go.

She avoided any discussion by opening the buttons of her dress. The heavy wool would provide no warmth in the water, but would only weigh her down and diminish the power of her legs.

"Are you sure?" Mary asked, with fear in her voice, clearly anxious about either answer.

"Yes," Flora insisted, revealing as much anxiousness in her own voice.

"*Flora, non, je te l'interdis*," Isabella pleaded, reaching up to grab Flora's hand.

"I have to, mama. We can't sit here. You know we can't."

Flora squeezed her mother's hand, then pulled away and struggled to pull off her dress, a task made far more difficult by the wetness of the material and the shivering of her muscles. Mary reached forward and helped until Flora was wearing only her petticoats, exposed to the bitter winds, and to unwelcome stares from the four men. They were incapable of swimming to shore, or at least unwilling, yet were eminently capable of displaying urges that appeared to be more powerful than their urge to survive.

Flora draped her wet dress over Isabella, hoping it might provide additional warmth. Isabella pulled her close and kissed her on the cheek.

"*Va avec Dieu*," Isabella whispered.

Flora smiled nervously, then turned to Mary.

"Watch the bleeding on her leg."

She turned and faced the harbor to the east. The distance wasn't impossible, but circumstances made it far too improbable.

"Go 'round the sails. Dinna get caught up in the riggin'," Jones advised her.

She nodded, then crawled along the side of the hull to the bow and searched for her target. Kaindler's Wharf. It was the largest wharf in the harbor and was sure to be a place where she could find help, even on New Year's Eve. She looked back at her mother one last time, and then dove into the dark water.

The shock of the cold was as emotional as it was physical. Already shivering, she had expected the water to be comparable to the frigid air. Instead, the iciness of the water penetrated her muscles and chilled her body to the bone.

Instinct drove her arms to strike against the waves and push her aching leg muscles to kick, while the struggle to keep her head above the churning whitecaps took as much energy as each stroke. A frantic fight against the waves would ensure a deadly cramp, and so she focused on slow, steady strokes. The choppiness of the surface left her unable to sense if she was making any progress, or merely waving her limbs in the same location. But she resisted the urge to look behind her, knowing it would be a wasted use of limited energy, and fearful that she might see the *Wild Pigeon* just yards away.

A distant shout caught her attention. She struggled to peer across the whitecaps and managed to glimpse three men on shore, one of them pointing in her direction, though she couldn't tell if the men had spotted her or the capsized schooner behind her. They weren't far from Kaindler's Wharf, by the boathouse of the Whitehall Boatmen's Society. Flora shouted back at the men, pleading for help in the loudest voice she could manage, then shifted course and aimed for the men rather than the wharf. She considered for a moment that she might be able to tread water until they could reach her in a boat. But she dismissed the thought just as quickly, realizing that the men from the Whitehall Boatmen's Society might have already started celebrating the coming New Year, just as Jemmy Jones had done before he'd left the safety of shore. Flora reached out and pulled herself through the waves with another stroke, certain that it was better to rely on her own strength than anyone else's.

\* \* \*

Flora watched as Dr. John S. Helmcken carefully stitched the wound in her mother's leg under the flickering light of both a lantern and the fire that crackled in the stone fireplace of the physician's cabin. She desperately wanted to move closer to the flames to warm her chilled body, but knew better than to block the doctor's light.

"I hope we don't keep you from Reverend Cridge's New Year's service," Flora offered.

"It's nothing to trouble yourself with. I'm quite certain Reverend Cridge will be thoroughly grateful I'm tending to a patient rather than adding my voice to the congregation's hymns, especially since the patient is your mother."

Flora nodded. Despite her polite question, she'd been far less concerned about the imposition they were causing Helmcken than about each hour that passed when they hadn't yet reached Elizabeth's bedside. She pushed her fears from her mind and leaned in to get a closer look at Helmcken's work. It had always fascinated her that human skin could be sewn together like the fabric of her dress. It was a fascination that her sister didn't share. Mary had placed herself on the far side of the cabin where she could see none of the doctor's efforts.

Helmcken had been a novice physician when he'd arrived at Fort Victoria from London in late 1850. Now, at thirty-four, he was the leading practitioner in the growing town, combining his medical practice with his political role as the Speaker of the colony's small and insular Legislative Assembly. The cabin that served as his home and office sat along the southeastern shore of the small harbor, making it the obvious destination for the Ross women as soon as they'd been pulled from the harbor's icy waters. Helmcken had set about treating the wound on Isabella's leg while his wife, Cecilia, had brought dry clothes of her own for the women to wear, insisting that their dresses be hung by the fire to dry before she'd allow them back out into the storm.

Helmcken tied off the ends of the last stitch and then turned to Isabella.

"In any other circumstances, I'd tell you to stay in bed for a week. But I understand the need to get to Nisqually."

"She is my daughter," Isabella replied, waving off her own medical concerns.

"Of course. And you have my deepest sympathies."

"Dr. Tolmie should be there," Flora offered. "Couldn't he look over mama's leg after we get there?"

"Yes, get him to take a look, make sure an infection hasn't taken hold. In the meantime, young lady, I'm counting on you to keep the dressing moistened with oil of turpentine. Also," he paused, reaching for a small bottle, "some blue pills, of my own concoction, which you all might need if the journey's rough. Though not as rough as today, let's hope and pray."

Flora felt herself flush as Helmcken handed her the pills, and she desperately hoped that none of the others had noticed. She had known Helmcken since she'd been a young girl. At barely nine years of age, she'd been sent by her mother from the family farm in Nisqually to join two of her brothers, to be schooled within the log palisades of Fort Victoria by the wife of Reverend Staines, Cridge's predecessor. In those early days, when the trading fort had been the area's sole settlement, the few girls who'd attended Mrs. Staines' school had been boarded in a second-story room above the Fort's bachelor's barracks, where Helmcken and the other single men resided.

Helmcken had seemed to Flora and her friends to be one of the Company's old men, at a time in her life when anyone over the age of eighteen was unquestionably ancient. But now, just a few months from turning seventeen, she had come to realize that some of the "old" men of the Fort—while still unquestionably old—were within an acceptable age for marriage to a young woman, and in some cases were even quite handsome. Of all the old-timers, the girls of Flora's age generally agreed that Helmcken was the most attractive. He was of average height for a Scotsman, with a square face that was framed by an unruly shock of black hair, a strong, dimpled chin, and a close-cropped beard. Although he often remarked that his head was too large for his own body, what people noticed most about him were the dark twinkling eyes that put every patient at ease—except, of course, those young female patients who found the twinkle to cause an embarrassing flush.

Flora was certain she wasn't supposed to notice such things about a man she'd known as her family's doctor and friend, particularly one who was now happily married to the Governor's eldest daughter. But she told herself that as long as such thoughts remained in her own mind, they were entirely harmless.

"Do you think you might have medication that could help Elizabeth," Flora asked. "Something Dr. Tolmie might not have that we should take with us?"

"A reasonable question, my dear, but it would surprise me to no end if there were anything in my cabinets that Tolmie doesn't have in greater quantities."

Cecilia brought cups of tea to each of the Ross women to help warm them inside.

"I sent our Indian boy up to John's farm to let him know you're here," she informed them, "but he just came back and said no one was home. I suppose that isn't a surprise on New Year's Eve."

John was the eldest Ross son who ran his own farm northeast of the town. He had been the family patriarch since Flora's father, Charles Ross, had died of appendicitis while overseeing the construction of Fort Victoria, leaving behind nine children and a pregnant wife. Flora, who was barely two at the time, had no real memories of her father. Her brother John, and family friends like Helmcken, Reverend Cridge, and Dr. Tolmie, had all filled the paternal role in her life.

"Now," Helmcken began, turning to Isabella while cleaning up his medical supplies, "I insist you walk as little as possible."

"We can get a wagon out to Muck Creek," Flora suggested. "Mama shouldn't have to walk much at all."

It seemed a logical solution, though the thought of finding a wagon at Nisqually wasn't a matter of immediate concern. They would have a much greater challenge finding a boat to replace the *Wild Pigeon*. None of them expected to locate a sober captain well into New Year's Eve who'd be willing to start the journey in the midst of a storm. And even finding a sober captain in the early hours of New Year's Day would likely prove a challenge. In the meantime, they would return to a farm that had been left in the hands of her three youngest brothers. Each had a weakness for whiskey, and all three were likely to be well into their own New Year's celebrations. An unannounced return might reveal the boys carousing with friends, or a farm that was entirely deserted.

Helmcken seemed to share her thoughts. "Well then, since we've already agreed that I won't be destroying hymns at church this evening, far better I get the horses hitched to the wagon and accompany the three of you back to the farm for the night."

Flora joined her mother and Mary in protesting the inconvenience his offer would present to him, but only for a moment. A cold draft whistled through the cabin and reminded her of the storm that still raged beyond the log walls. She stepped closer to the fire, confident that its light was no longer required for her mother's treatment, and relieved that she wouldn't be walking the two miles home in the rain.

* * *

Paul Kinsey Hubbs, Jr. gazed about the confines of his small log cabin and pondered whether he should tidy the scattered messes of books, papers, unwashed dishes, and similarly unwashed clothing. His guests—due at any moment—were unlikely to have any expectations for New Year's Eve other than free-flowing whiskey, particularly given that their host was a bachelor in his mid-twenties. But Hubbs was also the sole representative of the United States government on San Juan Island, and his half-dozen guests were the only other Americans on the island; each a gold miner who had claimed a small homestead on the island after failing to secure a fortune along the Fraser River. He decided that the appropriate measure of decorum required something more civilized than cheap whiskey served amidst dirty dishes and laundry, and proceeded to tidy the cabin.

For nearly two years since his appointment as Deputy Inspector of Customs for the archipelago, Hubbs had lived in the small cabin along the southern shore of San Juan Island, and had been the lone American in the area. Hubbs would fulfill his duties each quarter by issuing a tax notice to Bellevue Farm, the Hudson's Bay Company sheep farm located a hundred yards to the east, which he would nail to a fence post or doorframe. He always understood that the British company would ignore it and that the taxes would never be paid. His role had been intended as a figurehead position from the outset to ensure an official U.S. government presence on the island while the Northwest Boundary Commission attempted to resolve the last remaining disagreements over the location of the northern United States border. But he also felt a lingering frustration over the seeming pointlessness of his task and the loneliness of his setting.

Until recently, the only people who called the island home were the workers at the Hudson's Bay Company's farm, Hubbs, and the occasional encampment of local Indians, most often during the late summer salmon run. Despite the minimal population, it was a matter of general agreement that San Juan Island would be a strategic military post for whichever country was ultimately awarded its possession, as control of the island would ensure control of the Strait of Juan de Fuca, the American Puget Sound and the British Strait of Georgia. The strategic military potential of the island meant that there was far too much at stake to simply sit back and wait for the boundary commission to complete its endless negotiations and surveys.

Hubbs opened the door to his cabin and surveyed the weather. On a sunny day, his door would open to a view of the southern shore of the island, and the distant mountains of the Olympic Peninsula of Washington Territory across the vast Strait of Juan de Fuca. On this cold afternoon, the view was hidden behind a thick veil of grey rain. Were he hosting guests in a town like Port Townsend, such a hostile winter storm would have kept most invitees huddled in their homes, close to the fire. But the half-dozen Americans that Hubbs had welcomed to the island in recent months had survived the harsh conditions of the Fraser River gold rush. A little rain wasn't about to spoil their first New Year's Eve on their new island home.

More than thirty thousand Americans had trekked to the Fraser canyon in 1858, driven by dreams of gold. Nearly all would return disappointed, and most would pass through the archipelago on their return. If a half-dozen already had opted to homestead a claim on the island rather than return to a more distant home, then Hubbs was certain that dozens more, perhaps hundreds more, would arrive in the coming months. The more Americans on the island, the more difficult it would be for the boundary commission to award the island to the British colony of Vancouver Island. Possession could ensure title, of that Hubbs was certain. And until recently, it had been the Hudson's Bay Company's Bellevue Farm that possessed the entire island—apart from Hubbs' own tiny cabin—with scattered sheep runs, shepherd's cabins and cattle fields. But each American that arrived on San Juan Island could tip the issue in favor of the United States, even if the immediate result was increased tension between the two sides.

Hubbs had fought in several wars and skirmishes in his twenty-six years, both against and among Indians along the coast and throughout Washington Territory. A political war over a boundary might involve different tactics. Shots might not be fired and lives might not be lost. But it was a war, nonetheless. One side would win. One side would lose. And the winning side would possess and control the archipelago of islands that included San Juan Island.

A dim movement caught Hubbs' attention. Out in the strait, barely visible through the rain, a canoe traveled swiftly to the east. A large northern Indian canoe. Locals seemed unable to agree on a spelling for the proper name of the tribe from the Queen Charlotte Islands—the Hyders, the Haidah, the Haida—opting most commonly for "northern Indians." Hubbs had lived with northern Indians for three years, when youthful wanderlust and a falling out with his father had led him north for adventure. He had been accepted, had taken a bride, and had participated in all manners of tribal life, including warfare in canoes similar to the one passing in front of his cabin. But Hubbs was no longer a guest of the northern Indians. He was back among white society, even if his isolated cabin sat on the edge of that society. He was now an official of the United States Government. And he was a target.

The canoe passed in a straight line to the east and made no diversion toward shore. But Hubbs couldn't simply presume that the canoe would continue its trajectory. He grabbed his coat and musket, hurried out into the heavy rain, and scrambled along the muddy path that traversed the ridge to the east, toward the Hudson Bay Company's Bellevue Farm. The natives would be outnumbered by the farm's workers if they were to launch an attack, but a surprise attack could cause substantial damage and casualties. The farm had been Hubbs' refuge when the Clallams had attacked his cabin a year earlier. Despite their political differences, each would be expected to warn and protect the other.

Hubbs made no effort to remain hidden behind the low brush and grass that covered the hillside above the beach.

The occupants of the canoe would already know of his presence. Far better to stand his ground and perhaps give the impression by his confidence that he wasn't one lone man with a musket.

He slowed his pace as he reached the edge of Bellevue Farm since the canoe had already passed beyond the farm, and seemed unlikely to have San Juan Island as its destination. He considered continuing on to the farm to ensure that they were aware of the passing canoe in case it might return, but then noticed two of the farm's workers standing south of the cabins, watching the canoe disappear into the veil of gray rain.

Hubbs regarded several of the farm's workers as friends, or as close to the concept as he had come to find on the island. Perhaps now, with more Americans arriving on the island, there would be others to fill that role. He waved to acknowledge that they had all noticed the canoe, then turned back, suddenly concerned that the first canoe might have been a diversion to draw him from his cabin. He picked up his pace, recognizing that his paranoia was probably undeserved, but anxious to get out of the rain and back to his dilemma of frontier bachelor etiquette.

He considered his options as he navigated his steps along the muddy path, and concluded that hiding the dirty dishes beneath the soiled laundry provided the quickest means of tidying his cabin. It seemed the perfect compromise to ensure that the former miners would feel welcome in his home rather than intimidated by unnecessary pretensions, though the hidden dishes might also add additional odor to the unwashed laundry if he didn't get around to either of them soon.

Hubbs reached his cabin to discover that he had left the door open and lost the hours of accumulated warmth he had coaxed from his fireplace. He closed the door behind him and threw two more logs onto the fire as a defense against the winter storm that whistled through the cracks in the cabin's log walls. He calculated how long it might take to finish his remaining tasks, and concluded that he had more than enough time for a drink. The glass of whiskey that he poured wasn't an effort to delay his chores, he assured himself, but was a silent celebration of the year that lay ahead. Whatever the political ramifications might be, or however many Americans might settle on the disputed island, 1859 was certain to be a far less lonely year for Paul Kinsey Hubbs, Jr. than 1858 had been.

\* \* \*

Lucinda Boyce's water broke as she struggled to light a fire in the wind and rain, in an attempt to cook her dinner on the small patch of dirt outside her tent. She hadn't expected the baby to arrive for another few weeks, but pains that had escalated all afternoon had left little doubt that her third child would arrive with the New Year, in the midst of the storm. Nearly all of the residents who occupied the hundreds of canvas tents surrounding the fledgling town of Victoria were men, mostly American men, and gold miners without families. But Lucinda had managed to find a family a few days earlier that had agreed to take in her two sons for a day or two when the baby arrived. Frank, barely seven, and Orrin, only five, were the product of Lucinda's first two marriages, both of which had left her a young widow. The boys would be a burden during the delivery, so it had been a relief to find someone to watch over them.

Lucinda finally managed to get a small flame burning. She'd need to keep a fire going all night to protect herself and the newborn from the damp winter chill that was blowing in from the Pacific Ocean. The driving rain that poured down onto the soaked firewood made it unlikely that she'd have warmth for long.

Heavy clouds blanketed the winter sky and erased the last of the afternoon's light. It seemed another world from the vivid colors that had greeted her when she'd arrived from California a few months earlier, when the summer sky had been deep blue, and vegetation had glowed in vibrant greens. Now, it was as if the winter's chill had drained the color from her surroundings, leaving only variations of gray. There had been many days in the summer when the rolling hillsides of white canvas tents surrounding the small trading fort and its growing town had appeared romantic, when the hundreds of tents had gently fluttered in the breeze like petals of a massive flower unfolding in the summer's warmth. But in recent weeks, there had been far more days when tents had been ripped from their stakes by the winds, and when any pretense of romance had been lost to the harsh realities of facing winter with nothing more for protection than a thin sheet of canvas.

Lucinda had sent a neighbor to fetch the midwife—an Indian woman from the Songhees reserve across the harbor—once the contractions had confirmed that the birth was imminent. She had chosen the Indian midwife with the certainty that a woman who'd lived her entire life in a northern climate would be most able to ensure a safe delivery. Although Lucinda was a nurse by profession, she knew better than to deliver her own child without assistance. The child would be arriving in the midst of winter, in a tent city filled with restless miners who were all far drunker than usual on this eve of the New Year, where clean water was some distance away and raw sewage ran down every muddy pathway.

Her only fear was the possibility of complications, as Victoria had nothing in the way of hospital facilities for women. Reverend Cridge had opened a tiny infirmary a few months earlier, but it served only male patients, and just a half dozen of those at any one time. The few women who lived in the colony received medical attention in their own homes, even if that home was a tiny canvas tent.

She had never expected to be alone by the time the child arrived. Her husband, Stephen, should have returned from the Fraser River before winter had set in. Freezing temperatures and higher water levels made gold panning and sluicing nearly impossible and extremely dangerous. But Stephen had yet to return.

She silently cursed the hesitant flames as they consumed the kindling without making any impact on the two damp logs other than to generate a thick plume of smoke. She rummaged through her pile of firewood in the hope of finding a piece that was dry enough to catch alight just as a sharp contraction winded her. It was a strong one, but still far enough from its predecessor that it was clear she had a long night ahead of her.

* * *

Amor De Cosmos squinted through the dim lamplight at the type set for page two of the next day's *British Colonist* newspaper, the fourth edition of the new weekly paper. He had already set the type for the entire page when news had arrived that the *Wild Pigeon* had capsized in the harbor, with Mrs. Ross and two of her daughters among the passengers.

De Cosmos had only been in the newspaper business for four weeks, but it was enough journalistic experience to permit him to recognize that the capsizing of a vessel with the matron of one of the colony's founding families onboard qualified as "news," whereas most of the type already set into place qualified more as political protest or idle gossip. The editorial on the future of Victoria was untouchable. It had taken him most of a day to perfect his wording and he wasn't about to edit it down any further. The anonymous letter to the editor complaining about the ineptitude of certain government officials was equally sacrosanct, echoing (and not by mere coincidence) his own personal views. And while the piece congratulating the Sisters of St. Ann on the establishment of their new school was more than a month past the school's official opening, Bishop Demers had purchased an advertisement in the next two issues to announce the school's curriculum and tuition costs, taking up an eighth of a page. That sort of advertising support deserved a corresponding article regardless of its timeliness.

De Cosmos reluctantly opted to remove the list of recent steamer arrivals from San Francisco and Puget Sound, partly because the list accomplished no particular political goal, but primarily because it occupied a small area of space. It would take far less time to re-set the page with a short article about the capsizing of the *Wild Pigeon* than a long one, even if that meant omitting many of the details. De Cosmos adjusted his oil lamp, settled into his chair, and began removing the type.

* * *

Flora closed the door to Isabella's small second-floor bedroom, thankful that she and Reverend Edward Cridge had convinced her mother that she needed sleep. It was only when Alexander, the middle Ross brother, had returned home to announce that he had found a captain willing to make the journey at dawn, once he'd be relatively sober, that Isabella had relented and agreed that she could steal a few hours' sleep.

Isabella Ross was not a woman to be sent to bed by her children, no matter how serious an injury or illness might be. She had been born in the Michilimackinac region where three of the Great Lakes converge. She'd followed her husband across the frontier as he was posted to successive Hudson's Bay Company trading forts, traveling throughout Rupert's Land and New Caledonia, where there were neither roads nor colonial settlements. They'd defended themselves against hostile locals and established new trading posts in unforgiving climates. And she had birthed and raised ten children, the last of them born after she had already been widowed. A cut on her leg and a minor burn were not cause to rush to her bed, especially while her eldest daughter lay on a bed of her own—possibly her deathbed—just a short journey away. In earlier years, Isabella would have bundled the children into the canoe of local Indians she would hire for the journey. Company steamers had plied local waters for years, but the luxury of commercial vessels for both passengers and freight was a novelty that had arrived just a year earlier along with the gold miners.

Flora returned to the kitchen at the back of the farmhouse to find Cridge pulling on his overcoat by the fire.

"Can I get you a cup of tea before you leave?" she asked.

"Thank you, Flora, but I imagine Mrs. Cridge is waiting up for this old man, so I best be going."

Cridge wasn't old by any statistical measure, barely into

his forties, but his high forehead and choice of a beard with no moustache did little to contest his own assessment. He had a habit of referring to himself as an "old man" around his younger congregants and they rarely attempted to correct him.

Flora hadn't been surprised when Cridge had arrived at the house an hour earlier. Visits from Cridge were a regular occurrence, whether socially motivated or for the chance to sit and pray with the women of the Ross family. He would have heard of the capsizing during his New Year's Eve service, and there would have been no question in his mind that his pastoral care was required at the Ross farm. Dr. Helmcken would have tended to Isabella's physical injury, but the anxiety Isabella would carry from the fear that she might not arrive at Nisqually before her eldest daughter passed away was Cridge's territory to address.

"I trust all will go well in the morning and you'll be at Elizabeth's bedside before you know it," Cridge offered, with a tone that suggested more hope than certainty.

"I'm sure it will," Flora agreed with a similarly hesitant tone. She was relieved that Alexander had located a boat and captain, both for the certainty of knowing that their journey would resume in a matter of hours, and for the reassurance that there would be no reason for her to attempt to scour the docks at dawn for transportation. She was certain it would be considered thoroughly improper for her to be seen along the docks, inquiring among the smaller schooners, even under the dire circumstances.

The distinctive peel of Christ Church's two bells echoed faintly in the distance, announcing the arrival of 1859. Cridge smiled in relief.

"In my haste to get here, I forgot to ask anyone to tend to the bells. Perhaps I'm not as necessary around there as I like to think. Flora, my dear, may 1859 be a year of great blessings for you and your family."

Cridge's smile faded as he paused by the door, as if realizing that his wish to Flora had failed to adequately address her fears. "And I will pray for Elizabeth."

# Chapter 2

Wednesday 5ᵗʰ
Light northerly air, beautiful day, hard frost
during the night with a sprinkling of snow. –
All hands putting up log fence. L'Gamine
with oxen hauling logs. –

Bellevue Farm Post Journal, San Juan Island, Hudson's
Bay Company, Wednesday, January 5, 1859.

✳ ✳ ✳

"They all look so old," Mary Ross insisted while busily
poking a stick into a thicket of wild rose to knock its dusting
of snow to the ground. "Don't you think so? Dr. Tolmie,
especially. He's turned completely grey. Did you notice?
Flora, did you notice?"

Flora had noticed, but she was too preoccupied driving
a pickaxe into the hard, frozen ground to pay much
attention to her sister's ramblings. Besides, grey hair suited
Tolmie. Some people grow into the look that suits them the
most, and sometimes that look is being old and grey.
Tolmie had always seemed slightly odd in appearance, with

a prominent bald head protruding from a thick black beard and a mass of dark curls above his ears. It was a look that used to intimidate Flora when she'd been a young girl living at Nisqually, even though she'd known she had no reason to be afraid of the man who'd been a father figure to the younger Ross children. But now, with his look tempered by the change from black to grey, it made sense, as if all parts of his body had finally agreed on the image to present.

"I wonder if Mrs. Tolmie looks as old as him?" Mary continued. "She used to be so pretty."

"She's about the same age as Elizabeth. That's not old," Flora answered, before deciding that thirty was, in fact, rather old.

Flora drove the pickaxe into the ground a second time, wishing she had an easier way of breaking through the cold frost to reach the Sumac roots that she and Mary had been sent to gather. Sumac roots, dogwood bark, salal leaves and trailing blackberry roots were their task, each an ingredient for traditional indigenous medicines that their mother would prepare in an effort to cure Elizabeth's dysentery. By all appearances, it was a beautiful day for their task. The air smelled fresh from the storm that had passed, the sky glowed a deeper blue than usual, and a blanket of snow sparkled in the bright sunlight. But it was a sunlight that also taunted the girls; a low winter sun promising warmth that would never arrive, while warning of an imminent and rapid nightfall. Flora aimed the pickaxe at the cold soil for a third blow, but the hard ground refused to yield, as if determined to protect the precious roots.

A feeling of pointlessness pervaded her efforts. Elizabeth had shown no awareness of her mother and sisters' arrival, and appeared so weak that it seemed unreasonable to maintain hope for a recovery. There seemed little to do other than find the ingredients her mother required for her traditional remedies to complement each medicine that Dr. Tolmie had to offer. Flora was grateful for the opportunity to help, but hated to be away from the Wren farmhouse in case Elizabeth might have a lucid moment while they were away. Her anxiousness was tempered slightly by the peaceful silence of the forest in winter, broken only by the occasional gust of wind, and the more frequent gusts of Mary's social observations about the multitude of family members and close friends who filled the Wren farmhouse.

"And Uncle Henry looks old, too," Mary continued. "Well, he always looked old, I s'pose. They've all changed so much."

"I imagine they're all saying something similar about us. We look different now, too."

"But we look better."

Flora smiled at her sister's comment, knowing it was meant as humor, but also knowing that it was an accurate statement of Mary's views.

"And Mr. Wren's as handsome as ever."

"Mary!" Flora knew that Mary meant no disrespect to Elizabeth, to be commenting on her husband's appearance while Elizabeth lay dying. But it was poorly timed, rather inappropriate, and most of all, inaccurate. Flora had always found Charles Wren's appearance to be somewhat off-putting. If there was a handsome man behind the unruly hair, wispy beard and darting black eyes, he had perfected the art of hiding it. Flora understood the value of such a look in a society as rough as the one in which they all lived. But she also failed to understand what Elizabeth had ever seen in the man.

"I don't mean nothing by it. It's just what he is. Don't you think so?"

Flora considered whether Mary actually wanted to hear her opinion, or if she had only spoken her thoughts as a means of gauging her own reaction to hearing them aloud. She concluded that silence was the best response to avoid further discussion, then turned back to her task and drove the pickaxe into the soil a fourth time, finally breaking the stubborn soil apart and exposing the meaty roots of the young sumac.

\* \* \*

In the twenty-seven years since Dr. William Fraser Tolmie

had graduated from Glasgow University's medical school, he had always found the hardest task of his job to be the delivery of news that a loved one's illness would most certainly be terminal. But delivering news of this kind had never seemed as difficult as it would be to deliver to the members of the Ross family who filled the Wren farmhouse.

Tolmie had met Isabella and her family in the late 1830s, when he had travelled between Hudson Bay Company trading posts along the coast of what was then known as New Caledonia, but had since become known as British Columbia. Few men in the colonies performed a single occupation, and medicine had been only a part of Tolmie's duties with the Company. He'd spent his years since running Fort Nisqually for the Company's affiliate, the Puget Sound Agricultural Company, while raising a family with his wife, Jane, herself a product of the Hudson's Bay Company elite of Fort Victoria. Isabella had moved her family to the Nisqually area in 1846, two years after the death of her husband at Fort Victoria, and had resettled the family in a farmhouse on the delta. Known soon after as "Rossville," the farm became a social hub for the settlers of Isabella and Tolmie's generation. Two of the elder Ross sons became trusted employees of Tolmie's, and a bond was established with the entire Ross family that endured long after Isabella and the younger children returned to Fort Victoria in 1852.

Elizabeth, the eldest of the Ross daughters, was barely seventeen when the family moved to Nisqually. She had only just returned from a brief time in England, where her father had sent her and two of her brothers shortly before his death, in the hope that some time in the mother country would balance the harsh upbringing the older children had received at the Company's remote trading posts. Elizabeth had been strong and independent, like her mother, and after marrying Charles Wren in 1847, had helped her husband build a large and thriving farm on Lower Muck Creek. But it was a strength that Tolmie could barely remember as he gazed on her pale and sunken face. Elizabeth's body had been weakened by a difficult childbirth. She had survived the lengthy trauma, but the child had not. Once dysentery set in, Elizabeth had lacked the strength to fight, and no medicine that Tolmie might try was likely to alter the outcome. The plasters he applied were having no significant effect, but neither were the many remedies that her family members had been concocting. At least the Laudanum he administered, a derivative of opium, was helping to address any pain and anxiety. Even if that were the only benefit of his medicine, it was far preferable to deferring entirely to the traditional remedies that Isabella would apply.

Tolmie gazed out the window, desperate for a distraction. His eyes were drawn to the large barn that Wren had built several years before. It was the largest barn in the region, probably one of the largest in Washington Territory, and Tolmie was itching to get inside to look around. He knew he shouldn't be thinking such thoughts, but he relished the chance to escape mentally from the sickbed that was transitioning into a deathbed. The barn was almost outlandish in size, as if Wren had intended for it to advertise the wealth he'd acquired not just as a farmer, but also as a shrewd businessman. Perhaps it was jealousy that had inspired others to start the rumors. They were, after all, just rumors. But as the Superintendent for the Puget Sound Agricultural Company, Tolmie couldn't ignore his company duties simply because he was acting at the moment in his capacity as the Nisqually region's primary physician. The company's cattle, the cattle of settlers in the area, and horses, as well, had gone missing in numbers far higher than local predators could account for, while Wren's herd had seemed immune to the problems. Tolmie didn't want to judge Wren on the basis of rumors, but it hurt to be so close to the massive barn, yet unable to venture inside to investigate.

Tolmie turned back to face the bed where Elizabeth lay, struggling to breathe, cared for by Isabella and Catherine, the second oldest Ross daughter. Like Elizabeth, Catherine had married and remained in Washington Territory. It was a scene that Tolmie frequently encountered when caring for a member of a mixed-blood family, which were most of the families in this frontier region. Successive generations of women would care for the sick, teaching their daughters in the process. Medicine men still practiced their ways on the Nisqually reserve and elsewhere in the Territory, at least those who hadn't been murdered by kinsmen when they'd proven incapable of curing western diseases that frequently decimated their tribes. But Wren would never have allowed a medicine man to treat his wife, even though he was himself of mixed blood. Allowing Elizabeth's mother and sisters to make harmless teas would keep them occupied and limit their emotional outbursts. But a shaman in his house would have been an unacceptable intrusion.

The door opened and Flora entered, flushed from the cold outdoor air. Her eyes immediately fell on Elizabeth, searching for some sign of improvement. She turned to her mother.

"We found all of them."

Isabella rose from her chair and attempted to put weight on her injured leg.

"Mama, no, let me," offered Catherine, but Isabella steadied herself and brushed away the offer.

"*Je peux le faire*," Isabella insisted as she moved toward the door.

"I insist you let me help you on the stairs," Tolmie demanded, stepping forward to take Isabella's arm. "If you won't listen to me and stay off that leg, the least I can do is ensure you don't tumble down the stairs."

Tolmie guided Isabella down the stairs and into the entryway of the large farmhouse. As they turned toward the kitchen at the back they passed several family members in the parlor. Tolmie briefly caught the eye of Charles Wren, then quickly looked away, afraid that his expression would reveal that he had difficult news to deliver but hadn't yet found the courage to begin delivering it in the proper familial order.

Tolmie and Wren had known one another for nearly twenty years, and Wren had spent the early years of their acquaintance as one of Tolmie's employees at Fort Nisqually. Though Tolmie had often developed strong friendships with many of his employees, the Ross sons among them, he had always felt tension with Wren. That tension had escalated with the increasing rumors of cattle rustling, and it was present even as Tolmie tried to save the life of Wren's wife.

Tolmie escorted Isabella to the kitchen where Flora had already cleaned and sorted the roots and leaves she had gathered.

"Mama, look."

Flora held up a small bulbous growth emerging from the side of a sumac branch. Tolmie wasn't entirely sure of its purpose, but of all the ingredients spread out on the kitchen table, it was the one that hadn't yet been found and tried. Curiosity compelled him to step aside and watch Isabella prepare a decoction from the fungus and other ingredients, though he had little expectation that it would make any difference in the news he'd deliver when the moment seemed right. Many local remedies had become standard ingredients in the pills, plasters and other decoctions and concoctions that doctors would administer. But Tolmie was usually hesitant about adopting new ingredients into his own remedies until he'd experienced their effectiveness firsthand.

He watched Flora carefully peel the sumac roots of their dark, outer bark, only to discard the peelings entirely. The sought-after ingredient was the softer inner bark, which she gently peeled from each rootstalk and laid into a small pile, while Isabella carefully cut the bulbous fungus into small pieces. Tolmie knew enough about the medicinal practices that Isabella had learned from her own relatives to know that she would normally have worked with dried ingredients rather than fresh. But Isabella's supplies had been lost in the capsizing of the *Wild Pigeon*, and fresh pickings would have to suffice.

The laughter of young children outside in the yard distracted him for a moment, and he glanced out the window to see Mary showing Catherine's and Elizabeth's children how to make an angel in the few inches of snow that covered the ground. It was remarkable, he thought, how different the two youngest Ross daughters had turned out to be. When they were young girls living at Nisqually, Mary and Flora had seemed quite similar. But now, on the verge of womanhood, it was as if Flora was the older of the two. Mary had shown far less interest or ability than Flora in obtaining an education. And while both were quick to laugh and enjoy humor, Flora showed a serious and determined side that Mary lacked entirely. Mary's efforts to occupy the energy of the younger children were providing as much assistance as Flora's, but Tolmie felt certain that Mary was undertaking her task more as a personal means of escape rather than an effort to help the family.

Tolmie settled into a kitchen chair to watch Isabella instruct Flora on the proper method for pounding the pieces of Sumac fungus to open the flesh so that its healing elements would be more easily coaxed free by boiling water. He was anxious to learn, but also fully aware that he was using the demonstration as yet another distraction from delivering his news, in a way that was not unlike Mary's outdoor activities in the snow.

\* \* \*

Elizabeth's hand was cold and the skin shone, glossy and pale, stretched over blue veins and barren bones. Her body struggled to pull each raspy breath into her lungs, only to have the air escape moments later in a noisy and desperate struggle to free itself from her dying body.

Flora pressed both of her hands around Elizabeth's, hoping to transfer her warmth, but hesitant to squeeze too hard out of fear for its fragility. Three days had passed since she had arrived at the Wren farm with Isabella and Mary, and Elizabeth had yet to show any sign that she was aware of their presence. Flora couldn't shake an ominous feeling that had built from the moment she'd first set eyes on her sister. Elizabeth wasn't fighting. She had given up, and the disease was simply taking the opportunity she had provided.

Elizabeth had always been a fighter. She'd always been strong. She was the sibling Flora had wanted to emulate most. And she had given up.

Yet Flora was most troubled by the realization that she shouldn't have been surprised. The strength she remembered was strength from their youth. Elizabeth, the spirited young woman, and Elizabeth, the married wife and mother, now appeared to be two entirely different people. She knew some of the differences came from the misconceptions of childhood hero worship. Seeing her sister's married reality could only come as a disappointment by comparison. But most troubling was the feeling that Elizabeth had given up years before the disease had arrived, domesticated by expectations, by a notoriously difficult husband to please, by children to discipline, and by a lingering sadness.

Footsteps on the stairs announced an arrival. Charles Wren stepped through the doorway. His eyes rested on Elizabeth's body just long enough to see one noisy exhale announce that she was still alive. Flora looked up at her brother-in-law and searched Wren's eyes for any signs of sorrow for his wife's impending departure, as she had done each time he had stepped into the room. She saw only detachment, as if he had arrived to check on the status of dying livestock or a failing investment.

"Do you want to sit with her? I'm just holding her hand."

Wren made no eye contact with Flora, but simply issued a low, guttural noise that declined the invitation, then turned and left the room. He had obtained the update he'd come for and had no other reason to remain.

A feeling of powerlessness washed over Flora as she turned back to her sister. She had read that Florence Nightingale had revolutionized the British Army's treatment for dysentery in recent years, but remembered reading that it had been accomplished primarily through improvements to the sanitary conditions of military hospitals. The Wren bedroom appeared quite clean, leaving Flora to conclude that the most recent developments in European medicine would do nothing to save her sister. She only wanted to help her sister, yet the most assistance she could offer was to warm Elizabeth's cold hand between her own. It was a

34

devastating notion to accept, but she could see no other way to help a woman who seemed determined to die.

\* \* \*

**DIED**.

At her residence, near Steilacoom, Jan. 5th, of dysentery, Mrs. Wren, wife of Chas. Wren.
The friends of deceased and her husband are respectfully invited to attend her funeral at 1 P.M. this day, (Friday) from her late residence.

*Puget Sound Herald*, Steilacoom, Washington Territory, Friday, January 7, 1859, p. 2.

\* \* \*

The gravel beach along the southern edge of the Ross family farm was chilly even at the warmest times of the year, owing to the strong and near-constant winds that blew in from the Pacific. But it was especially bitter in the late afternoon in the middle of January. Not that Flora minded. She settled onto a sandy ledge overlooking Fowl Bay and gazed across the Strait of Juan de Fuca. She had finished her chores, as meager as they were this time of year with no crops in the fields. Now she needed to escape, to think. She'd considered paying a visit to her closest friend, Fanny, at the McNeill farm next door, but had concluded that what she needed most was some time alone near the water.

Isabella had purchased the farmland at the southern tip of Vancouver Island in 1852. The Hudson's Bay Company was dividing up the land bordering the Fort and selling it to the colony's founding families, and the opportunity had induced Isabella to move back from Nisqually with her youngest children. The purchase had made Isabella the first woman in the British territories west of Upper Canada to be a landowner under English law, whether white, Indian or mixed blood, though no one appeared to acknowledge it at the time, if they were aware of it at all. But the land hadn't proven to be the finest farmland in the region, given its location along the windswept shores of the strait.

Flora gazed across the restless bay and pondered the events of the week. She had returned from Nisqually by steamer the prior afternoon, with Isabella and Mary, three days after Elizabeth's funeral. They had found the farm to be much as they'd left it in the hands of the three youngest Ross brothers. And yet Flora couldn't shake the feeling that it all seemed different.

She pulled her coat close to protect herself against the chilly breeze. The late afternoon sunlight offered little warmth, though it had turned the snow-covered peaks of the Olympic Peninsula across the strait from a virgin white to bright amber. It was made all the more striking by the contrast of the deep blue winter sky. To the west lay the Pacific Ocean. To the south lay the Olympic Peninsula. To the east lay San Juan Island, the place of her birth, and behind that, the mainland of Washington Territory. They served as the boundaries of Flora's world as she knew it, and within those boundaries sat each of the three locations that had served as a home. Fort Victoria, the home for her earliest years and some later school years, lay two short miles to the northwest across a well-traveled wagon road, now surrounded by the rapidly growing town that sprawled beyond the Fort's log palisades. Nisqually of her childhood lay to the southeast at the southern end of Puget Sound. And the Ross farm of the prior seven years lay beneath her feet. It was a world filled with rugged beauty, but small, confined, and defined by towering mountains and a daunting ocean. A world as unforgiving as it was beautiful.

The world her father had travelled had stretched from northern Scotland to Upper Canada, across the prairies of Rupert's Land, through the hinterland and desolate coast of New Caledonia and the Oregon Territory, and finally to the southern tip of Vancouver Island. Three of her older siblings had seen a world that reached across the oceans to London and back. It was a world that Flora could only imagine. And of those family members who'd experienced such adventures, only her elder brother, Charles Jr., remained. First had been her father's death, then her brother Walter, and now, Elizabeth. For a moment she feared for Charles Jr., though she knew she had no rational reason to do so. She had just seen him in Nisqually where he had seemed perfectly well. Surely it was a coincidence, she assured herself, that the Ross family members who were gone were the ones who'd ventured so far beyond the limits of her own world.

"What'cha doing?" It was Alexander, her middle brother, who approached carrying driftwood for the fire in the kitchen. He was in his mid-twenties, old enough to be an adult in the family, as evidenced by his thick, dark beard, but young enough that he still fell within the younger half of the Ross children.

"Just thinking."

"About ..."

"Nothing. Everything. Elizabeth and Walter. What Mama looked like after they died."

Alexander dropped the driftwood onto the gravel and sat beside Flora. "She'd still tell you she's luckier'n most. Ten kids and she got to see every one of us grow up. Not many can say something like that."

Flora nodded, accepting the point. About a third of all babies born in the colony would die in infancy or childbirth. An outbreak of measles, scarlatina, diphtheria, or influenza could wipe out an entire brood. To have ten children survive to adulthood was a rarity. To be a mother who survived childbirth ten times over was a rarity, as well. To have both was nearly unheard of.

"Besides, if any of us weren't supposed to make it, it was you."

"Yes, I've heard."

Flora hoped that her tone of mild protest would prevent Alexander from repeating the oft-told story. It was told typically in late May, when the family would celebrate her unspecified birthday on whatever day was most convenient. It had been late spring of 1842, as Charles and Isabella had traveled to Fort Vancouver on the Columbia River, where

Charles would sign a new contract for his next term as Chief Trader for the Hudson's Bay Company's post at Fort McLoughlin. Charles hadn't learned until after arriving at Fort Vancouver that it would be his final term at the remote fort along the coast. It would be his task to shutter the fort and use as much of the lumber as he could transport to begin construction of Fort Victoria, hundreds of miles to the south. The new fort had become a necessity after establishment of the international boundary in 1846 had required the eventual abandonment of Fort Vancouver along the Columbia River.

Charles and Isabella had traveled along the rugged coast in the large cedar canoes of the Heiltsuk Indians that Charles had hired for the journey, then through Puget Sound to Fort Nisqually, and by land to Fort Vancouver. They'd brought with them three of their eight children, as Charles had deemed it unwise to leave the youngest children at the remote fort for a month, attended to only by their older siblings and Company employees. And Isabella accompanied her husband even though she was pregnant, certain as she was from the experience of her eight prior pregnancies that she'd easily complete the journey back to Fort McLaughlin before their latest child would arrive.

Near the end of the journey south, the party camped for the night on a wide beach in a large sheltered bay on San Juan Island, uninhabited at that time by anyone but the occasional Indian fishing encampment. That evening, Isabella went into a short and unexpected labor, and delivered the ninth Ross child in the middle of the night. The child had arrived early, as if determined to stake her claim to the remote island when the opportunity had presented itself. Although no one was thinking of such things at the time, Flora Amelia Ross had become the first person of at least partial European blood to be born on the island. And most likely the first of partial Ojibway blood as well.

As a child, Flora had passed along the southern shore of the island countless times on Company steamers and schooners traveling between Fort Victoria and Fort Nisqually. She could see the pale outline of the southern coast of the island if she walked out to Clover Point or climbed the hills behind the Ross farmhouse. But she hadn't been to the island since the day of her birth.

"Born early, a day or two away from Nisqually; even as a kid that age I knew you weren't supposed to make it. Maybe you've got some higher purpose to be here for."

A purpose. Flora nearly laughed, presuming he'd said the word in jest. The idea that a woman might have a purpose in life beyond motherhood was something few men would propose as a serious concept. Men had purposes to fulfill. They had careers to advance, families to sire, gold to pan, empires to build, mistresses to bed. Women had wombs. That was their reason to survive beyond infancy.

She realized that Alexander hadn't intended much meaning behind the comment. But it took a thought that had been circling in her mind in recent days, a thought that seemed to represent an inappropriate desire, and gave her permission to view it instead as a purpose. A purpose was beyond wants or desires. A purpose was ordained. A purpose justified action.

# Chapter 3

"You ever hear anything like it?" Mary whispered in Flora's ear, loudly enough to be heard several pews away.

Flora shushed her sister, partly because they were in church, and partly because she'd also never heard anything quite like it and didn't want any interruptions. The small choir sounded glorious, accompanied for the first time by a new barrel organ that had arrived recently from London to replace the congregation's simple melodeon.

For years, hymns at the church had been accompanied by an old fortepiano of questionable tuning, if any instrumentation at all. When the melodeon had arrived the year before, it had been welcomed as a wonderful addition. But the melodeon had offered only a thin, reedy sound, and was limited by the skills of its player, while the new barrel organ produced the same precise performance with each barrel that was inserted. It was limited only by the skills of the boy who'd been employed to pump the bellows of the small machine.

Mary craned her neck and gazed up at the choir in the gallery, as did most of the young women in the pews. The object of their attention wasn't the barrel organ or the choir as a whole, but one of the new singers, Arthur Bushby. Bushby had arrived from London the previous Christmas Day, bringing with him a pleasing appearance, an angelic high tenor voice, and unapologetic ambition. For the first few services after his arrival, his strong voice would turn heads in the pews. Now that he was a member of the choir, young ladies could at least pretend to be gazing upon the entire choir as they sang, even if it did cause greater strain on their necks. Agnes Douglas, one of the Governor's daughters, simply turned in her pew and faced the back while she sang, smiling at Bushby with a familiarity that none of the other young women could claim, while saving her neck from the ache the others would feel after the service had concluded. Flora found it more entertaining to observe the young women around her, straining their necks for a better view, or singing with particular animation in an effort to attract his attention.

Bushby's high tenor had arrived on the same boat that had brought a deep bass to the congregation, belonging to the Honorable Matthew Baillie Begbie. He was the newly appointed Chief Justice and, as yet, only judge, for the newly established mainland colony of British Columbia. Though Begbie's duties would require his presence on the mainland from time to time, traveling through the rugged wilderness to dispense justice, he had chosen to keep his residence in Victoria, as there wasn't yet any town of substance in British Columbia.

He initially had attended the Presbyterian Church, but had switched to the Church of England after receiving complaints that his voice was overpowering the rest of the Presbyterians. Whether it was because of or despite his powerful bass tones, the Christ Church congregation had determined that any man as important as the British Columbia Chief Justice should naturally be one of their own, and had welcomed him in.

The third male voice recently added to the choir, a strong baritone, belonged to John Butts, a ruddy Australian in his early twenties, whose colorful personality gave him the appearance of a height that his body actually lacked.

Butts had been a mediocre actor and a slightly less mediocre petty thief in San Francisco throughout his late teens. And though the crimes on his lengthy list had been minor, his well-publicized theft in 1857 of a leg of mutton and two jars of horseradish from a butcher had earned him the slightly mocking label "the notorious John Butts" from San Francisco newspapers, as well as several months on the chain gang. But it was his agreement to testify as the prosecution's lead witness in the murder trial of Judge Edward (Ned) McGowan that ultimately led to his decision to flee San Francisco, after he had become convinced that his own life might be at risk. The murder charge against McGowan had been trumped up by a vigilance committee that had carried out a minor revolution in 1856, by forming an army, hanging accused murderers without a fair trial, and banishing members of San Francisco's city government on boats to foreign countries. Though organized government of sorts had been restored in San Francisco by 1857, the lives that had been lost, the enmity that remained on both sides, and Butts' ineffective testimony at McGowan's trial, had left Butts feeling particularly vulnerable.

Since arriving in Victoria, he had insisted that he be called "John Butt" for reasons that he refused to explain. Most presumed it was an effort to distance himself from his life in California, particularly as Ned McGowan and hundreds of miners from both San Francisco factions had also traveled north to British Columbia for the gold rush. Their ongoing hostilities had, in recent weeks, caused minor battles among American miners along the Fraser River. But if anonymity had been the purpose behind the minimal nature of the change, it had proven to be futile, as nearly everyone continued to call him "Butts."

He had found work shortly after his arrival as the town crier and bell-ringer, a task well-suited to his gregarious nature and constant need for an audience, but poorly suited to his inability to filter whatever thoughts circled through his addled mind before spilling from his lips. And though Flora considered herself to be one who paid little attention to social gossip, she found it difficult to see him without instantly considering the rumor that he was one of those men often referred to in impolite conversation as a "boy" or a "molly." Whether or not the rumor was true, it wasn't appropriate for a girl of her upbringing to allow ideas to circulate in her imagination about the sexual acts certain men might carry out with one another, especially while she was listening to a hymn during a Sunday service. Butts had been in Victoria less than two months, but Flora had already concluded that he was yet another "character" to add to the lengthy list in the colony's small town.

Reverend Cridge stepped back to the pulpit as the choir concluded the hymn, and as the young women in the congregation reluctantly turned their attention back to the front of the church.

"And now, I ask for your indulgence, for your charity, as we pass around the collection plate. We know from Matthew, 25:31-46, that caring for the sick is one of our Christian duties and is among the qualities our Lord seeks to find in each of us when judging us for eternal salvation. And yet as our community grows, we leave far too many without care, without hope. Many of you have generously assisted in the creation of the small infirmary for men, but with the good Lord's assistance, we should be shortly announcing plans for a true hospital to care for the sick. It's my hope the Government, in its wisdom, will provide us with the funding we need. But I also appeal to all of you here today, to think about what you can do to help us fulfill this Christian duty."

Flora listened to Cridge's appeal, wishing she had an extra coin to place in the plate, and wondering if the topic could be a sign that her plans for that morning met with a higher approval. It was at least a coincidence. But even a coincidence would help ensure that she would follow through on the promise she'd made to herself while sitting at the beach several days earlier, pondering the possibility that she might have a "purpose" for her life.

As the service came to its conclusion, the congregation spilled from the front doors of the church in a procession that served as a reverse display of Victoria's social order. For the simple building's most noticeable testament to its

Company heritage was the organization of its pews, and the manner by which they demonstrated the order of society. The front pew was occupied by Governor Douglas and his family, and was separated from the pews behind it by a short, wooden wall. From there, one could easily determine the rank of each family in the colony by the location of their assigned pew in relation to the Governor's. Flora and her family occupied a pew a few rows behind the Governor's, with several of the Company's other original settling families between them. It was a position that reflected the fact that the Ross family had been one of the founding families of Fort Victoria, while acknowledging that the death of Charles Ross had diminished the family's role. Farther back sat the families that had arrived more recently, or lacked a high position within either the colonial government or the Company. And behind them stood the most recent arrivals, miners and merchants, packed right through the doorway and down the front steps.

Because the social order reflected by the pews was dictated by the hierarchy of Company officials, it meant that nearly every woman and child seated closest to the altar bore the features of full or partial Indian blood. Those who sat in the Governor's pew had the particular effrontery to bear features of both Indian and Creole heritage, the former through Governor Douglas' wife, and the latter through his mother. Many of the town's newer arrivals were openly hostile to the idea that they should stand at the back of the church while "Indians" should be seated in front of them. It was a hostility shown with equal venom toward Mifflin Gibbs, Peter Lester, and their families, negro merchants who had arrived with the first gold miners in 1858. Both men were among the leaders of a mass emigration of several hundred negro men, women and children, who had fled from an increasingly hostile climate in California as pro-slavery politicians attempted to align California's politics and policies with those of the southern states. The two men had established a thriving business in town, and shared a pew with their families. But they also shared the enmity of many white American miners and immigrants who had arrived with a far different hierarchy in mind than the one reflected by the pews in Reverend Cridge's congregation.

By the time Flora was able to exit the church, most of the congregation was already spread across the churchyard. She stood and watched the agendas that played out on the grounds below the bell tower, preoccupied by the agenda of her own that would unfold when the opportunity seemed right. The moments after a service provided each member of the congregation with the chance to be seen with the best people, to make connections for business or social engagements, and to flirt in an environment that offered both an element of safety and an appealing risk of scandal.

Flora hung back until the last few stragglers had thanked Reverend Cridge for his sermon before finding the courage to approach him, intimidated that the advice she would seek might impose upon the man's own expectations for her future.

"Reverend, I wonder if I could have a moment?"

"Of course, Flora. What did you think of the new organ this morning?"

"It sounded beautiful. The choir, too," she answered, in a near whisper. "But ... everything you said this morning about a new hospital, and our Christian duty to the sick ... I know how you help to hire nurses here in the colony when women are ill."

Flora stopped, realizing that the worried expression on Cridge's face might be a sign that he was misunderstanding the direction of the hushed conversation.

"I'm fine. We all are. I don't need a nurse. I want to be one. Mama's taught me so much over the years, and I helped take care of Elizabeth when we were there, as much as I could. I want to learn the new techniques, the Nightingale theories, the scientific approaches. I want to learn more. To help bring babies into the world, and help the sick and dying."

Cridge wrinkled his brow and exhaled a deep sigh that suggested the responsibility she had just placed on his shoulders.

"My goodness, child. It's an admirable goal. I'd be a hypocrite to question you in the slightest. But is that really the right direction for your life?"

Flora knew exactly what he meant. Shouldn't a girl like her put her faith in marriage? In a husband who would provide for her and their children? Shouldn't she strive to further the position of the Ross family name by joining it to the name of an ambitious new immigrant? It wasn't that Flora wouldn't consider marriage. She had shyly observed many young men about town in recent years who had struck her fancy and inspired harmless fantasies of matrimony. It was more her concern that a marriage of social privilege, of hosting afternoon teas with mindless chatter and needlework, would be neither a marriage that would consider her, nor a marriage she would consider for herself.

Just two years earlier, few Company men would have hesitated to marry a young woman of mixed or full Indian blood. Partly because of a lack of any other options. And partly because there was no established white society to enforce separation from the Indian communities. But upon the discovery of gold, more than thirty thousand miners had swarmed into the colonies, the Royal Navy's presence had grown in response, and businessmen and settlers had arrived from the United Kingdom and America with wives and families. All expected a colony that approximated the culture of their home country, and few tolerated contact with native communities.

Flora had felt the change at the balls that were frequently thrown to bring together the town's eligible young ladies with the eligible men of the Royal Navy. The darker a girl's skin, the fewer sailors who would ask her to dance. The few who did often did so more on a lark than out of genuine interest. And while Flora shared a native heritage with many of the other young women in the colony, she lacked the social advantage that had been granted by birth to friends and rivals like Agnes Douglas and her sisters. The men drawn to a life in the officer ranks of the Royal Navy were often the younger sons who would see no inheritance. They had turned to a naval career out of necessity, and were often drawn more to the connections a future father-in-law could offer than to the charms of a future wife. The prospect of marrying a governor's daughter helped many men overlook not merely the Douglas girls' Cree background on their mother's side, but even the Creole blood they had inherited from their father's side. Not that Flora envied any of the Douglas girls for their social advantage. Much better that any husband she might find would value her for what she had to offer as a wife, not what her family name had to offer for his advancement.

But if the most recent arrivals weren't viable prospects for marriage, from Flora's perspective, neither were the men born and raised in the colony. Most were, themselves, the product of mixed marriages. And while men of all backgrounds in the colony seemed prone to the combination of whiskey and irresponsibility, those who'd arrived from Great Britain or America seemed more able to carry on with a respectable life during their sober moments. Many of the men who had grown up in the colony, two of her own brothers setting a particularly pitiable example, seemed more prone to allowing whiskey to control their lives.

Flora was certain that her goal to learn nursing skills was driven by the desire to provide for those who were ill. It was fulfillment of the very Christian duty Cridge had spoken of that morning. But a competing motive was the desire to be able to provide for herself should she prove unable to find a suitable husband to provide for them both. It was an explanation that Flora was prepared to deliver, having rehearsed it for hours. But Cridge appeared far more willing to accept Flora's proposal than she had ever anticipated.

"I'm sure your mother's taught you well, but if you're serious about this, then you should go see the Sisters. They would probably welcome a pupil whose interest is in learning nursing rather than the alphabet and needlework."

The "Sisters" were the Sisters of St. Ann. They had arrived eight months earlier from Montreal to establish a convent and school, where they taught children of all races and ages in a small, one-room cabin. Equally important to their mission was their promise to provide nursing services to local women, and educate others in the field of nursing. Their efforts to establish both the school and the convent had kept the Sisters from actively providing nursing care in the community. But in recent weeks they'd begun to reach out to the sick and dying, had served as midwives, and had laid out the dead for burial.

"I tried to imagine all the advice you might give me, but never imagined it'd be to enroll at a Catholic school."

"You're almost seventeen if I'm remembering correctly. Mrs. Cridge has probably taught you everything she has to teach a young woman your age. She has many admirable qualities, but I say with no disrespect that her nursing skills are equivalent to those of the average wife and mother. If nursing is truly what you want, Flora, go see the Sisters."

\* \* \*

## BRITISH COLUMBIA.

Far away, under English rule, an English climate with its drawbacks gone; a rich soil that will grow in abundance any English crop; upon which currants and gooseberries, raspberries and strawberries run wild, and where cattle multiply; a country with coal seams and good harbors; ought to have drawn years ago many an English colonist towards Vancouver's Island. The island was granted to the Hudson's Bay Company for a short term that will expire next year. It was granted with the stipulation, that the Company should promote colonization, but with the foreknowledge that the Hudson's Bay monopolists have from the outset not only discouraged colonisation, but have, in some instances, put it down with a strong hand …

It is only a step from the island to the mainland of that western shore of British America which was called New Caledonia until within the last few weeks, but which Her Majesty has now named British Columbia ...

Great things are now anticipated. Vancouver's Island, in the North Pacific, is to become the seat of a noble British colony, and of a naval arsenal complete in every detail. If England pleases, she may build among the many islands in the sea between Vancouver's Island and the mainland a Cronstadt of the Pacific, and fasten with a mighty padlock—if such security be needed—her possessions on the western coast of North America, now regarded as of inestimable value.

*The Puget Sound Herald*, Friday, January 21, 1859, p. 1.

\* \* \*

Paul Kinsey Hubbs, Jr. struggled to pry a fragile cork from a fancy glass demijohn that was likely to contain mediocre whiskey at best. The contradiction between vessel and contents was a fitting contradiction for Hubbs, and one that the two dinner guests who'd gathered in his small cabin were too drunk to appreciate, even if they had begun to understand the degree to which Hubbs' appearance and character varied from the other. A first impression of Hubbs was typically that of an unkempt fur trader from an earlier era who was more at home in remote forests than in civil society, despite his government title as Deputy Inspector of Customs on San Juan Island. Most men in the region had abandoned out-dated frontier styles of clothing in favor of newly accessible imported textiles, but Hubbs continued to dress in buckskin, with his unruly hair and thick mustache adding to his rough, backwoods image. It contributed to the nickname given to him by many—the "white Indian"—which he wore proudly, though it had never been intended as a compliment.

But the physical impression Hubbs presented was altered on the barest of acquaintance by an air of self-importance bordering on arrogance. And after the briefest of conversation, he usually demonstrated that he was intelligent and well-educated, though also possessed of far more knowledge than common sense.

Hubbs pulled the cork free and filled three glasses with whiskey, hoping that his dinner companions had noticed the fancy glass container and might be sufficiently impressed by its appearance to be less critical of its contents. He handed the glasses of whiskey to Captain C.L. Denman and Edward Gillette, the two other men in the cabin.

"If I were paranoid," Hubbs began, in a tone that bolstered the possibility of his paranoia, "I'd say McNeill was here to intimidate us by hunting close by. Only way it makes sense that he and those Ross boys showed up the same day as you."

"Don't see how he'd know why I'm here, or care," Denman replied, looking up from unpacking surveying implements.

"He'd know you worked on Pemberton's surveys. He'd know there's more of us staking claims. Why else would you be here except to lay out claims?" Hubbs insisted, not about to give up on his theory.

Denman had been hired by several Americans living in Victoria to carry out a survey of the island for homesteading claims that they could stake in anticipation that the Northwest Boundary Commission might determine the disputed island to be U.S. territory. As the only official of the U.S. Government living on the island, and the only American to occupy any sort of remotely comfortable cabin that could keep out the February chill, Hubbs was the obvious choice for Denman to turn to for assistance. The number of Americans staking claims on the island had risen to more than a dozen in the prior month, with several arriving since the New Year, and though some were only on the island occasionally to protect their claims, most seemed intent on putting down permanent roots. Hubbs had staked a claim of his own on the far southeastern point of the island, two miles east of the government cabin he still called home. Gillette, an American engineer, had staked a claim less than a mile west of Hubbs' cabin. They were both to assist Denman with the survey in return for more accurate surveys of their own claims.

Hubbs was well aware that the activities of American settlers had been noticed in Victoria, and that tensions had been increasing between the two sides. He was firm in his belief that the timely arrival of William McNeill, Jr. and two of his friends, on the pretext of deer hunting, couldn't be a mere coincidence. McNeill was the eldest son of the Company's Chief Factor at Fort Simpson, far up the northern coast. His friends, Francis and William Ross were the youngest sons of the late Charles Ross. Both families were among the Hudson's Bay Company family compact that had settled the colony, and it was entirely conceivable to Hubbs that their sons would be on the island more to preserve the Company's interests in the land rather than hunt for the island's miniature variety of deer.

"Maybe they'll figure we're here for deer huntin', like them."

"They're not here for deer hunting. They're here 'cause gossip rounds the Fort like clap in a brothel," Hubbs retorted. "All it would've taken was one of the group who hired you to brag about the claim he's gonna stake here and the Company'd know about it in minutes. Sending over a hunting party to shoot over our heads is just the sort of thing they'd do."

Hubbs was far less trusting than Denman of the men who'd paid for the surveying expedition. Even the foolish ones should have understood the controversy Denman's assignment would generate at the Fort if the colonial government or the Hudson's Bay Company—still essentially the same thing for most purposes—were to become aware of the surveying efforts. But foolishness had a tendency to increase exponentially with each hour spent in a saloon.

Satisfied that he had led the conversation to his preferred conclusion, Hubbs turned his attention to his next priority and lifted the iron lid off a heavy pot he'd placed in the coals of the fire. The venison roast inside sizzled in its juices and gave off an intoxicating scent despite Hubbs' rudimentary cooking skills. The only recipe he had for roast venison required just four ingredients: a venison roast, salt, pepper, and a large quantity of pre-dinner whiskey. He was relieved to confirm that the roast was still far from cooked, since his guests were still far from ready to appreciate his cooking. Hubbs set the lid back onto the iron pot, reached for the demijohn, and ensured that his visitors' glasses remained full.

\* \* \*

SAN JUAN ISLAND. – We understand a number of Americans residing in Victoria and at other places on the Sound, have sent a Surveyor to San Juan Island—in dispute between the British and United States governments—for the purpose of pre-empting land according to pre-emption laws of the United States, believing that in the end this island will be declared to be American territory. It is looked upon as a speculation in which little is risked, and in case of success, the profit large. It is likely, unless this boundary question is soon settled, trouble may grow out of these movements.

*The Victoria Gazette*, Thursday, February 17, 1859, p. 3.

\* \* \*

Flora stood in the bedroom of her eldest brother John, and his wife, Genevieve, and observed the midwife from her position at the foot of the bed, hoping that the midwife would display a modern birthing technique that might soothe Isabella's bruised ego and justify Genevieve's decision to hire a professional midwife. Flora had tried to explain the rationale behind Genevieve's decision to her mother, but Isabella hadn't found the explanation to be convincing. She had birthed children in remote trading posts for nearly four decades, including her own, and was certain that her experience was every bit as reliable as any newcomer's alleged training or purported title of "nurse."

The midwife had been introduced as Mrs. Boyce, but she had immediately requested that they call her Lucinda, demonstrating an informality that identified her as American even if her accent hadn't. Flora watched as Lucinda examined Genevieve, anxious at the opportunity to learn, and ready to step forward to assist at a moment's notice. Isabella stood across the room, equally determined to step forward the moment the young American nurse displayed a lack of knowledge and competency.

A baby's gentle murmur pulled Flora's attention to Lucinda's own baby, who lay swaddled on the floor, fast asleep.

"If he wakes up, I could rock him back to sleep, if you're busy with the delivery," she offered.

Lucinda looked up from her examination and managed a slight smile. "If he wakes up, it'll be 'cause he wants something only I can give him."

"Two months old?"

"Ten weeks. Born on New Years Day. Maybe you remember the storm the night before? That's when I went into labor."

"My mother and I both remember that night well," Flora replied, wondering which of the women in the room would have the better story to share about the storm.

Lucinda lifted a cup of water to Genevieve's lips. "I imagine you want to get this over with, but this baby's not in any hurry to get here. Rest if you can." She turned to Flora and Isabella. "Perhaps we should have a cup of tea while we wait."

Flora could see how the suggestion bristled her mother. Isabella had likely been moments away from making the same suggestion, but as a host offering tea, rather than a new guest making a presumption that seemed far too familiar.

"I'll go make a pot. The kettle should be hot by now."

Flora left the room, realizing that emptying the kettle for tea would mean another trip to the pump in order to ensure enough hot water for the delivery. Tending to hot water was the sort of help she had always given her mother during deliveries of prior nieces and nephews, and it disappointed her to think that she might face such a limited opportunity to assist Lucinda as well.

"I'll give you a hand," Lucinda replied as she followed Flora to the kitchen, leaving her baby in the room with Genevieve and Isabella. Flora realized that Lucinda had also just left Isabella with another reason to question the judgment of the young American nurse.

Flora pushed the kettle to a hotter burner on the iron stove as Lucinda followed her into the kitchen.

"You mentioned you're learning nursing from the Sisters," Lucinda inquired.

"That was my intention. But so far we've only covered literature, French grammar, Latin, needlework … nothing particularly useful to nursing."

"Have they started providing services to the town yet?"

"Only in the last few weeks."

"Hmm, I'd heard a rumor about that. A shame for me. Less people pay a nurse if they can get help for free from the nuns."

"I suppose," Flora replied. "Though this is a mostly Protestant town. Don't underestimate the willingness of some women to pay money just to keep the nuns from their bedsides. You have spoken with Reverend Cridge?"

"You're the third person who's asked me that. I hardly think prayer's the way for me to find more people needing nursing services."

Flora smiled at the misunderstanding. "That's not why they told you to go see him. Reverend Cridge helps people find nurses when they need one. I suppose because he opened the infirmary for men. You should speak to him."

"I will, now that I know why."

Flora reached for the canister of tea leaves as the kettle began to boil.

"And would you do me a favor, Mrs. Boyce—Lucinda?" Flora asked, her voice lowered for privacy.

"I imagine so."

"Ask my mother's advice at some point."

Flora could see from Lucinda's smile that she understood the point, but she carried on regardless.

"She's delivered dozens of babies, including her own, and —"

"And me being here's an insult to her wisdom and knowledge."

Flora nodded, smiling.

"It's not my intention to insult the generation that taught me everything I know," Lucinda continued.

"Of course not. Thank you."

"I suppose it's the curse of getting older, that someone younger comes along and claims they can do it better. Perhaps it'll be you who pushes me aside some day."

"I doubt that entirely," Flora replied, pouring the steaming water into the teapot, but realizing that it was an idea that brought a smile to her face. "At least not at the rate I'm learning about nursing."

"So I've got nothing to fear if I pass on knowledge to you?" Lucinda asked with a grin.

"Nothing in the slightest," Flora replied, pleased at the suggestion that she had just found a potential mentor and teacher, if not a new friend. She only hoped that her mother wouldn't be too offended by the prospect.

# Chapter 4

Flora stepped through the front doors of Christ Church into the snowy morning and scanned the departing crowd that had gathered on the church lawn for their post-service socializing, undaunted by the light snow. At the base of the front steps stood her mother and sister, smiling broadly in conversation with Dr. Tolmie, who was visiting from Nisqually. She presumed their smiles were a sign that he was confirming what had been the gossip in town for weeks; that he would shortly move his family back to Victoria from Washington Territory.

The international border west of the continental divide had been finalized in treaty negotiations in 1846, by which the Oregon Territory had been confirmed as an American possession. A division of the territory in 1853 created a separate Washington Territory, and it had been understood that the new territorial government would someday refuse to recognize land claims asserted by the Hudson's Bay Company, and its affiliate, the Puget Sound Agricultural Company. Both had been instrumental in settling the region, but both were vestiges of British control. Once that day arrived, the Company's remaining farms and trading posts would be shut down. In recent weeks, it had been decided that Tolmie would oversee the four Vancouver Island farms belonging to the Puget Sound Agricultural Company, just as he had done with its operations in Washington Territory.

Flora descended the front steps and passed through the crowd. Family, neighbors, Company officials, and classmates. All of them so familiar to her. It struck her for a moment that she wasn't walking through a community of individuals so much as passing through a single entity. A single being that hummed in conversation around her. Family connections, intermarriages, and political affiliations were woven throughout the congregation like strands of a web, with Governor James Douglas firmly at the center, connecting all of them within his grasp. The publisher of one of the town's newspapers, Amor de Cosmos, had relentlessly attacked the entire group for months in the *British Colonist*, labeling them a "Family Compact," and claiming that they denied the colony fair and effective government. Flora had paid little attention to the attacks, because they were directed at men whom she knew, but she also knew that the attacks weren't entirely without cause.

She sensed movement behind her and looked back to see Governor Douglas and his wife, Amelia, exit the church, the last of the congregation to leave the warmth of the building on this cold and unexpectedly snowy morning. Douglas cut an imposing figure, tall and with a large build that was exaggerated by the stiff manner with which he held himself, as if posing to show authority simply by a lack of approachability. His insistence on wearing a uniform of his own design only added to his imposing figure. Douglas had no shortage of detractors, and no shortage of reasons to invite their criticism, but in this crowd he enjoyed a measure of popularity.

His most recent plan, announced a few days earlier, was to build new government buildings on the south side of Victoria harbor, and a bridge across James Bay to connect those new buildings to the center of town. It had been met with protests and ridicule, largely since many perceived the plan as an effort to use government funds to increase the value of his land interests adjacent to the planned government buildings. But there were also many in the community who were willing to overlook such schemes, for without his leadership, there might not be a Colony of Vancouver Island, or British Columbia. Threats of annexation by the United States had been rampant for years, fueled to a fever pitch by the discovery of gold and the arrival of more than thirty thousand American miners, many of whom considered it the God-given right of the United States to occupy the entire west coast of North America. Douglas, by sheer grit and determination, had put down many an effort to turn dissent into revolt or outright annexation.

As Douglas and his wife stepped into the crowd, Flora surveyed the reactions to his arrival. The web expanded the more she considered each group, enveloping civil government, the judiciary, and the Company within its reach. Dr. Helmcken, first son-in-law to the Governor and Speaker of the Legislative Assembly, was chatting with David Cameron, the Governor's brother-in-law. Douglas had appointed him to serve as Chief Justice of Vancouver Island's Supreme Court of Civil Justice, despite having no legal background of any kind. Alexander Grant Dallas, son-in-law number two, soon to run the Company's operations in the Western Department, was chatting with Dr. Tolmie, who himself was married to a daughter of H.B.C. Chief Factor John Work, a member of the colony's insular Legislative Council. Behind them stood Roderick Finlayson, another son-in-law of Work and Treasurer of the Legislative Council, conversing with W.A.G. Young, the new Colonial Secretary who'd been appointed by his wife's uncle, the Governor. Overseeing the entire congregation was Reverend Cridge, not merely the Company's official chaplain, but also Secretary to the Legislative Council. To the side stood Alice Douglas chatting animatedly with Charles Good, the Governor's private secretary, undoubtedly providing fodder for gossip. If Bushby hadn't been upcountry with Judge Begbie, he most certainly would have been at the side of

Agnes Douglas, furthering the potential for yet another strand of the web to begin to unfurl.

None of the strands that spread throughout the congregation included Flora within their grasp, yet she couldn't help but wonder; if her father had lived, would she be standing outside the church feeling separate and apart from the "Family Compact" that ran the small colony? A member by default, only by reason of the name she'd inherited from a man she couldn't remember? Or would she have become trapped in the sticky threads by a father deeply entrenched in the colony's politics, perhaps related more closely to other leading families by the marriage of a sibling, or perhaps a marriage of her own? She hadn't intended for a moment to feel relieved that her father hadn't lived to this day. But she also couldn't deny that she considered herself far better off for being able to walk away that morning without feeling the strands of a web trailing behind her.

* * *

Reverend Cridge stepped away from the spot where Dr. Helmcken and Alexander Grant Dallas stood, and paced off thirty feet in the grass. He looked back and imagined the building that would be constructed in the coming months. Then he imagined the reactions of Victoria's residents to the concept of placing their new hospital across the harbor from town, on an exposed point appropriated from the Songhees reserve.

"There's certainly a lot of space to work with." It wasn't a ringing endorsement, but it was the most he was willing to offer. The strong wintry winds that blew across the bay from the harbor's opening to the southwest hinted at isolation, if not desolation.

"It's by far the optimal location." Dallas stomped his boot in the frozen dirt, as if it supported his point by confirming the firmness of the land. "Away from the noise and dust of the town, and there's room for expansion, even if we do divide the reserve into lots."

Cridge responded with a noncommittal murmur and

wondered if it had been a mistake for the Hospital Committee to choose a businessman as its chairman. Dallas performed many diverse roles in the colony, each of them befitting his status as a shareholder of the Hudson's Bay Company. Serving as Chairman of the Hospital Committee was simply the latest. His original role, the role that had led him across the Atlantic, had been to report to the London headquarters about the Company's declining business concerns on Vancouver Island. It might have been a temporary assignment had Dallas not married one of Governor Douglas' daughters, Jane, in the Spring of 1858. It had hardly been a match of opportunism, given Dallas' substantial wealth. Instead, it was a match that created awkwardness within the Douglas family, as the reporting role Dallas had been sent to carry out required him to report to headquarters on the performance of his new father-in-law.

For over a decade, Douglas had run the Company's business under a lease from the British government that gave the Company exclusive rights to settle and exploit all of Vancouver Island, while also serving as Governor of the colony's insular civil government for eight of those years. The two roles presented frequent conflicts, exacerbated by the British government's decision to appoint Douglas to a third role; governor of the new mainland colony of British Columbia. In an effort to ensure that the Company's business interests wouldn't suffer under Douglas' increasing civil burden, the Company's London office responded by issuing a resolution appointing Dallas to take over his father-in-law's corporate position.

Cridge had heard many rumors about the tension the decision had caused in the Douglas family. That Douglas had unilaterally decided to postpone the transition to a future date of his choosing. And that Dallas had appealed to the London headquarters for assistance. The most recent rumor claimed that an instruction from London had arrived ordering an immediate transition of power at the Company, and that Dallas kept the document in his breast pocket, waiting for the least awkward moment to share it with his wife's father. The fact that this rumor made the document known to more people than just Dallas was the most awkward part of all.

Cridge pushed the rumors from his mind and returned his focus to the potential location of the future hospital. It had been a matter of significant dispute among Hospital Committee members for some time, and Cridge worried that Dallas' obvious intention of driving the matter to a decision that afternoon would only spark more strife at future meetings. Cridge and Helmcken had favored accessibility for Victoria residents, while Dallas had focused on locations far removed from where land values had skyrocketed after miners, and the businesses that followed miners, had poured into the town in 1858. Dallas' solution to reduce the needed funding for the hospital was to appropriate land on the Songhees reserve in exchange for the promise that the new hospital would provide services to all races and creeds. It had struck Cridge as a reasonable compromise from a financial perspective, if one ignored the fact that the principle of service to all, regardless of race or creed, had already been a foundational principle of the new hospital from the outset.

Cridge gazed across the harbor to the growing town of Victoria. It was a view he hadn't seen from such a perspective in nearly a year, and he was astounded by how much had changed. One year earlier, Victoria had been a small trading fort with a town of a few hundred people surrounding the log palisades, nestled along a hillside cleared of its virgin oaks, pines and firs. Since then, more than thirty thousand gold miners had passed through Victoria. Most had stayed only to secure transportation to the mainland and up the Fraser River, and to obtain rest, provisions, and prostitution before continuing their journey. But thousands had remained, whether intending to settle, or lacking the means to leave, resulting in a flurry of new construction, desecration of surrounding forests, and a tent city that cascaded across every visible hillside.

"Is it going to be enough?" he questioned aloud. "This little building we're proposing? It's what we need for today. But a year from now ..."

"We're limited by what we can afford," Dallas replied, "and there are days I'm not certain we have even that."

"All the gold that passes through here," Cridge mused. "It leaves us with the sick and the dying and the desperate. I fear we're destined to become a town filled with little more than the dreamers who failed."

The growth of the small town across the bay should have brought with it the means of establishing new infrastructure, and the opportunity for shared prosperity. Instead, misery and deprivation were most apparent. Cridge had marveled many times since the Fraser River discoveries at how a heavy, shiny dust could so readily reveal the extremes of humanity that religion, culture, and upbringing struggled to manage for the sake of civil society. The greed, the boundless hope, the envy, the optimism, the violence, the philanthropy, the despair; all of them aspects of humanity Cridge might witness at any time in the young colony. Yet all of them had been magnified to the point of collision by the mad rush to the Fraser in 1858. The loss of life had been enormous and showed little sign of abating. Hundreds of miners had died in their quest, some drowning in makeshift boats swamped in the choppy Strait of Georgia, some freezing to death or starving just miles from settlements. Some had died of dysentery in Victoria's tent city, or from gunshots or suicide. Others had ended their days in the tiny and temporary infirmary that Cridge and Helmcken had established. For those who made it up the Fraser, there were attacks from Indians, attacks from other miners, murders in the makeshift town, accidents in the river, starvation, disease, and suicide. The colony had always posed extreme challenges to newcomers. But all of them seemed exaggerated since the gold rush had begun, as if the land itself had thrown up defenses to the onslaught.

"I realize it burdens you to have to travel across the bridge to see the hospital's patients," Dallas remarked, ignoring Cridge's philosophizing. "Assuming of course that the bridge remains. But either way, this location is optimal for quarantine if necessary."

Cridge realized that Dallas had intended his bridge

comment for Helmcken, though he, too, would visit many patients at the hospital in fulfillment of his pastoral duties. But it was Helmcken who had proposed in the Assembly in recent weeks that the bridge across the north end of the harbor be removed to address citizens' concerns about the ease with which Songhees and other Indians could access Victoria. Helmcken's plan had been proposed as an alternative, if the Assembly didn't adopt his initial proposal to entirely relocate the Songhees village to San Juan Island, and permit a sale of the Songhees reserve for development and expansion of the growing town. It was an extreme proposal, if for no other reason than the certainty that it would escalate British and American tensions to forcibly resettle an entire native community on the disputed island. Helmcken insisted that he'd advanced the idea as a humanitarian gesture, though Cridge hardly considered the benefits that would flow to the town's business interests to qualify as humanitarian.

"The bridge isn't a burden. I'll visit many more patients in their homes than here in the hospital, and the journey to many of their homes is far more a burden than a permanent building here could ever be," Helmcken replied.

"And I suppose the quarantine issue is an advantage," Cridge furthered, accepting that there were many in the community who would value the ability to quarantine patients with infectious diseases across the harbor, closer to the Songhees village than to the growing town. And even if the Songhees reserve were to be subdivided, a sufficient perimeter could be maintained around the hospital once it was built.

"Well then, I believe we have our location," Dallas replied with a tone of conclusion.

Cridge nodded, less in agreement than in recognition that Dallas would drive the process to his own desired result. A resolution would still need to be written up and a vote of the committee would have to be taken, but Cridge understood that these would be mere formalities. The decision to place the new hospital on the Songhees' land had just been finalized.

\* \* \*

"My favorite was the farce they performed."

"*The Limerick Boy*."

"That's it."

"How could you like it? You kept laughing at all the wrong moments."

"You didn't laugh at all. I understood it better than you."

"My favorite was the Taylor Brothers."

"You should've seen them, Flora. They make the funniest negro men, and they're really good with the banjo and fiddle."

Flora wanted to interject herself into the Douglas sisters' frenetic reviews of the prior evening's theatrical performance by the Chapman Family and the Taylor Brothers, but the sisters' comments created so many questions in her mind that she had no idea which path of questioning to pursue. Nor did the sisters' commentary ever pause long enough to permit questions.

Another day at the Sisters of St. Ann's schoolhouse was over, and as with the end of most school days, a short walk with the Douglas sisters presented a chance to catch up on the local gossip from the town's best sources. Alice and Agnes were the daughters of Governor Douglas closest in age to Flora. Though she'd known the sisters for most of her life, she had never felt particularly close to either of them. They were girls who enjoyed privileges that Flora could only imagine, though with those privileges came a public life in a small community. It was a public life that, quite recently, had become subject to the judgments and critiques of a large number of new arrivals. Many a spurned suitor had reconsidered his pursuit of one of the Douglas sisters in recent months after concluding that they were uncultured, unintelligent, of "savage" background, or whatever other unflattering description might mend the suitor's bruised ego.

Flora had never inspired similar gossip about herself, as far as she was aware. She attributed it to her lack of a father in a high position, and to her ability to act according to her own relative status in the community. Gossip, she had concluded, was most frequently directed at those who attempted to occupy a place in society above the level assigned to them by others.

On this particular walk from school, the topic of conversation was the Douglas girls' attendance at the theatre the evening before, though "theatre" was a relative term in a town where the main room at the Assembly Hall had to suffice. The Chapman Family was a San Francisco acting troupe that regularly traveled throughout the west. They performed—or in the eyes of some self-appointed critics, "murdered"—a variety of plays, comedy skits and musical numbers. On this appearance, their first visit to Victoria, they had been joined by the Taylor Brothers, a duo who performed a minstrel act on banjo and fiddle while wearing black make-up and adopting stereotypical characteristics of negro men.

Flora wanted to ask the girls how they could find it funny to see two white men perform as negro minstrel singers, given that their own father was Creole, and given the frequent insults they would hear from American miners passing through town. She tried to imagine finding it funny to watch a white man perform as an Ojibway singer or dancer, in make-up and costume, and wasn't sure that laughter was the reaction she would feel. But the question Flora wanted to ask most was how the Douglas sisters could even attend a theatrical performance. The Sisters of St. Ann had specifically announced a rule against their students' attendance at dances and theatrical events for as long as they were enrolled. Dancing close to young naval officers would inflame improper desires, while the adult humor expressed at many theatrical performances would serve to corrupt young women's thoughts and emotions. Flora wanted to ask the girls how they could attend the performance, but realized that she already knew the answer. To tell the Douglas sisters that they couldn't attend a theatrical event would be telling the Governor that he couldn't take his family to such an event. Rules may well be written, but they were written for other people to follow.

"Who else went to the show?" Flora inquired instead.

She wasn't so interested in a list of which of the town's elite were in the audience that night, as much as learning whether any other students in the Sister's school were also breaking the rule on theatre attendance. If students without the privilege of the Douglas girls were breaking the rule, then perhaps Flora could take the chance as well. After two weeks of attendance at the school, she had found herself repeating lessons from prior years in a myriad of subjects, all while facing substantial impositions to her social life. Or at least the social life she aspired to. If the Sisters wouldn't provide her with the lessons in nursing that she sought, then she wasn't about to completely abandon the opportunities of the colony's social calendar.

"If you're asking if he was there, he wasn't. He went upcountry with Judge Begbie to hold court. Poor Agnes is beside herself in grief."

"I'm not beside myself. He'll be back, by and by. And it's not as though I've no other distractions."

Flora struggled to suppress a smile. She most certainly had not been asking whether "he" had been there. The social whereabouts of Arthur Bushby wasn't a topic that was high on her list of inquiries, partly because she was already well aware that Bushby wasn't in town. The comings and goings of the more prominent members of the small community were matters of general knowledge. It was known throughout town that Bushby had accepted an appointment to serve as private secretary to Judge Begbie, and that the two men were in the midst of Begbie's first judicial circuit throughout British Columbia, thereby instantly decimating the quality and attractiveness of the Christ Church choir. The mere fact that Bushby had never set foot in a court of law had apparently been unimportant to the Judge's decision to hire the young man, despite the need for him to serve as clerk of the court, assize clerk, clerk of the arraigns, and whatever other role might need to be filled in order for the court to function. Begbie's trials would be held in barracks, cabins, tents, saloons, or whatever other shelter might be available, assuming the weather even dictated the need for shelter. In many cases, a sturdy tree able to bear the weight of the convicted defendant was the sole requirement for a trial to proceed.

Flora also didn't ask whether "he" had been there because it was never clear at any particular moment which eligible young man in the colony might qualify as "he" to Agnes Douglas. Rumors abounded—all of which Agnes had refused to confirm, but coyly avoided denying—that she had accepted a secret marriage proposal from the son of a prominent Company official, even while she'd continued to encourage visits from not merely Bushby, but other suitors as well. Alice, on the other hand, was no less a flirt, but was far more discreet about the objects of her affection.

"I'm sure there'll be plenty of young officers to cheer you up at the naval ball next week," Alice offered her sister in a rare gesture of support.

"You're going?" It was more a gasp than a question that burst from Flora's lips. To attend a theatrical performance was one thing. The Sisters of St. Ann might overlook that, particularly since the Chapman Family were well-established and played in the best houses. But to attend a naval ball thrown by the Royal Navy in Esquimalt, and to dance with unmarried men in public, seemed a far greater infraction of the Sisters' rules. The dances had always been conducted with proper decorum, but they had also been evenings of amusement, laughter, and dangerous flirtations, the latter of which the nuns particularly frowned upon. She had asked her friends the question out of surprise, but she quickly realized that the Douglas sisters' answer should have been no surprise at all.

\* \* \*

We clip the following item from the *Gazette* of March 8th:

"Objections have been urged against Speaker Helmcken's proposed plan for removing the Indians to San Juan Island, on the ground that its possession is in dispute between the British and American Governments, and a step of this kind might cause a serious complication of national relations."

It would be strong evidence of a woeful lack of intelligence, on the part of the citizens of Victoria, not to urge objections against such an ill-advised proposition. We seriously object, on the part of the people of this Territory, to such a plan, and would warn the authorities of Vancouver's Island, in a spirit of friendship, against consummating any such act of folly.

*The Puget Sound Herald*, March 18, 1859, p. 2.

\* \* \*

Dr. Helmcken held a cloth to his nose and mouth as he examined the farm laborer's inflamed right hand. The smell of whiskey on the man's breath wasn't strong enough to mask the stench of the rotting flesh that blackened his forefinger to the knuckle. In most examinations, Helmcken would have been bothered far more by a patient's inebriation than by the nature of the injury or infection. But when amputation was the inevitable outcome, inebriation was a preferred quality in a patient. Chloroform would dull the senses for surgery. But alcohol dulled the fear.

"How did this happen?" Helmcken asked the patient in a gentle tone.

"I cut finger on axe."

The patient's name was Jacob. He didn't give a last name, and Helmcken understood that he might not have one. He was a Sandwich Islander, a Kanaka, who worked as a farm laborer at the Company's Bellevue sheep farm on San Juan Island, and he had come to Victoria that morning in search of medical attention for his hand. If only he had come three or four days earlier, Helmcken could likely have stemmed the infection and perhaps saved the finger. Instead, it would be lost. The entire finger, past the knuckle and into the hand, assuming that the first amputation stemmed the gangrene so that the entire hand wouldn't require removal.

"I cannot save your finger. The tissue is dead. I'll try to save the rest of the hand. Do you understand what I'm saying?"

Jacob slowly nodded, then took a long drink and emptied his flask.

Helmcken crossed his office, dragged a wooden box from under a table and lifted the lid. Inside were implements for an amputation. On top sat a wide saw that was used for thick, weight-bearing bones such as the femur. He pushed the saw aside and reached beneath it for a narrower metacarpal saw, which was used for thinner bones. Once he had cut away the skin and muscles tissue with a scalpel, the saw would be necessary to sever the bone with a clean cut.

The metacarpal saw, a scalpel, chloroform, a cloth to administer the chloroform, and straps to secure the arm and limit the thrashing that both the chloroform and the pain would induce. Helmcken methodically laid out each of the tools for the operation. He had time to prepare while he waited for a Royal Navy surgeon to arrive to assist him by administering the chloroform, restraining the patient, and helping to stem the blood loss. Once the surgery began, his careful preparation would limit the potential for errors.

Helmcken surveyed the implements and concluded that one tool was missing. He crossed the office and reached into a cabinet for a bottle of whiskey. It wasn't a standard tool for surgery, but Jacob had emptied his flask, and another drink or two might be necessary to control his fears before the naval surgeon arrived. If it served that purpose, then it was perhaps the most useful tool on the table. And once the amputation was complete, it might prove far more useful again by helping the two surgeons to forget the sights, sounds and smells of their afternoon's labors.

\* \* \*

His Excellency, the Governor, presents his respects to the very Reverend Mother Superior of Saint Ann's Convent, and acknowledges the receipt of her esteemed letter, dated the 15th of this month.

His Excellency learns with admiration the principles of rule which the Reverend Mother Superior proposes to maintain in regard to dances.

His Excellency desires to inform the Reverend Superior, that in general, he does not permit his dear daughters to frequent dances, but some occasions occur, as for example, the assembly of last Tuesday, when his position and public duty require his presence. Such occasions do not occur frequently, but if the Reverend Superior looks upon them as infractions of the Convent regulations, His Excellency will be reduced of necessity, though with regrets, to withdraw his daughters from the school.

Finally, his Excellency begs the Reverend Superior to accept his expression of very high esteem.

Government House, March 17, 1859
To the Reverend Mother Superior,
Saint Ann's Convent

\* \* \*

Flora struggled to decipher the handwritten title on the book she had been handed to read, a task made far more difficult by the dim light that was shed by a single oil lamp. Though she sat near one of the windows in the simple log cabin that served as the Sisters of St. Ann's schoolhouse, convent, and residence, the window was quite small and the glass was uneven and flawed. There were only four small windows on the side of the cabin that served as the schoolroom, and on grey winter days they offered far less light than the students needed to read either a book or chalk slate.

Only two days earlier, the Sisters' cabin had been crowded with students, and Flora had been one of more than a dozen teenage girls. Several of them had been her friends and classmates at Mrs. Staines and Mrs. Cridge's schools in earlier years, and each of them had become a student of the Sisters in recent months. But Governor Douglas' decision to withdraw his three daughters had caused an instant controversy in the community. Just as his decision four months earlier to enroll his daughters in the Sisters' new school had been seen as an official stamp of approval, his decision to withdraw them was proving influential. Several of Flora's contemporaries had failed to show up for school that day, and others were admitting in whispered conversations that their parents would withdraw the girls before the next naval ball.

While Douglas' actions would sway others, Flora understood that the mass withdrawal arose from a matter that was far more important to the town's elite than merely following the Governor's lead. Naval balls were a critical opportunity for parents to introduce their daughters to the eligible bachelors that filled the junior officer corps of the British Navy. Any girl of marriageable age who was denied the opportunity to mingle with the officers would see her options for a favorable marriage reduced, leaving only the hardscrabble immigrants flooding into the colony or, even worse, the men who'd been born and bred in the colony.

Another ball was to be held that night. She had heard several of the girls talking about it. The officers of two warships assigned to the region—the *H.M.S. Plumper* and the *H.M.S Satellite*—along with the members of the Northwest Boundary Commission, were the hosts of the evening. It would be the social event of the month. It would be talked about for weeks. And though many of Flora's friends, and her sister, Mary, were certain to attend, Flora would remain at home, attempting to convince herself that her decision to continue as a student of the Sisters was the better decision.

She knew it was unlikely she'd ever convince an ambitious young naval officer to abandon his post and settle with her in the colony, just as she was equally unlikely to be considered an appropriate bride to take home to the mother country. If a bride of "Indian blood" was increasingly viewed with disparagement in the colonies, then she'd cause outright scandal in certain circles on the eastern side of the Atlantic. But logic didn't entirely erase her reservations about missing such an event, especially because her education at the Sisters' school had yet to live up to either her expectations or hopes. Her first month had been largely a review by the Sisters, as they had sought to learn where Flora's prior education placed her among the array of students that filled the cramped cabin. She had spent most of her life obtaining a proper education, but some of the younger children were unable to read or write their own names.

The Sisters had quickly decided that the primary shortcoming in Flora's education was French grammar. French had been the language spoken most by Isabella to her children, but Flora's knowledge of the rules of French grammar was average. Most of the Sisters were French-Canadian by origin, and all four of them had spent their lives in and around the growing city of Montreal before coming to Fort Victoria. French grammar was a perfect meeting place between Flora's educational needs and the Sisters' teaching abilities.

French grammar hadn't been the purpose of her enrollment. But as she turned her eyes back to the notebook she had been given to study that afternoon, and began to understand its contents, Flora realized that her questions hadn't fallen entirely on deaf ears. Sister Mary of the Conception's notes from her own education in nursing practices were remarkably detailed, were written in French and, despite their lack of context, provided Flora with a great deal of information. It was information she might have been incapable of absorbing if she hadn't spent the past month focusing heavily on written French grammar.

# Chapter 5

"*Allons-y, Flora, vite,*" Sister Mary of the Conception insisted in a cheerful tone, without pausing to check if Flora was still behind her.

Flora hurried to keep pace and struggled to comprehend how a young nun who had only lived in the colony for less than a year could have become so agile on the muddy roads that branched out from the stockade around the Fort. Flora had always considered herself to be adept at navigating the treacherous mud pits that served as roads in Victoria. But compared to Sister Mary, she felt like a novice, though not a novice of the Catholic nun variety.

The last two weeks of March had been pleasant, but heavy rains and wet snow over the previous two days had turned the dusty dirt streets to mud. The mud made it a challenge for any lady to move through the town on foot, particularly on the streets that didn't have a wooden walkway. Despite the inconvenience, Flora considered the challenges of the mud to be far preferable to the dust that would engulf the small town during long dry stretches in the summer, particularly given how much of the dust would have originated in the overflow draining from poorly dug privies throughout town.

Flora followed Sister Mary to the front door of the home of David Forbes and his wife, Jane. It was a simple, two-story house on Collinson Street, built the prior year after Forbes and his wife had arrived from Montreal in the early stages of the gold rush to open a shop. The Forbes had arrived just weeks after Sister Mary, but under very different circumstances. The Sisters had left Montreal to answer a calling. Forbes had left Montreal in an effort to make his way in the world as a man of business, not charity.

Flora had never met Jane Forbes. But every woman in Victoria knew her on sight. For she had arrived in town at a point in her life when the peak of her beauty had coincided with both her knowledge of fashion and the social aspirations of her husband. She'd arrived not simply wearing a dress of the latest fashion, but also bringing with her a wardrobe far larger and more stylish than that of any woman in town. The quality of the laces and velvets advertised a status that few women in the colony could hope to match. But most noticeably, the skirts of Jane's dresses billowed out over hoops in the fashion popular in the Eastern colonies and U.S. states, while the dresses worn by most young women in town still rode over heavy petticoats, if they rode over anything at all. Jane Forbes had been noticed the moment she'd set foot on Vancouver Island by nearly every man in Victoria, but even more so by every woman.

By contrast, Sister Mary had arrived weeks earlier, but did nothing to change the fashions of Victoria; dressed in a simple black habit, and accompanied by Bishop Demers and her similarly attired Sisters from the convent of St. Ann. Each woman's impact on the small community had been significant, yet disparate, as would be their reason for meeting that day in Jane's second-story bedroom.

Flora and Sister Mary were welcomed into the house by the family's Chinaman, who silently ushered them to a narrow staircase that led to the second floor. Flora tried unsuccessfully to avoid staring as she passed him. Chinese men had started to arrive in mid-1858, after news of the gold discoveries had reached Asia, and their numbers had increased in recent months. Some had ventured immediately to the Fraser River, while others had remained in Victoria to pursue business opportunities or seek domestic positions to work off the price of their voyage. It was rude to stare, but she was fascinated by their distinct dress, their hair, their facial features. Everyone stared the first few times they passed a Chinaman in the streets. Families in Victoria that could afford domestic help traditionally had Indian servants, if less than a decade could be considered enough to establish a tradition. But Chinamen were rapidly becoming the favored candidates for domestic service. They were unique, they were cheap, and they weren't Indian.

Flora managed to limit her inquisitiveness to a quick glance as she followed Sister Mary up the stairs. The confidence with which Sister Mary invited herself into the couple's bedroom shocked Flora. Even though she understood that formalities can quickly evaporate in the face of a family illness, she would have expected an invitation from someone other than the family's domestic servant before entering a couple's bedroom, and certainly would have expected a nun to do the same.

Dr. Helmcken looked up as the two women entered the room, pausing from packing medical implements into his worn leather bag.

"Ah, good, Mr. and Mrs. Forbes, this is Sister Mary— oh, and Miss Flora Ross, who, I understand, has enrolled in the Sisters' school to learn about nursing."

Flora presumed that she wasn't expected to respond with a spoken greeting, but rather that she should remain in the background and defer to Sister Mary.

David Forbes stood by the window looking distinctly uncomfortable with Sister Mary's arrival. Across the room, Jane Forbes lay in bed, propped against pillows and looking pale and thin, but for the protrusion of her belly. She turned to Helmcken as he packed the last of his implements.

"I should hardly think I'm in a state that requires so many people to be hovering over me," she insisted. "Then again, I suppose if you asked the Sisters to be here rather than the Bishop, it at least means you're not anticipating last rites anytime today."

Helmcken smiled without responding and turned to David Forbes.

"Mr. Forbes, a word downstairs, if I might?"

Helmcken invited Sister Mary to join them with a gesture of his head. Flora started to follow, only to be stopped by a firm smile from Sister Mary. The instruction startled her. She hadn't expected to be allowed to participate in the most personal of family discussions, but neither had she expected on her first home visit to find herself alone with the patient in the most private of spaces, having to make small talk with a patient who was probably dying while the others discussed her fate in another room.

"Are you attending the philharmonic this evening?" Helmcken inquired of Forbes as they descended the stairs and faded from earshot.

The question nearly caused Flora to giggle, even though it had likely been intended to put Forbes at ease. It would be the philharmonic society's first concert that evening, made up entirely of local amateur performers and the Royal Navy's band from the *H.M.S. Tribune*, and it was certain to be well-attended. But an awkward air might have descended over Helmcken's discussion of his wife's medical condition if her husband had replied that, yes, he was planning to leave his dying wife at home in order to attend the affair, and was watching the time to ensure he wouldn't be late.

Flora attempted to offer Jane a comforting smile, but feared she only communicated discomfort at the circumstances.

"Well, Miss Ross, I presume you're one of the Isabella Ross Rosses."

"Yes, ma'am, her youngest daughter."

"Too young to be attending to someone like me, I should think."

"I'm almost seventeen." Flora was only nine years younger than Jane, but she understood that they were separated by more than just years. Jane's manner of speaking suggested an air of culture and breeding that was rare for a woman in the colony.

"Hmm. So then you're a novice?"

"Oh, no, ma'am. I'm just a student at the Sisters' school. I want to learn to be a nurse."

"Oh, yes, the doctor said that, didn't he? I've met your brother. John, I believe?"

"He's one of my older brothers."

Flora blushed as she heard her own reply. It would have been obvious to anyone who met them that he was older by twenty years, but she hadn't quite allowed herself to relax in this woman's bedroom, so the occasional awkward sentiment would have to suffice for conversation.

She discreetly gazed around the room, partly out of curiosity and partly to avoid looking directly at Jane. The house itself wasn't grand, but the bedroom showed the couple's taste and relative wealth by its furnishings and decoration, including the beautiful quilt that lay across the bed.

"So, then, Miss Ross, what would be your guess about this situation? I presume I'm dying, or they wouldn't be huddled downstairs, afraid of letting me hear anything. That's how these things go, isn't it? You tell the living that the patient's dying and invite the nuns to come over for support, but you certainly don't dare tell the patient directly that they'll soon shuffle off this mortal coil. It might be to keep the patient from giving up, but I suspect it's really to keep the family from having to deal with the patient's cries of despair until the inevitability is so obvious the patient's already figured it out on her own."

Were it any other topic of conversation, Flora would have found Jane's frankness to be invigorating. But a conversation about mortality on her first home visit only increased Flora's awkwardness, particularly since she could sense the fear behind the patient's ramblings. If Dr. Helmcken couldn't tell this woman that she was dying, then Flora was certain it shouldn't fall on her to bear the news. All she'd been told by Sister Mary was that the young woman had appeared to be pregnant, but that complications had ensued, and that it now appeared more likely that the growth inside the woman's uterus was not a baby, but a tumor. A diagnosis involving a large tumor proximate to the uterus left little doubt as to the outcome. Surely someone had told the poor woman this much.

"I'm sure you're going to be just fine, ma'am."

"I had so wanted a girl. I was sure it was a girl until the pains began. Then I decided it had to be a boy. Now I'd just be content if it's something that might pass. You're Catholic, Flora?"

"Uh, no, ma'am, mostly Church of England."

"Mostly?"

"Sometimes out here you can't be too concerned with whatever church is available to you."

"Well, I know it's blasphemy to say, but I've always felt we end up in the same place, no matter how we pray."

"I suppose I agree," Flora answered. "I've just never said it out loud like that."

"And nor should you, at your age. You'd only get yourself into trouble around here, I should expect, especially with the nuns."

Flora blushed, feeling Jane's eyes scanning in silent judgment.

"I'd never met an Indian until we arrived here," Jane continued. "We don't have them much in Montreal. Certainly not in the better parts. Is it true your mother owns a farm?"

"Yes, ma'am, just southeast of town."

"I can't quite fathom that it's allowed here."

"There are lots of farms on the edge of town."

Flora realized before finishing her sentence that Jane's disbelief hadn't been about the mere existence of farms near town, but about the idea that her Ojibway mother was the owner of such a farm. She briefly considered a second response, but opted instead to leave in place her more charitable presumption that Jane's inability to fathom Isabella's ownership of a farm must have been based on geography rather than race.

"*Flora, allons-y, s'il te plaît.*" It was Sister Mary calling from the bottom of the stairs. She was from an Irish family near Montreal, but seemed determined to speak French to Flora to further her language education.

"I'm sorry, I have to –"

"Well, this was a short visit, Miss Ross, but I've a feeling we may be seeing more of each other, if a nurse is what you are to become."

"I do hope so," Flora replied, before realizing the implications of her response. "Once you're feeling better."

She hoped it was a lie that Jane would appreciate, even though the falseness of the statement was obvious to them both.

Flora stood and hesitated, struck by the possibility that it wasn't Jane's cultured, eastern background that was intimidating to her, but the unspoken certainty that this young woman would shortly die. Flora was intimidated by the unseen tumor. But she was intimidated far more by the realization that, though she had escaped any detailed discussion about mortality at this first, brief visit, any future visit might require a more lengthy conversation about the fact that Jane would soon be dead. Elizabeth had been unconscious throughout her final days. Flora had carried on many conversations with her dying sister inside her own head during her vigil. But they had been conversations she could control. Surely the nuns would tend to all matters of spiritual questioning and issues of mortality. Yet she had been left alone with the patient during her first home visit, had been faced with the frightened woman's rambling fears, and had offered nothing more than untruthful reassurance. It was an aspect of nursing that she'd never considered before. And suddenly she could think of nothing else.

Flora smiled politely, hoping that her face hadn't communicated the flurry of uncomfortable thoughts that had rushed through her head, then hurried down the narrow stairs to where the family's Chinaman held open the front door for her.

\* \* \*

James Wright felt a sharp pain across the back of his skull as his head slammed against the kitchen floor at the back of the Ross farmhouse. The next feeling he noticed was a throbbing pain in his right eye, followed by a warm trickle of blood running down his cheek. The only other feeling he could identify as he struggled to get back on his feet was the urge to escape, only to have William Ross' fist drive into his jaw and send him sprawling once more.

Wright crawled across the floor in an effort to keep his face below the reach of his assailants' fists, and managed to wrench open the back door without receiving any more blows. Then he barreled out the door and stumbled across the snow-dusted field, certain that one, two, or all three of the young men would be fast on his heels, anxious to pummel him further. But only laughter trailed behind. Wright fell to the ground several times as he ran, partly from the whiskey he'd consumed in the Ross kitchen, partly from his inability to see out of his swollen right eye, and partly from his fear and confusion.

He was certain that he must have done something wrong on this cold Sunday morning to have justified the attack. Wright had always known he was different. The term "half-wit" was one he'd heard aimed in his direction many times over his forty years, and he'd heard it spoken that morning by the younger Ross brothers and William McNeill, Jr., their friend and neighbor. Wright had always preferred to refer to himself by the title of his occasional employment—a baker—but his weakness for whiskey meant that he was regarded far more as a half-wit "vagrant" than a "baker" by most who knew him.

Wright had gone to the Ross farm that morning hoping to find Alexander, hoping to secure some short-term work at the Ross farm. But Alexander wasn't at the farm, and neither were his mother nor his sisters. It was Sunday morning, and they were at church like most respectable people in Victoria. Instead, Wright found Francis and William Ross drinking at the back of the house around the kitchen fire with McNeill.

Wright had known all three men for several years. They had shared many nights in a cell at the Victoria gaol after arrests for public drunkenness or vagrancy. He couldn't exactly call them friends, but they had encouraged him to stay, and even handed him his own cup of whiskey. Wright had sensed a nervousness in the back of his mind, but it was a feeling he experienced whenever he tried to make friends. It was only when Francis slammed his fist into Wright's right eye that Wright understood that his nervousness was justified. His first instinct had been to pull himself up from the floor and run from the Ross farmhouse, but the fists and boots of all three men kept hitting him, each accompanied by laughter.

Wright couldn't outrun the young men, not when town was nearly two miles away. He needed shelter. A place to hide. It didn't cross his slow mind that he had left a trail of blood in the snow that would make it easy for anyone to find him before the last of the snow melted.

He scrambled down the bank of a small creek just outside the boundaries of the Ross farm and crouched in the shade beneath a small, wooden bridge. The ground was hard from the unexpected late spring frost, and it remained covered by the few inches of snow that had fallen overnight. The same shelter that had kept the sun from melting the snow also provided him with the illusion of the refuge he craved. It felt safe, and the babble of the creek was certain to help conceal him. Wright curled himself into the bank beside the creek, leaned his bruised and bleeding face into the cold snow, and then struggled to understand what he had done wrong so that he could be sure to never do it again.

*＊* ＊ *＊*

Judge Augustus Pemberton, stipendiary magistrate and police commissioner, stared down at Francis and William Ross from behind his bench, displaying both anger and disappointment.

"This is the second occasion on which you both have appeared before me on complaints of assaulting and maltreating near-helpless and harmless men. These were cowardly and brutal acts, and this latest outrage seems to stem from the leniency I showed you both on the last occasion. Therefore, I am fining you both five pounds, or in default of payment, two months imprisonment in the Victoria gaol. And be warned, if either of you come before this court again on a similar charge, I'll show little mercy. When fines fail to restrain the brutal propensities of bad men to commit aggravated assaults of this kind, I have the power to commit the accused to long gaol terms and to exact heavy bonds to assure good future conduct. I trust my words will be heeded this time."

Pemberton pounded his gavel and turned his attention away from the Ross brothers.

Flora watched from her seat in the small gallery and struggled to understand her own conflicted feelings about the sentence. Despite Pemberton's harsh words, a fine of five pounds was a light sentence that didn't fit the damage her brothers had caused. Pemberton had a history of issuing harsh sentences to men whose crimes were as simple as minor theft, public drunkenness, or the sale of whiskey to Indians. A punishment of six months of hard labor would have been likely if her brothers had been strangers to the colony. Newcomers could expect harsh sentences on their first charge. Indians could expect harsh sentences at any time. Wayward sons of Company families might be of mixed blood, but they were given many more chances to reform. It was as if a harsh sentence would serve as recognition that the system—that the Company—had somehow failed. William's youth was undoubtedly a factor in their favor, as he wasn't yet fifteen. To be drunk and violent at fourteen may well be a crime, but it wouldn't do to send the boy to months of hard labor when it was unclear whether he showed the promise of a responsible adulthood. Francis, on the other hand, was twenty-one. He had long ago run out of opportunities to explain away his behavior as youthful indulgence.

William McNeill had even less ability to cling to an excuse of youth. He was twenty-seven, a father of four, and was the McNeill son in charge of operating his family's farm, adjacent to the Ross farm, while his father ran a Company trading post along the northern coast of British Columbia. He still hadn't been arrested, and would likely stay in hiding long enough to measure the sentence handed down to the Ross brothers.

Flora loved both of her brothers dearly. Despite their differences, they were the brothers closest to her in age, while her older brothers had always seemed like substitute parents. But she also felt anger at their violent streak as she watched Wright limp out through the back of the small courtroom, his face swollen and bandaged. He hadn't asked for the burden of a feeble mind, and though Francis and William had similarly not asked to have a weakness for whiskey or a propensity to violence, Wright was undoubtedly the more sympathetic of the three. A brief flash of guilt also crossed Flora's mind as she realized that she also felt relief for her own circumstances. The possibility that the brothers might face a sentence of several months, just as they would be expected to help prepare the fields for spring planting, had created the fear in Flora's mind that her studies might be placed on hold so that she could help in their place. Pemberton had unknowingly saved her from such a fate.

Francis and William approached the benches expressing satisfaction rather than contrition, while Isabella's expression showed little in the way of relief.

"*Cinq livres. Je vais la payer, mais c'est la dernière fois. Compris?*" She would pay the fine for the brothers this time, but never again. Isabella turned and walked from the courtroom, ignoring the eyes that gazed on her with sympathy and judgment. Flora heard the determination in her mother's ultimatum, but wondered if her brothers had heard it as well.

She exited the courtroom to catch up to her mother, and found her in Bastian Square, engaged in conversation with Dr. Helmcken. He had treated Wright's damaged eye and had testified about the extent of his injuries.

"You're not doing them any favors by paying the bond," he advised as Flora approached.

"Prison is not better," Isabella replied.

"Perhaps Francis needs some time in Nisqually, at one

of his siblings' farms? It might do him some good to be separated from his brother for a few months."

Isabella dismissed the idea with a look. Five of her ten children had left the comfort of the nest, and two of those five were now deceased, one just weeks earlier. But it was also an idea that Flora had heard her mother raise before, after many sleepless nights. Charles, Jr. had a farm outside Nisqually and had the mouths of three children to feed. Perhaps the elder Ross brother would take Francis under his wing as a laborer, and serve as the disciplinary influence that Isabella had proven unable to be.

With his advice dispensed, Helmcken tipped his hat, offered a sympathetic smile, and then ventured across Bastion Square. Flora took her mother's arm just as John Butts' booming Australian voice echoed from Government Street.

"Town lots coming up for auction, Victoria and Esquimalt Harbor. Apply to the offices of Selim Franklin and Company. God save the Queen ... God save John Butt."

Flora and Isabella passed Butts on the wooden walkway as he lifted his hat and offered a slight bow.

"Morning to you, ladies. May you both have a thoroughly magnificent day."

Flora smiled and nodded. She would never have considered the possibility that a morning in court could serve as the start to a "magnificent" day. But Butts had a tendency to speak in superlatives, and she recognized that he likely was incapable of wishing them a "fine" or "decent" day. Such greetings were ordinary, for ordinary people to share. Butts seemed driven by a determination to never be seen as ordinary.

"Perhaps he'll be proven right, mama," Flora suggested. "Perhaps this can be a magnificent day after all."

Isabella huffed her disagreement. *"Ce garçon est un imbécile."*

Flora nodded, accepting that her mother's perspective was entirely different from her own. Isabella's sons would be home that night, which would be the wish of any mother. But soon they'd be drinking again. There'd be more fights, more arrests, more fines and eventually many nights spent in gaol. Flora considered her mother's perspective and accepted that there was little chance the day would ever be remembered as magnificent.

\* \* \*

# NOTICE.

I, ISABELLA ROSS caution all and every person that I will not be responsible for any debts contracted by my sons Francis or William Ross.
Victoria, 27th April, 1859.

*The British Colonist*, Saturday, April 30, 1859, p. 2.

\* \* \*

Beacon Hill Park had always felt like a private playground to Flora, lying south of the town, just to the west of the narrow wagon road that connected the Ross farm to Victoria. But as it was Queen Victoria's fortieth birthday, the park had become a playground for most of Victoria, crowded with over two thousand residents, miners and sailors, all anxious for the excitement of the annual horse races.

Flora and her friend, Fanny McNeill, had walked to the park with their respective older sisters, Mary and Matilda, but had become separated from the older girls. It was a circumstance that had been quietly intentional on both sides. None of the girls were particularly interested in the horse races. To merely watch a race between domesticated animals ridden by drunken men was a passive pastime. A far more interesting afternoon would involve a competition of their own, attracting the attentions of young sailors from the Royal Navy who were on leave for the day. Flora and Fanny shared Mary and Matilda's interest in the pursuit of frustrated and inebriated midshipmen, but also knew better than to try to compete with their older sisters, both of whom were accomplished flirts. Neither had put words to the thought, but Flora and Fanny shared a willingness to hang back at the edge of the crowd and scan for slightly less confident targets who might be overlooked by the two older girls. It was an interest that quickly faded when Flora's eyes fell on a far more interesting opportunity.

"Fanny, there's someone I need to go talk to."

"Who?"

"Over there. That woman with the baby. You don't mind, do you?"

Fanny shrugged her agreement and followed Flora across the field to where Lucinda Boyce reclined on a small blanket beneath an Arbutus tree. In the field nearby, two small boys rolled a hoop with sticks.

"Mrs. Boyce—Flora Ross. We met at the delivery you did a few weeks back for my sister-in-law, Genevieve."

"Of course. Very nice to see you again."

Flora introduced Lucinda to Fanny, and wondered if it would be polite to mention her surprise at finding the American woman celebrating the Queen's birthday. She kept the thought to herself, realizing that the vast majority of people in the park that day were likely to be American, and were likely using the official occasion as an excuse to enjoy a fine spring afternoon.

"I've been getting to accompany one of the Sisters on home visits over the past couple weeks," Flora proclaimed.

"Oh, that is good news. You must be learning a great deal."

"All I really do is watch what she does, and then twice I was left to just keep the patient company. I was hoping I could ask you some things."

Fanny tugged on Flora's sleeve and gestured toward Mary and Matilda across the meadow. "I'm going to …"

Flora nodded, realizing that a conversation about her afternoons with a dying woman couldn't compete with the midshipmen falling prey to the flirtations of Mary and Matilda. Fanny frowned a shy apology in Lucinda's direction and then hurried to catch up with the older girls.

Flora wondered if she had made the wrong decision to

so quickly abandon her afternoon plans for a conversation with Lucinda. The Sisters of St. Ann could prevent Flora from attending a formal ball, but nothing within their rules for decorum appeared to prevent her from chatting with a young sailor during a celebration of Queen Victoria's birthday. If the Sisters were to object at all, it would more likely be to the celebration of the British monarch than to an innocent discussion in a public park.

"Boys, stop fighting." Lucinda's reprimand was directed at the two boys playing with the hoop, and it pulled Flora from her distracted thoughts.

"They're yours, too?" she asked, already certain of the answer.

"Frank, the oldest, and Orrin, five." Lucinda smiled at Flora. "It's nice to have your company, but don't let me keep you from finding an interested shippy."

Flora smiled. "I'd rather talk with you. Chatting up the shippies is a little like fishing for bullheads in the creek. It seems fun until you catch one and realize there's nothing appropriate you can do except yank the hook out of its mouth and throw it back."

Lucinda laughed. "Fair point. I've met my share of sailors over the years, and I recall a frequent feeling of disappointment."

Flora hesitated, wanting to return the conversation to her list of questions.

"So, what is it that you can't ask the Sisters, but desperately want to ask me?" Lucinda asked.

Flora grinned at her own transparency.

"I just hadn't expected … I always thought of nursing as a physical effort—delivering a baby, applying a mustard plaster, feeding them, preparing a tincture—but that's only half the job. When I watched my mother care for someone, I just assumed the other half was my mother being a mother. But I have to do that, too. I have to talk to the patient, comfort her, help her understand what it means to be lying in bed … dying … at such a young age. And I'm just turning seventeen. How can I do that at my age?"

Lucinda reached out and took Flora's hand in her own.

"First, you listen. Patients are very good at telling themselves whatever they need to hear at any moment, whether it's searching for hope or adjusting to the need to face their mortality. You don't affirm a dying woman's hope for a miraculous recovery, or confirm a despondent patient's prediction of imminent death. You support them, whether that's holding their hand, listening to whatever they go on about, praying with them, or helping them sleep. And you do the physical side of your job to make sure they're as comfortable as you can make them. I may be a decade older than you, but I'm still overawed by the responsibility."

"I just worry I may not be prepared for it all."

"The fact you're worried is an excellent sign. Flora, some advice. Don't become friends with the poor woman. It's hard not to do, and you won't listen to me right away. But you'll find a nurse's life is harder if you become friends with every dying patient."

"My mother said the same thing, and I know it's good advice, even if it isn't easy to do."

A bell rang out across the park followed by a cheer from the crowd as another race began. The booming voice that barked the call of the race indicated that John Butts had expanded his duties from town crier and bell-ringer, though he called the race at a pace far more sluggish than the horses could possibly be running, peppered with irrelevant asides.

"I imagine there are many shillings and dollars being won and lost over there," Lucinda said, gesturing toward the crowd. "It means half my neighbors'll be drinking more than usual tonight to celebrate their winnings, and the other half'll be drinking even more to forget how much they lost."

Flora glanced across the park to the crowd that surrounded the flats where the races were underway, certain that Francis and William were somewhere among the celebrants, at the center of the betting, or at least the center of the drinking.

"Orrin, Frank, come here, boys," Lucinda instructed. Frank and Orrin looked up from their play with a rehearsed look of disappointment, anticipating that their afternoon in the park was coming to an end.

"Do you wanna see horses race around the park?" she asked them.

Their enthusiastic nods lasted only a moment before each began to run toward the crowd.

"Wait, boys. Wait!" Lucinda turned to Flora. "Will you join us? I could use a hand keeping track of the two of them in that crowd."

Flora glanced across the field and caught a glimpse of Fanny engrossed in conversation with Mary, Matilda, and a few young men from the Royal Navy, who looked as though they might be rather handsome if they were sober. For a brief moment she considered the fun she might have if she joined her friends for an afternoon dodging the drunken advances of overly insistent shippies.

"I'd like that," she answered.

"Off to the races, then?"

Flora nodded, certain that she was making the better decision, and followed Lucinda's lead into the crowd.

\* \* \*

Charles Griffin grabbed the paper nailed to the door of his cabin and ripped it free. It was a U.S. tax notice, a quarterly affair that seemed to represent the limits of action that the U.S. Deputy Inspector of Customs was willing to take on the island. Griffin glanced at the note's brief text. It claimed that the Company's Bellevue sheep farm owed the U.S. government $935.00 in taxes for its operations on San Juan Island during the prior quarter, and was signed "Paul K. Hubbs, Jr."

Griffin gazed across the farm in the direction of Hubbs' cabin. It sat a short distance to the west, beyond the farm's vegetable garden, and across the plateau above the Strait of Juan de Fuca. He felt certain that Hubbs was watching to see Griffin's reaction to the notice, but could see no sign of the American official. He considered tearing the notice to pieces, in case Hubbs was watching, but decided instead to forward the notice to Company officials in Victoria so that the Company could lodge an official protest with the U.S. government.

Griffin had just returned to San Juan Island on Jemmy Jones' new schooner, the *Carolena*, after having spent four days in Victoria on Company business. At thirty-two years of age, he still carried himself with a lithe athleticism and abundance of energy, somewhat tempered by his Presbyterian reserve and strong sense of duty to his position. He favored close-cropped mutton chops over the fuller beards that adorned so many of his superiors in the Company, and had managed to keep most of the hair on his head, which he maintained neatly trimmed. With thirteen years of Company service behind him, since arriving from Ireland, Griffin was a Chief Trader—a rank below partnership—and had been the clerk in charge of Bellevue Farm since establishing the post in 1853. He had no illusions that partnership with the Company lay in his future. He was a solid, reliable worker who managed an efficient farm, and the reward for solid, reliable workers rarely included a share in the business.

Griffin looked up from the tax notice to see Aleck Mcdonald, the farm's dairyman, approaching across the dirt road that ran through the middle of the small farm.

"Hubbs nailed it there yesterday, on the Queen's birthday of all days," Aleck called over as he neared the cabin.

"And it'll be ignored like all the rest. Seems I should think twice next time the Clallams are lobbing lead shot into his cabin and he needs someone to save himself, hmm?" It was Griffin's standard retort any time Hubbs annoyed him, referring to the protection Hubbs had received from Griffin and his employees when his cabin had been attacked by local Indians a year earlier. Posting tax notices hardly fit within the gratitude Griffin expected. Hubbs hadn't been injured in the attack, but the garroted bodies of two unfortunate white men had been found on the beach below Hubbs' cabin, most likely miners attempting to reach the Fraser River in a canoe. Americans were at a slightly higher risk along the west coast than British settlers. The attack on Hubbs' cabin rather than Bellevue Farm just a hundred yards away was a typical example of how most Indians up and down the coast showed a far greater preference for dealing with the "King George men" over the "Boston men" who had flooded into the colony since the discovery of gold.

Griffin folded the notice and made a mental note to send it to Dallas on the next boat to Victoria.

"How's the work on the granary?"

"It's comin' along."

Griffin nodded in satisfaction, though his face showed no hint of a smile. Aleck Mcdonald was one of a half-dozen white men at the farm—a mix of Scots, Irishmen and French-Canadians—who, like Griffin, had come to the island after years of service in other Company posts. Other workers at the farm, of which there were usually about fifteen, depending on the season, were Kanakas from the Sandwich Islands, occasionally a colored man or two, and several Indians. Aleck had been at Bellevue Farm for little more than a year, but had nearly a decade of Company service at trading posts in the New Caledonia region. He had shown particular skill at managing the farm's dairy cattle and was always willing to chip in wherever his labor was needed. But Griffin had harbored doubts about leaving the operations of the entire farm in Aleck's hands during a four-day excursion to Victoria. He was relieved and slightly impressed that he could report in the post journal he updated each evening that he had returned to find that all was well.

Griffin reached for the door handle to his residence and then hesitated, wondering if he should ask Aleck how his ailing wife was faring. She had been ill for several weeks though the cause was unknown. Instead, Griffin opted for the safer approach of assuming that Aleck would have raised the topic with him if there were anything he should know.

He turned his mind to the letter he would compose to Company officials. It would need to cover far more than just the demand for taxes. Tensions between Company farmworkers and American squatters were increasing with every interaction, and had escalated recently to scattered threats of physical violence. Several of Griffin's best sheep runs were being claimed as homesteads by squatters who had little knowledge or regard for the ongoing work of the Northwest Boundary Commission. The Clallams who'd attacked Hubbs' cabin had been driven by motivations far different than those driving the American settlers to stake claims to the island, but the risks each might pose to Bellevue Farm appeared far too similar.

Griffin entered his cabin, sat at his small desk by the window, and unfolded the tax notice. He understood that it was simply a political act intended to show an ongoing assertion of sovereignty, just as the formal protest to be lodged by officials in Victoria would underscore the British claim to the island. But he couldn't shake the feeling that symbolic acts might soon appear meaningless. He pulled a sheet of paper from his drawer, opened his inkwell, and pondered the best approach for raising his concerns with Company officials.

# Chapter 6

"Are you sure this is a necessary procedure?" Jane Forbes asked, her voice tinged with awkwardness as she looked away from Sister Mary and Flora.

"It will help to alleviate your discomfort," Sister Mary assured her.

"Will it, really? Or is it just elevating my discomfort so much more so that I'll be convinced it was reduced once this is over?"

Flora couldn't blame the poor woman. Jane was already in constant pain. The enema that Sister Mary had prepared might help in some respects, but Flora sympathized with their patient.

On any prior occasion, when Flora had been allowed to accompany Sister Mary on a home visit, it had been expected that she would stand at the side of the room to watch and learn. Most of those visits had been to the Forbes residence, but there had also been a baby delivered, and two visits to a dying woman at the Songhees reserve. This was her first opportunity to assist, and to demonstrate that she'd been paying attention. The fact that it involved the administration of an enema was something she would simply need to overlook if she was going to pursue nursing as a profession.

"Flora, go downstairs and ask their Chinaman for another towel."

"Yes, Sister."

Flora had noticed that Sister Mary would speak to her in English when around Jane, most likely to ensure that their patient wasn't disturbed by a conversation in French that might be about her. Even though Jane had lived most of her life in Montreal, she had lived in an English section and was far from conversant in French.

Flora walked downstairs to the main floor. She found the Forbes' Chinaman in the kitchen and realized, as she approached him, that she only knew him as "their Chinaman," as if he had no other name.

Flora found Chinese manners, clothing, and appearance to be as strange as everyone else found them to be. But she found it equally strange how Victoria's society dealt with the new immigrants. No one ever seemed to know the name of any of the Chinamen, as if knowing the term "Chinaman" was all that was ever needed. But now Flora would have to address the Forbes' housekeeper directly, and she had no idea what to call him, let alone how much English he spoke.

"Excuse me. Yes, hello, um, Mrs. Forbes, she needs another towel."

"Towel."

"Yes, towel, to dry, um … the cloth for –"

Her description was unnecessary, as he nodded and left the kitchen in search of a towel. She felt a flush of embarrassment for having presumed that she'd have to explain the concept, and even act it out.

Racial hierarchies had always existed in the colony, as far as Flora could remember, but until recently the simple hierarchy had been white men at the top, and Indians at the bottom. People of mixed blood were somewhere in the middle, depending on the social standing of their families and the visibility of their Indian features.

But the influx of Chinamen and negroes over the past year, as well as many miners from some of the stranger countries in southern and eastern Europe, had added so many dimensions to the racial tensions in the colony that Flora could hardly keep up. She had noticed distinctions between the races at play in shipping announcements found in the *British Colonist* newspaper. The arrival of a boat would be announced along with a listing of its passengers and cargo, such that a ship might be listed as carrying nine passengers, and a certain number of cattle, sheep or other livestock. But if two Chinamen and three Indians were also onboard, then the boat would be carrying nine passengers, various heads of cattle, sheep, other livestock, two Chinamen, and three Indians.

"A towel, Miss Ross."

The housekeeper held out a towel.

"Thank you …" Flora smiled in embarrassment and took the towel. It felt wrong to leave the phrase hanging without a name attached, especially when he had managed to learn her name. The front door opened just as she turned back toward the stairs. David Forbes entered, accompanied by a man Flora didn't recognize.

"And if we're lucky, we'll have that drink in peace without being disturbed by another nun or Indian having the run of the house."

Flora didn't need to be told that she was the "Indian" Forbes had referenced, in a manner not unlike Sister Mary's reference to their "Chinaman." But hearing herself referred to as "Indian" had become such a common occurrence that she showed no outward reaction, and focused instead on the immediate need to climb the stairs to return to the second floor. It would mean having to walk past Forbes and his guest in the entryway only moments after she'd been denigrated to a complete stranger. But there was no other way to reach the bedroom, and a prompt return would be expected. She took a deep breath, kept her eyes to the floor, and walked quietly to the stairs. She managed a meek smile of greeting as she passed the two men, and then climbed the stairs as quietly as she could. Not a word was spoken, nor an eye met by another. She felt relief to realize that, as Indian disturbances could go, it had been quite unremarkable.

* * *

Hubbs steered his canoe onto the muddy beach south of the Songhees reserve, across the small harbor from Victoria. He had paddled over from San Juan Island to stock up on provisions and further his connections with some of the Americans living in the colony. Though his official jurisdiction extended no farther than San Juan Island and its surrounding archipelago, and was limited to the task of levying customs taxes, he viewed himself as an ambassador for the interests of Americans in Victoria. Particularly for those who had an interest in staking claims on the disputed island. But provisions and connections could wait. Other requirements for the trip could not.

Hubbs secured his canoe high on the beach and walked along the thick mud toward the entrance to the harbor. Several flapping sheets of canvas were secured to the bushy salal along the beach to form crude shelters. A dozen young Indian women approached Hubbs and each beckoned him to follow them into the salal. Several exposed their breasts or lifted their skirts to advertise their wares. There was enough light left in the summer evening for Hubbs to conclude that most of the women were Songhees or Cowichan, and that he found some of them to be attractive. There would have been more selection along the northern edges of the tent city surrounding Victoria, particularly in the crude brothels that had been established in recent months, but he preferred this more informal location closer to the reserve. He had a type, and it was not the Chinese girls or pricier white women he could find closer to town.

Hubbs ignored the women's efforts to haggle him on price and continued to walk along the beach. He smiled when he realized that his persistence had been worthwhile. A girl in her late teens, bearing northern Indian features, and wearing only a blanket around her waist and a few bracelets on her wrists, stood apart from the other women. She looked down as Hubbs approached, and her hesitancy only added to her allure. Hubbs knew that her shyness could be an act. But he also knew that a younger and less-experienced girl could offer just as much pleasure as an experienced woman, but with less risk of syphilis. Far better to risk that the girl's shyness might be insincere than to assume every other risk that came with a look of experience.

Hubbs issued his offer to the girl in her native tongue, and she reacted in surprise at hearing her own language. He suspected that she'd never before met a white man who could converse in the Hyder's language, even if his dialect might differ from hers or carry the awkwardness of a foreigner. He hoped his pronunciations hadn't strayed in the years since he'd lived in the northern islands, and took the girl's hesitation as a sign that she was struggling to understand what it meant that he spoke her language, rather than struggling to understand the meaning of his offer. She looked up and nodded.

Several of the women farther down the beach yelled insults at the girl as she led Hubbs to a small clearing in the salal, away from the canvas shelters. She unwrapped the blanket from her waist and laid it on the ground, then stood and faced Hubbs in her nakedness.

Hubbs reached out and ran his hand through her hair, over her shoulder and down her arm, taking in the sight of her slender frame, and then moved behind her and took her in his arms. The scents of fish oils and charcoal that rose from her skin were intoxicating and emotionally overwhelming, instantly rekindling memories that were both beautiful and painful. He closed his eyes and he was holding her again. For a brief moment, the girl was Qawankie. As if she hadn't died the year before. He opened his eyes quickly, unwilling to allow tears to well by dwelling on the past. Emotions had no place in a commercial transaction. He caressed her small breasts and allowed one hand to linger while the other slowly reached down her belly. The smooth texture of her skin was as intoxicating as her scent, though Hubbs doubted that the rough calluses on his hands or his own rough scent were having the same effect on the girl. Not that it mattered, he told himself. He was paying her.

The girl turned around and smiled shyly, lowering her eyes. She wriggled from Hubbs' arms, lay down on the blanket and spread her legs. Hubbs grinned to himself, wanting to believe that she was in a hurry to feel him inside of her, but knowing that she was most likely only anxious to conclude the deal so that she'd have enough time to find one or two other desperate men before the pale light of the long summer evening faded to darkness. He shirked his suspenders off his shoulders and dropped his buckskin pants to his ankles. Then he waited, hovering over the girl until her look of anxiousness—either a request to begin or a demand to get it over with—gave him the encouragement he needed to kneel down between her legs.

* * *

Jacob understood that the wise approach would be to pick up his horse's pace and make it past the Cutlar place, and back to Bellevue Farm, without incident. Wise, at least, from the perspective of avoiding an opportunity for the new arrival to call him a "nigger" yet again and risking escalation into something far worse. Even though Jacob was from the Sandwich Islands in the Pacific, it troubled him to be called a "nigger" because he could hear the disdain.

Lyman Cutlar, a tall gangly Kentuckian in his mid-twenties, had arrived on the island a few months earlier, and had squatted on land northwest of the Company farm. His tiny cabin looked ready to be blown over by the first heavy wind, and his vegetable garden offered little potential for harvest other than a collection of scraggly potato plants. But Cutlar protected his claim aggressively, rarely to be seen without his musket at his side. All of the American squatters claimed their land with varying levels of aggression, but Cutlar sat at the far end of the scale. Jacob had concluded long before that avoiding Cutlar whenever possible would be the wise course of action. But to spur his horse to a faster pace would communicate fear, and he wasn't about to let this American squatter intimidate him on British soil.

Jacob gripped the reins tightly in his left hand, his anxiousness exaggerated by the awkwardness he still felt when using his left hand to hold the reins. For while the infection no longer spread through what remained of his right hand, the persistent pain and the missing forefinger had made it necessary for him to learn to ride with his left hand holding the reins.

The door to Cutlar's cabin opened and Cutlar stepped outside, likely having heard the approaching hooves on the hard ground. He looked as though he'd just risen, with his shirt hanging loose over his trousers, and his unkempt hair reaching out in various directions of protest. But he also held a musket in his hands, pointed vaguely in Jacob's direction. Not aimed, but ready, should a reason justify its use.

Despite the roving muzzle, Jacob's eyes were distracted to behind Cutlar, to the motley potato patch. One of the Company's large boars had sauntered into the patch from the brush nearby and had begun to root through the soil in search of the young tubers. Cutlar saw the direction of Jacob's gaze and spotted the boar.

"Son of a bitch."

He raised his musket and fired at the boar, striking the animal in the side of its neck. The musket's blast and the boar's squeal joined in a single noxious sound that shattered the peaceful morning. The boar turned to run, but dropped to the ground before it could reach the safety of the brush.

It was one shot. Only a pig had died. But Jacob understood that everything on San Juan Island had changed in an instant. Past tensions had been driven by arguments over land claims and sheep runs, by demands for recognition of each side's claim of national sovereignty over the island, and by disputes far too petty to justify the resulting anger. This was an act of violence by an American settler against a Company boar. Jacob had come across enough men like Lyman Cutlar in his life to understand that, in Cutlar's mind, it wouldn't be a leap to go from firing a musket at a trespassing boar to firing a musket at an offending person he had already denigrated with the epithet "nigger."

Jacob decided to give in to his original notion of wisdom and kicked his horse to pick up the pace. Cutlar stared with a look that screamed an unspoken insult, while his musket bobbed in his hands as if searching for its next target. Jacob took some comfort from the knowledge that Cutlar would need to reload, but the man likely had a pistol waiting just inside the door. He craned his neck to keep his gaze fixed on Cutlar as his horse carried him along the well-worn trail, knowing that exposing his back to the angry squatter would be the least wise course of action of all.

\* \* \*

Heavy rains during the night & showery all
day, light wind.
Shepherds packing wool, finished shearing
Ignace's flock last eve.g. –
Jacob & Lamane hauling logs. Robillard &
George sawing oak for hay carts, cradles &c.
– Inds weeding &c. –
Napoleon left for Victoria to have his
account settled. –
An American shot one of my pigs for
trespassing!!!
*Beaver* arrived wh Messrs Dallas, Fraser & Dr
Tolmie.

Bellevue Farm Post Journal, San Juan Island,
Hudson's Bay Company, Wednesday, June 15, 1859.

\* \* \*

Aleck Mcdonald paced across the front of Griffin's residence at the center of Bellevue Farm, too distracted to notice the new flowers that bloomed in the garden behind a short picket fence. As gardens go, it was nothing that would have attracted positive comments from any visitors. Mostly ox-eye daisies, bluebells, thistle, and others that had been imported from England and Scotland by Company men. But it added a minor touch of civility to the rustic farm.

Griffin approached from the northeast on horseback. He was accompanied by three men, two of whom Aleck recognized as Alexander Dallas and Dr. Tolmie. The third, he assumed, would be Donald Fraser, who was both a member of the colony's Legislative Council and a putative journalist for the London Times, though his stories served more as Governor Douglas' mouthpiece to the London press than legitimate journalism.

Aleck could feel Griffin's stare as the group approached, and expected that Griffin was questioning why Aleck would be standing outside Griffin's residence rather than tending to the dairy cows. Aleck hoped that the tension he could hear in Griffin's voice had nothing to do with him.

"It won't be easy to replace," Griffin insisted to Dallas. "Was a first class breeding boar. Sir, these Americans like Cutlar, they've no regard for our rights and property. We need to stop 'em from taking over our grazing lands, and keep the ones already here from interfering with our business. And with the threats he made, I'm worried for the safety of the animals and our workers."

Griffin was still upset about the earlier events of the morning. Cutlar had shown up at Bellevue a short time after the shooting and offered to pay three dollars for the boar, but an argument had ensued when Griffin demanded a hundred dollars in compensation.

Dallas, Fraser, and Tolmie had come over from Victoria on the *Beaver* that afternoon to oversee a shipment of sheep for the colony and to survey the status of the farm's operations. They'd arrived well before Griffin had gotten his anger under control. Aleck's inactivity as Company men arrived wouldn't help Griffin's temper, but Aleck felt he had little choice under the circumstances.

"Perhaps we can ride over there in the morning," Dallas replied. "We can have a word with Mr. …"

"Cutlar."

"I'd like to get a view of some of these squatters' claims as it is."

Dallas seemed relatively untroubled by the incident. Griffin's inability to inspire a sufficient level of anger in his superiors would only deepen his own frustration, and perhaps ensure that it was vented in Aleck's direction.

Griffin dismounted in front of his residence and thrust the reins toward Aleck in a manner that expressed his displeasure that Aleck was standing idle as the Company's men were arriving. Dallas dismounted and casually handed the reins to Aleck, as if assuming that Aleck wasn't shirking duties, but that it was his job to handle the horses. Aleck smiled a deferential greeting, then turned to Tolmie.

"Dr. Tolmie ..."

"Aleck, how are you?"

Unlike many of the Company officials, Tolmie could always be counted on to remember the names of the men who worked for the Company, at least the fellow Scotsmen who had as many years in service as Aleck had.

"Fine, thank you, sir. I was hopin' you could take a wee moment while you're here ... it's me wife, sir."

"Dr. Tolmie's not here on medical business, Aleck."

Tolmie held up his hand to stop Griffin. "It's all right, Charlie. There are few places I can go in the colony where there isn't some medical need. I'll join you gentlemen in a few minutes."

Tolmie turned to Aleck and waited for him to secure the horses to a post.

"What seems to be the issue with your wife? I'm not sure I know her name ..."

"Anna."

"Anna, yes."

Anna was the English name taken by the young Shuswap woman that Aleck had met while working at a Company post on the mainland. Indian names were always a disadvantage in white society, and Indian wives had enough disadvantages as it was without holding on to names that those around them could never pronounce.

"She's lost so much weight, and feelin' sick all the time, and says it hurts all 'round here ..." Aleck ran his hand along the right side of his own stomach, then paused, concerned that it wouldn't be proper to discuss his wife's condition any further outside the privacy of his cabin.

"Well, let's have a look then, shall we?"

Aleck led Tolmie to a small cabin on the edge of the

farm. It was built much like all Company buildings, in the "poteaux-sur-sole" manner. Thick, squared posts marked the corners and were spaced evenly along each wall. Vertical slots were cut into the sides of the posts, while horizontal squared beams, their ends tapered to fit into the slots, were stacked between the posts to form a thick wall.

Tolmie ducked to fit through the low doorway. The cabin was small, just a single room, and sparsely furnished. Anna lay on a bed, gaunt, and appearing far older than her twenty-four years.

"*Kloshe sun. Naika doctin copo lemesin.*" Tolmie greeted the young woman in Chinook.

If she had been Coastal Salish, Nass, or Kwakiutl, Tolmie would have been at least conversant in her own language. But Shuswap was a language he hadn't had an opportunity to study, which forced him to speak in the Chinook language that had developed along the coast to facilitate trade and communications.

"She speaks some English, Dr. Tolmie."

"Well, then, Mrs. Mcdonald, I'm Dr. Tolmie, and Aleck has asked me to conduct a short examination. So …"

Tolmie drew back the blanket and gently probed the young woman's lower abdomen, prompting her to cry out in pain. The examination took only a few minutes before Tolmie rose and motioned for Aleck to follow him outside. He paused just outside the doorway and gazed to the south, avoiding Aleck's eyes.

"There are most definitely some abnormalities. At least two enlargements that follow the path of her large intestine. And her liver is enlarged and protruding in a manner that suggests that the disease has reached the liver and done substantial damage."

"Meanin' what?"

"Meaning we can address her pain as it increases, and help her to feel as comfortable as possible, but I'm afraid that's all we can do for her. I have something I'll leave with you for the pain, and I'll send over some medications on the next boat. Is there someone here who can help you care for her?"

Aleck hesitated as his mind struggled to accept the news that his wife was dying.

"Everyone here's got more'n enough to keep themselves busy. I dinnae kin who ..."

"Then perhaps a nurse would be appropriate, when the time comes that you need assistance. Reverend Cridge oversees the infirmary and he places nurses for home care, often women from the reserve."

Tolmie offered a grim smile and a curt nod that wordlessly communicated the idea that they had covered all that needed to be said, then he strode across the clearing to Griffin's residence.

Aleck's mind raced as he struggled to digest everything he had just heard. None of it had been truly unexpected, given the extent of Anna's rapid weight loss and pain, though he had clung to the hope for a better diagnosis. But his wife was dying. Aleck looked back toward the closed door to his cabin, confused by the burden of having certainty about his wife's condition, yet uncertainty about whether or how to share such information with her. He turned and hurried across the farm to tend to his chores in the dairy barn. They seemed far less pressing, but they were the only burden he knew how to address.

\* \* \*

## Florence Nightingale.

At first I thought she was a nun, from her black dress and close. She was not introduced, and yet Edmund and I looked at each other the same moment to whisper, "It is Miss Nightingale, greatest of all now in name and honor among women." I assure you that I was glad not to be obliged to speak just then, for I felt quite dumb as I looked at her wasted figure, and the short brown hair combed over her forehead like a child's, cut so when her life was despaired of from fever but a short time ago. Her dress, as I have said, was black, made high to the throat, its only ornament being a large enameled brooch, which looked to me like the colors of a regiment surmounted with a wreath of laurel, no doubt some grateful offering from our men. To hide the close white cap a little, she had tied a white crape handkerchief over the back of it, only allowing the border of lace to be seen; -- and this gave the nunlike appearance which first struck me on her entering the room. Otherwise than in this Miss Nightingale is by no means striking in appearance. Only her plain black dress, quiet manners, and great renown told so powerfully altogether in that assembly of brilliant dresses and uniforms. She is very slight, rather above the middle height; her face is long and thin, but this may be from recent illness and great fatigue. She has a very prominent nose, slightly Roman, and small dark eyes, kind, yet penetrating; but her face does not give you at all the idea of great talent. She looks a quiet, persevering, orderly, lady-like woman. I have done my best to give you a true pen-and-ink portrait of this celebrated lady. I suppose there is a hum all over the world of "What is she like?"

*The Victoria Gazette*, Saturday, June 18, 1859, p. 1.

\* \* \*

Flora looked over at Jane Forbes, having had no reaction to the story she had just read from that morning's *Gazette*. She couldn't tell if Jane was awake or asleep. Her eyes were closed and her breathing was labored but steady. The veil of sweat on her face was to be expected in the oppressive heat that had blanketed the small community in recent days, though it was especially sweltering in the second-floor bedroom of the Forbes' home. Jane appeared gaunt and pale, but she hardly struck Flora as a woman who was dying, at least not when compared to the women Flora had seen die before.

"Should I read more?" Flora whispered.

"Does she ... inspire you?" She was still awake. "Miss Nightingale? Is she the reason ... you're learning all of this ... from the Sisters?"

Every word was a struggle. Flora hesitated before replying, not wishing to engage Jane in a lengthy conversation that might weaken her further.

"Perhaps a little. I think I'm more inspired by my mother. Watching how she cared for us, for neighbors, for my sister. It seems a better way to spend my time than baking biscuits or making lace."

Flora stopped, desperately hoping that Jane's pastimes before becoming ill had been neither biscuit baking nor lace making.

"You don't have to ... only read happy stories ... I'm aware that ... Europe's at war ... Victoria, too."

Flora wanted to tell her to save her strength. But for what?

"The world is ... not a happy place ... I don't mind if I must leave ... though when I'm better ... I do so want to see Europe."

Jane often spoke of impending death and an eventual recovery in the same conversation, as if both were as likely. Each time she did, Flora would carefully consider Lucinda's advice and avoid interfering with Jane's process of understanding and accepting her impending mortality. Discussing the events in the daily paper seemed far safer than discussing the progress of Jane's illness, though not all stories in the *Colonist* or *Gazette* seemed appropriate for discussion. Flora usually avoided reading anything to Jane about the war that was unfolding in Italy, threatening to engulf all of Europe, partly because it might increase Jane's anxiety, and partly because news from Europe was about three months old. She also hadn't discussed the efforts going on throughout the town to disarm Indians and lessen the violence that had escalated across southern Vancouver Island in recent months.

"I can still hear ... what goes on outside ..."

"It has been frightful at times," Flora answered, deciding that it might be better to remove whatever fears Jane might have imagined from a lack of knowledge about the situation. "There was an actual war last Sunday across the harbor. The Songhees and the Stickeens. They were shooting at each other for a few hours."

"Yes, David told me that was ... was the noise."

"When we came out of church we went down to the harbor and watched it from the bridge. Most everyone was there."

"Strange thing for ... for Sunday entertainment."

The same thought had crossed Flora's mind at the time. To leave church and then pass the time watching the Songhees and Stickeens attempt to murder each other in a volley of lead shot had seemed inappropriate for a Sunday afternoon. She had felt better about the day when it was reported that only one person had been killed.

"I must sleep ... Flora."

"Of course. Is there anything you need before I leave? Your Chinaman's driving me home in your carriage because of all the rumors and such."

"Good ... maybe some more medicine ..."

The medicine was Laudanum that Dr. Helmcken had provided. Flora had been instructed that Jane was to have a spoonful each time she asked. If she were lucid enough to realize she was in pain and request relief, then she was likely in need of the opiate.

Flora poured the medicine into a small glass, rather than risk spilling it with a spoon, and helped Jane swallow it. Jane managed a wan smile of thanks before closing her eyes.

Flora put the glass back onto the side table. "I'm sure Sister Mary will be by tonight to check on you, or at least tomorrow. And perhaps I will be as well, if she lets me. Good night, Mrs. Forbes."

She closed a curtain on the west side of the room to ensure that the late afternoon sun wouldn't interfere with Jane's rest, and then left the room and closed the door behind her. She paused at the top of the stairs and contemplated her emotions. After months of anxiousness to begin her nursing studies and accompany the Sisters on home visits, she had just spent the afternoon alone with a patient. And yet it left her troubled that nursing might not be the rewarding career she had hoped it would be. Anyone could read a newspaper to a patient. Anyone could empty bedpans. The point of seeking her training had been to learn skills that not just anyone could apply.

She repeated to herself words of advice that Sister Mary had shared after a recent visit.

"A nurse's job is not to fight death, but to fight pain, to fight anxiety, and to help the patient find physical and mental peace as God's divine will is revealed."

Flora wasn't entirely sure whether she accepted the advice. Surely she could do more than ease an inevitable outcome. But perhaps part of her education was learning the limitations of the profession from those who had previously tested its boundaries. She was leaving after an afternoon with her patient, and her patient wasn't writhing in pain or crying in misery. Perhaps she would simply have to accept such a simple outcome as a worthwhile afternoon. She pushed her remaining doubts from her mind and descended the stairs to find the family's Chinaman.

\* \* \*

Hubbs wondered if his eyes carried the same expression of ingrained boredom and frustration that he sensed in Captain George Pickett's, and concluded that they probably did. The two men sat at the dining table in Pickett's small home, a short distance from Fort Bellingham, having just enjoyed a dinner of salmon and potatoes, capped off with brandy. Hubbs had paddled across the strait from San Juan Island that afternoon, anxious to present Pickett with a statement he had induced Cutlar to write about his shooting of the pig, and resulting threats of arrest from British authorities.

Hubbs and Pickett had known one another briefly three years earlier during the Puget Sound War, when their companies in the Ninth Infantry had put down a series of Indian rebellions in the White River and Muckleshute regions. Since then, their lives had diverged in some respects, and run parallel in others. Both had been married to a northern Indian wife, though Hubbs' marriage had preceded the Puget Sound War. Both wives had died in the past two years. And both men had been left with a child. Hubbs' daughter remained with Haida relatives on the northern coast. Pickett's son, Jimmie, was being raised by a settler couple with no children of their own. It was something they had in common, both having, and not having, a child.

Pickett's eyes seemed to lack the fiery intensity that Hubbs remembered from when they'd first met. For the three years since the Puget Sound War, Pickett had commanded Company D at Fort Bellingham. The assignment involved political skirmishes with belligerent settlers, campaigns to prevent soldiers from deserting to seek a fortune in the gold rush, and never-ending battles with the slugs, skunks, and deer that raided the fort's vegetable garden. Company D's function had evolved into a domestic role, growing vegetables and raising cattle for other forts in the region. That type of command, Hubbs reasoned, would be enough to extinguish the fire in any officer's eyes. It was similar, Hubbs imagined, to what might happen to a man who traded a life of northern Indian raiding parties or U.S. Army scouting missions for an isolated island cabin, from which to perform a figurehead government position nailing tax notices to fence posts.

Pickett finished reading Cutlar's statement and dropped it on the table in a manner that communicated his low regard for the document.

"First of all," Pickett began, "I can't order anything of the sort. I have to raise it through appropriate channels."

"I know that," Hubbs replied.

"And a permanent presence seems beyond permissible as long as the boundary commission's still at work."

"Not if our settlers are being threatened with arrest."

Pickett tested his glass of brandy and considered Hubbs' retort. "What I could imagine are regular visits by one of our steamers, maybe even having a company cover the island on foot every few months, searching out encampments of northern Indians ..."

"That isn't enough to protect us."

"You're talking about having U.S. soldiers take over disputed territory. It could be years before the commission's done with its work."

"It *will* be years and we can't wait that long. And it's not just the settlers. Whoever controls San Juan Island controls access to the inland waterways. It's supposed to be American territory and we have to ensure it stays that way."

"I promise, I'll raise your concerns with General Harney when he's here next week."

Hubbs looked up with a start. "He's coming here?"

He could see from Pickett's expression that the Captain instantly regretted having divulged the General's plans.

"He's conducting a tour of some of the forts around the sound, and then a short detour to Victoria to meet Douglas."

Hubbs struggled to control his excitement. General Harney, the commander of the U.S. Army in Washington Territory, would end his trip in Victoria. Any boat returning from Victoria to Puget Sound would pass along the southern shore of San Juan Island. It would pass within sight of Hubbs' own cabin on the ridge, and it would pass disputed territory in need of U.S. military protection. Hubbs had paddled all the way to Fort Bellingham to lobby a Captain on his desire to secure U.S. troops for San Juan Island, when a General would shortly pass by his own front door. Hubbs smiled and tossed back the rest of his brandy.

# Chapter 7

Flora desperately wanted to leave the Forbes' bedroom. She felt unnecessary, incapable of providing any assistance, and on the verge of tears. Yet she knew she had no choice but to remain at the side of the room.

Jane hadn't been conscious in almost a day, and it appeared that she would be gone within hours. Her ragged breathing sounded far too much like Elizabeth's had sounded just a few months before, making it difficult for Flora to hold back tears, both in remembrance of her elder sister and for Jane's impending departure.

Flora and Sister Mary had arrived at the Forbes residence that morning, fully expecting that Jane Forbes would be another day closer to her last, but not expecting such a rapid decline overnight. Sister Mary had left immediately to locate Bishop Demers so that he could provide last rites for the patient. Flora felt that she should have gone to find the Bishop in order to ensure that an experienced nurse remained with Jane, though she had accepted the rationale that Sister Mary would have better knowledge of where to find the Bishop.

It wasn't the first time she would watch another pass

from this life. It wasn't even the first time that year. But it was the first time she would be an outsider participating solely because of a duty to assist, ostensibly without the emotional bond of the patient's family. But as Flora watched Jane's husband, she wondered if her own emotional bond with the patient had become stronger than his own had ever been.

Forbes sat across from the bed, silent, either listening to each breath or pretending he was somewhere else. Flora told herself that she had nothing to do with his manner, and that if Forbes were alone with his dying wife, he would still be sitting in a chair several feet from the bed rather than holding Jane's hand. But she also wanted to believe that he would have taken a moment of privacy to hold his wife close and express a deep and undying love, whether or not she retained any ability to hear him and understand.

Footsteps on the stairs arrived as welcome relief, along with the voices of Bishop Demers and Sister Mary. Their arrival would allow Flora to retreat further into the background, no longer the only outside presence in the room, and freed from the apparent lesson she'd endured by being the sole caregiver at such a difficult time. At least, she desperately hoped it would be the case.

\* \* \*

## DIED,

On Saturday afternoon, after a lingering illness, Mrs. Jane Rhoda Forbes, wife of Mr. David Forbes, aged 26 years. The funeral will take place this morning at 9, A.M., from her late residence, near the Catholic Church.

*The British Colonist*, Monday, July 4, 1859, p. 3.

\* \* \*

Flora had never felt anything akin to a sense of admiration for a dead body before. Yet Jane Forbes had retained much of her beauty, even in death. As tragic as it was for Jane to have died at such a young age, and as inappropriate as it felt to have noticed such a thing, Flora felt certain Jane would have appreciated the sentiment. Few people in the colony died in their beds, leaving bodies that could be viewed without sickening the mourners. Many were bloated after drowning and lying adrift in the water for days. Many were mutilated by murder, by accidents with farm implements or carriages, or when their own weapons misfired and exploded. Many more were maimed by ugly suicides, and still more were ravaged by brutal illnesses. Flora had seen more than enough examples of such unfortunate victims for someone who was only seventeen, and she assured herself that this made it perfectly appropriate to notice how Jane had managed to avoid such a fate.

There wasn't much to do as Sister Mary laid out the body and washed it, other than to replace the water in the basin on occasion and stand ready to assist.

"You'll miss her."

It wasn't a question. It was clear from her tone that Sister Mary intended it as a statement of the obvious, simply to underscore for Flora, as Lucinda had done weeks before, how nursing can take an emotional toll on the practitioner. But what Flora noticed most was that it had been spoken in English even though Jane was no longer around to hear it. Flora wondered if she could take it as a sign that she had proven herself in the young nun's eyes. As if perhaps Sister Mary viewed Flora less as a girl requiring instruction in French grammar, and more as a young woman showing her potential to serve the community as a nurse.

"Yes, I will," Flora replied.

"Flora, much of our work may seem to be mundane. The companionship. Helping with personal needs. Praying with her. Getting her to eat. To drink. But all of it serves the purpose of easing their final days. There are no measuring sticks. Only the perspective you have when you look back. You helped this poor woman."

Flora felt a rush of pride, but only nodded in response,

certain that she was expected to listen and absorb the advice.

"We all want to help these poor women to get better. But God has His plan. Just as He has His plan for you."

Flora nodded. God might have had a plan for Jane Forbes. That she could accept. But Jane had also had a plan for her own life, and the two plans had shared little in common. She recited a brief, silent prayer, asking that any plan God might have in store for her own life share far more in common with her own unfolding plans. It had been a silent prayer, and it had seemed almost blasphemous to consider. But she could tell as she looked back at Sister Mary that her face had communicated every word.

* * *

"It's about a hundred yards that way, past the vegetable garden."

Griffin pointed along the ridge to demonstrate the location of Hubbs' cabin, just west of Bellevue Farm, though Dallas needed no assistance in locating the cabin. The ruckus that drifted across the rolling hillside betrayed its location. It was just past 9:00 p.m. on July 4, 1859, and Dallas had come to San Juan Island on the *Beaver* earlier in the evening to oversee a further shipment of over four hundred of the Company's sheep. He and Griffin had shared a meal prepared by Griffin's Kanaka houseboy, followed by pleasant conversation over brandy, but had been drawn outside by the shouts and drunken laughter emanating from Hubbs' cabin.

"Aleck and Angus are over there, I imagine, seeing as they're both citizens," Griffin presumed.

"Citizens? Of the United States?"

"So they claim. Neither's likely to spend their entire career with the Company. It might make sense that they stake a claim somewhere in Washington Territory some day."

Griffin could tell that Dallas was bothered by the idea that some of the Company's Scottish workers were asserting

American citizenship. Management like Dallas, who lacked years of experience in the region, tended to expect national loyalty from Company employees.

"Something I didn't mention over dinner ..." Dallas began. "The Governor recently decided to appoint a new Stipendiary Magistrate and Justice of the Peace for the island."

Griffin looked over, more hurt than surprised. Magistrate and Justice of the Peace were positions he'd held since they'd been created years earlier by the colonial government. He'd never heard any complaints about his ability to ensure that justice was maintained on the island, even if those efforts had been limited largely to overseeing his own employees.

"You already have two dozen Americans here causing problems. There could be twice that by the end of summer. More even. And if this dead pig of yours has shown us anything, it's that the two sides aren't about to co-exist easily. You've enough to do running the farm. Holding the magistrate position at the same time creates the impression that your duties might be carried out more in the name of the Company than in the name of the colony."

"I've never done anything to—"

"I know that, Charlie. Douglas knows it, too. This isn't about you."

"Do you know who it'll be?"

"Name's John deCourcy. Major John deCourcy. A little stiff, from what I've seen, but smart, competent. You'll need to set up some sort of accommodations for him."

Griffin smiled more out of concern than amusement. The mere idea that a man as formal as Dallas would describe another gentleman as "stiff" suggested that the new appointee's personality might be ill-suited to the role of magistrate on the island. Griffin knew the land. He knew the Indians who established fishing camps along the beach in late summer. He had met the squatters and had remained relatively pleasant with most of them. He might lack the title of Justice of the Peace, but Griffin suspected that he'd continue to carry out most of the duties despite the "stiff" new appointee. He might even find that his lack of title would lead to more invitations to events like Hubbs' July 4th party he could hear across the prairie, since civil magistrates were rarely welcome guests at raucous gatherings. It wasn't much of a silver lining to lessen the sting of the demotion, but it would have to do.

\* \* \*

"McKay'll do the honors," Hubbs announced to the men celebrating in front of his cabin, "since he got the flag for us."

He nodded to his friend, Charlie McKay, who was securing the Stars and Stripes to a rough hemp rope that ran up a rickety flagpole the men had erected outside of Hubbs' cabin earlier that day.

"But before he does, remember, one week from today, here at one o'clock, we'll be voting for Governor of Washington Territory and a host of other positions right down to Justice of the Peace for these islands, for which this humble servant of yours is a candidate. And in case you're thinking of shirking your civic duties, you should know that one of the candidates donated a demijohn of his finest whiskey to help us get through the lengthy ballot."

The description of the whiskey as "finest" was a blatant exaggeration, if not an outright lie. But such was the nature of most campaign promises. The cheers that accompanied the announcement of the donation reassured Hubbs that most of the men celebrating Independence Day with him would return a week later to cast their ballots, assuming they were able to remember his announcement once the effects of the party wore off. He took comfort from the expectation that most of them would remain outside his cabin all night, passed out rather than asleep. He'd be able to remind them of the election in the morning.

"Here it goes." McKay grasped the rope and slowly hoisted the flag. No one remarked or appeared to notice that it was an older flag that lacked the thirty-second star for Minnesota, as well as the more recent thirty-third star for Oregon.

"Gentlemen, you should be standing as our flag is raised."

Hubbs' lecture brought most of them to their wobbling feet, though standing was a task far more patriotic than some of the men were able to perform after several hours of celebration. One of the more inebriated men remained in his seat and instead fired his revolver into the sky in a show of support for his nation's independence. Others followed suit, and soon several of the men were firing their weapons into the sky, or in one case, directly into the starry quadrant of the Stars and Stripes.

"Not at the flag! Not at the flag!"

Hubbs' shouts convinced a few of the less inebriated men to redirect their aim, and the damaged banner managed to reach the top of the pole without further injury. Against the pale evening sky, the bullet hole was barely visible just below the top row of stars. Hubbs sat back down on his rickety wooden chair and sighed. At least the flag had been the only casualty, so far. And perhaps if viewed in the right light the hole might appear to be the thirty-second star for Minnesota. He raised his glass of whiskey to the flag, silently celebrating the independence of his nation, and wondering if the country's founding fathers had faced as much difficulty organizing the support of the citizenry.

\* \* \*

Flora stopped on the trail and looked around.

"This seems like the perfect spot," she declared to Fanny and Mary.

It wasn't quite the highest point on the hill behind the Ross farm, but it was a spot that had open views to the northwest and southeast. They'd be able to view any fireworks that might be set off in Victoria, as well as whatever tiny bursts of light might be visible from Port Townsend across the strait.

Flora spread a blanket on the rocky ledge, Mary set the lantern down on the center of the blanket, and each of the girls took a seat along the edge. The pale light that filled the sky late in the summer evenings meant that they might have a long wait before any fireworks would begin, though the occasional random gunfire and explosions suggested that others were unwilling to wait for darkness before commencing their celebrations.

It felt odd to be celebrating in any fashion just two days after the death of Jane Forbes. Their relationship had been brief, yet unlike any other she had ever known. It was as if Jane's recognition of her limited time had freed them both to have discussions of the sort Flora couldn't imagine having with close friends. Regardless of the label she would place on Jane Forbes, it felt as though she had lost a friend, even if one she had known for only a brief time.

"Who's gonna watch which direction?" Flora asked, wanting to ensure that they didn't miss anything.

"I'll watch the north, you watch over the water," Mary replied, securing the right to watch the more interesting view.

"Where are you going to watch, Fanny?"

"I'm going to watch both. That way I won't miss anything."

Flora considered explaining the risk that watching both could mean missing everything, but opted to keep the thought to herself. She looked along the ridge to where William and Alfred McNeill sat against the trunk of a fallen tree, just in time to see William pass a small bottle of whiskey to his friend. She considered reprimanding her brother, but opted not to, knowing it would accomplish nothing. She found some satisfaction in having talked the boys into spending the evening on a hilltop by their family farms, where they could avoid the prying eyes of others who might see a whiskey bottle held by a fifteen year-old as another reason to gossip about the younger Ross brothers.

She turned to look south, and her thoughts strayed to Francis, barely into his first week working on their older brother's farm near Nisqually. He'd been left with little choice in the matter after having been arrested two weeks earlier for being drunk and disorderly. At least on this occasion there hadn't been any violence, if only because

Francis had been too drunk to stand. He'd been transported to the gaol in a wheelbarrow and dumped unceremoniously into a cell. The fine had been just a few pounds, including court costs, but this time Isabella had refused to pay it. Instead, she had offered to pay for a ticket to Nisqually. Flora's older bother, Charles, Jr., had agreed to take on Francis as a laborer on his farm for the summer, albeit reluctantly, and perhaps longer if the situation proved workable.

"I wonder if Francis is celebrating Independence Day?" Flora wondered aloud.

"Hard to imagine he wouldn't," Mary replied. "He's never shirked any reason before. Do you think mama'd let me go to Muck Creek for the rest of the summer?"

"To do what?"

"To help take care of the children, Elizabeth's children."

The speed with which Mary changed the topic to her own future suggested to Flora that the question had been on the tip of her sister's talkative tongue for some time. She wondered if Mary truly had any interest in taking care of her nieces, or just an interest in taking care of Charles Wren. Before she could respond, her attention was grabbed by a series of tiny flashes directly east from where they were seated, across the water on the southern edge of San Juan Island.

"Look over there," she exclaimed.

"Where?"

"Bellevue."

"Bellevue?" Mary replied. "Why would they light fireworks at Bellevue?"

"They looked like muskets or something."

Flora had heard that there were American squatters on the island, and she'd seen references to them in the newspapers in previous months describing the tensions they were causing between U.S. and Company interests. But the source of the small flashes had looked to be along the southern ridge, near where the Company's farm was located. She reminded herself that, just like Americans who had celebrated the Queen's birthday, many loyal subjects of her Majesty would celebrate Independence Day simply as an excuse to carouse in public. The distant flashes of gunfire were more likely signs of celebration than altercation.

Most businesses in Victoria had closed for the day, even many that weren't owned by an American citizen. And in a particularly odd display of celebration, the Royal Navy had given most of its men the day off, marking what one newspaper had described as the first time English soldiers had been encouraged to celebrate their country's defeat. Flora suspected that it was actually designed to ensure a large presence of English military on the streets of Victoria during the American celebrations, without officially posting them there. At least, that had been what Alexander had suggested to her earlier in the day.

A much louder string of explosions drew their attention toward Victoria, where several flashes beyond the trees suggested that fireworks were being shot from a boat anchored in the harbor. Flora glanced at the display for a moment, then returned her gaze to the southern end of San Juan Island, far too curious about the reasons for the possible celebration or altercation to look away.

\* \* \*

GEN. HARNEY.—This distinguished veteran, accompanied by his staff, visited Victoria on Friday last. He came on the U.S. steamer *Massachusetts*. On landing he was saluted from the Fort.

*The British Colonist*, Monday, July 11, 1859, p. 2.

\* \* \*

Hubbs and McKay stood at a semblance of attention on the gravel beach next to the Hudson's Bay Company wharf in Griffin Bay. The wharf was the only sign of settlement along the shore of the wide bay, where the beach quickly disappeared into thick forest to the west, and a wide sloping prairie to the south and east. Behind the two men, up the hillside and beyond the ridge that ran along the narrow peninsula, lay Bellevue Farm and Hubbs' own cabin, though neither were visible from the northern beach.

Ahead of them, in the middle of the vast open bay, sat the propeller barque *Massachusetts*. It wasn't the most impressive warship on the northwest coast, and was far smaller and less armed than most of the British naval vessels. But at nine hundred tons, with eight guns and seventy men aboard, it was easily the most impressive of the few American warships in the region.

Hubbs was surprised by the nervousness he felt as he and McKay waited for a small rowboat to reach the shore. He had watched all morning for the *Massachusetts* to appear on the horizon after leaving Victoria for Port Townsend, a path that would take the ship along the southern shore of San Juan Island, within direct view of his cabin. And as soon as the two men had caught sight of the approaching ship, they had raised the Stars and Stripes, despite having failed to repair the bullet hole.

It didn't much matter whether it had been the flag that had accomplished his goal, or whether Pickett had encouraged the General to stop at the island. Brigadier General William S. Harney was only a few yards from arriving on the beach of San Juan Island, rowed to shore by his crew. Hubbs and McKay would have the opportunity they had sought to present the grievances of the island's residents.

Hubbs' nervousness deepened as Harney came into view. The General cut a regal presence in the rowboat, surveying the island. Tall, with piercing eyes, snow-white hair and a neatly trimmed beard, Harney bore a grandfatherly appearance that belied his reputation as a ruthless hero of the Battle of Mexico City, and as the man who'd led the U.S. Army into the Battle of Ash Hollow, decimating the Sioux. Hubbs offered a rough salute as Harney stepped from the rowboat onto the beach, even though he hadn't been an active member of the U.S. Army in more than two years.

"General Harney, sir, welcome to San Juan Island of the United States. I'm Paul K. Hubbs, Jr., Deputy Customs Inspector for the island, and this here's Mr. Charlie McKay, one of the two-dozen American settlers who request your assistance."

Harney offered each of the men a handshake.

"Gentlemen, I assume one or both of you are responsible for our nation's Stars and Stripes that I saw flying across the ridge?"

"Yes, sir, that's the location of my residence, and I'd be grateful for the opportunity to show you and your men around and provide some refreshments."

Hubbs sensed Harney's hesitation, and noticed the General's eyes scanning the hillside above the bay.

"The British farm's over the ridge, sir, and the path to my cabin goes around the far side. They won't be disturbing us. I doubt they'll even know you're here."

"Then why don't you show me a little of the island, Mr. Hubbs."

Hubbs struggled to suppress a grin as he led Harney along the gravel beach and launched into his rehearsed speech.

\* \* \*

Hubbs moved his lamp closer to the paper and re-read the first sentence to himself.

"*The undersigned, American citizens on the island of San Juan, would respectfully represent —*"

Hubbs recognized that it wasn't quite "*We the People of the United States, in order to form a more perfect union,*" but he was pleased with the sound of it, nevertheless. Before he had departed the island that morning, General Harney had suggested that a petition from the settlers requesting military protection against future attacks from northern Indians might permit him to address the settlers' concerns. Hubbs had promised that such a petition would be prepared. There would be no reference to the deceased pig, no reference to the disputed border, and no reference to Bellevue Farm. It would be a simple petition requesting protection against Indian attacks, signed by each of the island's U.S. residents; though "residents" was a fluid category, as signatories would include Hubbs' father, Paul K. Hubbs, Sr., who was living in Port Townsend, as well as Aleck and Angus, both Scotsmen in the employ of the Company.

Hubbs dipped his quill into the ink and pondered the words that should come next, hoping that his earlier promise of a demijohn of whiskey would ensure that all of the island's settlers would show up for electioneering the next day, and hoping that the effects of the whiskey would ensure that each of them would sign the petition without question.

\* \* \*

Flora stopped at the corner of Yates and Government Streets, and gazed up at the painted sign over the door. T. PHELAN GROCERIES. She wondered if anyone had yet bothered to mention to Mr. Phelan that the advertisement for his store that had been running in the *British Colonist* for several weeks had consistently been spelling "glassware" without the "w." She contemplated mentioning it to him, but put the thought aside since she had other, more pressing business to address.

"*Nurse wanted, apply to T. Phelan*" was what it had said in the *British Colonist* that morning, in a paragraph listing new advertisers whose ads would appear in future editions. Flora considered it lucky that she had noticed the reference, since any other women who might be interested in the position might not be aware of the opportunity until the actual ad had begun to run on the paper's third page.

Two weeks had passed since Jane Forbes had died, and Flora already found herself feeling restless, spending her time engrossed in books that the Sisters assigned her to read instead of learning by watching the Sisters at work.

She entered the store and spotted Mr. Phelan behind the counter where he was busily wrapping a pound of butter for a middle-aged woman who looked vaguely familiar. Flora pretended to be interested in a bin of wild strawberries in an effort to avoid appearing impatient. The strawberries likely had been picked for Mr. Phelan by local Indians, and she imagined that the Indians must have become rather wealthy if the price demanded by Mr. Phelan for the strawberries bore any connection to the price he'd paid to acquire them.

The woman completed her purchase and bid Mr. Phelan a good afternoon, providing Flora her opportunity to approach.

"Mr. Phelan."

"Miss Ross, how may I assist you?"

"I'm inquiring about your advertisement. For the nurse."

"Oh, I wasn't aware it had started yet. Well, it's rather simple, really. The children are one and three, and my wife is finding them more of a burden than she seems capable of handling."

Flora stared for a moment, uncertain if she had understood him. "The children?"

"Yes."

"But, Mrs. Phelan ... she's well?"

"Quite well, yes. Tired, of course, as we all are."

Flora smiled, understanding. "Oh, I see. You're wanting a nurse for the children. A nursemaid."

"Yes. Was the advertisement not clear?"

"No. I mean, it likely is, or will be. Today the paper just said that there's a need for a nurse, without details. I'm sorry to trouble you, and I'm relieved to hear the family is well. Good day, Mr. Phelan."

"So, does that mean you're not interested in the position?"

"No, but thank you."

Flora left the shop and walked along Government Street, uncertain if she was relieved or disappointed. She wasn't certain she was ready to begin working as a nurse without supervision, but the opportunity had been far too tempting to ignore. Mrs. Phelan was a pleasant woman, there was no language barrier, and Dr. Helmcken would be nearby if Flora were unable to handle a particular matter. But she wasn't struggling to qualify as a nurse only to chase after small children, change their diapers, and clean up their toys. If those were her goals in life, she could focus instead on finding a husband.

The booming voice of John Butts distracted Flora as it echoed from farther down Government Street. His public announcement about the Government's latest franchise bill, and amendments being made to the right to vote, seemed by his delivery to be far more confusing than the bill could possibly be in reality. Flora paused on the wooden walkway and considered whether she should return to the store to mention the reference to "Glassare" in Mr. Phelan's advertisement for the grocery business, but concluded that surely someone had mentioned the misspelling long before she'd noticed it. And if not, Mrs. Phelan would soon have more time on her hands and might notice the spelling error while relaxing and reading the newspaper. Flora continued along Government Street, suddenly anxious that her afterschool diversion might have left her unable to complete her chores before dinner. The chores might not be part of a grander plan for her future, but they were most definitely part of her mother's plan for how the afternoon should unfold.

\* \* \*

Lucinda let the pail of water slip from her hand and spill onto the dusty pathway that wound through the tents, unaware it had even happened. For a brief moment, she had been consumed with fear as she'd approached her tent and caught sight of a man lifting her baby into his arms. She had told herself that it would be perfectly safe to leave the tent for the two-minute trip it would take to get water from the closest well. Frank was old enough to be relied on to watch Orrin and the baby for two minutes.

But it wasn't the brief moment of fear that caused Lucinda to lose her grip on the pail of water. Rather, it was the moment of recognition that followed. She ran to the tent, afraid to yell his name in case it was a mirage. But he was real. He smiled, and nodded at the baby in his arms.

"Does he have a name?"

"John Henry."

"Hello, little John Henry. I'm your father."

\* \* \*

Very calm & warm. –
Mr McKay & Mr Morris arrived here about
midnight last night from Puget Sound. –
Old Ignace & others returned from Victoria. –
Aleck: – left to see the doctor he was
suddenly taken very ill. –

Bellevue Farm Post Journal, San Juan Island,
Hudson's Bay Company, Sunday, July 24, 1859.

\* \* \*

"*Flora, viens ici, s'il-te-plaît.*"

Flora looked up from her efforts to slog through a dog-eared copy of Chateaubriand's *Génie du Christianisme* to see Sister Mary at the open door of the schoolhouse. Reverend Cridge stood outside, and she could see that there was another man behind him. Flora hesitated just long enough for Sister Mary to beckon her again with a more determined expression, as if insisting to Flora that she shouldn't keep the busy reverend waiting, even if he was with the Church of England.

Flora weaved carefully between her classmates and exited through the door.

"Reverend Cridge ..."

Cridge gestured to Aleck, standing behind him. "Flora, this is Mr. Aleck Mcdonald. Mr. Mcdonald, this is Miss Flora Ross."

"How do you do?"

Flora smiled in an effort to mask her uncertainty about the reason for the introduction. Aleck put a hand to his forehead as if tipping a hat, except that he wasn't wearing one.

"Mr. Mcdonald came to see me this morning. He's a laborer at Bellevue Farm."

"The dairyman, miss."

"Dairyman, yes."

Aleck had a simple, kind face, and the strong, husky body of a laborer. But there was something about his expression that struck Flora as odd. She struggled to think of the word that would describe the expression on his face. Incredulous. That was it. He looked at her with an incredulous expression.

"Mr. Mcdonald's wife is gravely ill and in need of a nurse …"

"Oh, I'm very sorry, Mr. Mcdonald."

"And it appears that her illness is terminal."

"But, Reverend," Aleck interrupted, "she's a lass, a student. She cannae be who you meant."

Flora suddenly understood why the word "incredulous" had come to mind.

"It's all right, Mr. Mcdonald. Flora is sufficiently qualified."

She would have preferred to hear Cridge offer a more ringing endorsement, but admitted to herself that her qualifications at this stage of her training couldn't readily be described as more than "sufficient."

"Mr. Mcdonald doesn't have much in the way of means to pay for a nurse, which is one of the reasons we've come to you. I spoke to Sister Mary, and she agreed that this could be a good opportunity for you to further your education with a sort of practicum."

"A practicum?" Aleck repeated. "This is me wife, Reverend."

"Yes, Mr. Mcdonald, and Flora is likely the only qualified woman I'm acquainted with who'd be prepared to provide nursing services at the rates we've discussed. She has no dependents to think of, and likely desires an opportunity to prove that she's ready to hold herself out to the community as a nurse. Since you aren't prepared to consider a nurse from the reserve, Flora is likely your only option."

"Mr. Mcdonald, if I may," Sister Mary interjected calmly, "Flora is still in the early stages of her training, but she has proven herself most capable at providing a patient with proper care and support. I would not have agreed to this if I did not think so."

An extended silence followed Sister Mary's comments as Aleck considered his response. Eventually, he simply nodded in resignation.

Cridge turned back to Flora. "Mr. Mcdonald came over this morning by canoe, and hopes to return as soon as possible. But I imagine you'd need a little time to think it over, assuming you're even interested in –"

"I'm most definitely interested, Reverend. I would very much like to accept. And I shouldn't think I've much to do to prepare."

Flora realized that this would probably have been the time to address the payment rate that Cridge had mentioned, but decided against it. If Cridge had already discussed a proposed rate with Mr. Mcdonald, it was most likely a rate that was fair, whatever it happened to be. She felt a surge of excitement at the anticipation of leaving for San Juan Island, while her mind frantically compiled a list of the things she would need to do before leaving.

"Perhaps we could leave in the morning, Mr. Mcdonald. I'm sure my mother would appreciate some time this evening to digest all of this before I leave."

"Your mother will need to do more than merely digest this, my dear" Cridge replied. "She'll need to approve it as well."

Aleck hesitated a moment, then nodded his agreement to the timing. Flora tried to not hold the hesitation against the poor man. She was, after all, only seventeen. And the patient was the man's wife, who was apparently dying. The disease in question was yet another detail that she should have asked about before agreeing to the task. It might drag on for months. It might be something she could contract. It might involve grotesque putrefaction of the woman's body. But now that she'd agreed, she would have to wait for that information.

She tried to push all doubts from her mind. Regardless of her readiness, she would be leaving the Sisters' school for a Company farm on the island of her birth. She would be a "nurse" in practice, even if the title hadn't yet been earned. Easing a patient's pain in her final days. And she wouldn't have to finish reading *Génie du Christianisme*.

\* \* \*

Pickett surveyed the efforts of his troops and concluded to himself that Fort Bellingham hadn't seen so much activity since August of 1856, when Company D had arrived in the area and commenced construction of the fort on a small, grassy hill. Three years later, the activity was deconstruction, as his men dismantled much of the fort and packed onto the *Massachusetts* and *Shubrick* as many of their weapons and provisions as the two ships could hold.

General Harney's orders had been simple and clear. Abandon Fort Bellingham and occupy San Juan Island. The implications of the orders for Fort Bellingham were far broader than simple abandonment of the fort. It meant abandonment of the town as well. As soon as merchants had received word that Company D was relocating, many of them set about dismantling their own businesses and making plans to relocate their stores as close to Company D as possible. Soldiers who received a government salary, albeit small and often delayed by months at a time, were more regular customers than many of the nearby settlers who were largely self-sufficient. Merchants had little choice but to follow the customers.

The doubts Pickett had initially harbored about occupying the island faded as he watched his men prepare for the journey. Whatever the politics might be of the Northwest Boundary Commission and its ongoing delays, San Juan Island would be American territory, the settlers would be protected, and it would encourage greater numbers to arrive and stake claims. Company D would ensure it.

\* \* \*

Flora and Isabella stopped at the low, grassy ridge that ran above the beach. Flora set her canvas bag onto the grass and turned to look back at the Ross farmhouse. She was nervous, but it wasn't for the journey, or the time she would be away from home. As a girl of only nine she had travelled from the family farm in Nisqually to attend school in Fort Victoria for several months at a time, and had felt far more excitement than nervousness even at that young age. But as a girl of nine she'd had no one's final moments of life as her impending responsibility. Her first thoughts the day before upon hearing of the assignment had been of herself. The risk of contracting the illness. Or the discomfort in caring for a dying woman at a small farm. Now she felt only concern for her own abilities, or lack thereof. Aleck Mcdonald's wife was dying from tumors in her intestines and liver. Sister Mary had advised Flora on the path the illness would likely take before Flora had left the schoolhouse for her last time the day before, and it had been intimidating advice. It would be a slow and lengthy decline as the disease would likely starve the young woman to death in a manner quite distinct from Jane Forbes' passing.

As they had crossed the field from the house, Isabella had said the comforting and encouraging words a mother would be expected to offer her daughter as she embarks on a new challenge. But there had been something about the thoroughly expected nature of such words of support from one's mother that had dampened their effect, even as the sentiment had been appreciated.

Aleck approached from his canoe, which sat along the gravel beach.

"*Kloshe sun*, Mrs. Ross. Aleck Mcdonald."

Flora could sense her mother smile at the gesture of a greeting in Chinook.

"*Klahowya*," Isabella replied with a welcoming smile.

"I can promise ya, your daughter'll be safe at the farm."

"I know Mr. Griffin from many years. My son was there."

"My brother, John," Flora interjected. "He worked at Bellevue five or six years ago before he bought his own farm north of town."

Aleck nodded. His expression betrayed that he hadn't had any interest in learning as much information about the Ross family. He reached for Flora's bag.

"Well, we should go. Wind's light now and back of us, but that's sure to change."

"Must we right now? My mother had wanted to offer you some tea before we go."

Aleck's expression again communicated more than his words would have done. The courtesy was unnecessary, and it clearly annoyed him that this young nurse who would soon hold his wife's life in her hands seemed more inclined to delay her arrival at Bellevue Farm in favor of tea and cakes.

"No, of course," she answered for him. "You've been away from your wife for a couple of days. We should leave."

She wondered how much of their future communication would be accomplished merely by reading his face after each comment she might make. When Charles Wren had offered so few words as Elizabeth lay dying, she had criticized the man in her mind for being so removed from each moment. When David Forbes had offered little more than barely concealed insults, she had assumed he was someone who allowed his prejudices to cloud his ability to recognize the kindness of those who were helping his wife. But as she watched Aleck carry her bag to the canoe, it struck her that this might instead be the only way that men were capable of responding to the prospective loss of their loved one. Women emote, provide comfort, congregate together and search for ways to help the one in need. Men block emotions, turn away from the illness, or even attack those providing the assistance they're unable to provide. She felt relief that she wasn't a man.

Flora turned to her mother and realized that her own expression was communicating words she seemed unable to say. She hoped that her hesitant smile told her mother it was time to leave, that she loved her, and that she remained nervous about her future.

"*Va avec Dieu,*" Isabella said while pushing a strand of hair from her daughter's eyes.

Flora remembered back to the last time her mother had

offered such a blessing. The last time Flora had been about to place her future at the mercy of the cold ocean waters. At least on this occasion only gentle waves lapped against the shore on a warm summer's day, promising a journey that was likely to be without incident. She hugged her mother until the sound of the canoe's hull scraping against the heavy gravel reminded her that Aleck was waiting impatiently. Then she turned, strode down the beach to the water, stepped into the stern end of the canoe that remained on shore, and carefully moved along the hull to the narrow seat behind the bow. Aleck pushed the boat away from the beach, climbed over the gunwale, and reached for his paddle. As he dipped his paddle into the waves, Flora looked back and waved at her mother. She felt self-conscious as she did, as if she were making far too much of this moment in her life. Her mother could see San Juan Island in the distance if she walked out to the point on the east side of Fowl Bay. But it would be weeks or months before she would see her mother again, and that alone made it feel like a substantial departure.

She looked forward, at the island that lay in the distance, then reached down into the hull for the paddle she had noticed. She gripped the paddle in her hands and dipped it into the water.

"What are you doin'?"

"Paddling," she replied, a little confused by the question.

"I dinnae need a lass' help."

She considered putting the paddle down. If she was just a lass in his eyes, then perhaps it was best to let him carry the burden. She'd be able to sleep that night without aching muscles in her back and arms. But the idea that he saw her as just a girl was far more of a reason to dip the paddle into the water a second time and draw it back with as much force as she could muster.

"I've been traveling in canoes my whole life, Mr. Mcdonald. I can't imagine just sitting here and watching the waves go by."

"Suit yourself, then."

She dipped her paddle into the water for a third time.

Her back and arm muscles would ache that night, and far more the next morning. But it would pale against the ache she would feel if she had done nothing.

# Part Two: Bellevue Farm

137

# Southern Peninsula of San Juan Island, July 26, 1859

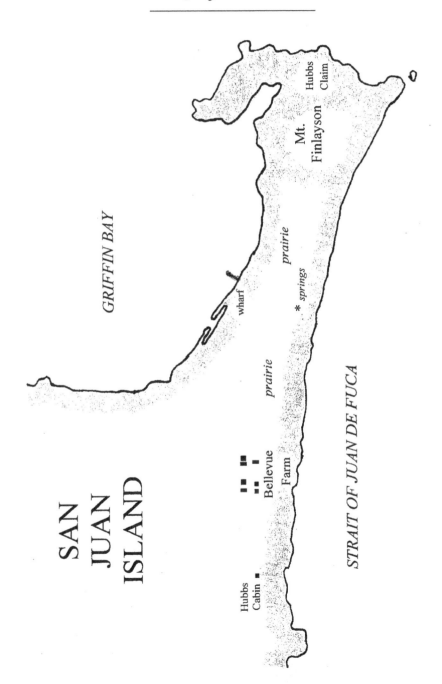

# Chapter 8

San Juan Island, July 26, 1859:

Aleck stepped into the shallow water and pulled the canoe high enough from the waterline to allow Flora to step directly onto the gravel beach. Flora gazed up at the hillside, half expecting the island to feel familiar. Instead, the steep hillside only appeared daunting.

She looked back to the west to where the southern coastline of Vancouver Island stretched out to the horizon in layers of diminishing blues. She couldn't pick out the exact location of the Ross farm, but found some comfort in knowing that one of the more faded layers of blue represented the hillsides of home.

"I was born here," she pronounced.

"Here?"

"In 1842."

"No one lived here then."

"I didn't say we lived here. I said I was born here."

"Here. On the beach?"

"Not this one. A large bay on the other side of the ridge."

"Griffin Bay?"

"I don't think it had a name back then. It was called Rodgers Island in those days, at least by some people."

Flora saw that look again. Incredulous. She could tell that Aleck was wondering if he'd made the wrong decision accepting her as a nurse for his dying wife.

"My mother said they stopped for the night while they were canoeing to Nisqually."

"Your Indian mother?"

"Three-quarters Indian. Ojibway. My father was Scottish."

Aleck shrugged as if he saw no difference between the two. It was a contradiction that Flora barely noticed. Men who had Indian or mixed-blood wives often looked down on any other woman of similar background. Aleck had told Cridge that he wouldn't accept a nurse from the Songhees reserve. He had felt the need to point out to Flora her own Indian blood. And yet his own wife was full-blooded Shuswap.

Aleck grabbed Flora's canvas bag from the belly of the boat and pointed toward the ridge at the top of the hill.

"Well, in case you dinnae remember from when you were here last, we're headin' up the ridge there."

Aleck started off along the rough trail that snaked up the hillside through thick, yellow grass and fading wildflowers. Flora hesitated before following, not because she had any option other than to follow, but simply because the enormity of her new task had suddenly registered. There were no nuns to consult. Her mother wouldn't be able to suggest remedies passed down through generations. Doctors Tolmie and Helmcken were several days away at best, given the difficulty of reaching them with a message. And each was unlikely to secure a vessel to come to the island solely to help an Indian woman whose illness was terminal. It would be up to her to help this man's dying wife, and her alone. Flora closed her eyes and silently recited a short prayer to ask for strength, and to ask that she do more good than harm in caring for Aleck's wife. Then she took a deep breath and followed Aleck up the hill.

\* \* \*

Griffin glanced up from his desk at the window to see Aleck returning from Victoria, followed by a young woman, if not a girl, who struck him as vaguely familiar. She was a daughter of one of the Company officials, nearly all of whom had daughters of mixed blood. Not a Douglas or a Work. Those daughters Griffin knew on sight. A McNeill? A Tod? A Ross?

He rose and walked out onto the porch of his residence just as Aleck and the girl passed by the small garden in front of his cabin.

"Feeling better, I see, Aleck."

"Much, thanks."

"Did the doc say what you had in you?"

"No, seems to've passed."

"Of course." Griffin waited for more.

"Uh, Miss Flora Ross, Mr. Charles Griffin."

Flora Ross. Griffin hadn't seen her for several years, and even then only in passing at the occasional social function at the Fort. At that age, she would have been nothing more than a curiosity to him, an amusing diversion as he'd search out the traits of a particular parent in her features or demeanor. Her older brother, John, had been an employee of Griffin's back in 1853, when Bellevue Farm was first established. It was the same family features that Griffin had always seen in young Flora. But she'd grown taller, slender, a young woman. Griffin looked away for a moment, fearful that he might have gazed too intently upon the new arrival.

"Miss Ross. I would'a hardly recognized yourself."

"Mr. Griffin. Very nice to see you again."

There was a moment of awkwardness as Griffin waited for a further explanation, but Aleck made no attempt to provide it. After an awkward moment, it was Flora who spoke up.

"Mr. Griffin, I don't know if you've heard, but I've been training as a nurse, with the Sisters."

"I hadn't heard."

"Yes, and it came to the Sisters' attention that Mr.

142

Mcdonald's wife is ill, and they felt it would be the charitable thing to send me to care for her. That way, Mr. Mcdonald can carry out his tasks here at the farm without too many interruptions."

Griffin struggled to suppress a smile. The girl was smart enough to know exactly which words would resonate with him, or with any Company Chief Trader tasked with running a farm at maximum efficiency.

"There's nothing in the farm's budget that could –"

"And there needn't be, Mr. Griffin. It's all been arranged so it'll be no burden to the farm."

Griffin turned to Aleck. "And she'll stay where?"

"I'm gonna bunk with Angus. She'll sleep in the cabin with Anna."

Griffin wasn't upset with the idea of a nurse taking care of Anna. She had reached a point in her illness where she needed assistance. He was upset that he hadn't been consulted, and that Aleck had thought it necessary to play ill himself in order to get to Victoria to find a nurse for his dying wife.

"Well then, welcome to Bellevue, Miss Ross."

"Thank you, Mr. Griffin. It feels a little like coming home."

"Home?"

"Says she was born here," Aleck interjected.

"Here?"

"Over there, somewhere." Flora pointed north toward Griffin Bay, across the other side of the peninsula from where she and Aleck had just landed in the canoe. "Or at least that's what I've been told all my life."

"Hmm. Well then ..." Griffin struggled to remember how old Flora would be. Perhaps seventeen, if he was remembering correctly the year of her father's death shortly after finishing construction of Fort Victoria. She was still a girl in so many ways. And no longer in so many others. He nodded with a terse smile, then turned back into his residence, anxious to finish balancing the books before breaking for a mid-day meal.

∗ ∗ ∗

Aleck's introduction was brief and simple. Anna. Flora. Flora. Anna. But it was an introduction that involved so much more than an exchange of names.

Flora thought she could read nervousness on Anna's face, and hoped that her own nervousness wasn't as visible. Anna was still able to walk, slowly and hunched over in pain, and she had greeted them outside the tiny cabin that was home to the couple. Flora knew that Anna was in her twenties, but it would have been impossible to predict her age if she hadn't known it. Her face was gaunt, her muscles were wasted, and her eye sockets had a hollowness that gave her the look of an old woman exhausted by her years. The disease was affecting her in ways that Jane Forbes had never experienced, and the image she presented left Flora with an ominous feeling about how the disease might progress under her care.

But the look in Anna's eyes that had struck Flora initially as nervousness seemed on reflection to be a look of confusion, almost bewilderment, as if this young woman who should have been in the prime of her life, planning a future with her husband, and raising a family, couldn't understand how she could be living inside a body that had become old and frail. Her body was leading her down a path that her mind and soul weren't yet prepared to follow.

Flora listened as Aleck explained to his wife how he had come to be returning with a seventeen year-old girl as her nurse, how Flora had just left school to accompany him to the island, and how Reverend Cridge had insisted that she would be an appropriate choice. She watched Anna's expression throughout, fearful that her new patient would show some of the same disbelief that her husband had shown, but Anna's face didn't betray any such emotion. Instead, she smiled and took Flora's hands in hers.

"Thank you to help me," she said in an insistent tone that appeared to be a struggle.

"Well, you're very welcome, of course," Flora replied, "though I haven't even started to help you yet."

Flora stopped, mortified that a completion of her thought would have been inappropriate. Of course Anna would thank her at the outset of her duties. There wouldn't be an opportunity to thank her when the task was done.

"Thank you for helpin' me," Aleck stressed to Anna, emphasizing his correction of her grammar.

"Thank you for helping me," Anna repeated.

"Oh, and you're welcome again," Flora answered, instantly feeling silly for answering the same question as an automatic response. Her mind was too busy trying to understand why Aleck would feel the need to correct his wife's English as she was dying. Proficiency in English varied between extremes in the colonies, and everyone was accustomed to having to make an effort to be understood at times. Anna's English appeared rudimentary, and Flora could see little purpose to be served by teaching her the proper conjugation of a verb. She wondered if it was merely habit for Aleck, or if it was a sign that he was refusing to accept the reality of his wife's condition.

"Come. Come."

Anna beckoned Flora to follow her into the small cabin. Flora hesitated for a moment, as if she still had one last opportunity when she could reconsider her acceptance of the job. Inside would be the room where she would care for Anna, where she would eat and sleep, and where Anna would die. It would be a room in which she would be tested. In which she would learn and grow. Or fail and disappoint. And either outcome would determine how a woman would spend her final moments. At peace or in pain. The weight of the responsibility was no longer speculation. Meeting Anna had made it real. And daunting. And despite her hesitation, Flora knew that she had made an irrevocable decision. As she had done only minutes before on the beach, she took a deep breath, recited the same brief prayer in her mind for the strength to fulfill her duties, and then followed Anna inside the cabin.

\* \* \*

Anna ate most of the food that Flora had prepared for her supper, a result that Flora considered a minor success given what Aleck had told her about Anna's lack of appetite. Flora sat next to the bed in the small cabin and held Anna's hand, as she had done so many times for Jane Forbes. When she'd first taken Anna's hand, Anna had squeezed tightly, suggesting a level of fear and anxiety that Jane had never allowed herself to show. Anna was far from her home on the mainland. She was isolated by language, confined in a small, dark cabin, and at a farm where the only other wives were Kanakas from the Sandwich Islands, or Indians from coastal communities rather than the mainland interior. Even with other Indian wives there were language and cultural barriers for Anna. The few women Flora had met at the farm since her arrival that morning had seemed welcoming, and had been providing Anna with care. But they couldn't replace family to a young woman dying before her time.

"Would you like to go for a walk?"

"No. Sleep."

Anna closed her eyes. Flora's few attempts at interesting conversation hadn't been particularly successful. Anna's English was too limited for discussions about religion, the war in Europe, or Florence Nightingale. Conversation had been Flora's primary contribution to Jane's care. But now, whatever stilted conversation she could cobble together from Anna's limited English, her own non-existent Shuswap, and their shared knowledge of the rudimentary language of Chinook, seemed to do little to ease Anna's pains and fears.

Anna's hand gently slipped from Flora's as she eased into sleep. Once Flora was certain that Anna was truly asleep, she cautiously rose, opened the door, and slipped out into the cool evening air. The sun hung low over the distant mountains of Vancouver Island, even though it was well into the evening. It was her favorite time of year, when a pale blue light would linger in the summer sky for several more hours.

"Miss Ross."

Flora turned to see Griffin seated outside the front of his residence, smoking a pipe.

"I trust you've everything you need for yourself?" he asked.

Flora took several steps away from the cabin, anxious that her response be quiet enough to not wake Anna.

"Yes, Mr. Griffin, I believe I have what I need, for the moment. Thank you."

She expected something in response, but Griffin merely puffed on his pipe.

"Anna's asleep, so I thought I might wander up to the ridge," she continued. "To get a sense of the view, if that's all right."

"Should be fine. Haven't been any sightings of northern Indians for a few weeks, so it's likely just all of us on the island … and a few squatting Americans."

She smiled and nodded, then walked north through the farm until she reached the gate along the fence by the dairy barn. The sloping prairie continued to rise for a short distance, and Flora followed the rutted wagon road past the gate and up to the ridge that ran the length of the narrow peninsula. As she crested the ridge, the view of Griffin Bay opened up before her. It was a wide, circular expanse, larger than Victoria's own harbor. To the north and northwest lay the vast majority of San Juan Island. To the east through the wide mouth of the bay lay other islands in the archipelago, dotting the horizon to the mainland, where the imposing visage of Mount Baker rose in the distance.

Flora turned and gazed to the southeast, along the ridge that ran down the center of the peninsula, to where the island came to an end at the gentle slopes of Mount Finlayson—more a hill than a mountain. When she had seen maps of the island, Flora had often thought that the southern peninsula reminded her of a tail on a kite, trailing out from the main body and serving little purpose beyond decoration. But standing on the peninsula's ridge, she was reminded more of the tail of a giant whale swimming along the surface of the water; sloping down on either side from its bulging central spine, and tapering to the broader tail fin. The slope was gentle to the south, where the farm lay, and much steeper to Griffin Bay on the north side, while the land on both sides of the ridge was open prairie covered in thick yellow grass that danced in the evening winds. Behind her, to the west, stood the island's forest, starting in a line so clear and impenetrable that it seemed an intentional demarcation to divide the peninsula from the rest of the island.

Flora felt remarkably exposed standing along the ridge. It wasn't much higher than the highest points at the back of the Ross property, but it was bare. The wind off the Strait of Juan de Fuca whipped across the ridge without any forest to engage it, and seemed all the more anxious because of it.

She gazed down at Griffin Bay and struggled to imagine a Heiltsuk canoe arriving seventeen years earlier with her father and pregnant mother onboard. Her mother's distress at the unexpected labor. Her father's worry. But for the small wharf built for Bellevue Farm, and the rough wagon road that trailed up the hillside to the ridge, the bay was likely just as it had been the day of her birth. It surprised her that she felt no profound emotion or sense of connection. It was a beautiful location to mark as the place of one's birth. And it was interesting to imagine the events of her entry into the world. But sated curiosity seemed to be the overwhelming emotion, and it left her disappointed.

She turned and looked back down the southern slope toward Bellevue Farm, at the large dairy barn, at the fenced corrals, at the cabins and cookhouse, and at the cabin where Anna lay asleep. A sudden fear gripped her once more. She exhaled deeply in an effort to push the tension from her belly.

"I can't help her if I'm afraid," she whispered to herself, then walked back down the wagon road to the farm, trailing her hand through the tall yellow grass.

\* \* \*

If Hubbs had learned anything from his more than two years living on San Juan Island, it was that a sudden banging on his cabin door in the middle of the night was rarely a positive development. It might be a passing northern

Indian, or a settler trying to escape passing northern Indians. But on this particular night, as Hubbs dragged himself from his bed, reached for his pistol, and called out to inquire who stood outside his cabin, he was pleasantly surprised to hear a man identify himself as Orderly Sergeant William Smith, of Company D, Fort Bellingham.

Hubbs flung open the door and was greeted by the sight of Smith standing just beyond the doorway, in full uniform and holding a lantern.

"Good evening, Mr. Hubbs," Smith began. "Captain Pickett is on the beach by the wharf in Griffin Bay and requests the pleasure of your company, sir. He's asked me to escort you to where he's waiting."

Hubbs had never dressed himself with greater haste. Within minutes he was accompanying the young soldier along the narrow path that led from his cabin, barely able to contain his excitement. As they emerged from the trees onto the gravel beach, Hubbs caught sight of the steamer *Shubrick* at anchor in the bay, just beyond the wharf. The *Massachusetts* lay farther out, surrounded by civilian boats. A short distance along the beach, Pickett and several junior officers circled a small fire. Hubbs struggled to keep his emotions in check and maintain his professional composure in front of Orderly Sergeant Smith. But it was a battle that he lost the moment he reached the fire and broke into gleeful laughter before embracing Pickett in a distinctly unmilitary hug.

The business conducted was brief—a quick consultation on the best location to establish a camp where Pickett would land his troops the following morning—and then, as with their dinner of four weeks earlier, Pickett considered it an occasion to be toasted with a bottle of brandy.

\* \* \*

Military Post, San Juan Island
W.T. July 27th, 1859

Order}
No. 1}

I. In compliance with orders from the general commanding, a military post will be established on this island, on whatever site the commanding officer may select.

II. All the inhabitants of the island are requested to report at once to the commanding officer in case of any incursion of the northern Indians, so that he may take such steps as are necessary to prevent any future occurrence of the same.

III. This being United States territory, no laws other than those of the United States, nor courts, except such as are held by virtue of said laws, will be recognized or allowed on this island.

By order of
Capt. Pickett.
signed James W. Forsyth,
2ᵈ Lieutᵗ 9ᵗʰ Infᵗʸ Post. Adjᵗ

\* \* \*

Flora's first thought upon waking was the discomfort she felt from having spent a near-sleepless night on a thin hay-stuffed mattress on the ground beside Anna's bed. Her second thought was to scratch at several itches that were likely the result of fleabites received during the night, if not bed bugs. And her third thought was that San Juan Island was far noisier in the morning than the Ross farm. It was a realization that made no sense. She had lain awake that night listening to sounds much like she would have heard had she been at home. The gentle rhythm of waves landing on the beach to the south. The constant hum of insects. The occasional call of birds, or lowing of farm animals from the nearby barns. The only unusual sound had been the low moans that occasionally escaped from Anna's throat as she slept. But there had been no reason to expect anything different with the arrival of morning.

Flora listened to the sounds and found that she could

distinguish between the spirited conversation of people nearby at the sheep farm, and much louder sounds from farther away that she couldn't place. They weren't sounds that made any sense to her. She concluded that it wasn't a typical morning at Bellevue, and that rising quickly and dressing herself would be a prudent course of action.

Anna remained soundly asleep, so Flora decided to leave her undisturbed while she investigated the commotion. She grabbed a small pitcher so that she could get water from the water wagon while she was outside, then left the cabin in search of an explanation for the distant noise.

The view to the southwest revealed a wave of dark clouds sweeping in from the Pacific threatening rain, but there was nothing out of the ordinary in such a summertime view. She turned to look north and spotted a dozen people standing beyond the fences, along the ridge where she had stood the evening before. Griffin, Aleck, and others—all farmworkers and their families—stood atop the ridge facing north toward Griffin Bay. She hurried up the wagon road to join them and understood the source of the morning's commotion the moment she arrived.

At least a dozen boats lay at anchor in the bay. Two were larger than the rest and appeared to be military vessels. But what all of the boats had in common was that the men onboard were busily unloading cargo.

Griffin noticed Flora's arrival. "American troops. Setting up camp on the beach, looks like."

"And merchants, followin' the customers," Aleck added.

Flora had read enough in the local newspapers over the previous months to understand that she was witnessing a significant event. Questions swirled in her mind, but she felt certain that it wasn't her place to ask any at a time like this. She was a newcomer, and a girl at that. Far better to listen and learn. Or so she told herself as she stood and watched the ships unload their cargo, waiting for Griffin, Aleck—anyone, for that matter—to offer something by way of a prediction or instruction. It was a long wait.

"Should someone go to Victoria to tell the Governor?" she asked, breaking the silence.

"They know already," Griffin answered. "You can't mobilize a whole company and its townies and move 'em across the water without word getting out. They know."

"Then if they know," Angus Mcdonald asked, "how come they're not here, too?"

No one had an answer. They were the first words Flora had heard from Angus since she'd been introduced to the farmhand the night before, when he had merely nodded in greeting. He was a Scot, like Aleck, and bore the same surname. While Aleck was stocky, Angus was tall and angular. Aleck had dark hair, while Angus had red hair and freckles. From her brief opportunity to compare the two friends and coworkers, it seemed to Flora as though the most they had in common was their shared last name and a thick brogue.

She turned back to deal with the more pressing events in the bay. She knew she should ask more questions, but she couldn't think of one that wouldn't likely be met with some sort of acknowledgement of its obvious nature. Instead, she stepped closer to Aleck.

"Anna is still asleep, and she slept well last night."

Aleck nodded his thanks but said nothing, whether too concerned by events in the bay, or unwilling to discuss the health of his wife in front of the others.

"All right, men, there's work to do," Griffin called out. "Looks like rain later this morning. Try to finish cutting hay at Grande Prairie before it gets here."

Griffin turned and walked to his cabin, leaving the others standing on the ridge, too entranced by the developments in the bay to begin their day of work. Angus was the first to turn away. Eventually the others followed, until Flora was the only one left, watching Company D establish its camp along the beach where she had been born.

She couldn't shake the feeling that the troops wouldn't be permitted to land without a response from the Royal Navy. An official protest. A demand to evacuate the island. An armed conflict. The latter thought sent a shiver up her spine. The American troops were just a few hundred yards below the ridge, just out of sight of the farm.

Flora felt instantly exposed and alone. The storm clouds sweeping in from the southwest seemed to amplify an instinctual sense of anxiety. She turned away and hurried back to the limited security of the farm's perimeter fence, and the protection of Anna and Aleck's small cabin.

# Chapter 9

## SAN JUAN ISLAND INVADED BY AMERICAN TROOPS.

We learn that a company of U.S. soldiers under command of Cptn. Pickett, were expected to land at San Juan Island yesterday, from Semiahmoo, in order to erect barracks and fortifications. They were ordered there by Gen. Harney, when up here a short time ago. We trust our government will call our insatiable neighbor to account for the unwarrantable assumption. The first thing that will follow will be duties and taxes imposed by the United States and Washington Territory, on British subjects, who may reside there, and serious disputes may grow out of it. When the title of the island is definitely settled in their favor, then it will be time to allow Americans to quietly garrison the island, and not before. It is desirable that the question of sovereignty should be speedily settled; but we hope that in the final settlement, Imperial politicians will not show such a disregard for British American interests as exhibited in the settlement of the northeastern and north- western boundaries, — by which New Brunswick lost millions of acres of land, and this side, all Washington Territory and Oregon to the Columbia River.

*The British Colonist*, Wednesday, July 27, 1859, p. 2.

\* \* \*

Flora surveyed the scene unfolding in Griffin Bay from the safety of the ridge above the farm and struggled to understand the implications. The *H.M.S. Satellite*, a Royal Navy corvette, had arrived in the bay earlier in the evening. Rather than steam into the bay in a hostile manner, with gun ports open, braziers lit, and cannons ready to fire, the *Satellite* had dropped anchor just beyond the American vessels still busily unloading supplies and building materials. Despite the closed gun ports, the *Satellite* was an imposing presence. Thick smoke from its boiler fires billowed above its masts and blended into dark storm clouds that spread across the evening sky. It was twice the size and weight of the *Massachusetts*, two hundred feet in length, with twenty-one 32-pound cannons. Whereas the *Satellite* had been designed as a first class warship, the *Massachusetts* had been intended to serve as a transport and had only been fitted with eight 32-pound cannons when it had been recommissioned and sent to the Puget Sound. If there were to be a war that night, it would be brief.

Flora tried to remember all of the other facts about the *Satellite*, the *Massachusetts*, and other ships in the region that had been thrown at her in conversation at past Royal Navy balls by nervous young sailors who seemed to believe that such conversation would impress a teenage girl. She wondered if any of the young men she could see standing on deck awaiting orders to launch a war were men who had asked her to dance at past events, then caught herself briefly hoping that it was only the ones who had spurned her for being "too Indian."

"There they go," Aleck announced, pointing down at the Company wharf at the foot of the hill.

Flora turned her attention to a small rowboat that slowly eased away from the wharf in the direction of the *Satellite*. A messenger had arrived at the farm shortly after the *Satellite* had dropped anchor, requesting Griffin's presence on the warship to brief Captain Prevost and Major John Fitzroy deCourcy, the new British magistrate for the island.

"Does it mean something that the cannons aren't visible?" Flora asked. "Do you think it means they won't start a war tonight?"

"Maybe it means they want the Americans to think they won't start a war tonight," Aleck suggested. "Maybe to catch 'em by surprise."

Flora looked along the beach to where Company D continued to set up camp, just beyond where merchants busily erected tents and unloaded supplies. She wondered if they considered the *Satellite's* non-threatening posture a reason to pause their efforts, or a reason to work twice as fast to establish their positions.

"Are you afraid, miss?" Aleck asked quietly.

"I should probably say I am afraid," she replied. "But I suppose I'm trying to be more hopeful this is something that'll end in a few days, once whatever misunderstanding it was gets sorted out."

"Cannae say I'm as hopeful," Aleck replied. "This island's too valuable. That bay down there's gonna be a naval base, jus' dinnae kin which country. If you ask me, there'll be a war. A real one."

"I'm pretty certain I didn't ask you," Flora replied with mild exasperation, imagining a sleepless night ahead of her thanks to Aleck's pessimistic projection.

Thunder rumbled loudly overhead, amplifying her fears. It had been raining most of the day, with intermittent thunder and lightning, as if foreshadowing the evening's events.

"If there's going to be more lightning coming, this may not be the safest place to be standing," she suggested, suddenly concerned about their exposed position on the ridge.

But as she gazed across Griffin Bay to the *Satellite*, and back along the beach to the soldiers of Company D, lightning strikes seemed the least of her concerns. Lightning could strike anywhere on the island, which seemed to lessen the risk that it might strike where she was standing. But if there were to be a war, it would most definitely happen within earshot, and within range of cannon shot. She turned and walked back toward the farm wondering if there was anywhere in the immediate vicinity that could qualify as a safe place to stand.

\* \* \*

Griffin stood in the light rain that fell on the deck of the *H.M.S. Satellite*, shook hands with Major John Fitzroy deCourcy, and understood instantly why Dallas had described the new British magistrate as "stiff." Griffin had learned over the years that some people offer a handshake as a gesture of friendly greeting, while others offer their hand aggressively to establish their superior standing in the social hierarchy. DeCourcy seemed to offer his hand as if he were doing the other person a favor.

Griffin responded with a smile of greeting, but immediately feared that his expression had instead betrayed the slight disturbance he felt by a closer examination of deCourcy's appearance. One eye seemed damaged, perhaps missing entirely under the damaged tissue, and Griffin looked away before concluding whether it was a battle wound or natural deformity.

He had found himself occasionally dwelling on feelings of resentment in the three weeks since he had learned that deCourcy would replace him as Justice of the Peace and Stipendiary Magistrate for the island. But while gazing at the American encampment from the deck of the *Satellite*, Griffin found that whatever offense had lingered was quickly fading into relief. He could step back from the unfolding political crisis and find refuge behind his responsibilities at the farm, while the new magistrate would be at the center of the dispute. DeCourcy would be responsible for the civil response, or lack thereof. He might not be a target for the Americans in any physical sense, but he most certainly would be a target for criticism from any colonial residents in Victoria who disapproved of the government's response. And there would be no shortage of those no matter what the response might be. Griffin realized that deCourcy's pretensions of superiority might be his best assets. He would be no less prone to criticism, but he might be far less troubled by it.

"My intention is to come ashore sometime mid-morning tomorrow. I'll request that you assemble all British subjects so there's a crowd to witness the proclamation of my commission."

It was an instruction despite deCourcy's use of the word "request." Griffin considered for a moment if he should have performed a similar ceremony when he'd first been appointed to the position, but he knew the idea would never have crossed his mind.

"We'll round up everyone," Griffin replied, "but be cautioned on expecting a 'crowd'."

"How many of your workers are British subjects?" Capt. Prevost inquired.

"Five or six, including myself. The rest are Kanakas and Indians. A few of their wives might be British subjects, and there's a young lady working as a nurse."

DeCourcy snorted at the idea of including women in any count of British subjects. Griffin wondered if the newcomer might already be reconsidering the wisdom in having accepted an appointment to serve as magistrate on an island where there were barely a half-dozen British subjects in need of the administration of justice.

"Just gather everyone you can," Prevost suggested, "The mere fact they live at the farm will demonstrate that they fall under the jurisdiction of the magistrate, regardless of their actual citizenship."

Griffin nodded, trying to accept the wisdom in losing so many hours of labor just to carry out a ceremony that appeared to be more about deCourcy's self-importance than the needs of the unfolding crisis. He needed his men working in the fields, not applauding speeches of government officials. The presence of Company D might have reduced the work required to protect the farm's cattle and sheep from marauding northern Indians, but the work that would be required to protect those same cattle and sheep from marauding Americans might be far greater.

"And what about the troops?" Griffin asked. "Is the navy gonna drive 'em from the island?"

"We're only here to deliver Major deCourcy," Prevost replied with a forced smile. "It's something of a coincidence, and not a military response to the arrival of the American troops."

Griffin nodded. He wasn't entirely sure he believed Prevost's claim. But if the *Satellite's* arrival wasn't intended as a "military response" to Company D's arrival, then it was likely there'd be a more provocative response still to come. It was a troubling thought. But at least war wouldn't break out that evening in Griffin Bay. At least not in the short time that he might continue to stand on deck of the *Satellite*.

\* \* \*

Lyman Cutlar finished buttoning his soiled shirt and followed Hubbs along the narrow trail away from his cabin. Hubbs could tell that the young Kentuckian was still confused by his explanation for the reason he was arresting Cutlar. The settler hadn't actually done anything wrong in the eyes of American authorities. But they were arresting him anyway to prevent his arrest by British authorities.

"So, what am I s'posed to do there? Sit on my ass and pretend you give a fuck 'bout a dead pig?" he asked.

"Seems better than getting arrested by John Bull for real and thrown into some hole in the ground at the Fort," Hubbs replied. "At least Pickett has plenty of liquor in his tent. Think of it more like an invitation to a soirée."

"To a what?"

"A place to drink and play cards."

Hubbs' arrest of Cutlar marked his first official act as San Juan Island's U.S. Magistrate, having been elected two weeks earlier in a whiskey-fueled day of electioneering. Once word had arrived in Pickett's camp that the *Satellite* had brought a new colonial magistrate to the island, Pickett had assumed that the purpose of deCourcy's arrival was to arrest Cutlar. Much better, Pickett had suggested to Hubbs, that Hubbs arrest Cutlar first and secure him at the American camp for a few days.

The American camp on the beach was coming into view through the trees when Hubbs grabbed Cutlar by the arm and stopped him in his tracks. Farther down the path, Griffin approached, accompanied by two British officers and a third man dressed in a dark blue coat that appeared to be covering a uniform of some kind. Hubbs assumed that all three were British officers on their way to arrest Cutlar, guided to his cabin by Griffin. For a brief moment, he considered escaping into the brush, certain that the knowledge he and Cutlar had of the island would ensure an escape. But from what Hubbs could see, the officers were armed, as were he and Cutlar, and running into the brush would expose their backs to the British firearms. Much better to face them down, he concluded.

"Stick close, keep me between you and them, and keep your hand on your pistol," Hubbs whispered to Cutlar.

In any typical arrest scenario, the arrested individual wouldn't have had a pistol at the ready. But Hubbs' arrest of Cutlar was far from typical. Hubbs put his hand on his own pistol and continued toward the advancing British authorities.

* * *

"This looks interesting. Do you know these, shall we say, gentlemen?" deCourcy inquired of Griffin as they approached Hubbs and Cutlar, accompanied by Captain Prevost and Lieutenant Peile from the *Satellite*.

"That's Hubbs, customs inspector, the shorter one," Griffin replied. "The taller one's Cutlar."

"The man who shot the hog?" deCourcy asked.

"Same."

"Doesn't look as though either's inclined to have a discussion at the moment."

"Hubbs wouldn't be stupid enough to draw as long as we let 'em pass. Don't know about Cutlar, though. He's not the smartest squatter on the island."

Griffin, deCourcy, Prevost and Peile slowed their pace. The two groups passed with barely a foot between them. Griffin looked back to ensure that Hubbs and Cutlar continued along their course, catching Hubbs' eyes for a brief moment as he looked back for the same purpose. The look of fear in Hubbs' eyes reminded Griffin of the look he'd seen the night Clallam Indians had attacked his cabin, except that this time, Griffin wasn't coming to Hubbs' rescue.

\* \* \*

Each step was a struggle for Anna. But once Flora was able to get her seated on the chair she had placed in front of the small cabin, she could see that the effort had been worthwhile. Anna's expression as she gazed across the strait was the closest to happiness that Flora had seen since she'd arrived. She draped a blanket around Anna's shoulders and promised herself that she would get Anna outside as many days as she could, if only for a short while.

The workers and their families were assembled next to Griffin's residence, in front of the Union Jack that flapped in the mid-day breeze. Almost everyone employed or resident at the farm was present: about twenty men, most of whom were Kanaka, along with a few Scots and French-Canadians, as well as a half-dozen Indian and Kanaka wives, and a handful of children.

Anna's chair was still twenty yards from the assembly, but Flora wasn't about to drag her patient across the farm just to ensure that one more wife of a British subject was closer to the ceremony. She assured herself that the presence of a young Indian woman who'd be unlikely to understand the pronouncements wasn't truly necessary to the ceremony's success.

Aleck approached Flora from across the small crowd.

"You sure she's fine like that, miss?"

"The fresh air will be good for her."

"Miss, you dinnae have to stay. We got no way to kin what's gonna happen here, but this is no place for a girl who's got no good reason to be here."

"I appreciate your concern, but I'm seventeen. I'm not a girl. And I have a very good reason to be here."

Aleck shrugged, as if he had done all he could to protect her.

Griffin emerged from his residence, followed by deCourcy and several men in uniform. Flora and Aleck stepped closer to hear the announcement.

Griffin cleared his throat. "I've asked all of you, all of Her Majesty's subjects and others, to assemble here so Lieutenant Peile can make an announcement about appointing Major John deCourcy as our new Stipendiary Magistrate and Justice of the Peace here on the island."

Griffin stepped back and deferred to Peile, a tall, bearded officer in his mid-thirties, who lifted a sheet of paper, surveyed the crowd with a critical eye, and then began to read his announcement. It was essentially the same terms that Griffin had just described, but in lengthier sentences filled with grandiose verbiage. The realization allowed Flora's mind to wander, and to question the wisdom in having so quickly dismissed Aleck's suggestion that she should return to the Ross farm.

She turned to check on Anna. Anna seemed to sense her gaze and smiled in her direction. There was happiness behind the smile, at being outdoors on a sunny day, at being a part of the day's events, and at being among her friends. But it struck Flora as a bittersweet happiness, tarnished by an understanding between them that Anna's sunny days were fleeting, and it surprised her to realize that a smile could break her heart.

She looked over at the men standing in front of Griffin's residence, puffing their chests, reading their proclamations, and staking their positions over what struck her as little more than a breach of military protocol. If the landing of American troops on the beach wasn't a full-blown crisis, they were certain to turn it into one. In the meantime, she reassured herself, the only crisis that mattered was that a young woman was dying as her body succumbed to disease. It was the reason Flora had come to San Juan Island, and it was the reason she would stay.

\* \* \*

Flora wrote as fast as she legibly could, dated the note July 29, 1859, and then blew across the ink to ensure it was dry. The *Satellite* had left the harbor the night before without serving any purpose other than to deposit Magistrate deCourcy on the island. The arrival the following morning of the Hudson's Bay Company steamer, the *Beaver*, was far less threatening and unlikely to spawn any rumors of potential conflict. But its arrival had prompted Flora to sit at the small table across from Anna's bed and write the note in haste. There might be a war, perhaps a skirmish, or at least a political quagmire unfolding a few hundred yards away, but she wasn't about to allow it to interfere with her responsibilities. She hurried outside as Griffin, Alexander Dallas, and a third man she didn't recognize, passed by the cabin. She looked past them, searching for signs of anyone else, but it was just the three Company men. Dallas paused when he noticed the anxious look on her face.

"Miss Ross?"

"Mr. Dallas, I'm sorry to trouble you. I was hoping someone from the *Beaver's* crew would have come to the farm with you."

"What is it, Miss Ross?"

"I need to get a message to Dr. Tolmie." Flora held out the folded note, hesitantly. "We need some medicines. Dr. Tolmie examined the patient when he was here last …"

Dallas hesitated, then took the note. "He's moving his

family to Victoria at the moment, so if you don't mind, I'll have it delivered to Helmcken."

"Thank you, so much. I know it's an imposition."

"I don't know if you understand all that's going on here, Miss Ross, but this is hardly a safe place for you to be. The Royal Navy is bound to respond to this provocation. I do hope you realize we can't assure your safety."

"You can't assure my safety in Victoria, either, Mr. Dallas. But thank you again for taking the note." Flora smiled her thanks and turned back into Aleck's cabin, surprised at how the confident tone of her response had so effectively hidden the fears she held inside.

\* \* \*

*Conversing with modesty and simplicity.* — Always seek to converse with gentlemen into whose society you may be introduced, with a dignified modesty and simplicity, which will effectually check on their part any attempt at familiarity; but never say or do anything that may lead them to suppose you are soliciting their notice.

An instance can scarcely be recalled of a lady, either by direct or indirect means, attempting to storm a man's heart into admiration, who did not effectually defeat her purpose, and instead of the coveted homage to her charms, awaken a feeling directly its opposite. What sight can be more pitiable or repulsive than that of a female, advancing in the vale of years, and leaving behind her all the youthful attractions she might once have possessed, and yet retaining her inordinate thirst for the society and admiration of gentlemen.

Thornwell, Emily, *The Lady's Guide to Perfect Gentility*, New York, 1856.

\* \* \*

Flora poked the grass with a stick, searching for any signs of a camas lily in the yellowed brush. The damp ground by the springs that lay east of the farm would surely hold the most promise for finding camas lilies, and she found the drying remains of several. Their blue flowers were long dead from the summer heat, but the identity of the plants was still evident from the yellowing stems. It was early in the season to harvest camas bulbs, but Anna's needs were immediate. Flora used her stick to break the soil and reach the bulbous roots, pulling one free and examining it in the sunlight. Cooking the bulbs into a rich, sweet paste would take considerable effort, but the effort would provide Anna with an easily digestible meal.

"I hope that isn't your supper you're digging up there."

Flora looked up with a start, frightened by the unexpected voice. She didn't recognize the speaker, and quickly assessed whether he posed a threat. The man was lean, of average height, mid-to-late twenties, and dressed in buckskin that reminded Flora of the clothing her brothers had worn when they were younger. His clothing suggested that he was civilian, and his accent suggested American, but it was hard to tell with accents since so many of the colony's residents were itinerant types who rarely stayed in one place for long. He had bushy, unruly hair that might normally be concealed under the wide-brimmed hat he'd just removed, and an equally bushy moustache. He smiled, though he carried rope and a musket, both of which complicated the welcoming nature of his smile. But what struck her most were his eyes when he smiled. They reminded her of Helmcken's twinkling eyes, and she felt a similar flush upon noticing them.

"Uh, no, this is—no, it's not for me," she replied. "But I see no reason why you should hope it isn't. It can be quite delicious."

"Are you here with the Bellingham settlers?"

"No, I'm not." Flora was unsure how much information she was prepared to divulge.

"I apologize, I'm being rude. Paul Kinsey Hubbs—junior—I'm the U.S. customs inspector—deputy customs inspector—and recently elected magistrate in these islands."

"Oh, I see. Am I in your way to reach the springs?"

"No, no. Not at all. I was just out at my claim, making sure no one had messed with the stakes."

"Your claim?"

"Out on the point." Hubbs gestured eastward to where the peninsula tapered past Mount Finlayson to the southeastern point of the island. "I've staked off a fine stretch of prairie just the other side of the hill, right down to the water."

Hubbs hesitated, and it seemed to Flora as if he were waiting for her to say something congratulatory or complimentary about his claim, until she realized that he was most likely waiting for her to reciprocate the introduction.

"Oh, uh, I'm Miss Ross, Flora Ross. I'm just at the farm for a few weeks as a nurse. Well, I shouldn't say a few weeks. I do hope it's longer than that. I'm sure it will be much longer. I should say she'll be just fine, but ..." Flora stopped herself, realizing that she was rambling, and certain that she had no reason to be doing so.

"Ross. I think I may know of two of your brothers. Cohorts of William McNeill's, if I'm remembering rightly. They were here deer hunting a few months back."

"Oh, of course." Flora smiled, relieved that her family name might only be associated with deer hunting in this man's mind, and not the James Wright beating, or any of the other escapades that Francis and William might be known for this far from home.

"Well, if you're heading back, I'm passing by the farm, I'd be happy to escort you."

Flora understood suddenly why she had felt a slight discomfort the moment she had set eyes on Hubbs. It wasn't so much the fear that he might be dangerous. It was the overly inquisitive expression on his face and in his voice, much like the look and tone she remembered in a young midshipman's ruddy face at a naval ball in late 1858 after a particularly spirited quadrille. The dance had ended, but he was just getting started.

"That's very kind, thank you, but I've a few more things I'm trying to find."

"It's not all that safe for a young woman to be alone out here." Hubbs gestured toward the crest of the ridge less than a hundred yards to the north, beyond which lay Griffin Bay and the encampment of Company D.

"I've spent my life in places where it apparently wasn't safe for me. But, thank you for your concern."

"Well, then, very nice to meet you, Miss Ross. I hope our paths cross again."

"Good day, Mr. ..." Flora had already forgotten the man's name.

"Hubbs. Paul Hubbs."

"Yes, of course. Mr. Hubbs. Good day."

Hubbs tipped his rumpled hat as he placed it back on his head, then continued along the prairie in the direction of the farm. Flora watched him depart, trying to remember what she had heard mentioned of this putative U.S. government official on the island. There had been comments about annoying tax notices, Indian attacks and an air of arrogance. But nothing else she could remember.

It wasn't until Hubbs disappeared from sight that she realized she had been standing still, replaying their conversation in her head, and forgetting her reason for being away from the farm. She looked around in all directions to ensure that no one else might be approaching, then knelt again to dig for more camas bulbs.

\* \* \*

APPLICATION OF ELECTRICITY TO MILITARY PURPOSES.— Experiments have been recently made with M. Grenet's electric pile for the purpose of producing an electric light to be used by night reconnoitering parties. The tries, which took place in the gardens of the Tuilleries and in

---



the Bois de Boulogne, are stated to have been highly satisfactory. This artificial sun may be extinguished or suffered to shine at pleasure, and will show, over a horizon of a mile and a quarter, all the movements of an enemy.

*The British Colonist*, Friday, July 29, 1859, p. 2.

\* \* \*

Flora ran quickly along the wagon road, overtaking several of the farmworkers' families in her anxiousness to reach the ridge and join the others. The sight that came into view as she reached the ridge was daunting. No actual war had broken out, but the ominous nature of the evening's developments quickly became clear.

Fires burned eerily in the braziers on the deck of the *H.M.S. Tribune*, ready to spark the fifteen 32-pound cannons pointed from the port side of the corvette toward the encampment of American troops on the beach. The orange light flickered across the water and along the white canvas of the American tents, marking them as easy targets. Onboard, sailors from the Royal Navy scrambled about, their long shadows thrown from the braziers to dance across the deck as the men prepared the vessel for their unannounced task. The insistent calls of the boatswain's whistle echoed up the hillside and added to the fearful anticipation that Flora sensed she shared with the farmworkers who stood beside her atop the ridge. Yet she was fully aware that her anticipation was undoubtedly a fraction of that being felt by the five-dozen American soldiers camped on the beach below.

The heat of the summer's day still hung oppressively in the air, despite the late hour, as the usual afternoon gusts of wind that would sweep across the island to ease the day's heat had never arrived. The long yellow grass stood still, erect, as if the wind were holding its breath, waiting for the island's fragile balance to erupt into a catastrophic battle at any moment.

Flora had left the cabin a short time earlier to give

Aleck and Anna some time together, only to discover the excitement that the *Tribune's* arrival had caused. The *Tribune* wasn't the largest British warship on the Northwest coast, but it was the most daunting, as it combined sails with modern steam-powered screw propulsion, and carried thirty 32-pound cannons and three hundred men. The navy's flagship in the region, the *H.M.S. Ganges*, was larger and carried more cannons, but its lack of steam power made it impractical for many purposes in modern warfare. The *Tribune* was more than sufficiently intimidating as it dropped anchor broadside to the American camp, facing down Pickett's two functioning 8-pound guns that, along with each soldier's musket, constituted the miniscule firepower of Company D.

Farther along the ridge, Griffin, deCourcy, Dallas, and the man who had arrived on the *Beaver* with Dallas—who Flora had since learned was George Hunter Cary, the colony's new attorney general—watched the same spectacle unfold in the bay, but from a vantage point just far enough along the ridge to separate themselves from the farm's laborers.

Flora stood between the two groups, curious to hear whatever snippets of conversation she might be able to pick up from Griffin and the others. She was unable to hear much, but understood that they'd decided to have Griffin deliver a message to the U.S. commander demanding that his troops abandon the Company's property, which in the Company's view meant the entire island. The wording they would use seemed to be an issue of disagreement, however, and caused Griffin and Dallas to turn back toward Griffin's residence to work out a proposed draft.

Flora tried to appear as though she hadn't been listening, though she knew it was unlikely that any of the men would have cared either way. Dallas paused as he and Griffin passed the laborers on the ridge, noticing Flora among them.

"Miss Ross, I expect the *Beaver* will return to Victoria tomorrow afternoon, in case this development encourages you to change your mind and deliver your message to Tolmie or Helmcken personally."

"Thank you, Mr. Dallas. I don't expect it will, but I appreciate the notice."

Flora caught several farmworkers glancing at her enviously, likely wishing that they, too, might have an option to leave the island. She turned back to the spectacle unfolding in the bay and struggled to picture herself boarding the *Beaver*, looking back at the island and the cabin where Anna lay, and finding relief in the prospect of returning to the relative safety of Victoria. It made eminent sense. But it would only ever happen in her imagination.

\* \* \*

Bellevue Farm, San Juan, July 30, 1859.
Sir: I have the honor to inform you that the island of San Juan, on which your camp is pitched, is the property and in the occupation of the Hudson's Bay Company, and to request that you and the whole of the party who have landed from the American vessels will immediately cease to occupy the same. Should you be unwilling to comply with my request, I feel bound to apply to the civil authorities. Awaiting your reply.
I have the honor to be, sir, your obedient servant.
CHAS. JNO. GRIFFIN.
Agent Hudson's Bay Company.
Captain Pickett, &c., &c., &c.

\* \* \*

Military Camp.
San Juan, W.T., July 30, 1859.
Sir: Your communication of this instant has been received. I have to state in reply that I do not acknowledge the right of the Hudson's Bay Company to dictate my course of action. I am here by virtue of an

170

order from my government, and shall
remain till recalled by the same authority.
I am, sir, very respectfully, your obedient
servant.
GEORGE E. PICKETT.
Captain 9th U.S. Infantry, Commanding.
Mr. Charles J. Griffin,
Agent Hudson's Bay Company, San Juan
Island, W.T.

* * *

Hubbs dropped a canvas sack filled with books outside the
open door of his cabin, then stopped and listened for any
sounds that might indicate if war had broken out across the
ridge. He heard only birds, the rhythm of the waves hitting
the beach below, and the pounding of his heart. The
bundling of his personal library in protective canvas was the
first step in his contingency plan to escape the island at the
first hint of British attack. The second step would be to
stash each bundle in the underbrush at the beach below his
cabin so that he could escape quickly in his canoe as soon
as the British cannons began to fire.

Less than an hour earlier, Hubbs had been loitering
around the edge of the American camp, coddling his injured
ego after Pickett had announced that he'd appointed Henry
Crosbie to serve as the U.S. Justice of the Peace and
Stipendiary Magistrate on San Juan Island. Hubbs could
hardly challenge Crosbie's qualifications for the job, as the
man had served as U.S. attorney in Washington Territory,
and as a Lieutenant Colonel during the Indian War; the
same war where Hubbs had served as a scout because of his
years spent living with northern Indians. He could also
hardly claim that his own election to the same position
barely two weeks earlier had been the finest example of a
functioning, sober democracy. But the idea that a military
authority would appoint a replacement civil magistrate over
the will of the people offended Hubbs on more than just a
personal level, even if the will of the people had been

inebriated at the time of its expression. That it had come from Pickett only deepened the offense.

The personal slight had led Hubbs to the edge of the camp to nurse his bruised ego, but left him unable to appreciate the nature of the conversation he'd then witnessed from afar—a heated argument between Pickett and a British official that Hubbs had wrongly presumed was Captain Geoffrey Phipps Hornby of the *H.M.S. Tribune*. If Hubbs had remained by the camp any longer, he would have learned that the man making blustery threats against Pickett was not a naval captain, but was Major deCourcy, a civil official who held no authority over the British cannons that lined the deck of the *Tribune*. Instead, Hubbs had hurried back to his own cabin, his misconceptions intact, to prepare for an evacuation to the safety of his father's house in Port Townsend.

Hubbs turned back inside to begin bundling a second sack of books, only to be startled by snapping twigs. He spun around and observed five men climbing the trail from the south beach below his cabin. He quickly sized them up while calculating the distance to his nearest firearm. They were civilians, city men, and they appeared unarmed.

"Afternoon, to you, sir. I wonder if we might have a word."

"Perhaps. You are ..."

"Amor De Cosmos, *British Colonist* newspaper." De Cosmos paused, out of breath from the hike up the hillside. "This is my colleague Mr. Higgins, as well as Messrs. Trahy, Cooper, Bell. We're here to inquire about the state of affairs on the island."

Journalists. At nearly any other time, Hubbs would have welcomed and even sought out the opportunity to meet local journalists in order to have his views recorded for publication. But doing so while anticipating the imminent arrival of 32-pound cannon shot didn't seem to constitute ideal timing for advancing the American side of the story, or his personal role in the unfolding crisis. On the other hand, Hubbs recognized that he had just given a Victoria journalist the opportunity to write a story about the terrified U.S.

deputy customs inspector preparing to flee from the military conflict he'd largely instigated. A measure of courtesy was in order.

"Gentlemen, welcome to San Juan Island, of Washington Territory. Paul Hubbs, Junior, deputy inspector of customs. Please, come in, come in. You look as though you're all in need of some refreshments."

Hubbs led the men into his cabin and set about pouring each man a large glass of whiskey, hopeful that his hands wouldn't betray a tremor as he poured, and thankful that he hadn't included his supply of alcohol among the first items he'd packed for evacuation.

"It looks as though you're in a hurry to leave, Mr. Hubbs."

"No, just being cautious. There were some rather hot and hasty words a short time ago between Captain Hornby of the *Tribune* and Captain Pickett. The *Tribune's* anchored broadside to the camp, fires burning, redcoats all over the deck. Just being cautious. Judicious."

"If we're interfering with your departure –"

"Not at all. Please, a toast … to the peaceful relationship between our two countries."

Hubbs downed most of his glass, hoping it might ease his anxious state.

"We noticed your American flag as we landed on the beach down below. That seems to be new."

"We raised it on Independence Day. And again on election day."

"You held elections here?"

"July 11th. Twenty American citizens voted here. I was elected magistrate for the island."

"Congratulations to you, sir." De Cosmos gestured with his glass while the others echoed his congratulations.

"Yes, well, I was informed this morning that I've been replaced by a Mr. Crosbie, whom you may meet at Captain Pickett's camp."

"Replaced? That hardly sounds like the result of a free and fair democracy."

Hubbs imagined the direction of De Cosmos' thoughts,

already composing a future article about the subjugation of U.S. democratic principles to American military objectives in the region. He concluded that it would be best to avoid mentioning anything further about the circumstances of his own election, and decided to focus instead on his preferred version of the events that had led to the arrival of U.S. troops.

"Gentlemen, more whiskey? We should raise our glasses to the memory of the poor, wretched animal that created this disturbance in our relations."

Hubbs could see from their reaction that they were unaware a dead pig had launched the affair, and were likely running through lists in their minds of possible politicians or other officials that Hubbs might have meant to describe as a "poor, wretched animal." Hubbs quickly launched into the tale of Lyman Cutlar's potatoes, the offending boar, and the British reaction, recognizing that he had a limited window of time to tell his story before he either ran out of whiskey, his guests ran out of patience, or cannon shot rained down on them all.

\* \* \*

"I dinnae imagine he'll show," Aleck predicted while peering through the dusty window of his cabin.

Flora looked up from across the cabin, where she was feeding Anna her dinner.

"It's still not six o'clock."

"Close enough he should'a been here by now if he's comin'."

Six o'clock was the time of the hearing that deCourcy had set on the summons he'd served on Pickett earlier that day, commanding him to appear at Griffin's cabin. And although Flora had noted that a few minutes remained, she shared Aleck's belief that Pickett was unlikely to appear.

Flora approached the window and looked to the south to where deCourcy, Griffin, and others congregated in front of Griffin's cabin. She wondered if any of them had any expectation that Pickett would show, and concluded that it was unlikely they did, since they all seemed to be relatively intelligent men.

"What d'ya think'll happen here, miss?"

The question surprised Flora, and for a moment she presumed that he must have changed the topic of conversation. Few men would bother to ask a woman her views on issues of politics or military adventures. Still fewer would ask a young woman they apparently considered to be merely a girl. And none would ask such a question of an Indian girl. She felt a tinge of nervousness, as if responding carried a heavy responsibility.

"I've no idea. I just worry they're all acting a little like my brothers get when they can't walk away from the whiskey." She didn't need to see Aleck's look to realize that she hadn't communicated a particularly clear concept.

"What I mean is, I've seen my youngest brothers when they get carried away with this idea that they have to prove their strength, their courage, prove they're somehow better than whatever other man shares the same space as them, even if he's a half-wit. I worry some of these men are similar right now. The American army can't back down and leave. The Royal Navy can't ignore what the Americans have done. Major deCourcy has a new position to carry out, as does that man on the American side. They're all too proud to just turn around and go home. If Captain Pickett doesn't show up, and we all seem certain he won't, does Major deCourcy try to arrest him? Does that ship in the harbor fire its cannons or land its troops so they can all feel they've shown what kind of men they are? I don't know what will happen, but I'm rather fearful of what might."

Flora gazed out the window toward Griffin's residence just as Griffin's Kanaka houseboy emerged with a tray of drinks for the men waiting outside. Flora took it as a definitive sign that they, too, were convinced that Pickett wouldn't be joining them that evening.

\* \* \*

Flora put down Anna's Bible once she realized that Anna

had fallen asleep during her reading from *Galatians*. The idea of allowing a Sunday morning to pass without something resembling a service had been inconceivable to Flora, and she hoped that Anna had appreciated her readings. The realization that she was missing the Sunday service at Christ Church, and all its social interaction, made her homesick for the first time since she had arrived the prior Tuesday.

Flora chose to feel relief at Anna's light snoring rather than offense, taking it as a sign that Anna was far more at peace than she'd seemed throughout the night when she'd been plagued by nightmares. Flora reached for a canvas sack and a stick for digging, and slipped from the cabin, anxious to use the opportunity to scour the gentle slopes of Mount Finlayson for herbs and plants. Her primary tasks were rose hips and salal that she would use to make a tea for Anna, but both were among the most common shrubs to be found on the island. The tougher task would be wild ginger, which Flora hoped to use as a remedy to ease Anna's intestinal discomfort.

As Flora passed the barns along the north side of the camp, and started along the ridge to the east, she realized that she'd been missing substantial activity while engrossed in the New Testament. Across the wide prairie east of the farm, by the springs, sat a dozen tents that hadn't been there the night before, while a line of U.S. soldiers traipsed along the wagon road from the beach carrying supplies.

She walked higher along the wagon road until she could see over the ridge and down into Griffin Bay. The *Tribune* still sat in the bay, broadside to the American camp, its fires still burning, and its gunports still open. But the American camp itself had been largely dismantled. The area above the springs, being just over the ridge, placed the new U.S. camp out of sight of the British guns, though not out of range. It made some sense to move the camp out from under the direct line of fire, Flora thought, but it also struck her that the British vessel could merely exit the bay and round the eastern point of the island, to the southern side of the peninsula. From there, the new American camp would be every bit as exposed as the old one, if not more so given the openness of the prairie. She presumed it was a possibility that had already crossed the minds of the American officers who were responsible for such decisions.

As she watched the U.S. soldiers establish their new camp, the warning Hubbs had issued two days earlier about the risks to her personal safety sounded somewhat reasonable. The American troops might seem preoccupied at the moment, but they were now just a few hundred yards from the farm rather than on the beach below the ridge. She paused and questioned the wisdom in continuing to the wooded slopes of Mount Finlayson on the other side of the new American camp.

"Miss Ross, is that you?"

The familiarity of the voice startled Flora. She turned to see Mr. Phelan, the Victoria grocer, out of breath as he trudged up the hill behind a collection of U.S. soldiers. Behind him trailed Mrs. Phelan and three gentlemen with their wives, all of whom seemed vaguely familiar. Each carried something in their arms, and for a moment Flora wondered in confusion why Mr. and Mrs. Phelan would be helping the U.S. army move its camp up to the ridge.

"We didn't see you on the boat, Miss Ross. Is there another excursion here already?"

Flora suddenly understood that the Phelans and their companions were not carrying supplies for the U.S. troops. They were carrying supplies for a picnic. A war between Great Britain and the United States might be unleashed at any moment on this very hillside, and these Victoria residents had thought it appropriate to come to the island for a Sunday picnic to see for themselves how events might unfold, all while resting on a blanket in the tall grass with cannons on one side and the targets on the other.

"No, I've been here several days," she replied. "There was a need for a nurse at the farm."

Mrs. Phelan nodded, catching her breath. "So that's why Mr. Phelan wasn't able to convince you to come work for us. We're still searching for a nurse, you know."

Flora hadn't known, or ever given the nursing position another thought. Her opinion of Mrs. Phelan had been altered enough as it was by the woman's apparent inability to care for two small children. That she clearly had the energy for a picnic in the middle of a prospective battlefield didn't help her case.

"Come, you must join us," Mr. Phelan offered. "Our Chinaman put together the most splendid picnic meal, and we have more than enough for all of us. Fresh strawberries, too."

"That's very kind of you," Flora began, but then paused. She wondered if they were the same overpriced strawberries she'd seen sitting in Mr. Phelan's store, unable to find a willing buyer. She hoped they weren't, since they'd be far past their best by now. She struggled to think of an appropriate and polite response that would free her from the need to take part in this bizarre ceremony, certain of the embarrassment she'd feel if anyone from the farm were to find her lounging on a blanket, whiling away a Sunday afternoon eating strawberries and waiting for a war to break out on either side of the picnic. Flora smiled and started to thank Mr. Phelan for the kind offer, but then realized that the summer's strawberry season had nearly passed and she'd yet to have a single berry. And a picnic meal prepared by a grocer's Chinaman was certain to be delicious. She looked back at the farm to confirm that no farmworkers were in sight, wondering if she could take the risk without facing either ridicule or cannon fire.

# Chapter 10

THE SAN JUAN EXCITEMENT.—The excitement concerning the occupation of Bellevue Island by American troops continues unabated, and forms the all-absorbing topic of conversation. The least important fact and the most absurd rumors are eagerly listened to and readily believed. Truly, very little reliable information is in possession of the public, as all attempts on the part of the press to penetrate into the secrets of State have provide futile. The *Satellite* returned to Esquimalt harbor yesterday afternoon, but she had little or no communication with shore, except on business with government officials, and what was the purport of her despatches has not transpired. The *Tribune* still retains her position at San Juan, and the *Plumper* is expected there with a reinforcement of 200 Sappers and Miners from New Westminster. What is to be the denouement of all this war talk is still shrouded in mystery, but the general desire is that no collision may take place, and that matters may be arranged satisfactorily to the honor and rights of the two nations, now assuming so belligerent an attitude toward each other.

*The Victoria Gazette*, Tuesday, August 2, 1859, p. 1.

\* \* \*

Hubbs wasn't impressed by the showmanship. He'd seen many dead bodies before. During the Indian Wars throughout the Puget Sound region. While participating in northern Indian raiding parties. Or on local beaches, where the bodies of waylaid gold miners occasionally washed ashore. And though most of them had still had the head attached, they'd usually shown signs of having been garroted, shot, disemboweled, or had their throats slit. The conclusion to be reached with each of them had been simple: death by Indians. Whether or not it was true, it was the accepted explanation for nearly all such discoveries. Crosbie's decision to hold a public inquest into the death of the young and as-yet-unidentified white woman whose decapitated body had been found on neighboring Lopez Island, with her head nearby in a blood-soaked canvas sack, struck Hubbs as grandstanding.

Nearly all of the bodies that had washed ashore in recent years, or been found drifting in canoes in the strait, had been of white men. The appearance of the body of an unidentified white woman was an extremely rare event, and for that reason alone Hubbs understood why Crosbie would want to inquire into her death to prevent rumors from circulating. But Hubbs hardly felt that the discovery justified Crosbie's decision to haul the poor woman's remains up the hill to the new American camp for an inquest in front of a large and curious audience, while British cannons remained pointed at the ridge.

Hubbs considered the large crowd to be proof of his grandstanding opinion. They weren't intruding on a private event. They'd been welcomed to witness a public spectacle. Only a few in the crowd were American soldiers. The majority of the spectators were civilians, roughly split between new settlers from the tiny village that had sprung up on the beach, and those who had come over for the day to witness the unfolding of an inevitable war. Crosbie had ensured that they wouldn't go home disappointed. There might be no cannon shot ripping across the prairie, but each would have a tale to tell of the headless body being dissected by the distinguished, older American gentleman who was most definitely upholding U.S. civil authority on the island.

Crosbie was delivering his message to an audience from both sides of the conflict without having to arrest a single individual who might protest his jurisdiction. He had found a means to demonstrate his American authority without actually exercising it, without risking conflict with deCourcy's competing British authority, yet ensuring maximum exposure. As entertainment, it was spectacular. As politics, it was brilliant.

Hubbs could easily have stomached more of the inquest, but he'd seen all of the political theatre he was prepared to stomach. He pushed his way through the excited crowd and wandered back toward his cabin.

\* \* \*

Flora had never been bothered by the sight of butchered animals, having grown up on her family's farms. But there was something oddly clinical about Griffin's dissection of two calves that he'd discovered dead in a field that morning that Flora found almost disturbing. Angus had found her in the cabin a short time earlier, and insisted that Griffin needed to see her immediately in the dairy barn. But as soon as Flora arrived at the barn, she'd realized that Griffin hadn't asked for her presence, but that her summons to the scene of Griffin's autopsy had been a prank that Angus had chosen to play on the newcomer. Griffin hadn't needed her, or anyone. Dissecting deceased animals in order to learn the reason for their death was a common undertaking for him. If his sheep or cattle were falling victim to a particular illness or poisonous weed, he wanted to ascertain the cause before large numbers of livestock perished. Flora considered leaving once she understood the reason she'd been allegedly summoned, but concluded that the better response to the prank would be to observe the rest of Griffin's spectacle as if nothing was out of the ordinary, even though a feeling of awkwardness hung in the air.

"Can you tell the reason they died?" Flora wasn't certain if Griffin was in a talkative mood, or so lost in his task that he'd pretend he hadn't even heard the question.

"This one's liver's inflamed. Looks from the stomach remains that it ate some arrowgrass. We'll need to check the fields, see what's out there so the others don't do the same. This one, looks like its throat's swollen. Could be skunk cabbage in the intestines, but hard to tell. Looks like it could've eaten some yarrow but that shouldn't have killed it."

"You're very thorough."

Griffin nodded and began cleaning the mess he'd created. Flora considered offering to help him clean up, but then concluded that she'd rather not remain in the barn long enough to find out if there would be veal in the cookhouse that evening.

She left the barn and walked up to the ridge to see what, if anything, had changed since her last visit the evening before. The American camp was complete, in its fourth day at its new location. Nearly two-dozen white canvas tents occupied the prairie, flapping madly in the wind and reminding Flora of the sea of tents that fluttered along the edges of Victoria. Three small cannons sat in the rough square formed by the tents, two that functioned, and one that clearly did not, as it served as a flag-stand rather than a cannon at the ready to fire on British soldiers. It was, Flora thought, a particularly apt sign that Company D recognized the inadequacy of their eight-pound cannons, compared to the *Tribune's* thirty-two pounders, as they saw no point in bothering to point the broken cannon in the direction of the British troops, even for show, if nothing else.

Flora had been on the island for a week, and in that time, it had gone from a quiet, windswept Company outpost to a bustling circus of military adventure and possible warfare. The *Tribune* remained at anchor in the bay, with fires still burning and its crew still actively ready to engage the U.S. troops at any moment. It had been joined a few hours earlier by the *H.M.S. Plumper*, which carried a contingent of Royal Marines and Engineers from the colony of British Columbia, and added twelve more 32-pound cannons to the British armaments in the bay. The crews of both ships were actively engaged in exercises to prepare for battle, or at least perpetuate the ongoing appearance of such. But the spectre of British weaponry had done little to slow the growth of the small village by the farm's wharf. A few days earlier, the settlers and merchants who'd arrived with the American force had established only a handful of tents on the beach. Now, small buildings were being constructed, most of them having been dismantled in Bellingham and brought over by the merchants who had followed the troops. It still wasn't much of a village, and the primary businesses other than the army's own sutler seemed to be a handful of whiskey tents and a collection of Indian women who had followed their customers to the island. But it presented Flora with a vision of the town that would undoubtedly grow if the American army stayed on the island.

The curious onlookers who continued to arrive by the dozens each day from Victoria, Port Townsend and other towns along Puget Sound, created an odd, carnival-like atmosphere across the hillside. British cannons still lay pointed at the ridge, ready to fire, while residents from Victoria and elsewhere picnicked on the prairie and wandered through Bellevue Farm, searching for stories to tell back home. Flora tried to imagine what it must have felt like for the soldiers on either side, to aim their cannons at the enemy, to be prepared to risk life and limb for country, and then see a dozen picnickers walk into the range of the guns, lay a blanket on the grass, and unpack a picnic lunch prepared by their Indian or Chinaman.

As absurd as each excursion of picnickers seemed, it also crossed her mind that an invasion of tourists far larger in number than the invading soldiers might be a factor that encouraged both sides to moderate their behavior. Flora felt safer walking along the prairie than she had done the day after Company D had landed on the beach. For all the talk of war, surely nothing serious could come from a skirmish where one of the sides was made up of only sixty poorly armed American soldiers, surrounded by dozens of picnicking British subjects. It was a thought that comforted her, whether or not it was a correct analysis of potential outcomes.

"Miss Ross."

Flora turned to see Hubbs approaching from the American camp, dressed as he had been when they'd met, and smiling at her in a way that felt less intrusive than their first meeting.

"Mr. Hubbs. Good morning, to you."

"And to you. It may be hard to see from here what's going on in the American camp, but if you're so inclined, Mr. Crosbie's holding an inquest into the death of a young woman whose decapitated body was found on Lopez Island. Though, I suppose most women are too squeamish for such a sight."

"I'm not all that squeamish. I've just come from an inquest of sorts as well. Mr. Griffin is trying to learn what killed two calves last night."

"He does enjoy slicing up a dead animal or two."

"We all have our different paths of curiosity to follow."

"And where does your path of curiosity lie, Miss Ross?"

It struck Flora as a rather impudent question to come from a man with whom she was barely acquainted. She hesitated, careful to consider what she might reveal in her response.

"I suppose mine is people. They do the strangest things, sometimes. I read a lot of books, but I keep finding that people in real life are far more interesting and strange than people in fiction seem to be. And your curiosities, Mr. Hubbs?"

"I suppose the one above all others is the ways of the Indian. I spent several years living with Hyders up north when I was younger."

"A Boston man living with northern Indians? I've never heard of such a thing. They trusted you?"

"I suppose I made them trust me."

Flora tried to decide if she was witnessing confidence or arrogance. She often found it difficult to distinguish between the two, especially with Americans.

"I'm surprised you still have a scalp on your head."

"I've some surprise about that myself," Hubbs replied, "given the skirmishes that went on."

"Well, I appreciate your offer to escort me to an inquest, but I hope you'll understand that I've some tasks I must attend to today."

"I can't be offended given the nature of the offer. I hope there'll be something more appropriate I can escort you to while you're here on the island. A young woman as pretty as you shouldn't be hidden away at the farm."

"I wasn't aware I was hiding. We've only seen one another out here on the prairie."

"I suppose that's true."

Flora realized that her response had thrown Hubbs. He'd likely expected bashful appreciation for the compliment, not a challenge to the idea that she needed his assistance to spend time away from the farm. She wondered why she'd responded as if it had been a criticism rather than a compliment, and decided it would be best to at least acknowledge the flattery.

"But thank you for the comment on my appearance, though I suppose you don't see too many women out here for any comparison."

"Well, I wasn't limiting my compliment to a comparison with women on the island. Please let Aleck know my thoughts are with him and his wife."

Hubbs tipped his hat and continued toward his cabin.

Flora turned back to the farm, but then hesitated, remembering Hubbs' description of the spectacle unfolding at the American camp. She started off along the ridge, curious about the possibility of viewing an inquest, and then paused once more, suddenly remembering the headless part of the story.

\* \* \*

## BOUNDARY QUESTION.

EDITOR BRITISH COLONIST :— ...

When the treaty of June 30th, 1846, was signed, neither Lord Ashburton nor Daniel Webster were fully aware that two channels existed. The only pass then used or positively known, was the eastern strait of Rosario, nearest the American continent, which had been explored by Vancouver; and it was the only one laid down on the map as a "strait," in opposition to the "Canal" de Harro, which figures on all the then existing maps, that I have been able to meet with, as a "canal" only. On most of them, indeed, it is closed up at its further or northern entrance ...

The treaty, however, once signed, it was gradually discovered that the Canal de Harro was as wide and regular a strait as that of Rosario, and American ingenuity now set to work to interpret—or rather misinterpret— the words of the treaty ... So evident, indeed, were the rights of England, that she willingly entrusted the examination of the question to the Boundary Commissioners, little suspecting the sharp practice about to ensue ...

I believe it would be much truer to say that General Harney has been delighted to find a means of obtaining notoriety, and thus making capital for the next Presidential election; but, whatever may have been the clap trap pretext, I know of nothing to excuse either the act in itself, or the pitiful

186

underhand way, in which, in presence of
stronger force, a stolen march has been
gained on the unsuspecting faith of Great
Britain, and a neutral island, sacred by
treaties, taken possession of by main force in
time of profound peace.

*The British Colonist*, Letter to the Editor, signed by
Alfred Waddington, Wednesday, August 3, 1859, p. 3.

* * *

Hubbs hesitated outside Pickett's tent, wondering how long
he would need to wait after the departure of the British naval
Captains before his entrance wouldn't suggest that he'd been
listening outside throughout the entire meeting. It wasn't
until he heard Pickett instruct his assistant, Lieutenant
Forsyth, to *"get Hubbs in here"* that he found the confidence
to step toward the tent flaps, running into Forsyth at the
entrance.

Hubbs entered the tent to find Pickett seated at a table,
with Lieutenant Howard standing behind him. He wondered
if it was just the dim lighting or if Pickett was as pale as he
appeared. The meeting had been tense. Three British
warships lay at anchor following the return of the *Satellite*
that morning, each with gun ports open and cannons aimed
at the hillside. Royal Navy Captains Hornby, Richards and
Prevost had started the meeting with courtesy and politeness,
but the mood had deteriorated steadily as Pickett had refused
to accept any of the proposals advanced by Hornby. Pickett
would not agree to withdraw civil magistrates. He would not
agree to any sort of joint occupation. And he promised that
he would attempt to repel any effort by the British to land
troops on the island, even though it was obvious to both
sides that his own company was thoroughly incapable of
repelling any force the British might muster, and would be
slaughtered in an instant.

Pickett told the Captains that he had landed on the
island under orders from Washington, following a decision

by the Northwest Boundary Commission to award the island to the United States. It was a lie, and it was likely that the Captains suspected it was a lie. But it was also likely that they'd be unwilling to risk hostilities in case it were true and Pickett had simply received his instructions first. The fact that it could take several months for news to travel from Washington D.C. to London and back to Vancouver Island gave Pickett the advantage. The naval Captains' decision to invade, or not, would be based entirely on local information, without any instructions from London, and would risk launching a war between the two nations. Yet the conclusion of the meeting had left the impression on Pickett and his men that an invasion was more likely than not.

Hubbs listened politely as Pickett recounted the meeting, rather than admit that he'd listened through the canvas. He wanted to interject and question Pickett's interpretation of the meeting on several occasions, but decided it would be preferable to just listen and feign ignorance.

"How many settlers are in camp?" Pickett asked.

Hubbs quickly counted the Americans he'd seen hanging about the fringes of the camp in the previous hours. "About a dozen."

"Round up the rest. I'm putting you in charge of settlers, a civil militia. Position them in the trees to the west of the camp, north of the farm, in a line about six paces apart. When the Brits land, fire in thirds, each reloading as the next group fires. If the Brits advance, fall back behind the farm and circle around to join us at the camp."

Hubbs nodded, though he had considerable reservations. Three-dozen cannons faced the hillside, and estimates placed as many as a thousand troops or more onboard the three warships, ready to land at a moment's notice. The thought of relying on his collection of settlers to repel a military assault with only muskets and bravado after they'd barely been able to raise a flag without casualties was troubling.

Pickett turned to Lieutenant Howard. "Make sure each man has three days' rations and sixty rounds." He turned back to Hubbs. "Our soldiers will be spaced out to the east of the camp, up the hillside and along the ridge. There won't be a solid target for their guns, and any landing will be surrounded by fire."

"Sir, what if they land, but not here?" Forsyth inquired. "What if instead of facing us head-on, they land troops on the north side of the bay and set up a camp of their own?"

"Then we grab our guns and walk around to the north side of the bay. No landings. I have my orders. We all do."

Hubbs' attention was pulled from the meeting by the piercing call of a boatswain's whistle that echoed across the water from the deck of one of the British warships. As he listened, he could hear heavy footsteps pounding across the wooden decks, and the squeals of pulleys as landing boats were lowered into the water. Hubbs hoped that the increased activity in the bay was designed to intimidate them, and nothing more. Even if that was the sole purpose, it was effective. But he couldn't entirely discount the possibility that it might be actual preparation for an attack.

\* \* \*

Flora kept hold of Anna's hand, afraid to let go in case it might awaken her. It had taken nearly two hours for Anna to fall asleep, fearful as she was that the King George men in the bay were about to fire their cannons in the direction of the farm. Aleck had come by earlier to tell Flora to stay indoors, as the American troops and settlers had fanned out through the woods just beyond the farm's northern fence. They were armed and ready to repel an anticipated invasion at any moment. The news had frightened Anna. And Flora.

There had been an argument. At least, that was the story that was circulating. An argument between Captains from either side. Angry. Posturing. Proud. And it seemed their egos might now lead to a war that should have been avoided. At least it would be short, she assured herself, given the imbalance of the two sides. Though she couldn't discount the possibility that it might turn out to be merely the first battle in something far more protracted between the two nations.

Since the American troops had first arrived on the island, Flora had tried to keep Anna from worrying by avoiding lengthy discussions about the standoff. But she hadn't appreciated how much Anna was hearing and understanding—or perhaps, misunderstanding—from the snippets of conversation and sounds of ongoing military exercises that filled the background of every waking hour. Anna seemed to understand that the disease spreading through her body left her with little time, and yet she was terrified by the prospect of danger that lurked beyond the ridge.

Flora listened to the night sounds and tried to imagine them from Anna's perspective, to appreciate the fears they could generate in the mind of someone unable to see the sources of the sounds. When Flora had arrived on the island, less than three-dozen people lived within a one-mile radius of the farm. Nearly all of them were employees of the Company. It was a situation that had lasted for only a few hours. Within a few days there were over a thousand people in the same area—including the British sailors and marines in Griffin Bay—all of them talking, moving, working. The result was a constant murmur of human activity, accentuated by piercing whistle calls, shouted commands, and shrieking pulleys. Usually twice each night there were gunshots, aimed not at an enemy, but at a tree stump, as the American sentries would discharge their muskets at the end of their shifts. Although it was expected, each gunshot carried with it a twinge of fear that made the listener search the night for any sound that might suggest whether another gunshot would follow, and perhaps many more after that.

Flora could leave the cabin each day and survey the situation for herself. Anna could only imagine the ships that lay across the ridge. Flora had assured Anna that the Royal Navy was well aware of the location of the farm, and would ensure that their cannons were aimed over the ridge to the east of the farm, directly at the American camp. But in her own mind, the farm was out of sight of the British ships, as was the American camp, and the cannons would have been aimed at their targets based on an understanding of where the target lay, rather than a visual confirmation. There was far too much room for error.

Flora had grown up learning to fall asleep at their Nisqually farm while childhood fears of Indians, soldiers or bears charging through the door would run through her mind. But she'd yet to tame this new fear that she shared with Anna, that there might be a thirty-two pound cannon shot accidentally aimed at her bed, ready to fire at any moment with no warning. It was understandable that Anna had found it hard to fall asleep that night, and Flora knew that she might find it even more difficult, since there was no one to hold her hand while she tried.

\* \* \*

"Aleck, Angus, we need all hands rounding up sheep this morning," Griffin called out across the farm. "Older ewes. As many as fit on the *Beaver*."

Griffin's instructions were shouted loudly enough to allow Flora to ascertain from inside the cabin that the *Beaver* had arrived at the wharf. She had spotted the small steamer a half hour earlier as it had passed the southern shore of the island, below the farm, before circling around the point into Griffin Bay. Its arrival lifted Flora's spirits. Whether or not Dr. Tolmie was on board, she hoped that the steamer's cargo would include the supply of opiates she'd requested. Anna's pain was becoming difficult to manage, and though Flora didn't want to see the poor woman dulled under the effects of opiates, it seemed a preferable state to being unable to sleep because of the pain.

Three days had passed since rumors about the tense meeting between Pickett and the British naval Captains had caused such excitement on the island, and the threat of attack had abated somewhat in the residents' minds, primarily for the simple reason that nothing had actually happened. The *Tribune* remained at anchor in the bay, guns ready to fire, but the *Satellite* and *Plumper* had left the harbor for the time being. It was a truce of inaction, but any change in circumstances could tip the balance in favor of war.

Flora exited the cabin and looked up the wagon road to see Tolmie approaching with Griffin, and trailed by Aleck. They were deep in discussion, so Flora stood back in the doorway and waited. As she had hoped, Tolmie paused when he passed Aleck's cabin.

"So I see you were anxious to get out of the classroom and into the field, young lady."

"It seemed like the right thing to do at the time."

"Not exactly typical times," Tolmie replied. "Mr. Griffin has the mail bag. I believe there are one or two letters in there for you, as well as the recent papers." Tolmie stepped past her into the cabin. "Now, let's see here. Good morning, Anna. How are we feeling today?"

"Much pain of belly." Anna struggled to sit up, but Tolmie gestured for her to remain lying down. Aleck entered the cabin behind Flora and stood by the door, his face drawn by worry.

Flora noticed a hesitation in Tolmie's approach as he sat on the chair beside Anna's bed, as if the mere sight of Anna's gaunt face and pained expression had already told him more than he could learn from the examination he would perform. And though Tolmie was gentle, Anna repeatedly cried out in pain as he poked and prodded her abdomen.

"Very well, then" Tolmie muttered quietly as he pulled Anna's blankets back over her. He offered Flora a grim smile that she took as confirmation that he saw no purpose to be gained from continuing the examination. Then he turned and addressed Aleck, in Anna's presence, as if there was no point in trying to hide the prognosis from Anna.

"There's certainly been a progression of the disease. Her liver is quite enlarged, much more so than before, and the pain's obviously far more intense. I have a few things with me that will help."

Tolmie reached for his leather bag and emptied a dozen bottles of pills and tinctures onto the small table by the window.

"She needs all that?" Aleck asked, surprised.

"Not necessarily. But given the circumstances, I can't

be sure when I'll be able to return or even send along more supplies. This should cover her needs for several weeks, and I'll make sure Flora knows the purpose of each."

Aleck thanked Tolmie and left the cabin. Tolmie organized the bottles on the table and explained the various medicines to Flora: which tinctures were for pain or liver function, which pills were for nausea, and which pills were for constipation or diarrhea. Flora was almost relieved when the instructions were completed and she could turn the conversation to lighter matters. A visit from Tolmie was as close as she was likely to get to a visit from home, even if it did feel somewhat inappropriate to turn the conversation from Anna's fatal disease to the comforts of home.

"You've made the move back to Victoria, I hear. It went well?" Flora asked.

"As well as moving six boys under the age of nine can go. We're building a new house, entirely of stone. In the meantime, we're living in an old cabin from the Fort that I had dismantled and rebuilt on our land. Not much bigger than this one. Again, six boys, eight years and younger. Coming to a war zone to retrieve a few hundred sheep feels like a holiday."

Flora grinned at the thought. "I should probably ask about Mr. Wren and the children. Did you have a chance to see them at all before you left Nisqually?"

She had heard rumors of recent confrontations between Tolmie and Wren that had led to charges against Wren for cattle rustling. She hoped the hesitation in her voice would communicate that she was aware of the sensitive nature of her question.

"I'm told that the girls are well," he replied. "As for Mr. Wren, I'll say only that he'd do anything to keep those girls safe, so you needn't worry."

Tolmie smiled and started for the door, then paused.

"No one would judge you if you decided to accept passage back to Victoria this afternoon. They might think it quite wise."

"You're not the first to offer. But I wonder how many of your own patients you wouldn't have seen over the years if you'd done the same? It's frightening at times, but how could I possibly leave?"

Tolmie smiled at the answer, then nodded and left. Flora followed him out the door and watched as he approached Griffin's residence, passing Hubbs coming from the other direction. She could only see Hubbs' face as the two men passed, but she sensed that they exchanged an uncomfortable greeting.

Hubbs carried a small bundle wrapped in canvas, and he smiled at Flora as he approached.

"Good morning, Miss Ross."

"Mr. Hubbs. This is a surprise."

"I hope you'll excuse my impertinence, but you mentioned the other day that you love to read, and I just happen to have what I expect is one of the only collections of books on this island that's anything other than a Company ledger. I thought you might appreciate borrowing a few."

Flora hesitated, reluctant to accept his offer, but well aware that she'd already re-read each of the three books she'd brought with her.

"May I see what they are?"

"Of course. Perhaps they're books you've already read, but they were just taking up space on my shelf. Let's see here ..." Hubbs put the bundle down on a small wooden bench and unwrapped the canvas, spilling sand that he brushed away.

"Goodness, are all the books on your shelf covered in sand?" she asked.

Hubbs hesitated, unwilling to explain that his library had spent the previous few days stashed by his canoe, awaiting a possible evacuation at the sound of the first cannon fire.

"I suppose I'm not the best of housekeepers," he replied. "There's Melville's *Pierre*, Hawthorne's *Tanglewood Tales*, Longfellow, *Hiawatha* ... *Moby Dick*, you've likely read that already. Thackery's *The Virginians*, Cooper, *The Deerslayer* ..."

Flora was familiar with all of the authors, and had read *Moby Dick* before, as Hubbs had predicted. She had tried once to get through *Pierre*, but had put it down after a few chapters. She imagined that with all the excitement on the island it would be even harder to find interest in the novel on a second attempt. She was especially relieved that the package didn't contain any of the religious French literature that the Sisters of St. Ann had expected her to struggle through.

"This is very kind of you. I'll enjoy them all, I'm sure, and I'll definitely return them when I'm done."

Hubbs' smile in response struck Flora as odd. It didn't seem to communicate a concept such as "you're welcome," so much as satisfaction at having accomplished a task. It crossed her mind that his simple act of kindness might have been intended more as a pretense to ensure a reason to speak again, and she felt herself blush as she considered the idea that his generosity might have been an initial and calculated step of courtship.

"Well, I should be getting on," Hubbs announced. "I have work to do on my claim."

"How much work does it take to hold a claim if you've already staked it off?"

"Staking a claim's a start. Building a home's more secure."

"But you have a cabin already."

"Government property. This one'll be my home." Hubbs pointed east. "I've staked off the best land on a small prairie along the water."

"Sounds very nice."

"I'd like to show it to you sometime."

Flora hesitated, unsure of the propriety of such an offer. It was unlikely she'd find anyone able to act as a chaperone, given that most of the island's few residents were preoccupied with staring each other down with cannons and muskets, loaded and aimed.

"I can't leave Anna alone for long."

"No, of course not. But perhaps that's something we can consider some day soon. Well, I must be going."

Hubbs picked up the bundle of books and handed them to Flora. Their hands briefly touched, and she felt a tingle rush up her arm, and a flush return to her cheeks. Once again, the memory of the spirited quadrille and the ruddy midshipman came to mind, but this time it was her reaction rather than the shippy's insistent gaze that seemed so familiar. Hubbs smiled, and Flora wondered if he had felt it, too. Or perhaps it was just a polite smile of parting, as he turned and strolled up the wagon road that would take him beyond the American camp to his claim on the point.

As Flora turned back to the cabin, she noticed Griffin standing outside his residence, looking in her direction. It was only a brief glimpse before he turned away, but she thought she caught an expression of disapproval. Had he heard the offer of an afternoon to be spent surveying Hubbs' land claim, or witnessed her blushing acceptance of the loaned library? She assured herself that any disapproval in his expression was merely a product of her own imagination, then entered the cabin to sort through her new trove of literature and opiates.

\* \* \*

The sound was unfamiliar. The sound of churning water. But mechanical. Rhythmic. It came from everywhere and nowhere, moving about in the thick fog that had enveloped the island overnight, leaving no certainty as to its source or location. Flora stood along the southern boundaries of the farm, accompanied by several farmworkers, and struggled to understand what was happening. But each time she thought she had pinpointed the direction of the sound, it seemed to shift in the wind.

Four more days of the stalemate had passed without incident. But on the morning of August 10, 1859, the residents of Bellevue Farm, the soldiers at the American camp, and the sailors and marines on the *Tribune*, had awoken to a thick summer fog that shielded the source and location of this new sound. The whole of Griffin Bay lay awash in an eerie orange glow from the braziers on the deck of the *Tribune*, their smoke thickening the fog, and their fires illuminating the mist in a flickering light that created a sense of other-worldliness.

The farmworkers that Flora stood with were the first

on the island to glimpse the source of the sound. Small windows opened and closed through the mist as the fog rose and fell in the breeze, each time revealing a little more to the residents. First was a glimpse of a small rowboat approaching the southern beach, out of the view of the British warship across the other side of the ridge. Then a glimpse of men in blue coats walking along the beach below the farm. Another of men climbing from a rowboat and hurrying onto the gravel. And finally, as the fog lifted further, it revealed the *Julia*, a large sternwheeler coursing back and forth along the south beach, and a line of more than a hundred U.S. soldiers snaking their way up the southern hillside to the American camp. A cheer rose across the American camp as Pickett's company realized that reinforcements had been landed in the form of four companies of troops from Colonel Silas Casey's 3rd Artillery in Steilacoom. Their arrival more than tripled the size of the American contingent on the island.

No one on the slope where Flora stood made a comment about the development. Any comment would have been only a statement of the obvious or a prediction of the unknowable. The number of U.S. troops occupying the island had just grown substantially. It was likely they were still too insignificant to pose a serious threat to any invading force that the Royal Navy might land. But it was, at the very least, an act of substantial provocation that had just upset the delicate balance of the previous two weeks.

# Southern Peninsula of San Juan Island, August 20, 1859

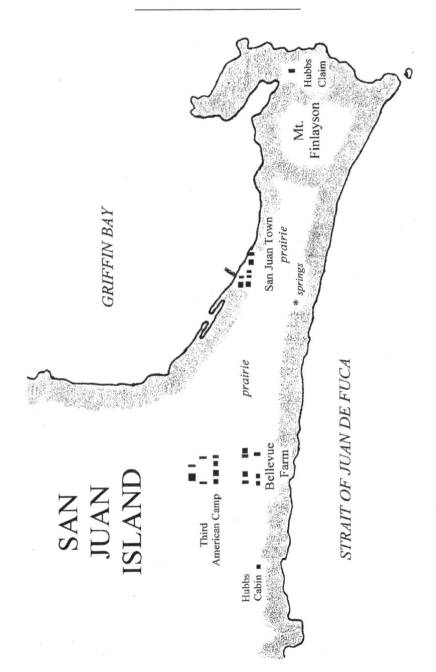

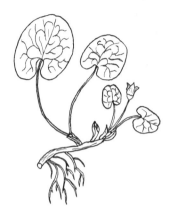

# Chapter 11

It wasn't until Flora stepped onto the gravel beach near the Company wharf that she decided it had been unwise to walk to the village on her own. It had seemed so close when she had looked down from the ridge, but she hadn't imagined how vulnerable she would feel as she walked through the growing community.

The village was still little more than a haphazard collection of tents and clapboard buildings, clustered by the wharf or spread out along the beach. But it had an energy that reminded Flora of the fringes of Victoria; the streets where the miners drank and whored, and from which girls like Flora kept a safe distance.

A few American soldiers strolled past and one muttered a comment under his breath. She couldn't hear the words, but she could sense the meaning by his expression. He was young and somewhat good-looking, though in a way that would quickly fade with his youth, and he looked at Flora with a smirking superiority. She could tell that he didn't assume she was a nurse, or educated, or from a well-placed family. Instead, he saw a young Indian woman walking alone into the village for a chance to earn a little income from a lonely soldier. It was a look Flora had seen before from miners that passed through Victoria. Newcomers who weren't familiar with the concept that a town's elite could have children bearing strong Indian features. She had never understood how men could want her to be the whore they imagined her to be, could want her for themselves and their own pleasure, yet deride her with the same look. There was a lot she didn't yet understand about men, and a lot about men that she wasn't certain she ever wanted to understand.

Farther along the beach sat several tents with small groups of Indian women gathered outside in all manners of clothing. Some wore fancy dresses that had seen better days, while others wore little more than blankets and skirts. Most of the tents offering women for hire were positioned next to a tent whose occupants peddled whiskey, ensuring an easy stumble for any drunken soldier looking to cap off a night of revelry.

Flora wondered if any of the tents were sitting on the same ground where she'd entered the world seventeen years before. She had pictured the beach in her mind countless times over the years, but she'd never pictured whiskey tents and prostitutes side-by-side on the sand.

One of the women caught Flora's eye. She appeared to be about seven months pregnant and made no effort to conceal her rounded belly. The woman returned Flora's gaze, though with an expression as unwelcoming as the look Flora had received from the soldier a few moments earlier. The woman's expression didn't communicate kinship or common identity, and Flora had no expectation that it would. In the eyes of the women along the beach, she was an outsider, a white woman who had no need to sell her body to soldiers in order to survive. For a brief moment, Flora considered offering her nursing services to assist with the future delivery of the child. But she just as quickly dismissed the idea, recognizing that none of the women in the tents along the beach would consider asking a white woman for medical help.

She turned and looked out at the *Tribune*, immediately appreciating how daunting its cannons must have seemed to the U.S. soldiers when they'd first camped along the water's edge. Even from the ridge, with its cannons pointed elsewhere, the gunboat had appeared threatening. But from the beach, so much closer and directly under the *Tribune's* gaze, the cannons appeared terrifying. She tried to imagine the same vision as it would appear at night, lit by the braziers on deck, and found it quite easy to understand the reason Pickett had moved his camp over the ridge. Mortality lurks nearby for everyone, but it's far less troubling when it isn't in plain view at all times.

Flora gazed along the beach and remembered the simple directions that Robert Janion had given. "All the way at the end," he had promised. Janion ran a commission merchant business in Victoria and had been part of a tourist excursion to the island that morning, wandering through Bellevue Farm in search of a story to share back home. She had known his family well enough that it was natural she would say hello. Upon hearing that she was working as a nurse, Janion had remarked that he had met another nurse shortly after the boat had arrived. Mrs. Boyle. Or Bierce. Or Price. He wasn't sure he'd heard it correctly, which had been obvious by the variations he had suggested. But she was here, with her husband and children, in a tent that was all the way at the end of the small settlement.

"Frank! Orrin!" Flora called out the moment she recognized the boys playing by the water, using sticks to carry out what appeared to be the serious task of torturing a small and unfortunate life form. Frank recognized her and ran along the beach, away from her.

"Mama! Mama!"

Orrin showed no signs of recognition, but just as quickly dropped his stick and ran after his brother.

It was just as Janion had said. The last tent along the beach. Among the newest arrivals. Lucinda stood over the hot coals of a morning fire, tending to a pot, and looked up to see Flora following behind her two sons.

202

"Heard a rumor you were here," Lucinda called out.

"For about three weeks now. I can't believe you're here. And with the children." Flora lowered her voice. "Are you sure it's safe for them?"

"Compared to what? Being surrounded by a few thousand drunk and desperate miners down to their last dollar? Growing up next to human waste running down the hillside and under our tent flaps? As long as the guns keep pointing up at the hillside, this is luxury."

"And Mr. Boyce," Flora started hesitantly. "He's here, too?"

Lucinda smiled. "Stephen came back a month ago. As soon as he heard about this debacle, he decided it was an opportunity to stake a claim and set up a business."

"Have you not seen what qualifies as a business along this beach?"

"He's gonna build a saloon. A proper one. With his partner, a Mr. Bowker. As Stephen puts it, panning for gold is like looking for a needle in a haystack. But finding soldiers who want to drink is like looking for hay in a haystack." Lucinda gestured to two rickety wooden chairs in front of the tent. "You'll join us for a meal?"

"I wish I could, but I can't stay long. The woman I'm caring for will be awake any time now, and I need to try to get her to eat something."

"Would she eat dumplings in gravy?"

"She might."

"Then sit. We'll eat and then you'll take a bowl to her."

"I couldn't take one of your bowls."

"You'll borrow it and you'll return it."

There was nothing more to be said. Flora took one of the rickety chairs and pulled it closer to the fire. She hadn't known Lucinda long, and she would have considered it presumptuous to call her a friend. But she also couldn't have thought of anyone from home whose arrival she would have preferred. Lucinda was an experienced nurse whose presence eased Flora's anxiety about caring for Anna. Lucinda was a resource. A mentor. And certain to become a friend.

Flora gratefully accepted a plate of dumplings from Lucinda and dug into the food as energetically as her manners would allow. She wasn't particularly hungry for lunch, but her appetite for the comforts of home was ravenous.

\* \* \*

THE WAR COUNCIL.—There is a report on the street that a "Council of War" was held at Government House on Tuesday; the subject, the difficulties growing out of the occupation of Bellevue Island by American troops, and more particularly their avowed intention of erecting fortifications. The "war party" have taken renewed offence at the proceeding of Lieut. Col. Casey to fortify the Island, which they declare under present circumstances is little less than an open declaration of war, and this Council was called at their instigation. The Council consisted of His Excellency Gov. Douglas, Admiral Baynes, Col. Moody, Judge Begbie, and Capts. De Courcy, Prevost and Hornby, and very exciting speeches are said to have been made.

Explanations from the U.S. officers were strongly insisted upon by several members of the Council, which, if unsatisfactory, then active hostilities were to be inaugurated. The final result was, that the "Fire-eaters" failed in their efforts, and the previously agreed upon course of waiting orders from home, was determined upon. We cannot vouch for the entire truth of these rumors and street conversations, and merely put them in print as portions of current history.

*The Victoria Gazette*, Thursday, August 18, 1859, p. 3.

\* \* \*

Hubbs whistled "Sacramento Gals" in a mixture of keys as he strode along the wagon road to Bellevue Farm after having spent the morning working at his claim. Time spent building his new home always put him in a good mood, and he had an absentminded tendency to whistle tunes from his youth in a thin, reedy sound against his upper teeth whenever he was in such a mood. Along the prairie, just to his left, the American troops were in the midst of dismantling their camp by the springs. Ahead several hundred yards, in a glen immediately to the north of Griffin's dairy and pig barns, the American troops were establishing their third camp. The troops had started the process of moving the camp the prior morning, on August 19th, by clearing brush and trees to make space for their tents and the few buildings they'd brought to the island. By this second day, most of the camp was being moved to the new clearing.

The official explanation for the move was the desire to shelter the troops from the cold winds that would whip across the open prairie from the Strait of Juan de Fuca, as the trees to the west of the new location would provide more effective cover. Hubbs wondered if part of the strategy was also to place the U.S. soldiers directly beside Bellevue Farm, much like a soldier might use a woman or child as a shield against his opponent, except that in this case there were far more sheep, cattle and vegetables than women and children at risk.

Hubbs walked through the farm just as Aleck emerged from his cabin.

"Aleck."

"Paul. I gotta get back to the harvest."

"Two quick things. First, I'm sorry about Anna's condition."

"Thanks."

"And, are you planning to stake a claim?"

"A claim? Here?"

"You've every right. The good lands are getting snapped up. You and Angus should have your own places."

"At the moment, I've more'n enough to think about."

Hubbs nodded. This wasn't the time to be pestering Aleck about future plans.

"I understand. But if you change your mind, I could help you pick a good piece of land."

The door opened and Flora stepped out, holding a bedpan covered with a small towel. Seeing Hubbs, she quickly put the pan back inside the door of the cabin.

"Pardon me. I'll take care of that later."

"Miss Ross, I was just over at my claim, and I thought you might appreciate a few more of these."

Hubbs dug into a bag over his shoulder and pulled out a half-dozen camas bulbs.

"Oh. That's very kind of you."

Hubbs turned to Aleck. "I understand they're something Anna will eat."

He handed the bulbs to Flora, who turned them in her hands and sniffed them.

"Did you notice the color of what was left of the flowers?"

"Uh, I think they were pale blue, perhaps."

"Blue? Not white?"

"I can't say for certain. Is that important?"

"Rather. The white camas is poisonous."

"Oh." Hubbs hesitated. "Then you should dispose of them. But there were a lot more over by the point. Tomorrow's Sunday, perhaps I could escort you there so we could harvest them with certainty?"

Hubbs struggled to interpret Flora's expression. Perhaps it had been too much for a man who had lived along the coast for nearly a decade to feign ignorance about the difference between the edible and poisonous varieties of camas? Still, she had yet to object and perhaps didn't mind his clumsy attempt at flirtation.

"Fine with me," Aleck interjected. "If it's only a few hours, I can watch Anna."

"A few hours?" Hubbs replied. "It's Sunday. It's her day off."

Aleck's hesitation betrayed his surprise at the idea that Flora might deserve a day off each Sunday.

"A few hours is more than enough," Flora insisted. "I'll ask around to see if one of the wives might agree to chaperone us."

"Chaperone?" Aleck grinned. "You're not in Victoria, miss."

"Yes, but ... what if someone saw me alone with Mr. Hubbs?"

"Paul. Please, call me Paul."

"Even worse, if they see me alone with him and calling him Paul? There could be dozens of Victoria residents here for picnics tomorrow. I could know all sorts of them."

"You tell 'em the two of you are gatherin' camas for me sick wife, and they won't think again about it," Aleck insisted. He turned to Hubbs. "What time are you plannin' so I'll know to be here?"

Hubbs turned to Flora. "Ten o'clock?"

"Well, I suppose it's settled, then," Flora declared in a disinterested tone, as if she had had no say in the matter. "Ten o'clock it is. Now, if you'll both excuse me, I've a bedpan to empty." Flora reached back in the door of the cabin, picked up the bedpan, and headed off to the privy.

\* \* \*

"... With all due respect to the character of our English immigration, we cannot but hold that it is not as well suited to the rapid development of a new country, as the Americans who would flock to the archipelago in the event of its being declared the possession of the United States. And certainly it is to the interest of these Colonies to have their vicinity peopled and its resources developed as fully and speedily as possible.

*The Victoria Gazette*, Saturday, August 20, 1859, p. 2.

\* \* \*

Flora all but forgot the camas lily pretense as she and Hubbs rounded the small hill known as Mount Finlayson and reached the tip of the island's peninsula. Stretching out before them lay a rolling expanse of pasture that hugged the eastern slope of the hill and tapered down to the ocean, dotted by tiny bays. To the north, beyond a patch of tall firs, sat the wide opening of Griffin Bay. To the east lay a narrow channel separating San Juan and Lopez Islands, through which the ocean ran like a river as the current rushed to fill or empty the inland waterways with each changing tide. And to the south lay the vast expanse of the Strait of Juan de Fuca reaching into Puget Sound, the mountains of the Olympic Peninsula across the strait, and, looming in the distance, the imposing Mount Rainier that had so dominated the landscape of her childhood Nisqually home. Other than its gentler slope, and its lower elevation just above sea level, the prairie was no different than the landscape by the sheep farm just a mile or so behind them. Tall, yellow grass swayed in the breeze, sprinkled with a few hardy, late-summer wildflowers. The forest was thick on the mountainside and along the northern beach, but there was only a single grove of trees on the southern half of the prairie; gnarled and twisted pines and firs at the southeastern point, huddled for collective protection from the wind, and leaning to the north as if the force of the constant wind off the strait made it too much of a burden for the trees to grow toward the sun. It struck her how open and exposed the area was, and yet isolated at the same time, cut off by Mount Finlayson, as if the end of the peninsula was its own island. And she decided that it was heavenly.

"All of this is your claim?"

"All the usable land."

"It's beautiful," Flora replied. "Though rather exposed."

"It's sheltered by the mountain."

"But open to the strait and the winds. I've some experience with a farm right on the water. The land's not as fertile as it is inland. The wind, the cold, the salt."

"But as pasture land it's fine. And up by the house, it's much more protected."

"Aren't you worried how isolated you are out here? All by yourself against any attacks?"

"I've handled my share of those in my cabin already."

"But over there you could escape to the farm for protection. Here there'd be no one to help you."

Flora stopped. Reciting Griffin's version of the Clallam attacks on Hubbs' cabin wasn't an ideal way to tend to Hubbs' ego. But he just smiled and shrugged.

"There's a few hundred American troops a mile behind us, not to mention British warships. I think I'll be just fine out here."

Flora followed Hubbs across the rolling pasture toward the north end of the property, where the beginnings of his home poked through the tall grass. His hand intermittently brushed against hers in a fumbling effort to hold it; fumbling in part because her reaction each time had been to pull away. There was no chaperone—no one else at all on the eastern side of the small mountain—leaving it entirely up to her to regulate their contact so that it wouldn't gather speed toward an outcome she might find herself unable to stop.

"Don't expect much yet," he cautioned, pointing toward the beginnings of his cabin. "I'm only just getting underway with it. It's mostly the stonework and starting on a couple walls."

Flora stopped in the grass and surveyed Hubbs' future home. The outline of the structure was defined by a low, stone foundation and roughly hewn driftwood logs, two high in each direction, secured by notched joints that seemed amateurish by their cuts. Three long pine poles were lashed together to form a tall tripod at one corner of the structure, from which hung a heavy iron pulley for hauling the logs into place. There were two openings for future doors, and a fieldstone chimney rose several feet along the southern wall. Flora attempted to complete the house in her imagination, then realized what it was that bothered her about the sight.

"You're building it with driftwood?"

"Mostly. There's perfectly good logs on so many of the

beaches on these islands. I go out in my canoe whenever I can and tie a log behind it."

"But the logs have worms in them."

"They're long dead. I'll fill the holes."

"I'm sorry. I'm being critical. My imagination sees a beautiful home sitting here someday. I'm sure it'll be lovely."

"The front parlor'll be here, a bedroom to the right. The kitchen'll be at the back, if I can find enough lumber."

"Well, why don't you hand me my bag and we can share a first meal in front of your parlor. It isn't much, but I figured we'd be hungry after we got here."

Flora motioned for the bag that Hubbs had offered to carry for her when they had started their walk. She sat on a log that lay in front of the house waiting to be used in construction and unpacked a small lunch. As they ate, Hubbs nervously filled their conversation with stories of his youth. He told her of his birth in East Tennessee, and of his infancy in France when his father served as a U.S. diplomat and took the family abroad for four years. He spoke of the French capital with an awareness of political and social upheaval that couldn't possibly have come from his childhood experience, yet was portrayed as wisdom acquired from his own observations. He told her of his adventures in California's gold rush country, of his rebellion against his father's expectations and his subsequent journey north, of his years of living with northern Indians, his time as a U.S. army scout during the Yakima and Puget Sound Wars, and his role in launching the arrival of U.S. troops on the island. He may have rambled, he may have stretched the truth many times, but by the end of the meal, Flora had decided that Paul K. Hubbs, Jr. was far more interesting than she had first presumed.

\* \* \*

From their new position along the ridge overlooking the bay, the 32-pound cannons that had once sat on the decks of the *Massachusetts* provided Company I of the Fourth Infantry with more protection for their arrival on San Juan

Island than the cannons would have provided had they still remained on the ship's deck facing the port and starboard sides. But it was a fact that was lost on the soldiers in Company I as the denuded *Massachusetts* carried them slowly into the foggy bay just below the *Satellite's* open gun ports.

Two weeks prior, shortly after landing his artillery companies on the south side of the island and taking charge of the U.S. military presence, Colonel Casey had brazenly landed supplies, lumber and the eight 32-pound cannons of the *Massachusetts* at the H.B.C. wharf. Troops had hauled the heavy cannons up the wagon road, still seated on their iron-wheeled wooden mounts from the ship. The undertaking had attracted a crowd, despite the risk of a British response at any moment, including excited children who ran alongside the cannons as smoke billowed from the overheated and overworked axels.

Pickett's Company D had landed before the arrival of British ships. Casey's infantry had landed on the south beach under the cover of fog. Reinforcements from the Third Artillery had landed recently at the Company wharf in the darkness of night. But Company I arrived in Griffin Bay in the middle of the day, gliding in plain sight past the *Satellite* and its cannons, brazenly intent on landing at the Company wharf. American cannons might have stood watch from the ridge, but the sole weaponry that remained on the *Massachusetts* was its relatively unthreatening signal gun that nevertheless stood at the ready, loaded by one of the soldiers with a tin can packed with nails, nuts and bolts rather than a signal flare or proper shot. The can was more likely to explode in the chamber than fire toward the British, but the intent was to fire something—anything—if hostilities broke out.

Nearly four weeks of peaceful occupation by the U.S. troops had created an impression among those on the island that the British Navy was unlikely to fire on the Americans, even under provocation. Daily life had taken on an odd acceptance of the normalcy of the situation. British and American officers exchanged courtesies, which even included invitations to U.S. officers to attend Sunday services and meals onboard the British vessels. They were invitations that were gratefully accepted given the superior quality of food available on the British ships. But whatever further provocations might be unleashed by one side or the other, including the arrival of Company I, most officers on either side understood that the standoff would not, must not, lead to war.

But it was an understanding that hadn't yet been appreciated by the soldiers of Company I as they climbed down from the *Massachusetts* into smaller boats to be rowed past the British guns of the *Satellite*, while their musicians played a desperate "Yankee Doodle Dandy" that telegraphed their nervousness by the lack of precise tuning.

But as they had done for nearly four weeks, the British guns remained silent. And as they had done three times before, American troops landed safely on the disputed island and further disrupted the balance of power.

\* \* \*

Charles Griffin emerged from his cabin, surveyed the horizon for approaching weather, and then turned his attention to the farm. Several Indians were driving carts of oats and peas to the barn for storage, while one of the French-Canadian workers repaired the wheel of a cart with the help of the *Satellite's* blacksmith. Beyond them, American soldiers continued to establish their new camp just north of the farm. Griffin's gaze turned to the water wagon sitting near the cookhouse, where Flora filled a jug with spring water. With each passing day since Flora had arrived at the farm, Griffin saw her less as the girl he had known from a distance and more as a young woman of recent acquaintance. He walked across the grounds in the direction of the sheep shed, then paused by the water wagon as if a question had just crossed his mind.

"Oh, Flora, how's Anna doing?"

Flora looked up from her task and frowned.

"She's in a lot of pain, but she doesn't like taking the medicines Dr. Tolmie brought because they just make her sleepy. I imagine as the pain gets worse, she'll come to appreciate whatever we can do for it, even if it just makes her less aware of it all."

Griffin nodded. He'd already heard as much from Aleck, but had wanted to start the conversation with something other than his intended topic. He waited just long enough to make it sound like an afterthought.

"I noticed Paul Hubbs has been paying you lots of attention."

"I suppose he has."

"It's not my business to say," he said anyway, "but your family's nowhere around right now, so I feel almost responsible. Paul's a decent man, though we don't see eye-to-eye on much. But he won't be looked on kindly back in Victoria. Not after helping to start this whole mess. Your family is Company, and this island—this farm—it's Company. He's been fighting all of that since the day he got here. I just thought I should say as much."

Griffin looked down, bracing himself for the response. He had been right to speak his mind, but he wasn't sure Flora would appreciate either his frankness or his assessment of Hubbs.

"Thank you, Mr. Griffin. I suppose I don't know him well, not yet," she began. "But he is well-educated. He seems perfectly capable of handling liquor in a responsible way. And he seems to not care in the slightest that I have Indian blood in my veins. Those are three qualities I've rarely found in one man, and never in one who wanted to be so acquainted with me for much more than a dance. Anyway, not that it matters. I'm seventeen and I didn't come here to be pursued by a lonely American official. But there's no harm in the time I spend with him."

Griffin nodded and decided that he'd likely regret anything more he might say on the topic. He lacked the youth and swagger that Hubbs could offer to a girl as young as seventeen, at least by his own critical self-assessment. Only five years separated the two men. But in Flora's eyes, Hubbs was almost her contemporary, while he'd been a grown man since she'd been a child. He might be seeing her as the girl blossoming into a woman, but it was likely that she still looked upon him as an older man.

"I imagine you're right. My apologies if I overstepped. Do let me know if there's anything you need for helping out Anna." Griffin turned and walked to the sheep shed, wishing he'd said nothing at all.

\* \* \*

Hubbs had no one but himself to blame for the crowd of people waiting to greet the newly elected Governor of Washington Territory on the dusty square at the center of the third American camp. But he had plenty of people to blame for the place he'd been given to stand, far from the front of the ceremony. Just six weeks earlier, he had stood on an empty expanse of beach with his friend, Charlie McKay, to greet General Harney and to petition for the intervention of troops. Six weeks later, he was stuck behind the Governor's civilian entourage, which itself was behind rows of military officers. Out in front, Colonel Casey rode back and forth on his horse, attempting to appear far more heroic than Hubbs believed the man had any justification to claim. Hubbs wanted, as much as anyone—more than anyone—to secure the island as U.S. territory, and to secure his own land claim under U.S. laws. He had petitioned, supported, and encouraged each of Pickett's aggressive stands when it was just Company D on the island; objecting only to Pickett's appointment of Crosbie as unelected magistrate. But Colonel Casey's conciliatory efforts since he'd taken command were leading to increased rumors that a joint occupation might be in the island's future, and that title to land claims might remain uncertain until a final boundary resolution could be reached. And yet the Colonel rode back and forth on his horse as if he were a conquering Roman general.

Over four hundred American troops were spread out across the prairie, organized by their nine companies, standing in crisp formation and in full uniform. At the edge of the new American camp, becoming known to most as

"Camp Pickett," stood the officers awaiting the arrival of Governor Gholson, blocking much of the view of the small contingent of civil officials that included Hubbs. The worst offenders were the women in the Governor's entourage, with tall hats that might have been fashionable in Olympia, but effectively blocked Hubbs from the ceremonies. The townies lining the wagon road from the wharf had a better view of the proceedings that would unfold. Even the residents of Bellevue Farm had a better view, at least those who had walked to the edge of the farm north of the dairy barn.

A light cheer from the wagon road signaled the arrival of the Governor before Hubbs could see anything. Eventually, between heads and hats, he caught a glimpse of Governor Gholson being escorted closer to the waiting corps of officers. The agenda was fairly simple. The Governor would be received by the officers, after which he would carry out a brief inspection of the troops. It wasn't clear to Hubbs if there would even be an opportunity for him to introduce himself.

All he had asked for was a company of soldiers to protect the residents from northern Indian attacks, and implicitly, from arrest by the Hudson's Bay Company for shooting errant pigs. He hadn't asked for over four hundred troops to turn the island into a military base surrounded by British warships. He hadn't asked for an unstable political environment that would imperil the validity of land claims asserted by settlers like himself. And he hadn't asked for developments that would transform the Deputy Inspector of Customs and former duly-elected Magistrate and Justice of the Peace from the preeminent U.S. Government official on the island to an afterthought lost behind a collection of fashionable headwear. Hubbs craned his neck once more, realizing that he was not so much reaching for a better view, as reaching to be viewed at all.

\* \* \*

Flora watched Governor Gholson approach the American camp from her position north of the dairy barn, where she stood flanked by the wives and children of several of the farm's laborers. Even if this wasn't the governor of their own colony, his visit was a spectacle that didn't carry a risk of imminent cannon fire. Instead, it offered a chance to see ladies from Olympia in bright, fashionable dresses, as well as all the pomp and ceremony that was missing from the daily drudgery of the troops' exercises on the island.

Flora searched for Hubbs in the crowd, and thought she managed to catch a glimpse of him at the back of a group of civilian officials from Olympia. She felt for him, stuck behind rows of dignitaries and their wives, and hoped it wouldn't dampen his mood if she saw him later.

There was a pause in the proceedings after Colonel Casey greeted the Governor, and a slight murmur spread through the crowd as if everyone was waiting for something to happen. That something turned out to be the firing of five 12-pound howitzers. The blasts were louder than any gunfire that had yet been heard on the island, and it terrified several of the smaller children watching from the dairy corral who screamed in fear.

Flora could hear the sounds of the guns being reloaded, and then the realization hit her. This was a salute of multiple guns. Perhaps twenty-one, or seventeen? She wasn't sure of the number for a ceremonial occasion such as this. But it meant reloading and firing again. And at least twice again after that.

Flora ran across the field to the cabin, tempering her speed slightly to avoid the fresh cow manure that dotted the field, and cursing herself for wanting to escape her duties for a chance to see the spectacle. Anna had been asleep when Flora had left the cabin. But now she would be awake, unaware of the reason for the cannon fire and the screams of children, and becoming more terrified with each successive explosion.

The door to the cabin was already open as Flora approached, and she burst inside to find Aleck rocking Anna in his arms.

"She's fine," he said softly, not looking up.

"There'll be more guns any second now."

216

"We know."

The howitzers fired again, sounding every bit as loud inside the cabin as they had by the barn. Aleck hugged Anna close and whispered in her ear, comforting her.

Flora stepped back outside, realizing that it wasn't a moment when Anna needed a nurse. She could do many things to help care for Anna, but replacing her husband wasn't among them.

\* \* \*

## SCARCITY OF WHITE WOMEN.

... The proportion of white men to white women here is about twenty to one. This vast disproportion of the sexes injuriously affects this country in various ways. ...

The intermarriage of whites with Indians is fraught with many and serious evils. It has been asserted that it elevates the Indian at the expense of the white race. While we question the fact of its *morally* elevating the Indian race, we are fully sensible of its demoralizing influence upon the white. The effect of this species of amalgamation, as seen here, and, we believe, everywhere else, has been an almost instantaneous degeneracy of the white, with no visible improvement of the Indian; while the offspring are found to possess not only all the vices inherent in the Indian, but unite with them the bad qualities of the whites.

*Puget Sound Herald*, Friday, August 26, 1859, p. 2.

\* \* \*

"She's strong enough to carry lumber. No wonder you always go for Indian brides."

Flora glanced over in time to catch sight of Hubbs as he punched his younger brother, Charles, in the arm, quickly silencing him. She understood that Charles had intended the comment as an insult aimed more at his brother than at her, but she also found a measure of pride in the idea that the women Charles Hubbs might know in Port Townsend wouldn't have helped move a shipment of lumber from the beach. If that made her "Indian" in his eyes, so be it.

"What? She knows she's Indian," Charles protested, though in a quieter voice.

Flora had just met Charles a few minutes earlier. He was barely a year younger than Flora, but as with most boys that age, he acted far younger. Like his old brother, Charles was the holder of a claim for one hundred and sixty acres, farther west on the island. But unlike his brother, Charles had had little to do with the establishment of the claim. His brother had staked out the land in Charles' name in an effort to increase the number of purported U.S. settlers on the island.

As yet, the teenager had shown little interest in securing his rights to settle the land. But Hubbs had nevertheless convinced his younger brother to spend a few days on the island to help with construction of the cabin after he had splurged on a small shipment of lumber. Aleck had insisted that Flora take the afternoon off, since it was Sunday, and so Hubbs had two helpers to carry the lumber from the beach where it had been dropped. Flora wasn't about to merely watch and feign fragility while the two brothers carried the lumber by themselves. Much of it was narrow clapboard, and Flora could easily carry a few boards by herself. The only difficult part was climbing up the bluff from the beach. After that, it was just rolling grassland.

"You don't have to do that, Flora," Hubbs insisted as he passed Flora on her return to the beach to collect more of the boards.

"I've helped my brothers repair the barn before. I'm not worried about splinters."

"I'm only worried you won't want to return next Sunday."

It was only a week since Flora had first seen the beginnings of Hubbs' new house, yet there had been substantial improvements since then. Hubbs had cajoled several settlers to help raise additional logs into place for each of the exterior walls, and the stone chimney now rose above the future roofline, requiring far less imagination to see the home that would someday be completed on his claim. Hubbs had expressed a determination to have walls and a potentially watertight roof on the two main rooms of the structure before the heavier rains of the fall and winter would arrive, allowing him to finish the inside of the house in any weather. The kitchen would likely have to wait. There would be a fireplace in the front parlor, and Hubbs could cook his meals there at least until the following spring.

Charles' "Indian brides" comment rang in Flora's mind again as she climbed from the beach and started back to the house with another load of wood. It wasn't a statement about prospective intent, but of habit. He had teased his older brother for "always" opting for Indian brides, not for holding out until he could find the right one. The realization was sudden, and she chided herself for not having given the idea any thought before. Hubbs had lived with northern Indians for three years. He'd taken part in war parties, if his stories were to be believed. He'd been a young man in his early twenties. Of course he had taken a bride. Or brides.

She asked herself which would be preferable: if he had taken only one bride, and had developed a deep relationship with the girl over several years before abandoning her, or if he had taken a series of companions, never remaining with any of them long enough to form a strong emotional bond. She wasn't entirely sure of the reason why, but the idea of several successive brides felt less threatening even if it might be deemed scandalous in certain circles. The more troublesome question was whether to follow Charles Hubbs' statement by asking Hubbs a direct question about his marital past. She decided to opt for the polite option of pretending that she hadn't heard the comment at all, and saving the question for any future discussion she might have with Hubbs about marriage.

The thought stopped Flora cold and the lumber nearly fell from her hands. "Marriage." To merely think the word was jarring. The concept had been woven throughout her thoughts of the previous few minutes, but somehow the word had avoided her conscious detection. But there was no denying its presence. She was contemplating the competition of Hubbs' past relationships, the threat that they might pose to his next relationship, and whether she might be the one to enter into that relationship—marriage—to a man she'd known barely a month. He was an interesting character, and someone who'd shown her a fair amount of kindness. He'd flattered her with attention, and she enjoyed walking with him to where he'd staked his claim. But she was seventeen. She'd only just begun to establish herself as a nurse. And yet there was a part of her mind busily worrying if she could compete with his memories of past Indian brides; brides he had left, perhaps abandoned, or given a reason to abandon him.

Flora watched Hubbs as he approached from the cabin on his way back to the beach. Was he wondering if she had once had other paramours courting her? Was he considering the possibility that Flora might someday be his next "Indian" bride? She found it hard to complete the thought, as if she were presuming too much, uncertain if she feared that such a possibility might arise, or that it might not. She secured her grip on the lumber lest she appear too weak to be of real assistance. Hubbs grinned as he approached. He reached down and picked a small wildflower, a purple wild bergamot, and gently inserted the stem into Flora's hair above her left ear.

"There. Two things of beauty."

Flora smiled, though more from realizing that the flower was hardly a thing of beauty. It was a late summer survivor that should have died weeks before, and seemed to acknowledge that fact by the browning and wilting of its petals. But it was a simple act that brought a smile to her face.

"You're sure it's not too heavy for you?" Hubbs reached out to take the lumber from her arms.

"No. Really. I can manage by myself." Flora smiled her thanks and continued her trek to the house with the lumber securely in her arms, still certain that she could manage by herself, but a little less certain of whether she wanted to.

# *Chapter 12*

The hole where the lead shot had entered the sow's skull was just below the left ear, as it had been for most of the others. She was the twelfth in less than a week. Her heavy carcass was slippery from the relentless rain that had soaked the island all morning, making it a struggle for Griffin and Aleck to heave it onto the wagon. But Griffin was determined that the sow wouldn't go to waste. The killings had been almost nightly, frequent enough that he would send someone out first thing each morning to check the sows in the fields, expecting to find that one, two, or even three, had been shot during the night.

"Makes no sense. Why leave 'em here?" Aleck asked. "I seen the food they eat. If it was me, I'd be shootin' a sow every night for supper."

"This isn't about food. Pure animosity's what it is." Griffin set out across the far side of the field in search of more victims. "The ewes we've lost, the lambs, those were food. These are symbols."

In the three weeks since the *Massachusetts* had landed the Fourth Infantry's Company I at the wharf, the military situation had remained largely unchanged. Nearly five hundred U.S. soldiers now occupied the island, and they had started to dig in their position by constructing massive earthworks along the ridge, an earthen fort defended by the 32-pound cannons taken from the *Massachusetts*. The *Satellite*, meanwhile, had remained at anchor in the bay, gun ports open and cannons aimed at the ridge. The pretense of civility remained in all official dealings, but there were far too many conflicts below the surface to convince Griffin that there wasn't still a substantial risk of escalation.

The troops onboard the various British men-of-war had access to fresh and varied food supplies from both Victoria and Bellevue Farm, while the U.S. troops relied on limited produce from farms around Puget Sound, and army rations that were little more than maggot-ridden hard tack and salt pork. The presence of Bellevue Farm, with a large vegetable garden, cows, sheep, pigs, and more, only yards away from the American camp, was a temptation that invited mischief. Yet the massacred sows left to rot in the fields were the primary casualties of the standoff thus far.

"Maybe you should post a few of us out here at night and catch the bastard in the act?"

"And someone would get shot, and that's how wars start. I already told Powell to round up the whole drift today and bring 'em in. We'll keep 'em up at the barns till we figure out something else. Maybe we can put 'em up at Friday's, far enough from all this mess." Griffin pondered the logistics of moving the entire drift such a distance, and then dropped the idea, favoring the easier access of the barns at Bellevue.

"Have you seen Hubbs when he's around Miss Ross?" Griffin hoped Aleck would see the question as one of concern for Flora's wellbeing.

"A few times. Why?"

"You think he treats her right?"

"Seems to. Any reason to think he dinnae do well by her?"

Griffin shrugged. "You think he deserves her?"

Aleck hesitated. "Not sure I go with the idea we get things we deserve in life."

Griffin mentally kicked himself. "Sorry, that was careless."

Aleck was the last person he should have asked to comment on such a concept. He had always struck Griffin as an honest, hardworking man. He couldn't have deserved his own present circumstances. But if he'd been offended, he didn't show it. Something had caught Aleck's eye, and he strode across the field for a closer look.

"Another over here."

Griffin joined him and examined the carcass, partially hidden behind a salmonberry bramble. Unlike the others who'd all been granted a quick death with a shot to the head, this one had been shot in the shoulder and appeared to have run for shelter, where she'd bled to death.

Griffin considered the motives and sanity of the perpetrator. Did he presume that Company or colonial officials in Victoria would learn that a few pigs were being shot each night as some form of political protest? Or that they'd care? Did he think it would affect the outcome of the dispute? Did he walk away from the carcasses each night with a sense of satisfaction? Or a feeling of power amidst a political and military confrontation in which most of its players were entirely powerless? Griffin could only guess at each of the answers, and it could be any one or any combination of those he'd considered. The one certainty he took with him, as he and Aleck heaved the last slippery carcass onto the wagon and started back to the farm, was his own relief that the only victims of the meaningless acts of protest thus far had been scattered livestock.

* * *

Flora jumped at hearing Aleck's gentle knock on the door, knowing that the knock meant that Hubbs had arrived outside the cabin. She turned toward the bed, anxious that Anna might have stirred, and was relieved to see that she remained in a deep, opiate-induced slumber.

A muffled exchange of greetings outside the door confirmed that Hubbs had arrived, precisely at the time he had promised, to escort Flora to a ball in the fledgling village. Hearing his voice just feet from the door elevated Flora's nervousness. She had been to many other balls, most often thrown by the Royal Navy. But she had always attended with other girls, usually following Mary's lead. While Flora had been the more academic of the two sisters, Mary had acquired a confident understanding of men and their unspoken social cues, along with a fearless drive to socialize. Tonight was the first time Flora would attend a ball in the company of a gentleman, rather than her sister, and it made her miss her sister's social guidance all the more.

Flora had expected to suffer certain deprivations when she'd agreed to come to the island, but had never imagined that one might be the struggle of preparing for a town ball with neither a mirror nor her finest dress, particularly since there had been no town on the island when she had left Victoria. She had come to Bellevue Farm with only three plain dresses, none of which she would have ever considered wearing to any social event at home. Rotating them since her arrival had meant increasing their wear and tear and introducing stains that refused to fade.

Her resulting fear of embarrassment was one of the reasons she'd hesitated when Hubbs had invited her to the ball, even though it was obvious from the moment he'd issued the invitation that the event would lack the usual social expectations of any similar event in Victoria. The town had steadily increased in size in recent weeks, as merchants had continued to follow the growing U.S. military presence on the island. But it was still little more than a rough collection of tents and buildings thrown up without forethought, serving as shops for whiskey, dry goods, and prostitution. Its populace lacked any form of social elite that could cause a girl to judge herself a failure for attending a dance in the same dress she might wear to dig camas bulbs or administer a sponge bath. It was a point that Hubbs had driven home when he'd reminded Flora of the business carried on by nearly all of the other women on the island, and had insisted that she would stand out as one of the cultured women from the big town of Victoria.

The dress Flora had chosen to wear had a stubbornly permanent stain near the collar that had been caused by Anna in a manner that Flora preferred not to consider. Rose Robillard, the Kwakiutl wife of a French-Canadian laborer on the farm, had offered to lend Flora a lace shawl to cover the stain. And though it was hardly fashionable, Flora had gratefully accepted it. Even with the shawl, the dress remained an outfit she would have been humiliated to wear in the company of her friends to anything social at home, especially if she had explained the nature of the partially hidden stain. But under the circumstances, it would have to do.

Anna's declining condition was the second reason that Flora had hesitated to accept Hubbs' invitation. Even though Aleck would be by his wife's side for the evening, and able to summon Flora within minutes, she felt that it was improper to even consider an invitation to a dance while her patient lay so close to death. But Lucinda had convinced Flora that proper attention to pain medication before the event would ensure a few hours when Flora could be just a seventeen year-old girl.

She was relieved that Anna had fallen asleep before she began her preparations for the dance. She couldn't have allowed herself to prepare for a night of dancing if Anna had been watching. It felt far too wrong to enjoy life in front of one who was in the midst of seeing life slip away, even after her experiences with Jane Forbes. Jane had always wanted to hear news of Flora's life, of life in the town outside her windows, and of stories that could only have served to remind her of everything that was ebbing from her grasp. Flora understood the concept of living vicariously, of holding tightly to the promise that life goes on outside the four walls of a patient's confinement. But it seemed to her that every joy that might be found in hearing of another's ongoing life would be darkened many times over by the reminder that the patient would never again share such an experience herself.

Flora took Anna's hand in her own to gauge her patient's circulation. It was cold. A coldness that felt unnatural. She gently placed Anna's hand back on the bed, then took a deep breath, uncertain if the tension in her stomach was a product of guilt or fear. Everything appeared to be in place. In the cabin. And in her personal presentation. And even if it wasn't, she assured herself, the lack of a decent mirror meant that she'd never know. She turned to the door, practiced a relaxed smile, made one final check for stray hairs, and then reached for the doorknob.

* * *

The tent that billowed in the breeze was larger than any other structure that had been erected in the tiny settlement along the beach, and yet it seemed to Flora as though it couldn't possibly be large enough to hold a dance for all the people who were milling about outside. Several bonfires had been lit along the beach, and dozens of people more interested in whiskey than dance were huddled around the flames, appearing ominous in the flickering light and shadows. Flora glanced from the *Satellite* anchored in the bay, with its own fires burning on deck, to the top of the hill to her right, where the American cannons pointed down at the bay. The tent, the crowd and the village, sat between the two rows of cannons, seemingly oblivious to their precarious setting. And yet, the mere organizing of a ball for American settlers and soldiers, on a disputed island, under the watch of a British warship, seemed as much an act of aggression as the landing of American troops had been. Flora imagined that anyone arriving on the island that night might presume that the fires on the deck of the *Satellite* were meant as part of the spectacle, and not a threat of firepower. With such a perspective, it made the firelight that danced along the shimmering water seem almost romantic. It was an idea that she decided to adopt for the evening to feel more at ease.

"You'll have to excuse my footwork tonight. I'm a little out of practice," Hubbs explained as he and Flora approached the evening's event.

"I suppose you and the rest of the squatters haven't had many dances on this island before," Flora teased.

"Residents, Flora. In this crowd tonight, they're residents."

"Of course. I didn't mean to take sides. I'm just used to the terms I hear up at the farm."

Flora took a closer look at Hubbs as they walked past the flickering light of a large bonfire and noticed the effort he had made for the evening. Gone was his typical buckskin, replaced by woolen trousers and a linen shirt. He had tamed his hair, at least as much as his hair seemed willing to be tamed, and had even trimmed his moustache. She smiled, pleased to see that his years on the edge of society hadn't destroyed some of the lessons he had learned in his cultured upbringing, and she wondered whether he had made the effort for her, or for the sake of appearance in the small community.

The tent was already crowded with soldiers, squaws, squatters, and townies. Flora relaxed upon seeing that the vast majority of the women in the tent were clad in their everyday clothing and were in search of a soldier for an evening of work, if they hadn't secured one already. She assured herself that her dress was more than adequate by comparison.

Despite her initial fears, it was the men in the tent who presented the latest developments in fashion, as most of the U.S. soldiers wore the new "plug" hats that had arrived only a few days earlier. Some also wore their new black uniform trousers if they'd been able to get them altered in time for the dance, though a few wore the new trousers even though it was painfully obvious that they'd located neither needle nor thread. The new uniform was only a partial replacement—the hat and pants—but the hat was a vast improvement over its predecessor, providing a wide brim for protection from rain or sun, that was rolled up at one side and secured with a pin. The changes presented a crisp, formal presence that almost masked the extent of drunkenness that already consumed most of the crowd.

She turned her attention to the few dancers who circled

the middle of the tent in a Virginia reel, courtesy of a ragtag band. Two townie couples appeared to be sober and quite serious about demonstrating the proper form of the Virginia reel. Many of the soldiers gave the impression that they would have been certain of the steps if they were sober, while their partners did little more than awkwardly follow in drunken imitation. Such a spectacle would have been deemed scandalous at any of the past balls Flora had attended, but it provided most everyone present at this ball with rollicking entertainment.

Abuse of whiskey had arisen as one of the earliest challenges to order on the island after Company D had landed, and remained a considerable problem despite the awkward agreement between competing magistrates deCourcy and Crosbie to cooperatively ensure that whiskey sellers wouldn't secure a foothold on the island. Each successive upstart establishment that attempted to sell whiskey had been shut down by the pair over the previous few weeks, yet the liquor still managed to flow in considerable quantities. The American camp's prison tent was filled most days with soldiers who woke to discover that their night of drinking had ended with their arrest, while absence from duty among the troops had become a substantial problem for both efficiency and morale. Yet it was clear to Flora that access to whiskey wasn't proving to be the least bit difficult on this particular evening.

"Looks like Hubbs brought his *klootchman*."

It was said behind their backs, but loud enough to ensure that they both heard the comment. "*Klootchman*" was Chinook for "woman," but it had become the accepted term in white society for any Indian woman that a white man might keep around for more than a few nights, carrying an implication of possession. Flora turned to see two American privates behind them, both smirking with drunken self-confidence. Hubbs turned to face the privates.

"Gentlemen, may I introduce you to Miss Flora Ross. Her father, Charles Ross, built Fort Victoria, and her mother owns a large farm just across the Canal de Haro. Miss Ross is a nurse at the Company farm."

For reasons that were most likely a product of excessive liquor consumption, both privates found Hubbs' comment to be hilarious. Flora ignored their peals of laughter and chose to demonstrate her social standing rather than discuss it with strangers. She touched Hubbs' arm and gestured across the tent to where the band had struck up a new tune.

"It sounds as though they're playing a French country dance."

Hubbs smiled and extended his hand. "So they are. May I have this dance?"

Flora took his hand and followed him onto the dance floor, quickly discovering that the pebbles, grass and shells that were strewn across the sandy ground presented hazards she'd never encountered at any past ball. It had been more than nine months since she had danced in public, thanks to the Sisters' ban. But compared to the other couples who stumbled across the sandy ground, they stood out as a particularly accomplished pair.

As their third dance came to an end, due to the abrupt realization of the band that two of their musicians weren't playing the same tune, Hubbs took Flora by the arm.

"I want to introduce you to someone. A friend of mine."

He led her through the crowd until they reached Captain Pickett and Lieutenant Forsyth, and then exchanged formal introductions. Pickett offered a slight bow.

"Your humble servant, Miss Ross."

"Captain, it's a pleasure, I'm sure." Flora smiled at the officers, surprised by the degree of intimidation and nervousness she felt. She had met many Captains, and even a few Admirals and Vice-Admirals of the Royal Navy while growing up in Victoria, but this was the first time she'd been presented to an officer not as somebody's daughter, but as somebody's prospective paramour.

She realized that part of her intimidation also stemmed from the immediate observation that it was Pickett, far more than any other at the ball, who set a standard of fashion that would play upon her fears of inadequacy. His uniform was perfectly pressed, and his Southern accent gave him an air of sophistication. But, even more so, it was his grooming that set him apart. Pickett's long, dark hair was slicked back, falling down to his shoulders in long ringlets, while his Van Dyke was perfectly waxed. Flora realized that a light floral scent she had detected was most likely emanating from Pickett's hair. Even at a Royal Navy ball, Pickett would have stood out as a dandy, perhaps even gossiped about as a possible molly, and Flora found herself tempted to ask if Pickett's grooming supplies could be bought from any of the fledgling merchants in the tents along the beach.

"Paul has told me a great deal about you, Miss Ross. He tells me you're a nurse to a young woman at the farm."

"Yes, Captain. One of the farmworker's wives. I'm afraid she's in her final weeks."

"Perhaps our company surgeon could be of some help. Dr. Craig. I'll ask him to arrange a visit."

"That's very kind of you, Captain. Dr. Tolmie has seen her a few times, but I'm grateful to know there's a doctor much closer to the farm who might be willing to examine her."

"Consider it done. And in the meantime, I hope you're helping to keep this man out of trouble."

The comment unnerved Flora. She sensed that Pickett had intended it as a subtle commentary on Hubbs' past.

"I wasn't aware he'd been causing trouble," she replied.

"He hasn't been lately, and I presume you deserve the credit for that. Excuse me." Pickett smiled and turned to leave.

"Captain," Flora interjected, "if your company has any need for the services of a nurse, I'm still learning of course, but —"

Pickett laughed with a tone that offended Flora even before he responded with words.

"I surely doubt any of my soldiers will be giving birth or dying of old age anytime soon, Miss Ross." Pickett nodded to Hubbs, then turned to leave once again. Flora started to interject, part from offense and part from the need to insist that her skills might have some use for his troops, but Hubbs grabbed her arm to ensure she understood that further comments wouldn't be appreciated, either by Pickett or him. She held her tongue as Pickett and Forsyth moved on through the crowd.

Flora pushed the offense from her mind. "I don't know how much you had to do with his offer about the camp doctor, but in case it was anything at all, thank you."

"It was something I asked him about. I wanted to let him tell you."

Flora sensed an awkward tone in Hubbs' voice that suggested his claim of credit hadn't been entirely truthful. A little white lie, perhaps, and she gave it no more thought. She turned and gazed across the tent, recognizing that the event's already limited sense of decorum was quickly evaporating. Most of the soldiers were far too inebriated to dance any longer, while most of the women were waiting to take advantage of the soldiers' drunkenness in order to obtain some American currency, whether it be earned or simply lifted from a pocket.

A wave caught her attention. Lucinda sat across the room with John Henry swaddled in her arms. Flora presumed that one of the two gentlemen talking beside her would be Stephen Boyce. She turned to Hubbs.

"It's my turn to introduce you to someone."

Flora beckoned for him to follow her through the crowd, pleased at the opportunity to introduce Hubbs to a friend whose first impression of the man wouldn't be tainted by his years as the U.S. government representative on the island, or by the gossip of his time with the northern Indians. It would be the first time she'd introduce a man to anyone as her own paramour. Her earlier feelings of intimidation and nervousness returned as Lucinda rose to greet them, just as the band struck up a quadrille of questionable tuning.

\* \* \*

The music from the tent wafted up the hillside as Flora and Hubbs wandered up the rutted wagon road toward the ridge. There had been several times during the walk back to the farm when Hubbs' hand had grazed against her own, as had happened on their walks before. She considered reaching out and taking his hand in an effort to put him out of his misery, but was taken by surprise when he stopped in the path and firmly took her hand.

"Is this alright?"

Flora nodded hesitantly and continued to walk slowly along the trail, forcing Hubbs to resume his pace beside her. She assured herself that there would be less risk of an improper moment if they remained in motion.

"I had a very nice time tonight. Thank you for bringing me, even if you did have to put up with a dance partner in a tragically horrible dress."

"I had the prettiest dance partner in the room."

"Prettier than Captain Pickett?"

Hubbs laughed. "Do not expect me to answer that."

Hubbs stopped again, forcing Flora to choose between pulling her hand from his or stopping beside him. She chose the latter, and realized as she stopped next to Hubbs that they were just short of where they would come into view of the American earthworks on the ridge above. It was their last chance for a measure of privacy, and the realization sent a flush to her cheeks.

"I know it's not right to ask you this out here in the dark, all alone, but I so much want to kiss you."

Flora hesitated, uncertain of the appropriate response. Several of her friends had kissed their paramours, and in some cases done far more. Agnes Douglas had regaled her with stories of having kissed several of her gentlemen callers, but it was something that Flora had thus far only imagined. Though she had never imagined it happening on the wagon road, at night, fifty yards below a line of 32-pound cannons. In her imagination, Hubbs had kissed her as they picnicked on a blanket near his half-built house, surrounded by tall yellow grass and wildflowers. And in her imagination, Hubbs had made his advances with suave confidence, not asked her permission with awkward nervousness. But she was old enough to have learned that nothing in life ever turns out quite like one imagines it will.

She blushed and nodded slightly. Hubbs leaned in and kissed her. It was a simple, gentle kiss, until he put his hand against her back and pulled her close. His mustache tickled her face, and nearly made her laugh. It was when she felt Hubbs' hand slide down to her hip that it became clear that, although Hubbs had initiated the kiss, it would be up to her to decide when to end it. She pulled back and smiled, unable to look him in the eye, and yet wishing she could have allowed the kiss to continue.

"I don't think you've been told often enough how beautiful you are."

Flora blushed and looked down, embarrassed.

"I'm not sure I have the features most men consider beautiful."

"Like I said, you clearly haven't been told enough. Maybe someday I'll get you to believe it." Hubbs leaned in and kissed Flora again. This time, he kept his hands from roaming too far, allowing Flora to feel comfortable with a longer kiss. She pulled back only when she felt her own ability to maintain decorum slipping from her grasp.

"We should be getting back," she whispered, then turned and continued up the wagon road. Hubbs followed reluctantly, yet quickly enough to ensure that his hand didn't stray from hers.

\* \* \*

Mary watched nervously as her mother poured hot tea into the cup she had set on the table before Reverend Cridge, and waited for the proper moment to plant the seeds of her idea. She reached for an oat biscuit and a pot of jam to calm her nerves.

"John Butts is a fool. He will not win election," Isabella pronounced confidently as she set the teapot down onto the table.

"But a crafty fool," Cridge replied. "The good Lord might not have blessed him with wisdom, but the young man has a ridiculously strong belief in his own importance. In politics, that's often enough."

"I think he's funny," Mary interjected. "Not that he's trying to be. But he just is."

The rumor that John Butts, town crier and bell-ringer, would offer himself as a candidate for the legislative assembly had circled the town in recent days, creating a flurry of discussion that had, in the opinion of many, been the sole purpose behind Butts' announcement. The outgoing Australian might not have a future in politics, but he was, yet again, the center of conversation. It was his favorite location.

"Have you heard from Flora in recent days?" Cridge inquired.

"Letter three days ago," Isabella replied. "The woman, her patient ... *elle est très malade.*"

"But she's safe, with all that's going on there?"

"She says it's exciting," Mary interjected. "I almost envy her. To be right in the middle of all that nonsense. To take care of someone. To feel needed. I could use some experience like that myself."

"Without the dangers involved," Cridge replied. "It worries me to no end having sent her there."

"We also received a letter from Mr. Wren," Mary added, unwilling to allow the topic of her own needs to vary off course. "He had much to say about the girls. How they're coping without Elizabeth. They miss her very much. I don't suppose Mr. Wren can properly raise them on his own and still run the farm. It seems like so much work for a man to do alone."

"Do they make final your contract?" Isabella asked of Cridge, offering him the plate of oat biscuits, and frustrating Mary with the change of topic.

"Not in the slightest," he replied while taking the smallest biscuit on the plate. He paused to take a bite, and emitted a muffled sound that signaled an intention to continue his response as soon as he could finish the first bite.

Mary reached for another biscuit, recognizing that Cridge was certain to embark on a lengthy discussion about the controversy that had erupted in recent weeks over the pending expiration of his contract as the official Company clergy, the efforts of some to have the colonial government agree to an extension at public expense, and the implications that it created for the colony's separation of church and state. It would be several minutes before an opportunity would arise when she could once again plant the idea in her mother's ear and seek the support of Reverend Cridge. Surely the man who had sent her younger sister into the middle of a brewing war would have little objection to the idea of Mary undertaking the care of her motherless nieces. And of Charles Wren. It would be caring for family. It would be charitable. It would even be God's work, she assured herself, testing the phrase in her own head before concluding that it might be best to leave God out of her plans.

\* \* \*

It was shortly after the toast given by his father that Hubbs began to understand that the reason he'd been summoned to a family gathering at his father's home in Port Townsend hadn't been to celebrate his twenty-seventh birthday, nor his brother Charles' sixteenth birthday three days earlier. Rather, the promise of a birthday celebration had been subterfuge to ensure his attendance.

It was the first time in months that so many of the Hubbs clan had gathered together, an event that had been possible only since his father, Paul Kinsey Hubbs, Sr., had moved from California to Port Townsend in 1858 with his new and youthful wife, the former Maggie Gilchrist. Charles Hubbs had accompanied his father and stepmother on the journey north, along with a newborn half-brother, Bayard, born to Maggie only months before the move. It was a move inspired by the years of intermittent violence that had plagued northern California ever since San Francisco's Committee of Vigilance had taken control of the city. Within a few months of their arrival in Port Townsend, Hubbs Senior had established himself as one of the most prominent attorneys in Washington Territory.

The supposed celebration of Hubbs' birthday hadn't been limited to family members, which provided Hubbs with his first clue as to the true purpose of the event. Morris C. Frost sat directly across from him at the family dining table, with his wild hair, his red, puffy face, and his wide barrel chest giving the appearance of a man whose innards were under some sort of internal pressure and might burst from his body at any moment. Frost had recently secured the appointment to serve as U.S. Inspector of Customs for the region, making him Hubbs' direct superior. And it was while digging into one of the best meals Hubbs had tasted in months that he obtained confirmation that the purpose of the dinner wasn't to celebrate that he was turning another year older, or to welcome him home as the conquering hero protecting U.S. sovereignty, but to pressure him.

"You've probably noticed," Hubbs Senior began in lecturing his son, "we certainly have, that most of the commerce to and from the island is running through Victoria."

"Cattle, produce, even some of the lumber for our U.S. boys has been comin' out of Victoria," Frost interjected.

"Which, I don't need to tell you," Hubbs Senior continued, "is in direct violation of the customs laws of the United States. The laws are clear, son, as you well know. Imports from the British colonies have to be cleared through customs here in Port Townsend, and all import duties have to be paid in full before the goods can be landed anywhere else in the territory."

"Even those damned fool picnickers are part of the problem," Frost added. "Some of them are doin' business on the island, makin' contacts, makin' sales."

Maggie smiled and passed Hubbs the bowl of potatoes as if wanting to pretend that this was still just a friendly family dinner.

"And of course," Hubbs Senior continued, stating the obvious, "you're the resident deputy inspector of customs on the island."

"Which means," Frost interjected, "need I even say it,

that it's your task to make sure nobody lands if they haven't first submitted to a proper inspection here in Port Townsend. I wrote out your instructions in a letter in case anyone disputes your authority. It's in my overcoat. I'll get it for you after we're done here. And it's a mighty fine meal, Maggie. Mighty fine."

Hubbs dug into a fresh helping of potatoes, hoping that concentration on his meal might somehow erase the offensive turn the evening had taken. He had come to the dinner expecting to be honored. Not just as the eldest son of a prominent family passing another milepost in life, but as the instigator of a campaign to occupy San Juan Island with U.S. troops, thereby strengthening the U.S. claim to the entire archipelago. He had paddled more than twenty nautical miles across the strait in a driving rain, arriving soaked and shivering. He had expected to be showered with praise, but instead had been showered with orders that undoubtedly would be received on the island with controversy, if not outright confrontation. Surely these educated men of worldly experience understood that to stand in the way of trade and travel would elevate the tensions and increase the risk of outright war? Hubbs started to form the words of his question, but then heard the answer just as quickly inside his own head. For them, commerce was the war. A gain of territory would be meaningless if the development profits were realized elsewhere. Hubbs held his tongue, dug into his potatoes, and tried to ignore the realization that the conquering hero was merely a pawn in his father's and Frost's business campaign.

\* \* \*

Flora fidgeted nervously as Dr. Craig examined each bottle of medicine that she'd organized on the heavy table by the front window of the cabin. He'd said very little since his arrival, but she was certain that his serious expression served as critical judgment of her nursing skills.

"Has she received any medications today?" he asked without looking up.

"A dose of Laudanum, just an hour ago." Flora pointed at one of the near-empty bottles of opiates that Tolmie had left her six weeks before. She couldn't tell from the sound that came from Dr. Craig's throat if her answer had met with approval or scorn. She looked over to Lucinda in the hope that her eyes would confirm which emotion he had expressed, and caught a wink that she interpreted as encouragement.

Dr. Robert O. Craig, Assistant Surgeon for the U.S. Army in Washington Territory, was the full title he had announced at the door a few minutes earlier, with the crisp Yankee accent of a well-bred upstate New Yorker. Flora wondered if he had announced himself in that manner because of military discipline, or because he felt it necessary to make up for his youthful appearance by declaring the longest title he could claim. Although if it were the latter, Flora decided, he should drop the "assistant" part of the title. There are certain professions where service by an "assistant" may seem just as acceptable as service from one who no longer assists, but surgeon wasn't one of those professions.

"How often do you administer it?" he asked.

"Whenever she asks for it. About three times a day now. Maybe four. It mostly puts her to sleep for about six hours or so. Well, not really sleep, but ..." She looked over at Lucinda, hoping to elicit some assistance. Lucinda offered only a smile of support and returned to her task of bouncing young John Henry in her arms in an effort to keep him from interrupting the examination.

Dr. Craig pulled back Anna's blanket, then reached under Anna's shift and felt around her abdomen. She moaned, but seemed barely aware of the examination.

"She's passing stools?"

"About once a day. It usually causes her a lot of pain."

"Vomiting?"

"Maybe once a week, but not for a few days."

Dr. Craig felt around Anna's neck and under her armpits, then carefully lifted her eyelids, one at a time and held up a lamp to get a clear view of her eyes.

"It would have been preferable if she were fully conscious for this, so that I could get a better sense of where she's feeling the most pain."

"I'm sorry. I didn't know you were coming today."

He paused, then reached his hand across Anna's body to pick at something small. He held up his hand to reveal a small bedbug that he squished between his thumb and forefinger. Flora blushed at the implied criticism.

"I do search for those, several times a day," she insisted, "and for fleas, of course. I thought I was getting most of them."

"When was this bed last made?"

"It's a couple months old, but lately the idea of moving her to another bed long enough to re-stuff the mattress ..."

Dr. Craig nodded. "Probably not worth the effort." He rose and searched through his medical bag.

"The diagnosis you described from her prior physician appears correct. There is a substantial growth along the descending colon, and the liver is grossly enlarged. The disease is depriving her body of nutrients, no matter how much you've attempted to feed her. Her lymph nodes are swollen, and she's having serious problems with blood circulation and swelling in her feet and lower legs."

"I've been massaging her lower legs every day."

"Keep doing that, twice a day if you can. Her greatest risk right now is intestinal blockage, and that would be an excruciating end."

"How will I know if that's happening?"

"She'll begin frequent vomiting, fecal vomiting even, along with severe abdominal pain and swelling."

The thought of being responsible for a woman going through such trauma sent a shiver through Flora.

"What should I do if that happens?"

"If she's able to swallow, give her more of this." He handed the bottle back to Flora. "I'll send another bottle along. You'll also need it in a form you can inject, once she's no longer able to swallow anything or keep it down—that is, if you own a syringe?"

"Flora can use mine, Doctor," Lucinda interjected.

"Good," he replied. "I have only one here on the island, and can't afford to lose it."

Flora ignored the implied criticism that his syringe would be at risk in her possession.

"Do you have experience with a syringe?" he asked.

"I've seen how it's done."

"Hmm, then I suppose I'll have to come by again."

"You needn't burden yourself, doctor," Lucinda interjected. "That's something I can teach her."

"Good. Very good. Well, then." Dr. Craig secured the latch on his medical bag and turned to the door.

"Thank you, Dr. Craig." Flora opened the door for him. "Thank you so much for coming to see her."

Dr. Craig replied with a grim smile that seemed both an apology for having been unable to do more for Anna, and an expression of his dissatisfaction at having had to tend to a dying Indian woman at the command of Captain Pickett, under the care of an inexperienced Indian girl. He nodded curtly and then left the cabin.

Lucinda examined the doctor's bottles of medicine. "I thought you handled him well."

"I thought you were going to do more to handle him for me," Flora replied.

"And how would you learn from that?"

"I'd learn from watching you."

"Which would teach you how to be excellent at watching others. When the time comes to use the syringe on Anna, you won't learn by simply watching me do it."

"You want me to experiment on her?"

"Better than experimenting on me." Lucinda's expression softened into a smile. "I'll be here to throw out bits of help from the corner, just like today."

A sudden urge to run back to the safety of her family farm gripped Flora, more than it ever had when British naval vessels had sat broadside to the shore with their cannons displayed and ready. Anna was dying, and it would be a miserable end. An experienced nurse would ease her pain so much better than Flora could hope to do. An experienced nurse would offer confidence and comfort.

Flora could offer the best of intentions and the earliest stages of training, but the inability to promise anything more for her dying patient terrified her more than any fear she had faced before.

# Chapter 13

The laundresses. They were the logical choice to approach first. Flora could have troubled Dr. Craig, but he had left the impression that she'd already been enough trouble, so she opted for one of the laundresses instead.

She had heard the name of the first one who'd arrived with Company D—Catherine McGeary, wife of a private. Ever since the Americans had established their third camp, Catherine and her family had occupied a tent across the fence from the farm's dairy barn. And they had recently started construction of a small cabin next to their tent.

Catherine was outside her tent chopping wood as Flora approached. She stopped the moment she saw Flora, and looked her over with suspicion.

"Excuse me, I wonder if I might trouble you for a moment?" Flora asked in the most formal manner she could muster. She had learned over the years that a formal introduction was often necessary to allay any concerns a first glance might raise about her origins or intentions.

"I'm told there's a priest who's come to the camp. I'm nursing a woman at the farm who's in great need of spiritual guidance."

Catherine relaxed. "Ya mean Father Rossi?" she asked in a thick Irish accent.

"Yes, I suppose that would be him."

"He's stayin' behind the armory. I'll show ya."

She embedded the axe in the stump she'd been using as a base for her chopping, picked up a small baby from a bassinette by the tent, and motioned to a girl about four years of age playing nearby. "Mary, come 'ere, sweetie."

The girl took her mother's hand, and Flora followed them into the sea of conical tents that surrounded the main buildings of the camp.

"Thank you for your help. I'm sorry to pull you away from your work. I'm Flora … Flora Ross."

"Catherine McGeary. So yer a Brit?"

"I suppose. I'm not sure, really."

"How can ya not be sure?"

"I won't know for certain until they decide who owns this island. I was born on the beach down there."

"Don't say that too loud 'round here, or you'll have hundreds o' soldiers tryin' to pitch a tent on ya to claim ya for their side."

Flora looked up, slightly shocked by the image, until she saw the grin on Catherine's face and joined her in the laughter.

"It's that tent there." Catherine pointed to a white canvas tent, indistinguishable from the other tents that were set in long, straight lines.

She turned back to her quarters, then stopped. "There's not too many o' us around here—women, I mean—so if ya need help with anythin' for your patient … for anythin' at all …"

"Thank you."

Flora approached the tent Catherine had identified.

"Excuse me. Hello, Father Rossi?"

There was no answer.

"Father Rossi? Hello?"

"Who is this who looks for Father Rossi?"

Flora could tell from the thick Italian accent that she had found him. She turned to see Father Rossi approaching through the maze of tents. He was tall and thin, in his mid-forties, and dressed in black robes and a wide-brimmed black hat. His smile looked as though it masked a strong pain, a notion that was bolstered by his posture, as if he was protecting himself beneath his hunched shoulders. She'd heard that Father Rossi was Italian, but nothing about his appearance would have told her that he was Italian, other than his priest's clothing. Instead, he reminded her of several prominent Victoria residents who had recently organized the town's Hebrew Benevolent Society.

She noticed a look in Father Rossi's eyes that told her that he was also sizing her up, and was probably wondering how much Indian blood ran through her veins. She smiled in recognition that they were sharing an important step in their introduction, a step that had no words, yet told each of them so much about the other merely from their respective appearance and mutual prejudices.

"Father Rossi, my name is Flora Ross. I'm a nurse at the farm next door."

"Please, please, sit, sit." He motioned to a log in front of his tent, but Flora hesitated, sensing displeasure in his voice.

"Thank you, but I can't stay. I'm here because the patient I'm nursing at the farm is dying, and she's Catholic, and I thought maybe, if it's not too much trouble, if you could just come to the farm and –"

"Of course. Of course. We go now. One moment." Father Rossi ducked into his tent and returned seconds later with a Bible. He gestured toward the farm. "Now we do God's work, yes?"

Flora smiled, relieved that she could bring to Anna a level of spiritual support that she'd been unable to provide. She led Father Rossi back through the maze of tents and past Catherine's skeletal cabin, though Catherine was nowhere to be seen.

"I realize you're here for the American soldiers ..."

"I am here to reach God's children. Even some British are God's children." He smiled, though Flora sensed that, despite the smile, he had intended the insult that was implicit in his comment.

"I should probably mention, as well, that Anna—that's her name—she's Shuswap Indian, but Catholic, too."

Father Rossi nodded with a grunt of disapproval, though he followed it with a smile that Flora interpreted as his acceptance of the unpleasant complications that God's work sometimes presented.

"And you are not Catholic?"

Flora blushed, feeling inadequate in a way that the question had never made her feel before. "No, I'm not. But I went to a school this year that the nuns run in Victoria. The Sisters of St. Ann?"

Father Rossi nodded. "I have come to learn in this country that European separation of the faiths is not the way here. Many of the church I build, we build with money from the Protestants, as if more religion, of any religion, is good for them."

Flora smiled and nodded, sensing that he wouldn't have cared for her views on the subject. As they left the grounds of the American camp and reached the rutted road to the farm, she noticed Major deCourcy standing in the road, watching them, intensely curious.

"Good morning, Father. The name's Major John Fitzroy deCourcy, English magistrate on this island."

"Father Louis Rossi. A pleasure, sir."

"Louis Rossi? A French first name and an Italian last name?"

DeCourcy started along the wagon road, leading Father Rossi into the farm's compound. Flora followed behind, feeling ignored.

"I am Italian, born in Ferrara. Luigi by birth, but work much of my life in France, so, now I am Louis."

"Ferrara is a beautiful town. What brings you to our camp?"

"A *sauvage* woman who is ill."

"Oh, yes. Of course," deCourcy replied, as if he had hoped for a more interesting reason to explain the visit.

Father Rossi's use of the term "sauvage" rang in Flora's ears. She was accustomed to hearing the word "savage" spoken nearly as often as the word "Indian," and often spoken in her direction or with no regard to her presence. She told herself that the word "sauvage" sounded less offensive in the French form and when spoken with a heavy accent, but still wondered if bringing Father Rossi to the bedside of a dying woman whom he might look upon as something less than a child of God might have been a mistake. She stopped by the cabin and gestured to Father Rossi.

"And I believe she is there," Father Rossi presumed.

"Yes, that she is," deCourcy replied. "When you're done in there, my quarters are that cabin at the end. Please come by and we can talk about your home country."

"Very kind of you."

Father Rossi turned to Flora.

"You say her name is Anna?"

"Yes. Anna Mcdonald."

Father Rossi entered the cabin without waiting for a further invitation. Flora followed him inside, relieved that she had managed to bring a priest to Anna's bedside, but troubled that she might have found one with insufficient regard for the patient.

\* \* \*

Hubbs climbed over the railing of the *Caledonia* as the steamer's passengers gathered on deck.

"Good morning, ladies and gentlemen," he began, "I am Paul Kinsey Hubbs, Jr., the deputy inspector of customs in this region. May I see your permits, please?"

The question was met with a chorus of confusion and protest from the passengers.

"Since when d'we need a permit to bring in a picnic lunch?" one man protested.

"The only way we can be certain you're bringing nothing more is by carrying out an inspection, sir," Hubbs replied. "I'm sorry, but U.S. law is clear, and I can't allow you to land until you've obtained the required permits.

A tall, slender man pushed through from the steamer's wheelhouse.

"You'll address me if there's a problem, young man."

"And you are?"

"The Captain o' this vessel, Captain Broderick. What the hell's this about?"

"U.S. law requires that this boat clear customs in Port Townsend before proceeding to this island. I have to ask you to turn this boat around and –"

The remainder of Hubbs' instructions were lost beneath a chorus of protest from the passengers.

"Young man," Broderick replied with annoyance, "I've been landin' this steamer here for months with no need for any permit. This island's as much British as American, and you've no right to stop us."

"I have the right of U.S. customs laws, and the force of the U.S. army behind me. Anyone who lands on the island without having cleared customs in Port Townsend will be subject to arrest."

"Military arrest," Broderick queried, "or civil arrest?"

"Well, it would be civil unless the individual is –"

"So it'd be Magistrate Crosbie who's behind you threatenin' to arrest my passengers, not the army?"

"I can't get into the specifics of how the laws will be enforced."

"And you've no authority of your own to arrest anyone."

"My authority is the enforcement of U.S. customs laws."

"So why isn't Crosbie here to back you up?"

"If I need to appeal to Magistrate Crosbie for assistance, I'll do so. But for the time being, it's sufficient to instruct you and your crew to return to Port Townsend for inspection."

"And if we refuse, Mr. deputy inspector?"

"A report will be filed with my superior in Port Townsend, and he will –"

Hubbs was cut short by the realization that his spirited defense of U.S. customs laws had blinded him to movement happening along the port side. He turned to discover that two smaller boats had pulled alongside the *Caledonia*, and that more than a dozen of the *Caledonia's* passengers had already climbed down into the smaller craft. One of the boats pushed free and was rowed toward the wharf, while several more passengers climbed into the second boat.

Hubbs stared for several seconds, uncertain of the response that would both address the infraction and preserve what was left of his professional dignity.

"You were sayin' …" Captain Broderick baited.

Hubbs carefully considered his response.

"Under the circumstances, I'll overlook your failure to obtain a permit on this one occasion, and treat this as a warning to you, and all future visitors to this island or any other port in Washington Territory."

Hubbs nodded to Captain Broderick without looking the man in the eyes, then turned back to his own rowboat secured to the starboard side, thinking back fondly to just two months earlier when the enforcement of U.S. customs laws had involved little more than nailing a notice to Charles Griffin's door.

* * *

"You had no right to do such a thing," Crosbie fumed, pacing angrily across the front of Colonel Casey's desk. "This is a delicate situation and you're acting like a petulant child."

Hubbs struggled to maintain his composure in the face of Crosbie's lecture, but he couldn't keep his eyes from darting angrily about Casey's tent, giving him the demeanor of a cornered animal rather than petulant child. Casey focused on papers strewn across his table, as if determined to ignore Crosbie's upbraiding of Hubbs, while Pickett kept his attention focused on Crosbie in order to avoid returning Hubbs' wild stares.

"It's my responsibility to enforce the customs laws of the United States on this island," Hubbs replied. "My duty. I've been doing it here for more than two years, and I'll continue to do it."

Hubbs glared back at Crosbie, pleased at the opportunity to stand up to the man who'd taken his magistrate position without any democratic process.

"These islands are disputed territory," Crosbie replied.

"Which doesn't stop you from enforcing U.S. laws on this island," Hubbs answered. "You're here to advance U.S. laws, and so am I. You don't get to decide what U.S. customs laws should be, or how I should enforce them."

"Mr. Hubbs, I'm not overly concerned with the activities of a handful of picnickers here for the day, and neither should you be," advised Colonel Casey without looking up from behind his desk. "Whatever minor points you might think would be advanced by forcing the *Caledonia* to detour to Port Townsend, pales next to the advantages I see of having the elites of Victoria's society coming here and seeing a growing and thriving American community, fully in control of this island."

"I have very explicit instructions, Colonel."

"As do I, and where our instructions, or as I like to call them, orders, might diverge, I must ensure that mine take precedence. Now, if you gentlemen will excuse me, I've more important matters to address with Captain Pickett."

Hubbs grabbed his musket and stormed from the tent. His anger increased with each step that his feet pounded across the camp, while a deep redness spread across his face. As he passed the last tent on the edge of camp, he yelled in frustration and slammed his musket into the ground, repeatedly, until the wooden stock cracked on the fourth blow. The realization that he had broken his weapon froze him in place. He stared at the split stock, embarrassed at his own loss of control, and hoping that no one from the camp or farm had noticed the manner of his departure.

He turned away from his broken musket and looked down toward Griffin Bay through a break in the trees, at the boats of merchants and tourists that plied the harbor, free of customs restrictions. He felt the anger building once again and turned away from the bay. This time his eyes fell on Bellevue Farm, and he realized that what he needed most was a sympathetic ear.

\* \* \*

Flora placed a hand on Hubbs' shoulder and then froze at the realization that it might be too forward a public gesture when she had only meant to show support. She hesitantly pulled her hand back, which meant instead that her fingers traced an unintentional line down his upper arm.

"But if it's your job to collect the taxes, then they should just let you do your job," she offered, hoping her words would explain the awkward trip that her hand had taken along his shirt sleeve.

"That's what I told them," Hubbs replied.

"And whoever tells the American boats that they have to go to Victoria for a customs inspection, should be allowed to do their job, too," Flora continued.

"Nobody tells American boats to go to Victoria."

"Isn't Victoria where American boats are supposed to go first when they come into the colony?"

"It's a free port. And they're not coming into the colony when they come here. They're still in the United States."

Flora started to point out that not everybody involved in the present dispute shared Hubbs' certainty that the island was American territory, and even fewer supported the policy of acting as if there was no boundary commission attempting to resolve the dispute. But she stopped herself when she realized that it wouldn't be the type of support Hubbs had so clearly hoped to obtain from her.

She hadn't expected to spend her Sunday afternoon discussing U.S. customs laws, but instead had expected to accompany Hubbs to the point to help him finish the roof on his house. But by the time Hubbs had arrived at the farm after his customs encounter it was mid-afternoon, and Flora had told Aleck that she would watch Anna for the rest of the day. Going to the point was no longer an option, and sitting on a bench in front of Aleck and Anna's cabin would have to suffice. Flora told herself that it was for the better, given Anna's condition. Her pain was almost beyond management, and the higher doses of Laudanum kept her unable to communicate anything more than cries of pain.

"It must be difficult for you," Flora began, uncertain if she should finish the thought, "to have been the only government official on the island, and to now have to be a part of this whole process."

"It's frustrating, is what it is."

"But, it's a sign of your success." Her comment was met with a challenging look, though she understood that it was meant as a challenge to continue her train of thought, so as to echo his own beliefs. "It's because of you that there are all these other officials on the island. If you hadn't been doing your job, none of them would be here."

"But they don't see that."

"Maybe you need to make them see it." Flora stopped herself, wondering if moving beyond sympathetic ear to encouraging voice was a wise move.

"I thought I was. The enforcement of customs laws is one of the most important parts of our argument to show our claim to these islands. I can't back down. I can't."

Flora regretted that she had lost the chance for another Sunday at the point with Hubbs. Seeing progress by the end of each day made him grin like a boy on his birthday, and Flora found it endearing. Watching him pout over the difficulties he encountered while enforcing customs laws was far less endearing, and she was sorry that their only time together this Sunday would be spent bolstering his certainty about the importance of his work.

Anna cried out from inside the cabin, jarring Flora from her thoughts. She rose from the bench with an apologetic smile.

"I'm sorry, but I need to get inside."

"I know. I know. I'll figure this out. I will."

Flora entered the small cabin leaving Hubbs on the bench outside. She reached for the bottle on the table that would ease Anna's distress, and then paused and looked back through the open door, worried for a moment that Hubbs might search out a bottle of another kind to placate his own distress. She wondered if perhaps there was something more she should have said. But Hubbs was already gone.

\* \* \*

## Notice

As the revenue laws of the United States are now in force on this, and all the islands east of the Canal de Haro, Captains of vessels bound to this Port are hereby notified that they must enter and clear their vessels at the Customs House, Port Townsend, before landing goods on this island –

All persons found landing goods without the proper permit are liable to have their goods confiscated –

Given under my hand the
27th day of September in
the year 1859
sd/ Paul K. Hubbs Jr.
U.S. Inspector of Customs
for the island of San Juan

\* \* \*

Hubbs stood in the small rowboat and cautiously steadied himself against the pitching waves, then raised his hand in a futile effort to stop the *Julia* from proceeding further into Griffin Bay. Boarding the *Caledonia* was a task that had involved little threat to Hubbs' safety. It had been at anchor when Hubbs had boarded it, and the greatest risk had been the potential for falling into the bay while climbing aboard. The *Julia* wasn't at anchor. The wide-hulled paddle wheeler was steaming into the bay with Hubbs standing directly in its path. For a few tense moments, Hubbs couldn't tell if the boat's captain had any intention of stopping or if he could even see Hubbs standing in his pitching rowboat. Veering around him wouldn't be an option for the massive and ungainly steamer. And though the vessel had slowed substantially since it had come into the bay, it still carried enough momentum that Hubbs most certainly would be on the losing end of any collision.

"Stop the vessel, by the authority of the United States Treasury Department."

Hubbs doubted he could be heard inside the pilothouse over the sound of the churning paddles. But he felt the need to offer some explanation for his decision to stand in a small rowboat and face a large paddle wheeler as it bore down upon him, especially for those curious passengers near the front of the boat who'd taken notice of him.

He wondered what his father would think if he was drowned beneath the *Julia's* hull and mangled in the blades of its paddles while trying to further the goals of Port Townsend's business elite. Would he be proud of his son? Would he disclaim responsibility? Would he even remember that he and Morris Frost had pushed his son to stake out such a position?

Hubbs reached for the oars in the hope that he still had time to haul his rowboat far enough from the steamer's path so that he'd be tossed to the side, rather than pummeled under its shallow hull, when a sudden burst of metallic clangs and a heavy wooden groan told Hubbs that the captain had taken drastic action to slow the ship's progress. By the time the two boats slowly collided, Hubbs was able to grab the bow of the *Julia's* hull and remain standing in his ostensibly authoritative pose as he was pushed across the water.

Several passengers peered down over the bow.

"You tryin' to get y'self killed, lad?" an older man yelled, clearly enjoying the apparent idiocy of the man who had stood firm against the large sternwheeler from the confines of an unstable rowboat.

"Are you the boat's Captain?" Hubbs asked, even though it was abundantly clear to him that none of the men peering down at him were the Captain.

"Says he's to talk to the Cap'n," the older man yelled back toward the pilothouse, while the man next to him tossed a rope over the side. After a few awkward starts that nearly sent Hubbs into the cold bay, the passengers succeeded in hauling him high enough that he was able to throw his legs over the rail and land on the deck.

Hubbs quickly pulled himself to his feet and brushed off his canvas pants, anxious to offer as official an appearance as his ordinary clothing and awkward entrance could permit.

"What the hell d'ya think you're doin'?"

Hubbs presumed the angry man approaching him was the boat's Captain.

"Paul Kinsey Hubbs, Jr., Deputy Inspector of Customs. I'm informed that this boat has come from Victoria without clearing customs at Port Townsend, which is required under the laws of Washington Territory. So, I can't allow you to land until you've first gone to Port Townsend and cleared the vessel at the Customs House and obtained the proper permit."

The initial response was a chorus of muttering and swearing among the passengers who'd overheard Hubbs' speech. Hubbs looked away from the angry glares, only to find his startled eyes fall on Lieutenant Forsyth, Pickett's junior officer.

"Lieutenant," Hubbs blurted out, losing his air of authority to one of surprise. "Surely you recognize the need to assert U.S. laws on our territory?"

Forsyth shook his head disapprovingly, unwilling to involve himself in the unfolding fiasco. Hubbs turned back to the Captain of the vessel.

"I've had the authority to uphold these laws on this island these past two years," Hubbs continued, "and it's never been more critical than –"

"You, sir, do not have any authority to make such demands on this island," came a booming Irish voice from across the deck.

Hubbs looked over to see Major deCourcy pushing his way through the small crowd of passengers.

"Major deCourcy, welcome back to U.S. territory, sir."

"This is disputed territory, and you'd do well to follow the example Mr. Crosbie and I've established, neither of us upsetting the delicate balance that exists on this island."

"You have your orders, Major, and I have mine, and they're to ensure that this boat turns around, now, and proceeds to Port Townsend."

"Or what, Mr. Hubbs?" deCourcy asked, his anger building. "Are you going to ask Lieutenant Forsyth here to launch an attack on the rest of the passengers to collect U.S.

taxes, or will you sink this boat with the force of your own arrogance?" DeCourcy turned to the boat's Captain. "This man has no authority to stop you from landing at the wharf. He's bluffing. I assure you, there'll be no interference from the authorities."

"Captain, Major deCourcy is a civil magistrate for a foreign government," Hubbs replied. "This steamer's an American vessel. It's been running for, what, three months since arriving up here? Are you prepared to see this boat impounded next time it docks anywhere in Puget Sound, unable to earn back its construction costs until you pay a sizeable fine for breaking U.S. Customs laws?"

The Captain turned angrily to deCourcy, hoping the Irishman would have a better response than his prior assurance that Hubbs was bluffing.

Hubbs had only had a few encounters with deCourcy, and had mostly viewed the man from a distance. He had felt a measure of fear when they'd first passed along the wagon road, when Hubbs had carried out his theatrical arrest of Lyman Cutlar two months earlier. But that fear had been caused by the firearms each side had carried, and the risk that either might feel the need to use them to prove a political point. He had never imagined that simply standing across from deCourcy could engender the same feelings of fear, or that the fear would be caused not by a rifle or pistol, but by the sense that the normally stiff and reserved deCourcy was about to explode. Even shielded as deCourcy's face was by his thick black beard, a deep redness was visible as it spread across his cheeks, while his good eye widened under the clenched muscles of his forehead.

Hubbs own anger had festered in the weeks since receiving his instructions from his father and Morris Frost. But as he gazed upon the far more visual expression of anger that deCourcy displayed, he felt a surge of pride at realizing that he might be responsible for one of the most significant confrontations in the boundary dispute since Pickett's tense meeting with three British naval Captains two months before. Ever since the initial days of the confrontation, each side had operated under a veil of civility, as if courtesy and manners could distract their attention from the fact that the American army and the Royal Navy were on the verge of taking their two nations to war over a small archipelago of islands. It was a veil of civility that frustrated Hubbs because it weakened the American case. He had taken the first step in bringing U.S. troops to the island, and now he would take the next step in asserting U.S. civil laws without deference to a colonial counterpart. For his father, the dispute might be about profits for local businessmen. But Hubbs had found the means to turn his enforcement of U.S. customs laws into a major gain for U.S. sovereignty.

"God damn your soul to hell," deCourcy blurted in anger. He turned and stormed past several startled passengers to the rail.

"Seaman!" he yelled at a young sailor in a passing launch from the *Satellite*. "Boy! Pull alongside. I've a shipment of my personal effects to be taken to the *Satellite*."

"Yes, sir, Major," the young sailor replied, steering the launch toward the *Julia*.

DeCourcy turned back to Hubbs.

"If you want to waste your time playing games with your own countrymen to inflate your status on the island, be my guest. The Royal Navy'll be landing my things this evening, and if it leads to a confrontation, it'll be on your head."

DeCourcy turned and bolted into the passenger compartment.

Hubbs grinned at the theatrical exit, taking it as proof that his boarding of the *Julia* would be remembered throughout history as the moment Paul K. Hubbs, Jr. secured American sovereignty over San Juan Island.

* * *

Hubbs rowed closer to the *Satellite*, rehearsing his speech and cursing his countrymen in competing streams of thought. He could barely remember his earlier feelings of triumph, stung by the humiliations that had followed. Forsyth had been the worst betrayal. To have gone to

Victoria to purchase goods in the first place, rather than Port Townsend or Steilacoom, was a betrayal by any U.S. soldier. But all the more so by someone serving as a second lieutenant of Pickett's company. Hubbs had expected foreigners like deCourcy to object to his efforts to uphold U.S. customs laws, but he had expected a second lieutenant of the United States Army to show support for U.S. law. The refusal by Forsyth to acknowledge Hubbs' authority had left him no option but to grant the passengers a waiver for this occasion only, as he had done with the *Caledonia*, solely to avoid undermining any further the authority he had as Deputy Inspector of Customs. But then Forsyth had gone straight to the American camp to report on the events to his own higher authorities, followed a short time later by the *Satellite's* Lieutenant Peile launching an official complaint by the Royal Navy.

It had been a frustrating afternoon, and it was only going to get worse. Hubbs rowed closer to the *Satellite*, his guts twisting from his anger at the betrayal. He didn't know which was worse, the embarrassment of having had Pickett—Pickett, of all people—upbraid him in front of other officers, and then have Colonel Casey demand that he personally apologize to deCourcy, or the embarrassment he was about to face in a few moments, retracting his position in front of the stiff and arrogant Irishman.

Hubbs was sufficiently lost in thought that he was in a near daze as he obtained permission to board the ship, climbed the rope ladder to the deck, and announced to the *Satellite's* boatswain that he wished to see Major deCourcy. He could feel the eyes of the seamen falling on him with judgment and scorn. He wondered if any of the seamen were those who had broken into his cabin a year earlier to steal a keg of rum, and if he could justify an air of superiority by making such a presumption.

After an anxious wait of several minutes, Hubbs was ushered into the quarters of Captain Prevost, where he found Prevost and deCourcy awaiting him. Prevost handled the introductions with a professional courtesy that bordered on friendliness, while deCourcy stared angrily from the side of the cabin. Once courtesies were exchanged, Hubbs made the decision to get to the point in an effort to make the painful meeting as brief as possible.

"I wanted to speak to Major deCourcy, to follow up on our discussion earlier on the *Julia*. After consulting with colleagues on the island, we've decided to permit the landing of Major deCourcy's personal effects without compliance with U.S. Customs laws, this one time."

"One time!" DeCourcy caught himself mid-explosion.

"It's my duty and obligation to enforce U.S. customs laws, and that includes preventing landings of this sort." Hubbs reached into his breast pocket and extracted the letter that Morris Frost had given him at his birthday dinner. "I thought you might wish to see this letter, from my immediate superior, Mr. Frost, outlining my duties in situations such as this."

Prevost reached for the letter and glanced over its wording.

"I have no interest in hearing whether or not you're prepared to overlook the application of customs laws this 'one time'," deCourcy retorted while Prevost reviewed the letter. "You have no authority over me or any British subject. I can land my own personal property at any time, with or without your permission, and with the military support of the Royal Navy if necessary."

Prevost handed the letter back to Hubbs, having scanned it so quickly that it appeared more a superficial show of courtesy than a reading of its contents.

"Nevertheless Mr. Hubbs," Prevost interjected, "both Major deCourcy and I appreciate that you're willing to overlook your own instructions on this one occasion, whatever we each may think about whether you have any authority in these islands to act in such a manner. Now, may I offer you some brandy? And have you been on the *Satellite* before? Perhaps a tour is in order before you depart?"

Hubbs felt his shoulders lower as the tension in his upper back eased. It was clear that the humiliation he'd faced at the American camp had been far worse than what he had just experienced on the *Satellite*. No one had criticized him personally. No one had yelled more than a few words. And now Prevost was offering him brandy and a tour. Perhaps next time they might even acknowledge his authority in matters of importation and customs duties. Hubbs accepted the glass of brandy from Prevost and took a sip, realizing that he had managed to complete the discussion of customs duties without actually apologizing to anyone.

\* \* \*

## Why the Caledonia was not Allowed to Land.

SAN JUAN ISLAND,
Sept. 30th, 1856.
EDITOR BRITISH COLONIST:—

SIR—In your issue of Monday the 26th inst., appears an editorial, headed "*Another Outrage – Excursion to San Juan.*" &c., in which you have, (perhaps inadvertently) made several unjust accusations, and some actual mistakes. So far as the article is correct in its strictures, we plead guilty to the charge, and herein furnish you with our defense, in mitigation of the sentence a just public never fail to pronounce. ...

The causes of this piece of impoliteness can be summed up in a few words: A certain set of traders, residing in Port Townsend, are very jealous of the growth and position of this place, and fearing that their town will be moved over here – and to prevent the same, they called on their *intelligent* collector, to enforce the revenue laws, by which species of sharp practice they expect to sell all the goods consumed here, and prevent any trade between us and Victoria merchants.

The collector readily concedes to their demands, and promptly orders his constable residing here, to carry out their wishes regardless of consequences. ...

In fact, what more could be expected of a man who has spent a lifetime teaching *bears how to dance*, for public exhibition; or one who was educated in a *menagerie*, and his affection for *animals*, accounts for the selection he made in his appointment of Inspector for this Island. But I am sorry, however, you thought proper to publish our Inspector's name; I would not attempt to put it again in print, for fear of disturbing his equilibrium; for a little fame in this way would, without doubt, cause the cerebral termination of his spinal cord to collapse, and then we would be deprived of his invaluable services.

*The British Colonist*, Letter to the Editor, signed by "Justicia", Monday, October 3, 1859, p. 2.

\* \* \*

Flora could see the pain disappear from Anna's face as the opiate was absorbed into her bloodstream, and she feared for how much worse Anna's condition might get before her life was over. Every moment that Anna was in pain was a moment when Flora was proving unable to give her the comfort she'd been hired to provide. Even if Hubbs had come calling in recent days, and he hadn't, she would have felt unable to leave Anna alone except for the briefest of moments.

She picked up the basin that she used as a bedpan and left the cabin to empty it, stopping outside the door when she noticed the scene unfolding in front of Griffin's residence. Griffin was shaking hands with an older gentleman with wild grey hair and a barrel chest, while Hubbs stood behind the man looking as though he had just been reprimanded in school. Griffin and the older gentleman started up the wagon road, with Hubbs glumly following behind. Griffin paused near the front of Aleck's cabin.

"Well, Mr. Frost, thank you again for stopping in to speak with us."

"My pleasure. And please, it's Morris. And if there are any more difficulties, don't hesitate to raise 'em with Paul, here, so we don't have any further misunderstandings." Morris Frost smiled and continued up the wagon road. Hubbs hesitated to follow his superior just long enough to glance over at Flora and force a smile that she took as an apology for not stopping to visit. Then he turned and followed Frost past the farm's gate toward the American camp.

Flora waited. Griffin would want to say something to her. He had commented to her about Hubbs whenever he'd found the opportunity in recent weeks, and Hubbs had created more than his share of opportunities for commentary in the previous few days. The stories of his efforts to stop British arrivals from landing on the island had been retold in far more versions than could possibly reflect the truth. But in some respects, it didn't matter which version was true, because in each of them Hubbs was mocked for his efforts to enforce U.S. customs laws on a disputed island. Flora hadn't been able to decide if she was willing to be the sympathetic ear to Hubbs once again, if he were to come calling. But she also worried that she might have said something to encourage him the last time he'd been by to see her, and concluded that it left her no choice but to offer him at least a willingness to listen. But since he hadn't visited since the event, it didn't matter much whether she would prove capable of displaying sympathy or not.

"That was Morris Foster—no, Frost—or Foster—Inspector of Customs. The direct superior to your friend, the deputy inspector."

Flora tried to remember when Hubbs had gone from being Griffin's friend to being only her friend.

"He says that whole mess was a misunderstanding—Hubbs' misunderstanding—he promised there won't be any interference with our farm. No customs duties on sheep or cattle. All just a misunderstanding."

Griffin was gloating, and it bothered her. It bothered her because it seemed personal. It bothered her because Hubbs had been instructed by that same man, whose name Griffin couldn't remember correctly, to enforce American customs laws that were now, apparently, just a misunderstanding. And it bothered her because it made her realize that she wouldn't hesitate to be a sympathetic ear if Hubbs ever bothered to come by again for a visit.

\* \* \*

STORE BREAKING. — On Wednesday evening an attempt was made to break into the store of T. Phelan, corner of Yates and Government streets. The burglar had opened the door about half way, when he was disturbed. He ran into Broad street, stumbled over a pig, and dropped an empty sack, but finally escaped pursuit.

*The British Colonist*, Friday, October 7, 1859, p. 3.

\* \* \*

John Butts dropped his wheezing body onto the wooden walkway along Wharf Street, certain that nobody had pursued him. He reached into his pocket for the apple he had stuffed inside the moment he'd entered T. Phelan Groceries, but it was no longer there. Butts cursed the pig that had tripped him, and imagined the animal enjoying the crisp, red apple that had inspired Butts to jimmy the door after he'd spied the crate through the window. He could easily have paid for it if he'd had the patience to wait until morning, but patience and a willingness to pay for his acquisitions were two qualities that Butts had never enjoyed.

At least his flask was still firmly in his breast pocket, though nearly empty.

A footstep jarred him and he looked up to see a man approaching, though he quickly concluded that it was more a boy trying to act like a man. Sixteen year-old William Williams approached with a wide grin on his handsome face. The young Brit was a recent arrival in the colony and had conversed with Butts on several occasions with a familiarity that Butts found intimidating. Young men as handsome as Williams were rare in the colony, and even rarer if they paid Butts any attention.

"Damn pig, huh, John?" Williams took a seat next to Butts and flashed a knowing grin.

"I've no idea what you're implying. You bet your life about that. John Butt is just sitting here enjoying a pleasant drink. Watching the world go by."

To underscore his alibi, Butts pulled the flask from his pocket and unscrewed the cap. He lifted the flask to his lips, but was stopped by Williams, who grasped Butts' hand holding the flask. Butts froze at the contact.

"Ain't it more polite to offer me a drink first?"

Williams pulled the flask from Butts' hand and took a long drink. He handed him back the flask with little more than a sip of whiskey remaining inside.

"Much obliged, John. Much obliged."

Williams patted Butts' thigh in a manner that might normally have been viewed as a simple gesture of thanks if his hand had rested closer to the knee, and if his fingers hadn't then tickled a path along the inside of the thigh. Butts glanced at Williams. The tone of the knowing grin had changed somewhat, but was still most definitely knowing. Butts quickly downed the last sip of whiskey in his flask, roughly calculated the odds that his cabin-mates might still be carousing around town rather than home in bed, and concluded that it was undoubtedly a risk worth taking.

\* \* \*

Flora watched Anna's labored breathing, reminded by every breath of the final struggles Elizabeth and Jane had gone through. Aleck stared stone-faced from his chair beside the bed. His wife's hand rested in his, but his fingers seemed afraid to grasp it. Neither Flora nor Aleck had spoken for some time, almost hypnotized by Anna's irregular, gasping breaths, even though any conversation would have helped to cover the painful sounds.

Father Rossi had administered last rites a short time earlier in a brief, rushed ceremony. Flora wasn't certain that Rossi would still be on the island, as she'd heard him discussing a pending return to Port Townsend, but was relieved that he had remained and would be able to conduct any services after Anna had passed.

She struggled to keep her mind on the present, but it was clear that her present was about to change. It felt wrong to be imagining the next steps in her life, but it also felt like a permissible wrong, as Anna's condition worsened by the hour. A return to the Ross farm and the chance to further her training with the Sisters seemed the most obvious path, but she wasn't certain she could leave the island just yet. She hadn't spoken with Hubbs in more than a week, since the public scandal of his efforts to enforce customs laws, and wasn't sure if she could even consider herself to be the subject of his courting any longer. But she also wasn't sure it would matter. At seventeen, one man's awkward courtship shouldn't stand in the way of her own plans.

Letters from home had been scarce in recent weeks, though she didn't fault Mary or Alexander for writing less since they'd be preoccupied with the harvest. But the absence of letters had made her feel all the more distant from her family, and even more reliant on the new friends she had made on the island.

In the space of nine months, she had helped ease her sister's passing, assisted with the care of Jane Forbes, and nursed Anna through her final months. Such experiences would be common throughout her life as a nurse, and she wondered if she were truly prepared to deal with the emotional toll of so much loss. Lucinda's advice from several months before rang in her head. She hadn't quite become friends with Anna, not as much as she had been friends with Jane. But it had been a circumstance that had less to do with Lucinda's advice than with language barriers and personalities. If she could have assisted with a birth on the island, had there been any, would it have allowed her to feel the two sides of a nurse's career? The balance of the beginning and ending of life. Perhaps facilitating the joys of birth, at least, those in which the mother and child both lived, would diminish the pain of each loss, and provide a sense of fulfillment. For with so many other patients, her sense of fulfillment would be realized only upon the patient's death, and the accompanying realization that her efforts to ease their journey were no longer required. So many paths that she could choose would promise far different moments of fulfillment. Seeing a child mature into an educated adult. Harvesting a season's crops. Serving her family a meal that had taken hours to cook. Hosting needlework parties over tea. They were paths for a future that seemed simpler and less emotionally challenging. But none of them would provide her with the feeling that she was taking the path she was meant to take.

Aleck carefully placed Anna's hand on the bed, rose, and left the cabin without a word. Flora wanted to call after him to tell him that it might not be a good time to leave Anna's side, but she was far too inexperienced to measure the time Anna might have left from the nature of her tortured breathing. Flora moved over to the seat Aleck had vacated and picked up Anna's hand. It took her back to Elizabeth's final moments, and the frustration she'd felt at being unable to do anything more than warm Elizabeth's hand in her own. It had inspired her to become a nurse. And yet she was back in the same position, feeling the same frustration, tempered only by the realization that she had already done everything a nurse could be expected to do.

She gently squeezed Anna's hand.

"I'm doing the best I can."

Anna couldn't hear her. But she hadn't spoken the words for Anna's sake.

# Chapter 14

Wednesday 12th
Weather fine & clear but chilly.—
Forenoon men as yesterday – afternoon the
above three men making a coffin & digging a
grave for Aleck's wife who died about 11 am: –
*Julia* arrived from Victoria. –

Bellevue Farm Post Journal, San Juan Island, Hudson's
Bay Company, Wednesday, October 12, 1859.

\* \* \*

It was the first time she had touched a dead body. When
Jane Forbes had died, Flora had only watched Sister Mary
wash the body, and helped from a distance. When Elizabeth
had died, her mother and sister, Catherine, had tended to
the body. But now there was no one to observe as she
washed Anna's body. It was her task to carry out alone.

Aleck was missing. The last few nights he had stayed in
the cabin, holding Anna at night. But when she had finally
passed that morning, he had run from the farm, overcome
with emotion. Angus had gone searching for him, expecting

that Aleck would be drinking wherever he could find whiskey in the village. But neither of them had turned up since. The emptiness of the small cabin was almost overwhelming, but it allowed Flora the privacy to have her own breakdown, a breakdown driven by mourning for Anna, and relief for the completion of an overwhelming responsibility.

She picked up the basin and left the dark cabin to get fresh water. The bright sunshine and brisk cold jolted her dulled physical senses, as if she needed a reminder that life went on all around her even though her attention was focused on death.

She stopped as she rounded the corner of the cabin. Hubbs was sitting on a chair in front of Griffin's residence. He leapt to his feet as soon as he saw her, then hesitated. Flora broke the silence.

"If you're looking for Mr. Griffin, I believe he's down on the *Satellite* for the afternoon."

She hadn't intended to start their first conversation in nearly two weeks with a dismissive tone, but she was hardly in a mood to measure her words.

"I was waiting for you."

The idea struck her as more offensive than flattering. Surely he hadn't come by to offer an explanation for his absence, not at a time when he had to know she was preparing Anna for her burial. But men can be like that sometimes, she had learned. She didn't have a great deal of experience with them, but she had enough to know such a thing.

"I'm preparing Anna—washing her body."

"I know. That's why I didn't want to knock." Hubbs approached with a look on his face that Flora couldn't interpret.

"I'm sorry about Anna. I hear Aleck's disappeared."

"He's probably in town. Angus went to try to find him."

Hubbs hesitated again. Flora wondered if that was it, and if she should simply thank him for his concern and continue with her task.

"I'm also sorry 'cause I've been an idiot over the past few days or so. It wasn't that I didn't want to come by. I did. But I know what people've been saying, about me, and I didn't want to risk seeing a look in your eyes like the one everyone else has been giving me."

"You were doing your job." Flora stopped, wary of offering anything that might once again inspire him to action.

"It's not much of a job anymore, since we pretty much agreed to let anyone land anything on the island."

"Well, perhaps that gives you more time to finish your house." Flora waited for an answer, but all she observed was a shrug. "Paul, I don't mean to be rude, but I'm sort of in the middle of something rather delicate."

"I know. I'm sorry."

Flora smiled awkwardly, unsure of what else to say, then turned and continued to the privy to empty the basin.

"Flora. What are you gonna do now?"

She stopped. No one had asked her this yet, and she hadn't reached any decision in her own contemplations, even though the options seemed rather limited.

"I suppose I'll return home, after the service tomorrow."

"Please don't. If you go back I'll hardly be able to see you. Working on the house without you there, it's just not the same. I want to make it up to you."

It was more than she'd expected from him. So much of Hubbs' courtship had seemed to come from a place of flirtation and friendship. Now he seemed willing to admit that he needed her.

"Aleck will want his cabin back, and there's really nothing else for me to do here. There's more I could learn from the Sisters. And if I'm going to find another nursing position, it'll be in Victoria most likely."

Neither spoke for a moment, hoping the other might offer an obvious solution.

"I must finish this. We can speak later?"

Hubbs nodded as Flora turned and disappeared behind the cabin. By the time she returned, he was gone.

* * *

Flora had hoped for one of the sunny days of recent months, days when Anna had felt well enough to sit outside and gaze across the strait to the mountains of the Olympic Peninsula, her pain overshadowed by serenity. Instead, it was a cold, grey, windy day so typical of the coastal autumn. As Flora stood beside the open grave, she gazed up at the dark clouds and made a brief plea that their threats of rain remain unfulfilled.

All of the farm's workers and their wives were in attendance for the funeral, except for a few of the temporary Indian workers who were out in the fields digging potatoes. Flora allowed her eyes to pass across the people gathered by the grave. Aleck was inconsolable, to such a degree that it surprised her. When she had arrived on the island, Aleck had seemed stoic, almost detached. And then during Anna's last few days, he had shown a fear that seemed to leave him incapable of functioning. Now, he could barely stand, though she acknowledged that it was likely due in part to excessive drinking the night before.

Hubbs, Father Rossi, and Lucinda with her infant son, were the only attendees from outside the farm, although at the start of the service Flora had noticed Catherine McGeary watching the proceedings from across the field, outside her tent. Hubbs hung back at the edge of the group, as if he was concerned that his attendance might not be welcome.

Father Rossi began the service in Latin, spoken with a thick Italian accent. Flora was grateful for his presence. He had visited Anna several times in her final days, though Flora had often wondered if his visits were driven by the exercise of his Christian duty, or an excuse to sit with deCourcy afterward and talk of European affairs over a glass of sherry. But regardless of the motivation, his visits had done much to calm Anna in her final days, which was all that had mattered to Flora. Watching him wander from Aleck's cabin to deCourcy's after each short visit would remind her of something Mrs. Cridge had once told her in school, several years before; that many of man's most noble achievements are the result of ignoble intentions.

She struggled to pull her attention back to Father Rossi's service, but found it difficult to keep her mind from wandering, as it so often did during Latin services. Aleck had come to see her before the funeral, to thank her, but had been unable to express more than a few words. What he had managed to say was that he couldn't move back into the cabin yet. He couldn't sleep in their bed without Anna, knowing it was where she had died, knowing that he was alone.

It was an opening she hadn't expected. As long as Aleck was unwilling to sleep in his own cabin, she could perhaps delay making any decision about her own future. She had no idea if the Sisters would consider her time on San Juan Island to be confirmation that she was ready to work as a nurse, or merely another step in her education. She felt certain that Reverend Cridge and Dr. Helmcken would help her find other patients to care for if she were to return to Victoria. But she was far less certain that she could find any work as a nurse on San Juan Island if for no other reason than the limited population. Most of the men on the island were soldiers who would be cared for by Dr. Craig. Most of the women were working in tents along the beach and would be unlikely customers for a nurse. And then there was Lucinda, her friend and mentor. Would any woman hire a seventeen year-old girl with limited experience when Lucinda was living a few hundred yards away? Flora felt certain of the answer.

She hadn't spoken to Hubbs since their conversation the prior day, and she wasn't sure what she would reveal to him whenever they did speak again. Aleck could decide at any moment that he had to lie in his own bed, or Griffin might object to a young woman staying in a Company cabin without contributing to the farm's bottom line, which was a likely concern on any Company farm. She might not need to leave yet, but neither could she make any plans to stay. At least, not long term plans, she told herself, as a possible temporary solution played itself out in the back of her mind.

It surprised her to suddenly realize that the service was over. Aleck placed Anna's Bible on top of her rough casket, and then two of the farmhands shoveled dirt to begin filling the grave. The group of mourners slowly broke up and wandered back to the farm. There would be a semblance of a wake over lunch, and then everyone but Aleck would return to work for the afternoon.

Flora took a moment by the grave, watching as dirt slowly concealed the casket. She felt as though she should find more meaning in the moment, but accepted that her moments of meaning with Anna were behind her. Then she turned back to the farm to discover that Griffin had waited for her, but Hubbs hadn't.

"I know this isn't the time to ask," Griffin started, "but I will anyway. I assume you're returning to your family as soon as you can?"

"I'm not sure."

"I know Aleck doesn't want to go back to his cabin right now, but we'll be shuffling people around. That cabin's for workers with families, and Aleck'll move to one of the men's cabins, once he's ready."

"I understand," Flora answered. "And I wanted to ask you, I heard you say a few days ago that you're hiring some more Indians for the rest of the harvest."

"We do that every harvest."

"I wondered if you'd hire me as one?"

"You're joking."

"I'm quite serious."

"But you're not an –"

"I grew up on a farm—two of them. Whether it's harvesting turnips or potatoes or oats, I know how to do it."

"And how am I supposed to explain myself hiring a Ross as Indian labor?"

"You hire them without going through Victoria for any contract. Just count me as another one hired. No one has to know."

"They'll find out. And we hardly pay 'em much of anything."

"Which might be more than I've already been making. I don't need to work every day. Just when you need another hand. If Aleck wants to return to his cabin, I could sleep on the floor in the cookhouse."

"You can't sleep on the floor."

"I've spent the last two months sleeping on the floor. A thin mattress, but on the floor."

The expression on Griffin's face told Flora that it had never crossed his mind to ask where she'd slept each night.

"We could have set up some sort of bed in there."

"There was no room for another. Please, I don't think I'm ready to go home."

"Because of him."

"Because of me."

As the words escaped her lips, she realized she had spoken them more from defiance than certainty. She would stay for her own needs, but because her primary need was to figure out her feelings for Hubbs, and whether Hubbs shared those feelings for her. She could return home after more time on the island, perhaps knowing her heart had been broken. Or his. But with certainty. But she couldn't return home now only to pine for a man who might never visit, and who she might not actually love.

Griffin shook his head in disbelief. "Our Indians start on the turnips tomorrow, first thing." He turned and walked back to his residence.

\* \* \*

Flora rose reluctantly from her warm blankets, and stretched muscles that ached from her first day harvesting turnips. It felt wrong to wake up alone in Aleck's cabin. She had no right to sleep alone while so many others shared cramped accommodations at the farm, even if she was still sleeping on her thin mattress on the floor, leaving Anna's bed empty. But she was grateful for the temporary refuge.

The quiet of the cabin was still odd to her. She had gotten used to the constant struggle of Anna's breathing, and to being aware of another's presence. But the difference was much more than the silence. It was a void created by Anna's absence, but also by an absence of the meaning Flora had found in the opportunity to care for her. Instead, she was rising from bed with little expectation that she'd find meaning in a turnip harvest. It was a thought that was interrupted by a yell from outside that sounded as though it had come from the American camp a few hundred feet away, and that sounded like the word "invasion."

Flora hurried outside to see several of the farm's residents rushing up the slope to the crest of the hill. Beyond them, she could see soldiers scurrying for position at the American camp. She ran up the wagon road as quickly as her sore legs would carry her, anxious to find out if there truly was an invasion underway. There had been no sounds of gunfire, no cannon shot ripping across the prairie. Even as Flora picked up her pace, she was already certain that it was just another false alarm among many.

She reached the crest of the hill and joined Angus and the others gazing down at the harbor. There was still no gunfire. But at the American camp to their left, U.S. troops fanned out across the hillside, while troops mobilized around their cannons at the heavily armed earthworks still under construction to their right. Down near the beach, British marines moved along the gravel and into the trees west of the village. They lacked the appearance of anything Flora would have described as an invasion, yet it was the first time that British troops had landed in any non-ceremonial capacity along the southern shore of Griffin Bay. That, alone, made the moment feel significant. Moments after the marines disappeared from view into a grove of trees, several of the trees began to shake, while concussive sounds echoed across the hillside. She quickly understood that the British troops weren't attacking Americans. They were attacking the trees.

Griffin and deCourcy reached the ridge and joined the others, attempting to make sense of the spectacle. Flora deferred to listening to the others, realizing quickly from their own questions to each other that none of them had received any advance information about what these troops were doing. There'd been times in the past when a few troops had landed to cut trees for lumber or firewood, but those had been farther from the American camp.

Was it a new road to the farm? A road to the American camp? A path for a future invasion? Or just a need for firewood? Many theories were offered, but nobody had any answers. The only certainty, confirmed by the response of the U.S. troops, was that it was an unannounced provocation of some kind. But not an actual invasion. Not yet.

"All right, people, the turnips won't harvest themselves," Griffin pronounced with a tone of boredom. "If war breaks out, you'll know."

Flora smiled at Griffin's assurance, and at how accustomed they had all become to the idea that a war could be unleashed at any moment, yards from their home. They all seemed certain that it wouldn't, but had learned to live with the idea that it could. No matter how hard she'd tried to allow life to carry on, there had always been a part of her brain listening every moment for gunfire, for orders yelled to troops, or for anything that might signal the realization of her greatest fears. It had always been a challenge to put those fears aside. But Flora accepted that her greatest challenge of the day had just begun and would involve not gunfire, but a field of turnips and the aching muscles in her back and legs.

She turned to follow the others, only to have her eyes fall on Hubbs, approaching along the road from the American Camp. She presumed he was heading to his claim to work on the cabin, and wished that she could trade a day in the turnip field for a day helping Hubbs with his construction tasks. He smiled hesitantly as he reached her.

"You're not organizing the locals to repel this possible attack?" she asked. It had been an attempt to sound light and cheerful, but she instantly feared that it had come across as a critique of his attention to personal matters in the face of a British incursion.

"I've concluded I can do more to secure the island for my country by focusing on my own patch of land and leaving the army to fight over the rest, thanks to some wise advice." His smile relaxed as he spoke. "Perhaps you can secure a small portion of the island for Her Majesty by tending to the turnip crop."

"I'll try to convince myself there's such a high purpose to my work."

Hubbs took a step, as if the conversation would be nothing more than simple pleasantries, then stopped and hesitated.

"I've missed you. And I've no one to blame but myself. I just wish I knew what to say to make you understand that I never wanted to be away from you."

"I suppose you just did."

There was a lengthy silence before Flora understood that Hubbs was hoping for a response that echoed his sentiments.

"We suspend the harvest on the Sabbath," she began. "Perhaps you could show me all you've accomplished on the house over the past couple weeks?"

"I'd like that," he answered. "I'd like that very much. Till Sunday."

His smile widened to a grin, and he tipped his weathered hat before continuing along the wagon road. Flora watched him as he walked away, relieved that they had reaffirmed their shared interest in spending time together.

\* \* \*

Flora scanned the sentence in her sister's letter before reading it aloud, to ensure that the meaning was clear.

"'Big news is, Cary and Ring in duel,'" she read. "'Now Cary running from law. Do you get newspaper there'?"

She put the letter down and looked over at Hubbs, who was busy chinking large cracks between the logs that formed the front wall of the house with a mixture of mud, lime, and dried grass. The room was beginning to take on the appearance of a main parlor, though it was a label that seemed slightly pretentious in a house that would start out as only a parlor, a bedroom, and, if all went well, a rudimentary kitchen.

"Did you meet Mr. Cary?" she continued, uncertain if he was listening. "He was here at the farm right after the troops landed, just for a few days. Strange man, I thought. I suppose it is odd that the attorney-general is running from the law because of a duel."

Flora turned back to the letter and struggled to interpret a paragraph describing how unhappy Francis claimed to be, living in Washington Territory with the family of his older brother, Charles, Jr. Mary's letters always presented a challenge as they lacked accurate spelling and grammar. She had never shown an interest or ability at academics, and so it had never been forced on her. But despite the flaws, Mary's letters always made Flora homesick.

As Flora read, Hubbs continued his work on the front wall. She enjoyed watching him work, although she had come to the conclusion that his construction skills weren't particularly accomplished. His upbringing as the son of a merchant, diplomat, attorney, and politician had taught him many things, but the proper use of tools wasn't among them. What was important, she told herself, was that the home would be comfortable. Perfect right angles weren't necessary for comfort.

A cold autumn storm brought steady rain that pounded on the roof and dripped onto the floor in several locations, as if mocking Hubbs' belief in the integrity of his construction skills. The fireplace was complete, but the fire within it was forced to compete with the winds that whistled through the many cracks in the unfinished walls. Yet Flora found herself able to imagine that the house would someday be a warm and comfortable home for Hubbs.

"'William helped Alexander with harvest, except for nights in gaol. Usual reasons. Marie –'" Flora turned to Hubbs. "Marie is John's new baby, about seven months," she explained before turning back to the letter. "'Marie crawls, smiles lots. Wish you can see.'"

Flora got up from the floor, envying Mary for having finished the season's harvest at the Ross farm, as her own muscles ached from the five days of work she'd been given by Griffin, all of them spent harvesting turnips. She had taken part in many harvests since she was a small girl, but keeping up with her brothers had never been as exhausting as trying to keep up with the Indian workers that Griffin had hired.

"I'm being selfish." Hubbs stopped working on the wall and approached Flora.

"How?" Flora asked.

"Convincing you to stay, keeping you from your family."

"Perhaps I convinced myself to stay. And I wouldn't have stayed if I didn't want to."

"But you miss them."

"Of course I miss them. And I could practically see them if I had a telescope on a clear day."

"Maybe you should go home for a visit?"

"After the harvest is done."

"Griffin can find another—" Hubbs stopped before saying 'Indian'.

Flora struggled to understand the point to his suggestion. A week earlier he had seemed to pressure her to stay on the island, and now he seemed certain that she needed to go home.

"I stayed because I chose to stay. Besides, this house of yours is just getting to the point where it's going to need a woman's touch."

"It's not just my house that needs a woman's touch."

Flora pretended to be shocked, but found herself laughing as Hubbs pulled her close and kissed her. It was affection that he hadn't shown in weeks, but it felt as welcome as it did surprising. Mary's letter fell from Flora's hand as Hubbs pushed her back against the wall and pressed his lips firmly against hers with an aggression that was new, intoxicating and frightening. The isolation of the cabin lost its romantic appeal, as Flora contemplated that they were at least a mile from the closest neighbor. She struggled to pull back from the kiss and stared into his eyes, trying to read the intensity that they signaled. She forced a smile from her lips.

"And that is as far as this woman's touch is allowed to go. Especially on the Sabbath."

Hubbs grimaced in disappointment and weakened his grip.

"Do you want me to finish the letter, or not?" she continued, changing the topic.

"Yes, I want to hear all about Marie learning to crawl."

It was a lie, but he'd delivered it convincingly enough before turning back to the half-finished wall. Flora picked up the letter and struggled to find the paragraph where she had stopped reading, overcome by the emotions of the moment. She was shocked by the aggression he had shown, yet pleased that his affections had resumed, and anxious at the realization that a part of her hadn't wanted the moment to end. She located the paragraph where she had stopped reading, and then scanned the next two sentences to gain an understanding of what Mary had intended before attempting to read them aloud.

\* \* \*

> Some wicked rascal says "that he has invented a new telegraph." He proposes to place a line of women, fifty steps apart, and commit the news to the first as a very profound secret.

*The British Colonist*, Monday, October 24, 1859, p. 1.

\* \* \*

"It's only a rumor."

"More'n a rumor. East coast papers are all sayin' he's on his way."

"So if it's in a paper, it's fact?"

"T'is when it's in 'em all."

Flora didn't know who they were, the two men talking loudly behind where she and Hubbs sat on a rough bench, waiting for the show to begin, but she was tempted to turn and ask them to keep their voices down. It wasn't as though either had revealed anything new. Everyone in the tent had been talking about nothing else since they'd arrived that evening, as rumors had started earlier in the day that General Winfield Scott was travelling from Washington to negotiate some form of resolution to the standoff.

In the prior few days, the rumors passing across the

island had centered on far simpler fare; such as which plays, skits and songs the Chapman Family would perform in the tent they had erected at the edge of the village. Flora wasn't particular as to which type of performance the traveling theatrical troupe might choose, just as long as she was able to attend. She had made certain that Hubbs would take her since the Sisters no longer had any role in limiting her entertainment options.

She couldn't blame the men behind them for being excited about the rumors. General Scott was the grand old man of the U.S. military, and an officer who'd previously commanded General Harney in the Mexican war. If it were true that he was to arrive in the region any day, then the tenor of the standoff was about to change entirely. Harney and every officer below him would have to defer to their superior, a man who had already earned the nickname "The Great Pacificator" for his role in negotiating resolutions to U.S.-British boundary disputes in the eastern states and colonies. Governor Douglas would have to adopt a more conciliatory tone to match the approach that Scott was expected to bring. And regardless of the variations in rumors that spread through the crowd, the expected outcome was the same: some form of joint occupation of the island, if not an outright withdrawal of all military forces.

"Well, I don't know about you, but I hope they perform a farce," Flora commented to Hubbs in an effort to start a light conversation. It had been clear from their past conversations that he considered a joint occupation to be a defeat of everything he'd worked to obtain; a retreat from the bargaining position of sole occupation. Flora feared that she would see a return of Hubbs' depression and anger once General Scott's visit had played itself out.

"I'm thinking I'm gonna focus on trying to get the kitchen built before winter sets in," he pondered, without prompting or context. "At least a roof and a few walls so we have some protection from the wind and rain."

"We." It was the only word that registered with Flora. She had allowed herself to indulge in occasional harmless fantasies of marriage as a means of measuring her own feelings, at least in the weeks before Hubbs' encounters with the *Caledonia* and the *Julia*. But Hubbs seemed several steps ahead of her, simply by his use of "we" in a comment about his future kitchen, and it made her realize that returning to Victoria after the harvest to search for another nursing position had instantly become a more complicated proposition. It also made her realize, as the first performers strode onto the small stage, that perhaps the Chapman Family didn't need to perform a farce that evening to lift Hubbs' spirits. Perhaps she could accomplish that all on her own.

\* \* \*

Flora watched the young couple wandering away from the tent after the Chapman Family's slightly disappointing performance. She didn't know them, but felt as though she had seen them so many times before. Not the same two people, but the same image of the white man and his *klootchman*, and the same emotions passing between them in public. It wasn't the affection a drunk soldier showed a woman he had hired for a few hours. It was affection shown by a man toward his wife, regardless of any difference in their race. It was far more than Hubbs had shown toward Flora in public, and it was far more than she would have allowed in their courtship. But for a brief moment, she envied the young woman who hadn't been raised within the same societal limitations.

She had to wait until they were a safe distance from the crowd before asking the question that swirled in her mind once again, driven by Hubbs' earlier reference to "we". But the anticipation and nervousness built with each step until she could no longer hold her silence.

"Did you love them?"

"Who?"

She hesitated, worried that she lacked the courage to finish the conversation.

"It's whispered that, well, that you had Indian brides when you lived in the Charlottes."

"Only whispered?"

"Only whispered in my company."

Hubbs hesitated for a measure of time that seemed troubling.

"When I went up there, I didn't even know if they'd welcome me. But they did, as more than just a visitor. I was young, alone … lonely … eventually I was married to a young woman by their traditions. Not in a Christian sense. And it wouldn't have been recognized by the law down here since she was full-blooded Haida. But she was my wife."

"Was?"

"She died a little more'n a year ago. A fever and I don't know what else it might've been."

"I'm sorry. That must have been so difficult."

"Does it bother you to hear all that?"

Flora pondered her feelings before answering.

"No. Except it bothers me for you, that you lost her like that. But I'm not bothered for me, if that makes sense."

She knew it wasn't an entirely truthful answer. Part of her had wanted to hear him insist that he had only ever loved one woman, and that she was standing before him. To hear that she had become his first love. But she also wasn't certain she could have promised the same feelings in return if he had spoken them aloud, not after the emotional confusion of the previous few weeks.

Another question circled in her mind. Surely if their marriage had produced children, he would have them with him, on the island. But he'd said nothing of children and had none to be seen. It was information she wanted to confirm, but she couldn't bring herself to ask the question.

Hubbs took Flora's hand as they started up the wagon road to the farm. He squeezed it and then flashed her a smile, either intended to reassure her about his answer, or to ensure an end to their conversation about his past. She returned it, hopeful that their next conversation to touch on the topic of love would have less to do with his past, and far more to do with her own future.

\* \* \*

## Bellevue Gossip.

The Washington correspondent of the S.F. Bulletin contains the following on the Bellevue matter:

Be assured that the Administration do not feel itself very grateful to General Harney for his course in taking possession of San Juan Island, and thus tying up a very troublesome diplomatic knot ...

Neither General Harney nor the United States Boundary Commissioner, Mr. Campbell, had any authority to occupy the island by a military force. But it is one thing to take such a step and another to retract it.— Hence the quandary of the Government, and hence the appeal to General Scott for his advice and aid. The Government cannot openly rebuke General Harney, because that would be an admission of doubt as to our title to San Juan – an admission of which British diplomacy would be sure to make the most. Nevertheless, General Harney's conduct is considered rash and impetuous.

It is supposed here that General Scott will conclude a negotiation, whereby the forces of both parties will be withdrawn, and leave matters thereby as they were before the occupation by Capt. Pickett; and unless the "Downing street" gentlemen are in for a war, all matters can be and will be amicably settled.

*The Victoria Gazette*, Thursday, October 27, 1859, p. 3.

\* \* \*

"It's almost as if I'd gotten used to the idea there could be a war right here at any moment," Flora began from her perch on one of Catherine McGeary's chairs, "and now I just feel even more confused about what might happen."

Flora looked over to Lucinda and Catherine for confirmation of her thoughts, while bouncing Catherine's seven month-old son on her knee. The baby was the same age as her youngest niece, and holding him furthered the ache of homesickness.

Catherine stood at the wood stove and slowly poured heated tallow into a cast iron pot of lye, carefully measuring the right amount to produce the soft laundry soap used to wash the soldiers' laundry. Her new cabin was hardly more finished than Hubbs' rambling construction, but it was solid and would make the winter more tolerable for the family.

"Yer startin' to think like an army wife," Catherine said. "Nothin's ever the same long enough to get used to it. First time ya hear there's a war or some fight with the Indians, it seems like that's yer future. But it's always changin'. Ya can never know what to expect."

"Thank God there's change," Lucinda added. "Maybe if we had some peace around here, Crosbie would stop trying to put my husband out of business."

"'Cept if there's peace, he's got no customers," Catherine replied, eliciting a frown of agreement from Lucinda.

Lucinda placed ten-month old John Henry onto the plank floor where he crawled about investigating his new surroundings. Outside, Lucinda's and Catherine's older children played together in the tall grass. Flora had brought Lucinda to Catherine's cabin in the hope that they would become friends. Both women were American, both were about the same age, and both had young children. It seemed natural that they'd develop a friendship.

It had been nearly two weeks since rumors had circulated that General Scott was in nearby waters onboard the *Northerner* and refusing to come ashore in order to avoid offending the British with any act that could be seen as a proclamation of U.S. claims to the island. Negotiations were allegedly underway in writing between Scott and colonial authorities, but that was as much as the rumors confirmed by their commonality. After those simple facts, the rumors diverged in all possible directions of war, peace, capitulation, and deadlock. The only confirmation of progress had been the arrival of an officer from General Scott's entourage that morning to order a cessation to construction of the redoubt, the earthwork fortification housing cannons along the ridge. Catherine's husband had shared this information with her earlier in the day, though Flora had a feeling that Catherine shouldn't have been sharing it with her and Lucinda. Nevertheless, it provided a sign that some arrangement was being finalized.

"Do you think it's true that absence makes the heart grow fonder?" Flora asked hesitantly.

"Missin' yer family?" Catherine asked.

"Of course. But I mean between men and women." Flora turned to Lucinda. "You and Stephen were apart more than a year."

"It's a silly expression," Lucinda replied. "My heart didn't grow fonder. It ached more and more every day he was gone. Some days I was angry. Some days I thought about leaving. The moment I saw him, I just felt relief more than anything else. And then we had to get to know each other all over again."

"Durin' the Indian wars I wasn't workin' as the laundress," Catherine interjected. "Me and Ed had been hitched little more'n a year, and Mary'd just been born, and I didn't see him for six months. Same sort o' mixed feelin's. And when he did come home, it was just like that … like parts o' us were strangers."

Flora nodded, though they'd given her precisely the answer she'd feared. Catherine smiled, understanding Flora's concern.

"It's a short canoe across the water. He'd come see ya."

"I know he would, occasionally at least. But would we feel like strangers each time he did? I feel like I'm just beginning to understand him."

Lucinda laughed. "The moment you think you understand a man is the moment you're in big trouble."

"Understandin' a man's like tryin' to figure what a stew with dumplin's is made from," Catherine added. "Ya can see the fluffy dumplin' on the surface—the good part—but there's a whole mess o' stuff bubblin' away underneath. It could be choice cuts or it could be knuckles, and only it's maker really knows."

Flora smiled, accepting Catherine's point about the layers men like Hubbs kept hidden, layers she might never understand.

"Don't you want to go back home to get more nursing experience from the Sisters?" Lucinda inquired.

Flora hesitated. Harvest would soon be over, and with no patient under her care she would have no justification to remain at the farm, and nowhere else to stay. Every woman on San Juan Island could be grouped into one of three categories: a handful of wives to settlers or farmworkers or soldiers; prostitutes; and a young nurse who no longer had a patient under her care. The island was no place for a seventeen year-old girl without a husband or a role to play at the farm.

"I thought I did. But you can teach me anything I'd be able to learn from the Sisters," Flora answered, hoping it might not be too much to suggest. "I just keep thinking that the only way to know how I feel is to spend more time around him. I can't get to know someone if they're nowhere near me."

"Maybe what ya need's more time to get to know yourself," Catherine suggested.

"I've had seventeen years of that."

"Seventeen years is nothin'. Have ya even kissed him yet?"

Flora blushed, giving away her answer.

"And how'd it make ya feel, other'n shame and guilt?" Catherine asked with a grin, accurately predicting the first two thoughts in Flora's mind.

"It made me feel special, safe. He isn't courting me because of my father's name. He isn't disappointed that my eyes are dark, or my skin isn't pale. He makes me feel … wanted."

"And d'ya wanna raise his kids, cook meals he'll complain about, wash his dirty laundry, care for him when he's sick, put him to bed when he's drunk and pissed himself, and listen to him ramble on about all he could'a done with his life if only the good Lord and the entire universe hadn't worked against him?"

Catherine's list surprised Flora by its tone. She had considered several of the items already, though in gentler terms, and had concluded each time that her answer was probably agreement. But it intimidated her to hear them all at once, summarizing Catherine's idea of what it meant to be married to a man.

"Isn't it also laughing with him, loving him, supporting him, building a life together?" Flora answered.

"Same list, Flora, just different words said by a girl thinkin' ahead to a weddin', not a wife o' six years lookin' back at it all."

Flora smiled, relieved that the main difference in their lists might be the perspective of years. She glanced around the McGeary's small cabin. At the piles of laundry that Catherine had to wash that day. At the children crawling across the floor. At the toys scattered across the room. It was entirely consistent with everything Catherine had listed, or everything Flora had answered with, but it surprised her to realize that it might be everything she could want for herself.

\* \* \*

"Time gone. You go."

Hubbs rolled over and smiled. He wasn't about to let his needs be controlled by an old watch that the squaw had probably lifted from a drunken soldier. He reached over to the pants he'd left in a pile beside them and pulled a silver coin from the pocket, taking note that the rest of his cash was still safely in place.

"Now we've got lots more time."

The young woman, more a girl, took the coin with a forced smile, and Hubbs hoped her hesitation had nothing to do with the idea that he'd be staying longer. He lightly traced his fingers down the side of her torso, hoping to elicit an unconscious smile or giggle from his touch. Every woman's reaction to being tickled would vary, but he held a personal belief that a girl who worked in the business of pleasuring men could unwittingly reveal her level of experience by how readily she'd find his touch to be ticklish. He was pleased to see the girl grin and squirm back from his fingers before he'd reached the bottom of her ribcage, and found himself wondering if Flora would react as quickly. He had barely asked himself the question before deciding that she'd probably find it ticklish before his fingers even navigated through her clothing.

Everything was so much simpler in a tent along the beach with a girl like the one who lay beside him. The expectations of both sides were understood and complementary. There were no social rules of courtship, no questions over whether he could touch her, when, or where. Flora was the first girl that Hubbs had properly courted, a social necessity given her upbringing, but a difficulty given his own lack of experience. His past companions had been the result of negotiation more than courtship. In so many ways, Flora was the perfect prospect for a wife. She had the dark features that fueled his desire. She had the name of a respectable family in the colony, to the extent that her youngest brothers hadn't yet destroyed its respectability. She had intelligence and education. She had experience running a farm, which was something that Hubbs had never attempted. And he imagined that she would make a caring mother. Her upbringing might have stifled her natural ways, but surely she'd open herself to him as his first wife had done, once she'd have the societal approval of marriage. She might have no experience yet with physical passion, but with a little instruction and the chance to release the fears and shame she'd been taught, perhaps she could be everything he'd need in a wife.

And if she weren't, there was no shortage of other options to replace her shortcomings.

Hubbs reminded himself that the time he had with the girl was slipping away with the ticking of an old pocket watch, risking his hopes of obtaining everything else he desired for the afternoon without reaching into his pocket

288

for a third coin. He moved his hand more forcefully down the girl's torso until reaching her hips, then gripped her buttocks and pulled her close, willing himself to begin their second session of the afternoon.

\* \* \*

LIEUT. GEN. SCOTT.— We are informed by Mr. D.B. Foster, Purser of the *William G. Hunt*, that Gen. Scott has quietly taken up his quarters on Fidalgo Island, where he will probably remain during the pendency of the dispute regarding San Juan. Fidalgo Island is on the eastern side of Rosario Straits, which the British claim as the dividing channel between the two countries. He therefore occupies ground not in dispute. As will be seen by the Victoria news, elsewhere, he has communicated with Gov. Douglas.

*The Puget Sound Herald*, Friday, November 4, 1859, p. 2.

\* \* \*

The flowers that Flora placed on Anna's grave were the last of the season from Griffin's garden, and they were poor excuses for flowers. A cold wind off the strait blew the dried buds off the dirt mound the moment Flora set them down, as if offended by the inadequacy of the offering. Dr. Tolmie retrieved the flowers and lodged them securely between two of the rocks that supported a small wooden cross.

"I suppose you realize by now that you've chosen a career that deals constantly with the entries and exits of life." Tolmie stepped back from the mound.

"I think that was what drew me to nursing from the start."

"And was it all you imagined it would be?"

"I hadn't imagined being someone's nurse while a war threatened to break out just feet from the door. But it felt like I thought it would feel. To be pleased I was helping her, to be afraid that maybe I wasn't really helping her enough given my inexperience, and to feel her appreciation even when she couldn't say anything."

"I suppose there are few things in life that we experience in the manner we imagine." Tolmie gestured toward the farm to suggest that they return along the narrow path. "I gather you've been spending time with that Hubbs fellow."

"You don't approve?"

"It isn't my place to approve or disapprove."

"But you have an opinion."

"I always have an opinion. It isn't always proven to be correct, however, nor always proper to share."

"I know he isn't popular at the Company."

"A lot of men aren't popular with the Company."

Flora stopped in the path and threw him a frustrated stare to protest his efforts at avoiding any meaningful answers. He paused and considered his wording.

"I've no right to question you. But I've known you since you were taking your first steps, so I feel I've some obligation to your late father to express what he might've said, and to your mother who isn't here to measure the man for herself. Paul Hubbs is an adversary. Adversaries are usually driven by the same motivations as we are. He's gone to great lengths to try to make this American soil, and we're doing what we can to ensure otherwise. We're usually more like our adversaries than we are different. Perhaps that's the only reason I'm hesitant. He treats you right?"

"As right as anyone ever has. He has moods sometimes. But he makes me smile. He makes me laugh. He's not always trying to, but he does it just the same. He's staked a claim out on the point, and there's just something about how I feel when I'm with him out there ..."

"Seventeen is still young."

"And some say twenty is too old, and it'll be here before I know it. And anyway, he hasn't asked me —" Flora caught herself, having revealed more than she'd intended.

"And your devotion to nursing?"

"I can still be a nurse here. Maybe not as much as I can in Victoria. But I know it's my calling."

"Well, I expect we'll be leaving tomorrow afternoon once the ewes are loaded. If you decide you'd like to be home for a while to have time to think it all over, there'll be space for you, as always."

"I suppose that offer tells me what you think of Paul."

"No, my dear. Only that whatever choice you make, it should be made with every option open to you, so you'll always know you made the choice you wanted to make."

Flora smiled her thanks, then noticed Angus running along the wagon road toward the farm, waving his arms wildly.

"What in heaven's name ..."

"I've a feeling we should go see what this is all about," Tolmie suggested.

Flora nodded and followed Tolmie across the field to the clearing in front of Griffin's residence, where many of the residents had gathered upon hearing Angus' yelling. By the time Flora and Tolmie were within hearing range, he was already close to the end of his news.

"Just one company—Pickett's—that's it. And one British company." Angus was out of breath from the run and unable to finish long sentences. So many questions were thrown at him that he held up his hands in protest. Then he started over.

"General Scott's in the harbor, on the *Massachusetts*. Some Lieutenant came onshore, announced a settlement, joint occupation, just Pickett's company here, one British company somewhere else on the island, no U.S. civil authority over Brits, that's all I know."

Everyone was silent, digesting the news. A small cheer erupted in the distance, though Flora couldn't tell if it had come from the far side of the American camp, or perhaps from the *Satellite* in the harbor. Everything had changed in an instant, and it was a change that could be cheered or dismissed by people on either side of the conflict. U.S. soldiers might be pleased about returning to a fort on the mainland, just as sailors on the *Satellite* might be pleased to return to Esquimalt Bay. But with just one U.S. company of soldiers on the island, the new town that had been built on the beach would lose most of its captive customers, as would the hundreds of squaws plying their own trade, and as would Stephen Boyce's efforts to establish a thriving and legal saloon.

Flora's first thoughts were about Hubbs. He was supposed to come by the farm to accompany her to his claim for the day, where they planned to work on the outside kitchen walls at the back of the house. She had no idea if the man who would show up would be angry, morose, or philosophical. Would he spend the day using her as a substitute target for his anger, or as a chance to escape the island's politics and enjoy their time together? She hoped it would be a day that would confirm the choice she expected to make about Tolmie's offer for passage on the *Otter*, rather than sow new doubts. But it was an outcome that was largely beyond her control.

*  *  *

"The important thing is that it's Pickett who's staying. He won't hesitate to stand up for our interests when he needs to."

Hubbs hammered nails into the board that Flora was holding for him against the posts of a future kitchen wall. She listened less to his words than to his hammering, as she had noticed that the way he handled tools was a reliable indicator of his emotional state. He could be joking with her, but hammering with such force that he'd bend more nails than he'd drive into the wood, informing her that he was upset about something. Or he could be having a serious discussion, yet hammer his thumb until it was purple, indicating that he was focused more on their conversation than his own work. And while she was generally pleased whenever he was focused on their conversations, she had also learned that hammering his thumb could instantly destroy his otherwise genial mood. On their prior Sunday at the claim, he had responded to a blow to his thumb by screaming angrily and driving the hammer through the board he had just fastened to the interior wall.

On this day, he seemed calm, careful, and particular

about getting each board secured properly in place. Flora took it as a positive sign, since it suggested that he wasn't angry about the joint occupation agreement. Perhaps the weeks of rumors had prepared him for the inevitability of such an arrangement.

"It doesn't mean we lost the war. It was just one battle. Now we'll just reconfigure, focus on what the commission's up to and keep them vigilant, use political channels, make sure Buchanan or whoever follows him'll press America's rights. A handful of John Bull sailors sitting somewhere else on the island won't change the fact that this is American territory. We're not done yet."

"So half the island thinks we have peace, and the other half thinks we've got a different kind of war?" She instantly questioned the wisdom of challenging his perception of the deal.

Hubbs lowered his hammer and grabbed a handful of nails. "When the boundary is final, making this an American island, then the war'll be over."

Flora considered it a positive sign that Hubbs had shown up at the farm that morning, precisely when he had promised. He wasn't morose over news of the settlement, but instead led a cow by a rope and carried two apple tree saplings. He had purchased the cow that morning from a man in the village who'd imported a small herd to the island, and he planned to keep it at the house. But since he'd yet to build any sort of barn or shelter to protect livestock in inclement weather, it meant that the cow would be kept in the kitchen for the meantime, though 'kitchen' was a label that was more applicable to intentions than fact. It was little more than a partial post-and-beam shed attached to the back of the log frame of the house, with a half-finished roof over a dirt floor. It was far from ideal to shelter a cow in the future kitchen, but Hubbs had explained to Flora that having some kind of agricultural activity going on at the claim was important to protecting its size, since a house without cattle or crops would have no need for acreage. A single cow and a two-tree orchard was a start.

As much as Flora understood the need to get the kitchen

constructed, she would have preferred to help with improvements to the enclosed rooms of the house where it would have been less exposed. It was mid-day, yet the temperature hovered just above freezing, while a cold wind tossed low, dark clouds across the top of Mount Finlayson behind the house. It could have rained at any moment. Or snowed. What they weren't expecting was the violence of hail.

"Do you hear that?" Flora asked, as the first pellets hit the roof.

Hubbs was already reacting, running to grab the cow's hemp lead to guide the animal into the relative safety of the half-finished structure. He secured the rope to a corner post, allowing the cow to remain protected from the hail, then turned to Flora.

"What do you think? Keep working out here, or inside? At least the hail can't hit us as long as we stay under the roof."

"I'm fine either way," she answered, despite a clear preference. "I know how much you want to finish this before the weather gets colder."

Hubbs turned back to the task at hand and then paused. "I'm not so much trying to get this done for the weather as trying to get this done for you, so you could have somewhere to live instead of sleeping on the floor at the farm, so you don't have to feel like you need to go back to Victoria ... so *we* could have somewhere to live."

Flora froze. She had no idea what the proper response would be since it felt as though he'd communicated only half a thought, and the second half of the thought at that. It suggested so much without actually asking her anything.

She broke the silence. "Dr. Tolmie offered me passage on the *Otter*. They're going back tomorrow."

"And?"

"The harvest is over, and I can't stay at the farm much longer if I don't have something to do or someone to take care of."

"So you want to go home?"

"I do, but I don't."

"He'd let you stay a couple more weeks."

"And then what?"

"And then we move here. A couple weeks should be all we need to find someone to marry us on this island."

"Heavens, no. No, we can't. There's only one man who can marry me, and that's Reverend Cridge."

Hubbs stepped back, as if confused, until the entire statement sunk in. "Reverend? You mean, get married in Victoria?"

Flora realized that she had responded with planning details rather than a firm answer to a question that had been merely implicit throughout the conversation, and still remained unspoken.

"Well, if that's something we're thinking about doing at some point. And getting it organized would take more than a couple of weeks. And the faster it is, the more people would talk." Flora hesitated, confused by the manner in which the conversation was unfolding. None of her daydreams had involved such an indirect conversation about the topic. "That is, if you're asking me?"

Hubbs smiled and took Flora's hands in his.

"Yes, Flora Ross, I am. I'm asking you. Will you be my wife?"

Whenever Flora had imagined the possibility of a proposal, the question had been delivered with more definite intention under far more romantic conditions. And she had always been quick with a firm answer, trying out each option in her imagination. But now that the question had finally been asked, she found herself unable to form any response at all, stunned by the magnitude of the decision she faced. Questions, warnings, fantasies and doubts fought for her attention. The distance from her family. The risks to her developing nursing career. The isolation of living out at the point. The pressure of competing with the memory of his late, first wife. Whether she really knew the man she would marry? It was too much to consider, which is why she found herself incapable of giving the matter any consideration at all, and instead heard a simple response fall from her lips.

"Yes, Paul Hubbs, I will."

Hubbs took her in his arms and kissed her with more conviction and passion than she'd ever allowed him to express before. The questions and doubts faded from her mind as she accepted his passion as proof that she had given the right answer. She kissed him back, tried to communicate the same level of emotion, and struggled to ignore the odor that the cow had just introduced onto the dirt floor of their future kitchen.

# Chapter 15

Flora squeezed Hubbs' hand for support as she stepped over a gurgling stream that trickled down the steep southern slope of Mount Finlayson to the beach a hundred feet below. The path from Hubbs' claim was a series of narrow, meandering tracks that had been carved across the hillside by the hooves of cows and horses over the years. On prior occasions, she had kept a polite distance from Hubbs even though she sensed that he wished to hold her hand, and had found little difficulty navigating the path on her own. She had never imagined that placing her hand within his firm grasp would actually deprive her of balance and make each step a more difficult challenge.

Flora followed the path that ran just a step to the right of Hubbs, but nearly a foot higher on the steep hillside. With each step, their bodies rose and fell according to their respective uneven path, never entirely parallel, and never predictable. It left her unable to rely on his hand for stable support, yet she was unable to let go. It was only as they rounded the southwestern slope of the hillside and reached the gentler prairie stretching across the peninsula that she was able to relax and enjoy the feeling of walking hand-in-hand with her new fiancé.

They could hear the sounds of activity in the bay long before they reached the ridge, where the scene came into view. At the wharf, below, a company of U.S. soldiers loaded tents, armaments, and supplies onto the *Massachusetts*, while civilians loaded personal possessions, inventory, and parts of dismantled buildings onto smaller craft. It was as though the previous months had been thrown into reverse, with troops and merchants pulling back from the beach like retreating tides.

"Angus," Hubbs announced, nodding his head toward the wagon road below. Flora turned to see Angus hurrying up the road toward them.

"Angus," Flora called out as he approached. "We have news."

"I heard already," he replied, excited and out of breach. "Everyone's talkin' about it."

"They can't be."

"Why not? Sendin' Pickett away's big news."

"Sending Pickett away?"

Hubbs' question was three words long, yet Flora could hear the anger build with each word, as Hubbs came to understand the implications of Angus' announcement.

"Pickett's out," Angus replied. "Captain Hunt's company is stayin' instead. Word is the Governor objected to Pickett since he did Harney's biddin'. So Company D's shippin' back to Fort Bellingham, or what's left of it. Ain't that the news you had to go on about?"

Flora couldn't answer. She watched Hubbs' expression, fearful that he might explode in anger, but he managed to contain it.

"Angus, do you think you could accompany Flora back to the farm? I'd like to get some more work done on the cabin before it gets dark."

"Of course."

Hubbs words had been controlled, but the effort that it had required of him had been obvious. He lifted Flora's hand and kissed it, then offered a forced smile of apology.

"I will visit tomorrow."

"I look forward to it."

Flora knew that her own expression communicated worry, but it would be best to say nothing more. Hubbs would need time alone to process the news and address his anger. He let go of her hand, nodded to Angus, and turned back along the ridge in the direction of his claim.

Angus started along the path.

"I guess he and Pickett are friends?"

"More or less, I suppose. I think he found consolation in the idea that Company D would remain, since he convinced them to move here in the first place."

Flora stopped in the path, suddenly realizing how the departure of Company D would affect her own friendships.

"I have to go. I'm sorry."

Flora ran from Angus, hurrying along the road in the direction of the American camp. If Pickett's company was leaving, then Catherine was leaving. As she reached Catherine's quarters, the door swung open before she could raise her fist to knock. Catherine smiled from inside the cabin.

"You're leaving?" Flora cried.

"But we're not," Catherine replied, with a grin. "Come inside. Yer gettin' wet."

Flora hesitated, not having noticed that the rain had started again. She stepped inside.

"But, the news. Surely you've heard …"

"Hunt's company don't have their own laundress," Catherine explained proudly, "so they're gonna transfer Ed to Company C so they won't all be stuck with filthy drawers and no one to wash 'em."

"Oh, I'm so relieved. I would never have imagined … transferring a man between companies because of his wife's job."

"Ed wouldn't mind how it sounds. Most privates don't have a wife who can hoard a bit of silver for the future. But the real reason yer here is to tell me yer gettin' hitched."

Flora stared, confused.

"Ed heard from someone who heard from someone else that yer man's gonna marry the Indian nurse he's been courtin'. Who else'd it be?"

"But he only just asked me."

"Apparently, he'd been plannin' for it."

"And they say women are gossips."

"Are ya happy?"

"Terribly, I think."

"Then I'm happy. I hope it lasts—the happiness, I mean." Catherine pushed a pair of soldier's uniform pants under the soapsuds. "Don't mind me. The water gets cold fast on days like this. Ya set a date yet?"

"No. We're going to Victoria in a few days so he can meet my family and we can arrange everything with Reverend Cridge. And he wants to ask my mother's permission. But we want to do it as soon as we can. The house is more or less ready. The windows and doors aren't all in yet, and the kitchen's more of a barn at the moment, and the wind gets through all the cracks between the logs. But you have to come see it. It would be such a beautiful place to raise a family—will be. And we're going to be neighbors. Not as close as now, but still close."

Flora continued on about her plans, about the house, about the crops they would plant and the livestock they would raise. She talked about the wedding she wanted, and the wedding she would have to accept. She talked about having children. And she talked about finding a way to still work as a nurse despite all of it. She knew that her ramblings might come across as naïve. But Catherine wouldn't stop her, since she had likely rambled on in the same way a half-dozen years before, only to discover that many of her hopes and dreams had been nothing more. As she heard the excitement in her own voice, she told herself that it confirmed that she was in love. And that she had made the right decision.

\* \* \*

Much has been altered since my last letter ... General Scott on his arrival, very properly and very promptly, undid most of the foolish and indeed disreputable performances of our silly stupid Commander Harney. He ordered the troops off the island, including Captain Pickett and his company, who were first sent here by Harney four months since, to work upon a huge field. Work was given up at once and heavy guns shipped off.

One company only (my own) was designated as the temporary garrison of the island upon the ground promise of protection to the settlers against Indians. ...

I am confident that this whole imbroglio is a disgraceful plot involving General Harney, a dull animal, Mr. Commissioner Campbell, a weak, wordy sort of man; Captain Pickett, to some extent, whose main fault perhaps has been bad judgment in allowing himself to be used as a tool by the main conspirators. ...

All this wretched performance of Harney is the legitimate result of popular government. It was to please the dear people that Harney made his *coup*, and he did please the people, silly, blind fools that they are.

Excerpt of letter from Captain Lewis C. Hunt, Company C, to Mrs. McBlair, November 18, 1859.

\* \* \*

Hubbs stood on a table, lifted the paper containing the fruits of his afternoon's labors, and faced the dozens of American settlers who crowded into the near-empty building in the village.

"I'll read this next resolution in its entirety, and then we'll take a vote. It reads: 'Resolved: That the title set up by Great Britain—to justify an invasion of American soil, to kidnap and try by a foreign court an American citizen—the

attempted occupancy by a British fleet, blockading the port
of San Juan—is futile and preposterous in the highest degree.
Geography and hydrography clearly point out the boundary
line defined by the treaty. That the channel of the Canal de
Haro is the one alone therein referred to straightest and most
direct, much the wider, deeper and the better of navigation
as proven by the soundings. There can be no doubt of the
American title. That the doubt, if any exist, is entirely
dispelled by the language of the treaty, surrendering as much
of Vancouver's Island as lies south of the forty-ninth parallel
to Great Britain. That such was the meaning of the treaty,
and such has ever since been recognized, in the erection of
countries in the Territory of Oregon and Washington, and
the exercise of judicial jurisdiction for years over said Island.'
All those in favor?"

Nearly every hand in the small warehouse reached for
the leaky ceiling.

"Opposed?"

No hands were raised.

Flora stood at the back and watched Hubbs preside
over the public meeting that he and a few others had called
for all American residents of the island. They had
assembled at the newly constructed warehouse of Baker &
Roberts, one of the many new businesses on the island that
risked seeing its investment destroyed by the departure of
American troops. The threat of war might have caused
countless sleepless nights, but it had also fattened plenty of
wallets. Many of the island's new residents had arrived in
the hope of finding the fortune that had eluded them in the
Fraser River gold rush, and they were not about to watch
passively as a second chance at fortune slipped away in the
name of peace.

Flora felt a sense of pride that Hubbs was one of the
organizers of the meeting, bringing the community together.
But she had also never seen such angry passion unleashed at
authorities, whether British or American, and it made her
worry for the future of the island, regardless of which flag
would be flown over its soil.

"The resolution is passed unanimously," Hubbs

announced. "I'm going to turn over the chair to Fitch, who'll present a resolution to nominate General Harney as the Democratic candidate for U.S. President."

A cheer rose up across the warehouse, not for Fitch, but for the idea that Harney could be the next President of the United States. Flora shuddered at the thought of putting a country of so much wealth and promise into the hands of a man who had demonstrated such a careless approach to diplomacy. But it wasn't the first time she'd heard suggestions that Harney should run for President. Rather, it was such a common suggestion that there were those who claimed that the entire San Juan affair had been part of a campaign by Harney to portray himself as Presidential material.

Hubbs walked to the back of the warehouse and joined Flora, taking her hand in one of his first public showings of affection.

A man standing in front of them turned and reached out to shake Hubbs' hand. "You should run for the Assembly next time. The whole island'll vote for you."

Hubbs returned the handshake. "Oh, I don't know. There are plenty of qualified men on the island to do that."

Flora smiled at his answer, recognizing it as a poor attempt to disguise his ambition, then turned her attention back to the front of the room where the future of a far more ambitious man was being subjected to a vote. As with the prior resolution, its passage was a foregone conclusion, and of entirely no consequence.

* * *

Flora gazed about the empty saloon and imagined the diverse characters that might have once consumed liquor, played cards, and done whatever other forms of carousing were whispered about in judgmental conversations. She had seen inside the doorways of saloons before, in Victoria, glancing inside while quickly walking past, certain to not pause long enough that it might be seen as loitering. Each time she had caught the odor of the establishment in a quick breath that she'd immediately exhaled as soon as she was beyond the doorway. Cheap whiskey. Stale smoke. Stale humanity. The same smell hung in the air of Stephen Boyce's empty saloon in San Juan Town, though with far less intensity since it had only been open for three months.

"Was it what you expected?" Lucinda asked, pouring a cup of tea from a teapot that Flora imagined had seen little use.

"I suppose. The few times I've glanced inside a saloon before I never noticed what the building looked like. I was so busy looking at the people. Now that it's empty it's just an ordinary building."

Lucinda's eldest children played at the back of the small room, likely unaware of the building's former service. The saloon was a casualty of the war that never was. Although a willing clientele had been immediate and sizeable, there hadn't been time to generate enough income to pay off the substantial setup costs before the joint occupation had been announced and the customers had begun to depart the island. The added pressure of the dual magistrates—Crosbie and deCourcy—and their combined efforts to shut down the island's whiskey peddlers, had further saddled the business. And the weeks of anticipation for General Scott's settlement meant that arrangements had been in the works for the reduction of American troops on the island, ensuring prompt departures of several companies as soon as the settlement was announced. An equally prompt business decision was made about the saloon. Stephen Boyce and his partner, John S. Bowker, recognized that the fifty or so U.S. soldiers who would remain on the island could never support the business, and so the saloon would be shut down before further losses could mount. It was a decision that had been repeated by businesses throughout the village in recent days, as tents and buildings disappeared, prostitutes dwindled in number, and merchants of all kinds followed their customers back to their respective forts.

Flora hesitated with the question she'd been desperate to ask all morning. "You're not going to leave the island, are you?"

"Worried you're going be left all alone here?"

"Rather worried, yes. A month ago there was a new town being built under our feet. Next week it might be an empty island with nothing but a couple farms, a few hundred sheep and a few dozen troops staring each other down."

Lucinda shrugged. "We'll probably stay a while to see what happens, see if the claim we staked out holds up. But the boys need to be in school, and now the chances of setting up one here are far less certain if more families leave. We're all setting down roots just as the island's losing its every comforts of civilization. Doesn't seem too wise."

Flora hesitated, having never considered any business in the tiny village to fall within her definition of a comfort of civilization. But she hadn't expected to hear herself expressing such uncertainty just weeks before her own marriage, or hearing Lucinda echo it back to her.

"I suppose I won't have children for years, so the lack of a school isn't a problem for me," she replied in an effort to counter her prior comments. "And we're going to be out on that point by ourselves. I suppose it won't matter much if the rest of the island is filled with people, or if it's empty."

"After a few months of marriage, you'll want to spend time with other people. I promise you that." Lucinda smiled and patted Flora's hand. "He seems a good man. Smart. I know Stephen wouldn't have asked him to settle these affairs if he didn't think so."

Flora looked across the room to where Hubbs sat at a table, between Boyce and Bowker, pouring over the financial records for the business. The business partners were still on speaking terms, but little more, and had decided that an amicable liquidation of their business would only be possible if they hired someone to arbitrate the remaining disputes over the division of assets and unpaid debts. Hubbs wasn't a lawyer, but he was well-educated, he had a government position on the island that related to financial matters, and his father was a lawyer. That made him the most likely candidate to arbitrate their dispute on an island with few other options.

"I don't imagine he'll finish before we leave tomorrow,"

Flora cautioned. "He's planning to come back after we meet with Reverend Cridge. But by the time I come back, I'll be a married woman."

It sounded peculiar to say aloud, as if she needed to practice it more times to get used to the sound of the words spilling from her lips. As if she needed to say it aloud as a means to measure the reactions of the listeners, and the emotions of her own that she still struggled to understand.

"Mrs. Hubbs," Lucinda proclaimed with a grin. "Sort of rolls off the tongue."

"Mrs. Hubbs," Flora repeated, with less certainty. "I just don't feel like a Mrs."

"You never do. It'll always sound like they're talking about your mother-in-law or some other old woman."

"My mother-in-law's not much older than you are—not that you're old, of course. I mean you're both quite young. Never mind me. I'm just a little muddled today. There's so much change right now."

Flora tested the tea in her cup and found that it had cooled more than she preferred while she'd been busy talking. She took a long sip and let the concept of change circle about in her mind. Her home. Her friends. Her name. Her marital status. The direction for her entire future. She had set it all in motion with a simple answer to a complicated question, just as the entire island was undergoing material changes of its own. But change was everywhere around her, and she would need to adjust to all of it.

✳ ✳ ✳

Everyone at the table was silent as Isabella delivered grace in French. Flora hadn't seen such a spread at the Ross kitchen table in years. She'd left San Juan Island feeling the pressure to impress the family with her fiancé, but it was clear that her family felt at least as much pressure to impress Hubbs, as if an ordinary dinner might spoil the entire engagement.

"So's it true what they say 'bout you, stoppin' those

boats?" William reached across the table for the pot of stewed beef.

"William! Shush!" Flora sank in her chair, having feared just such a question from William.

"It's in the papers," he insisted, to justify his question.

"You can't believe everything you read in the newspapers, William," Hubbs replied.

"I do if it's 'bout me. Only way I know what I got arrested for," William replied, with a smirk that bordered on outright pride.

"Flora said in a letter you're building a house on the point," Mary said quickly, trying to silence her brother.

"It's just about ready to live in," Hubbs replied.

"Which means it'll be challenging for the first few weeks," Flora added.

"Do people ask what you're doin', marryin' the enemy?"

"William!" Flora stared him down, knowing it would do no good.

"There are no enemies for our family," Isabella offered, more for Hubbs' benefit than William's.

"Exactly," Alexander added, looking directly at William. "You lived half your life at Nisqually, making you as much American as him. If Paul's the enemy, then half of you's your own worst enemy, too."

William had already proven the point by being his own worst enemy on regular and repeated occasions. It had never crossed Flora's mind before when Hubbs' younger brother had helped build the house, but she realized how similar William and Charles were. She made a mental note to ensure that her marriage to Hubbs didn't bring the two young men into any more contact than necessary, concluding that each could prove to be a terrible influence on the other.

As the family passed the dishes around, Flora surveyed her family members and kept a mental scorecard on how Hubbs was doing with each. Mary clearly adored him from the start, although Flora thought she also detected a hint of jealousy. William was on the fence, as if he hadn't yet baited Hubbs enough to see what he was made of. But his support would take time, since Hubbs wasn't about to stand up to him too aggressively at his first meeting, especially with Isabella and the rest of his family present. Alexander seemed more intimidated than impressed. They were about the same age, but Hubbs had the east coast and European upbringing that could be intimidating to a man born and bred along the coast, as well as having a government position to his name. And Isabella spent less time reading Hubbs than reading Flora, searching her daughter for signs that she was happy. Enough smiles had passed between them already that Flora knew Isabella was seeing everything she needed to see.

Across the table, Hubbs regaled Alexander with his tale of stopping and boarding the *Julia*, and his subsequent visit to the *Satellite*. He told the tale from the point of view of the story's hero, and ensured that every detail secured his position in that role. Flora found herself smiling at her earlier insecurities. Of course her family would love her fiancé. He exuded charm when he wanted to make the effort, he had stories to share that would impress any audience as long as they didn't know which parts were true, and he had doted on her in a manner that was loving, yet within acceptable boundaries.

Flora turned her attention to a second helping of turnip mash, realizing that she remained nervous about the meeting they would have with Cridge the following morning. Dinner with her family would be good practice for Hubbs, to prepare for the more serious and probing inquiries he could expect from Cridge. And as she watched her family react to Hubbs' self-aggrandizing yet entertaining tale, she concluded that her fiancé was well-prepared to deal with Cridge's critical eye.

\* \* \*

"And you've never been married before, Mr. Hubbs?" Reverend Cridge asked politely, noticing the reaction on Flora's face. He hoped that her expression was a result of the directness of his question, rather than the possibility of

Hubbs' answer. But the potential for such surprise was precisely why he insisted on meeting with every couple he would marry, and why he asked questions that one betrothed might not ask the other, whether out of politeness, ignorance, or fear. Having such meetings at his residence over tea seemed to lower the defenses of each putative husband and obtain more truthful answers.

"Widowed. Almost two years ago."

"Oh, my deepest condolences."

"We were married in the Charlottes, by their traditions, so of course it wouldn't have been recognized under the law in Washington Territory. Nor in your church, I imagine."

Cridge nodded. A marriage to Flora would be Hubbs' first legal marriage under Washington's restrictive marriage law, since her Indian background wasn't more than fifty percent of her blood, unlike her predecessor's. And while 'widowed" was likely an important concept for Hubbs to recognize, it was irrelevant to the propriety of a wedding in the Church of England if the first marriage had been merely a frontier marriage. A sin, certainly. But not a bar to a subsequent marriage. Any contrary policy would preclude a legal marriage for half the men in the colony.

"And I take it the two of you haven't yet known one another in a biblical sense?"

"No," Hubbs replied with a delivery that barely disguised his disappointment.

"Heavens, no, Reverend," Flora exclaimed.

"It's a question I must ask, my dear." He wondered if Flora had noticed just how different their reactions had been to his simple question, though it was a difference in tone that was typical of most couples he interviewed. "Of course, I'm sure you both understand the very serious undertaking of a marriage between a man and his wife. In the eyes of God, you're making a sacred commitment to one another, and to Him, to care for each other, mind, body and soul, till death do you part."

Cridge sat back and attempted to read Hubbs. He wished he'd been given more warning about the meeting so that he could have discretely inquired around town about the man. From what little he knew, it was clear that Hubbs wouldn't be a quiet husband who would bore Flora with repetition or silence. A restless energy bubbled beneath the surface, and it seemed clear that he would challenge Flora as much as she could be expected to challenge him. Cridge presumed that Flora would need such a man to be happy, and he expected that Flora had already figured this out for herself.

"Flora, my dear." Mary Cridge entered the Cridge's front parlor and reached out to hug Flora.

"Mrs. Cridge. I missed you so much."

Mary Cridge pulled back slightly from the hug, took Flora's hand, and placed it on her belly. Flora looked up excited, questioning.

"I think it'll be a girl," Mary said, smiling.

"Oh, I'm so happy for you."

Cridge felt a mild blush creep onto his cheek, surprised that his wife would share such an intimate detail when she hadn't yet been introduced to Hubbs. The introduction was a formality that Flora addressed while Cridge pondered what other private matters his wife might reveal in conversation. The news that they were expecting their third child had come as welcome news, as both of them wanted a large family. But it had also come in the midst of a battle over Cridge's contract renewal, and the resulting uncertainty about whether he would continue to receive a salary from the government. His worries about feeding his family were only exacerbated by the pending arrival of another hungry mouth.

"Is there a date for the ceremony yet?" Mary Cridge asked.

"We're hoping for something very soon, so we can be together over the winter," Flora replied. "It won't be a large wedding. If I start inviting the daughters of Company officials to Mr. Hubbs' wedding ... well, I'm sure you can appreciate why we have reasons to keep it to family and close friends."

"What dates have you given them, Edward?" Mary inquired.

"I've given them no dates, yet, my dear. We're still discussing their commitment to one another, their commitment to the good Lord, and such other matters as fall within my bailiwick."

"Well, figuring out the date so we can start planning is enough in my bailiwick as well," Mary answered. "I presume it'd be ... January?"

Mary Cridge leaned over her husband's desk and thumbed through his appointments calendar.

"Early December, if possible, ma'am," Hubbs offered. "Before winter sets in."

"The week of December 5th, perhaps? Edward, your calendar is fairly open that week."

"Perhaps Tuesday, the 6th?" Flora suggested. "So it won't interfere with your Wednesday service?"

"Fine, the 6th it is," Mary Cridge confirmed, entering it onto her husband's desk calendar.

Cridge smiled in slight annoyance at his loss of control over the proceedings. "Very well, we have the critical task of the date out of the way. Now, about your eternal salvation ..."

\* \* \*

A serious insurrection broke out at Harpers Ferry, Virginia, on Sunday night, October 16th. The parties engaged in this outbreak were a body of two hundred and fifty Abolitionists and a gang of negroes under command of a man named Brown.—The first acts of the insurrectionists were to stop the trains going East and cut the telegraph wires. The first intelligence received was from a station east of Harper's Ferry. Intense excitement prevailed in Baltimore, Washington, Richmond, Frederick and Martinsburg, and all through the adjoining States, and immediate steps were taken to pour into Harper's Ferry a military force to quell the insurrection, while

precautionary measures were adopted against
a general uprising of the blacks.

*The Puget Sound Herald*, Friday, December 2, 1859, p. 2.

\* \* \*

The *General William S. Harney* lay on its starboard side in the uncommonly heavy surf, while much of its cargo—at least the cargo that floated—was scattered across Griffin Bay. A few dozen soldiers from Company C scrambled to save the livestock that had been onboard, mostly cows and sheep that struggled to keep their heads above the churning waves.

Griffin, Aleck, and Angus watched from the water's edge to see if they could be of assistance, having hurried to the beach as soon as word of the wreck had reached them at the farm. The schooner *General William S. Harney* had been hired to carry the remaining property of Pickett's Company D back to Fort Bellingham. But just as the ship had been fully loaded, a winter storm that had been building all morning reached fever pitch, and gale force winds blew the boat off its anchors until it capsized.

It became clear as soon as the men reached the beach that the situation was more under control than the initial calls for assistance had suggested. Without a boat at their disposal, Griffin and the others could do little but watch as the last of the surviving livestock were rescued by the soldiers. The realization that no lives, human or animal, appeared to be at stake any longer allowed Griffin to relax and find a lesson in the wreck.

"Seems almost poetic. The General's namesake, carrying away the last of Pickett's things, driven off its moorings and foundering on the rocks."

"Harney wasn't foundering when they nominated him for President the other night," Angus responded.

"Fools vote for fools. But this island's the only place where there's enough of 'em to push a candidate like him. He's got no more future than that scuttled schooner."

Griffin wondered if any of the troops also would

describe the wreck as poetic, or opt instead for divine judgment. Pickett's departure with Company D a few days earlier had coincided with Mount Baker erupting a massive volcanic plume into the sky, directly over Fort Bellingham. It had spooked many of the soldiers as they'd boarded the *Massachusetts* for the voyage, terrified that it was a sign in judgment of their actions. For that to be followed by a storm so severe that it scuttled the *Harney* and destroyed many of their possessions on the very beach where they had landed four months earlier was certain to further their fears.

Griffin watched a moment longer, until it was clear that the soldiers had rescued all of the remaining livestock, then he nudged Aleck and Angus to follow him back up the hill. The storm was only going to worsen, and they had livestock of their own to protect.

✳ ✳ ✳

Hubbs was certain that he'd never been colder. He hadn't planned on paddling his canoe to his own wedding, but the unexpectedly harsh winter storm had made it impossible for him to find passage on any of the usual schooners that plied the waters between the island and Victoria.

Wet snow and salt water mixed in the bottom of the canoe, soaking Hubbs' trembling legs. He had left before dawn and had paddled much of the morning, yet he was barely halfway across the Canal de Haro. Every few minutes he would need to put down his paddle, bail out the icy water, and then warm his hands before resuming his paddling.

He hadn't seen a winter storm this severe, this cold, since he'd lived in the northern islands, when he would have had the good sense to not go out in such a blizzard. In a canoe. Alone. But he couldn't turn back. In a matter of hours he'd be married in Victoria. If he made it there. The guest list might have been rather modest, but his presence was most definitely expected.

The only consolation was that the storm came from the

Northeast. It was colder than a storm from the West, but the winds hit his canoe broadside, or at times acted as a tailwind. A headwind this cold and fierce would have made the journey all but impossible.

Hubbs could barely feel his fingers any longer, but hoped that the exertion of the paddling would keep enough blood flowing to them to prevent any permanent damage. His father and brother should have arrived in Victoria the evening before, but he found himself repeatedly daydreaming that the steamer they would have taken from Port Townsend would come alongside his canoe at any moment and rescue him from his miserable plight. It gave him something to occupy his mind and distract his attention from the misery that occupied his body. Hubbs dug his paddle into the waves and pushed his canoe forward, hoping desperately that he would arrive in time, and that the service at Christ Church would be his wedding rather than his funeral.

* * *

Flora searched for her pale reflection in the vestry window, hoping to confirm that Mary had adequately repaired the damage that the snow and wind had caused to her hair. The long walk to the church through deep snow had been unanticipated, but necessary, after their wagon had become stranded before they'd even reached the edge of the Ross property. She worried that her hair seemed far too flat in her faint reflection, but assured herself that it would improve as it dried.

"I think Elizabeth would love knowing I'm there," Mary insisted, "The idea of her daughters being raised by her sister—or sisters, if Catherine helps out—but I'll live with them, so I'll be there for them all the time."

Flora listened to her sister ramble on about her plans. It was entirely in keeping for Mary to hold back news like this until the morning of Flora's own wedding in order to ensure that she would garner an appropriate share of the attention. Initial reactions from other family members had been hesitant. Some were troubled by the idea of Mary living with her sister's widowed husband, even if it was on the pretense of taking care of the children, while others expressed an open dislike for Charles Wren that they'd kept to themselves as long as Elizabeth had been alive. Yet Mary seemed unmoved by any contrary opinions.

"You do realize," Flora cautioned, "that many will see this as scandalous. To live with him, but not as his wife."

"I'm the children's aunt," Mary protested. "There's nothing scandalous in family caring for family. Although, if he were to fancy me, perhaps marriage could be in our future."

Flora looked up with relief to see Reverend Cridge enter the vestry.

"Is he here?" she asked, with a hint of desperation in her tone.

"Not yet, my dear. But I'm sure it's only because of the storm. Mary, would you mind giving us a few minutes?"

"I'll let you know if he gets here." Mary rose and left the vestry.

Flora noticed the "if" in Mary's parting words and wondered if it had been an intended slight. She assured herself that if Mary's planned courtship of Wren should come to fruition she would feel no similar jealousy for such a union.

Cridge sat across from Flora and took her hand. "I've been waiting four years for the chance to marry off one of the unmarried Ross children. It never occurred to me that you'd be the first."

"Please say you approve."

"How could I do anything but approve of a marriage performed in the eyes of our Lord?"

"He's a good man. And I'm still going to be a nurse. I promise. Lucinda's going to be one of our closest neighbors. They staked a claim just north of Bellevue, and she's going to teach me so much—at least, if they stay on the island. But she's married, and she's still a nurse, and she has three children, so I know I can do it, too."

"There, there, don't get all worked up before the

ceremony, child. I've no doubt you'll do that and more to fulfill your Christian duty. I've never doubted it."

Flora smiled and relaxed, relieved to feel that her nuptials wouldn't tarnish her in his eyes.

"So then," Cridge continued, "I take it that sending you to care for Mr. Mcdonald's poor wife was the right thing to do."

Flora realized that in all the talk of marriage and the details of the ceremony she had never fully explained to Cridge how the experience on San Juan Island had gone for her. She told him about Anna and her illness, about Aleck and the difficulty he had shown in expressing his emotions until Anna was gone, about Father Rossi and his attitudes toward anyone with Indian blood, not to mention anyone from the Church of England, of the assistance of Dr. Craig, of her reconnection with Lucinda, and finally of Anna's death. It was a lengthy story that passed the time until Mary returned to announce that Hubbs had arrived. It was the first opportunity Flora had had since Anna's death to hear herself tell the story and truly understand what it had meant to her. And it was an extremely effective distraction to keep her from worrying about the groom's unexplained absence.

\* \* \*

"I require and charge you both," Cridge continued, "as ye will answer at the dreadful day of judgment when the secrets of all hearts shall be disclosed, that if either of you know any impediment why ye may not be lawfully joined together in matrimony, ye do now confess it. For be ye well assured, that if any persons are joined together otherwise than as God's Word doth allow, their marriage is not lawful."

As Cridge spoke, Flora glanced back at her family. Her mother was uncharacteristically in tears. William shuffled his feet out of boredom, only to be elbowed by Alexander to stand up straight. John and his wife, Genevieve, looked preoccupied and tired, most likely from eight month-old

Marie in Genevieve's arms. Mary, standing next to Flora as her maid of honor, sniffed back tears of her own.

Across the aisle sat one of the few new in-laws to attend, Paul Kinsey Hubbs, Senior, the father of the groom. He had left his pregnant wife and small child in Port Townsend for fear that the voyage on storm-driven waters would be a difficult journey for them. Charles Hubbs stood next to his older brother, his best man and witness, with a smile of mockery that seemed to be something of a permanent fixture on his face.

"Paul Kinsey Hubbs, Junior, wilt thou have this woman to be thy wedded wife, to live together after God's ordinance in the holy estate of matrimony? Wilt thou love her, comfort her, honor, and keep her in sickness and in health; and, forsaking all others, keep thee only unto her, so long as ye both shall live?"

"I will."

Flora was certain that she harbored no doubts, yet she was terrified by the realization that she would now be asked a similar question, except with the addition of the command to obey and serve her husband. She thought that she'd detected a tremor in Hubbs' response, but reassured herself that it would only have been from the cold. They had delayed the wedding a further twenty minutes after he'd arrived, just to ensure that he could warm up by the stove long enough to stop shaking.

Cridge turned to Flora and smiled. It was a smile of approval and pride, and Flora imagined that her father would have looked at her with a similar expression if he had lived to see the day.

"Flora Amelia Ross, wilt thou have this man to be thy wedded husband, to live together after God's ordinance in the holy estate of matrimony? Wilt thou obey him, and serve him, love, honor, and keep him in sickness and in health; and, forsaking all others, keep thee only unto him, so long as ye both shall live?"

"I will." The words escaped from her mouth with ease, as if she'd played no part in the decision to speak them aloud. The remainder of the service passed as if in a dream, and Flora found that she was listening to herself recite her vows while noticing flakes of snow falling outside the windows.

As Cridge led the guests in prayer, Flora realized that the ceremony was over. The ring was on her finger. The vows had been recited. She now was, and forever would be, Mrs. Paul K. Hubbs, Jr.

\* \* \*

## SAN JUAN QUESTION SETTLED.

A correspondent has favored us with the following important information:—

A joint occupation of the Island of San Juan has been agreed upon. The preliminary arrangements are already made, and the dangerous question settled at the altar of Hymen. Paul K Hubbs, Esq. U.S. Revenue collector for the Island of San Juan, on the part of the United States, and Miss Flora Ross, a true and loyal subject of Her Majesty Queen Victoria, resident of Bellevue, on the part of Great Britain, have agreed to enter into a matrimonial connection, and jointly occupy the Island. Therefore the high and mighty dignitaries of the two nations may congratulate themselves upon so happy a termination of that vexed and dangerous question, which threatened to involve two of the greatest nations of the earth in a terrible war. How long they will continue to peaceably enjoy a joint occupancy depends entirely upon the affection and respect each shows to the other. May the question of their boundary line never again be misunderstood, so as to call for the arbitration of our countries' courts.

*The Victoria Gazette*, Wednesday, December 7, 1859, p. 2.

# Part Three: Floraville, 1865

# Southern Peninsula of San Juan Island, 1865

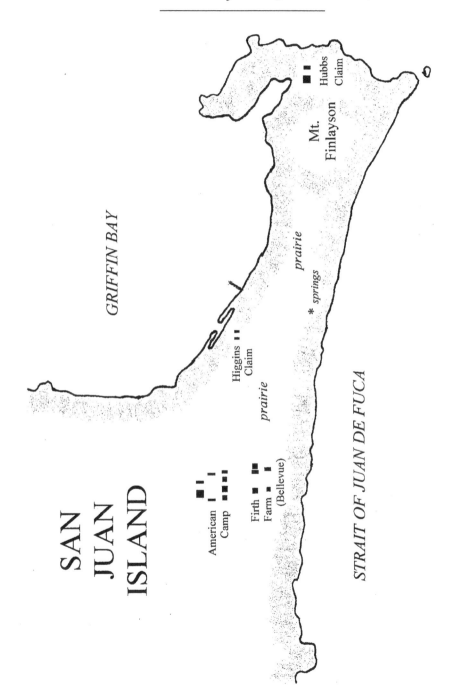

Chapter 16

San Juan Island, February 2, 1865:

Flora shut the front door. The interior temperature of their home was almost as frigid as the morning's winter chill outside, but that had been the purpose in leaving the door open for ten minutes. The interior air had felt heavy, stale and warm, but the outside air carried the fresh scent that always followed a night of heavy rain, and the breeze that had swept into the cabin had surely helped to purge the air of harmful elements.

A ragged cough pulled her attention back to the small bed in the corner, where Paul K. Hubbs, III, a few months shy of turning three, fought an illness that still seemed difficult to identify. The symptoms were common in childhood illnesses. His throat and tongue were raw and coated, his cough was violent but sporadic, and his fever was constant. Flora's only consolation was that the child lacked the rashes or other skin ailments that would suggest scarlet fever (or scarlatina), measles, or diphtheria, and it allowed her to cling to the hope that he was suffering from a far less aggressive fever that would pass.

The winter had already taken the lives of many small children throughout the region, especially in the more heavily populated towns of Victoria, Olympia and Portland. Reverend and Mary Cridge had lost their youngest child, Frederick, two months earlier, at only ten months of age, most likely from scarlatina. And word had reached Flora in recent days that other children in the Cridge household were now fighting the illness as well.

Flora placed the back of her hand on Paul's forehead. His temperature felt unchanged, but she was certain that the fresh air would at least help his throat and lungs.

"*True nursing ignores infection, except to prevent it. Cleanliness, fresh air from open windows, are the only defence a true nurse either asks or needs.*" They were words written by Florence Nightingale in her seminal *Notes on Nursing*, published in 1859, reflecting wisdom that Nightingale had accumulated while caring for wounded soldiers in the Crimea. And they were words that Flora had adopted as a fundamental rule of her own nursing practice. She had administered mercurous chloride to help purge Paul's body of toxins, and she'd given him teas of blackberry root and poplar bark to ease the pain in his throat and lessen his cough. Had her mother, Isabella, or Dr. Helmcken been present, she was certain that both medicines would have been among the first prescribed treatments. But neither would have been as effective in a room of stale air.

She placed another log in the fireplace to ensure that the fresh air wouldn't turn Paul's fever into a chill, and then lay on the small bed to add a mother's comfort to her remedies. She assured herself that most afflicted children survive such illnesses. But she couldn't let go of the fear that Paul might be her sole opportunity to have a family. Conception had proven more difficult than she had expected. And though she and Hubbs had tried to have more children since Paul's birth, their efforts had failed.

Flora had blamed herself for an inability to conceive or carry a child to term in the first years of their marriage. She now accepted that Hubbs' frequent and lengthy absences were at least as much of a cause as any physical flaw, but blamed herself for whatever she had done to lessen her husband's interest. At only twenty-two, she was no longer the girl that Hubbs had married, but neither had she allowed herself to become matronly. That wouldn't have been possible while running a farm single-handedly while her husband pursued other endeavors.

Hubbs had been gone for nearly a week and was unaware that his son was ill. She had no way to reach him, primarily because she had no idea where he was. Throughout the five years of their marriage, Hubbs had pursued a series of careers that often took him away from the island. For several years, he had served as Justice of the Peace for the San Juan archipelago. For a time, he had been Postmaster, followed by an attempted stockbroker business. He had set up a ferry across a river west of Bellingham, and he had been a participant in the island's developing limestone quarries. Until recently, he had continued his post as deputy revenue collector. He had even been elected to the Washington Territorial Legislature, where he'd served during the Tenth Session in 1862-63 as a House member for Whatcom County in the Assembly, while his father had served concurrently on the territory's senior body, the Legislative Council. That position had been the highlight of his years of struggle, and Flora could take credit for much of that success. She had worked hard at elevating his attire and appearance, had chatted with wives at community events, and had ensured whenever possible that Hubbs' speeches had suggested confidence rather than arrogance.

But it had been a short-lived political career, lasting only one session. Hubbs had insisted that he would manage to return for a future term. And since most elections in the young territory were prearranged acclamations, he often traveled to Olympia to further his connections to the territory's power brokers in hopes of obtaining their blessing for a return to the legislature. His efforts had proven fruitless thus far.

Flora often wondered what her husband had done to alienate those who could have lengthened his time in politics, particularly given the advantage he had from his father's dominant role on the Legislative Council. It seemed that his increasing favor for whiskey had followed the failure of his political aspirations. But perhaps it had been the other way around? Although it didn't much matter either way. Hubbs turned to whiskey for support instead of turning to his wife. His absences grew and were increasingly unexplained.

A distant beating of hooves pulled her from her thoughts and sent her mind running through the list of most likely visitors. She rose from the small bed, confirmed that the musket was leaning by the door, and then peered through the front window to see Robert Firth approaching the cabin on horseback.

Firth was a stocky Scotsman in his mid-thirties who had taken over management of Bellevue Farm from Charles Griffin three years earlier, after Griffin had accepted a transfer to Red River. By that time it had become a pale reflection of the thriving farm Flora had seen on the first day she'd arrived on the island. It had been diminished in size by the growth of the American military camp and by the competing land claims of settlers across the island, deprived entirely of its vast sheep runs and grazing fields. The Company's reasons for operating Bellevue evaporated as quickly as the farm's acreage, and it had made the decision to lease the remaining lands and buildings rather than operate it as a Company business. Firth, and his wife, Jessie, had run the farm as their own ever since. Flora still found it odd to visit them, finding that images of the people who'd once lived at Bellevue Farm would flash across her mind, as if demanding to be remembered.

Flora opened the door and stepped onto the small porch. "Good morning, Robert."

"Mornin' to ye, Flora," Firth replied with the thick accent of the Orkney Islands. He didn't dismount, suggesting that it would be a brief visit. "I'm huntin' up a stray calf. Gone missin' through a break in the east fence. Thought it might'a dandered this far."

"I haven't seen it, but then I've only been to the barn this morning for chores. Please look wherever you wish."

Firth nodded toward the cabin. "How's the boy?"

"No real change in the past two days, but that's positive news. And Lexie?"

"She's mendin'. The lass'll see her fourth birthday, day after morn'."

"I'm sorry I haven't been able to visit to check on her. But I can't leave Paul alone, and I can't bring him with me."

"Lucinda's been by."

Flora nodded and struggled to suppress the feelings of inadequacy that she'd felt in recent years. Lucinda and Stephen Boyce had moved back to Victoria shortly after Flora's marriage to Hubbs, to enroll their sons in school. And for a period of a few years, Flora had experienced the opportunity to provide nursing services across the island. But ever since the Boyces had returned to the island and settled a mile to the northwest of their original claim, the island's residents had turned to Lucinda's greater experience. No one who was traveling to the south end of the island in search of nursing care would pass Lucinda's farm and ride an extra two miles for a less experienced nurse.

Lucinda had always been more than willing to act as a mentor, but Flora's opportunities to learn from her friend were diminished by her responsibilities running the farm. Hubbs knew nothing about farming and had no interest in learning. For so many years, Flora had wanted to believe that she was answering a calling as a nurse. But in recent years, it had more often felt that she had become a farmer, like her mother.

"I was about to put on a kettle for tea. Would you like to warm up before continuing your search?"

"Very kind o' you, but I should be gettin' on. Jus' wanted to kin if all's well here."

Flora smiled her appreciation. Hubbs' absences were no secret among her friends, and the Firths were her closest neighbors. Robert Firth had given her frequent and invaluable assistance with so many tasks that were beyond Flora's physical ability to carry out alone. She couldn't help but quickly run through a mental list of possible assistance she might seek from him while he was there.

"Thank you for looking in. I'm sure as soon as Mr.

Hubbs returns and can watch over Paul, I'll be back out there helping Lucinda."

Firth smiled and spurred his horse to ride on. Flora entered the cabin and closed the door behind her. Paul was asleep, his hoarse breathing seemed slightly less ragged, and she took his condition as an opportunity to make the tea she had suggested to Firth, but for her own benefit. The fire hadn't yet raised the temperature in the cabin, and unlike Paul, she wasn't shielded from the cold by a heavy quilt. She hung the kettle over the fire, placed another log onto the flames, and pulled her shawl closer, wondering if Florence Nightingale had ever questioned the wisdom of her own advice after returning from Crimea to the cold, damp air of London.

* * *

Doctor Helmcken sat on the side of the bed and took Cecilia's hand in his. It felt colder than it had seemed just minutes before. Her breathing was just as noisy, but less even and less frequent. Even if he hadn't had years of medical training, Helmcken would have understood that his wife was dying. She was only thirty, and had given birth to six surviving children. But the arduous and painful birth of their most recent child, a boy they had named Cecil, had left her body unable to heal. Pneumonia had set in, and she had no strength to fight the disease.

Helmcken had seen so much death in his years as Company surgeon, and had so successfully hardened himself to the concept, that he found himself unable to express any emotion while watching life slip from the body of his own beloved. His experience told him that Cecilia would be gone by nightfall, or by the following morning at the latest. But he couldn't wait in vigil for her passing. Children all across the city lay sick and dying from scarlet fever or diphtheria. He couldn't afford the luxury of holding his wife's hand for her last hours if it meant that several children might die without his medical care. He assured himself that he might come to a different conclusion if he held any hope for the possibility that she might awaken and be aware of his presence. But it wouldn't happen.

A brief cry of protest from the tiny lungs of Cecil drew Helmcken's attention across the room, to where Alice Good, one of Cecilia's younger sisters, held the infant in her arms. Once Alice Douglas, she had married Charles Good, her father's private secretary, in a scandalous elopement four years earlier, though the couple eventually returned to Governor Douglas' favor. She, her mother—now Lady Douglas following her husband's recent investiture and retirement—and her youngest sister, Martha, had been caring for Cecilia and the child in recent days with the assistance of Dr. Israel Powell, while Helmcken had tended to sick children around town and maintained his duties as Assembly Speaker. It had always been his practice to rely on other physicians such as Powell to attend to his own family members, but it was a practice that had never before left him feeling so emotionally torn.

"If she were awake, she would tell me to tend to the others," he expressed more for his own benefit than for Alice's or Martha's.

"She would," Alice assured him. "And perhaps she'll awaken after you return."

Helmcken nodded despite his certainty that she would not. He turned back to his wife, wishing that his final memory of her could be of a smile, the brightness of her eyes, or her hearty laughter. He leaned down, kissed her, and then rose from the bed and reached for his black leather bag.

\* \* \*

Hubbs realized that it was morning only when he felt the girl slip from under the blanket. He smiled to himself, knowing that she wasn't leaving, but that she was rising to prepare their morning meal.

He opened his eyes just enough to see her slender body move across the tiny cabin, dimly lit by the remains of the fire and the rays of morning light that shone through the sole window and through the many cracks in the rough wooden walls he'd constructed. The light had a bright, white tone that informed him that snow had fallen overnight. The girl's breath hung in the air as she'd yet to revive the fire enough to chase away the chill, yet she remained naked. She knew that Hubbs was watching. Her actions betrayed that knowledge by the way she moved about her routine. Hubbs wanted to believe that she was displaying herself to give him pleasure, but he understood that she was using the only means she had of asserting a measure of control of him. And he didn't mind in the slightest.

The cabin was little more than a lean-to, and Hubbs was somewhat surprised it had remained standing throughout the early months of the winter. Yet it was where Hubbs felt at home. Close to nature. Free of responsibilities. And at peace. He'd regaled the girl with his stories of life with the Haida, a tribe that her own people feared. They were the same stories he had told Flora. But while his wife had reacted with shock and apparent disbelief, the girl had reacted with awe, and ever since had accorded Hubbs the position that a man in her society would hold in a marriage. His job was hunting, warfare and the spoils of war that he would bring to her, even if that involved only a fishing net or the warfare of capitalist ideology. Her job was everything else.

Hubbs reached out and pulled her onto the bed, thinking that he'd caught her unaware. She grinned and pulled back the blanket to reveal a body that displayed how much he wanted and needed her. She reached down and took him in her hand, carefully balancing pleasure and control in tandem. Hubbs lay back and enjoyed the pleasure, until deciding that the moment had arrived to roll his body onto hers and reassert his own illusion of control, even though he understood that, no matter the physical position, she already held him firmly in the palm of her hand.

\* \* \*

Reverend Cridge relinquished his place on the edge of the bed to Dr. Helmcken, and instead lowered himself into a chair beside the bed of his son, Edward Scott. Each tortured breath that the seven year-old struggled to pull into his lungs tore at Cridge's heart. He considered losing himself in the solace of prayer, but prayer hadn't kept their son Frederick from dying of what had most likely been the same illness two months earlier. Prayer hadn't given Edward Scott the strength to fight the fever since it had set in. And prayer hadn't kept scarlet fever from attacking the bodies of their son, Eber, only six, lying in a bed across the room, and their daughter, Grace, just two, in the room next door.

He could feel Helmcken turn in his direction, but he couldn't bring himself to look into his friend's eyes. The two men had tended to so many men, women, and children who had died in the young colony—one tending to their medical needs and the other to their spiritual needs—that they had developed an unspoken language between them. He knew well the silent look that Helmcken would give him when there was nothing more a medical doctor could do beyond tending to pain, and only the spiritual needs remained. It was a look so familiar that he didn't need to raise his head to know that it was the look in Helmcken's eyes after examining Edward Scott.

Cridge hadn't needed a doctor's analysis to know that his son was dying. The boy had been vomiting the same putrid, blackish substance that Frederick had purged in his final days. His extremities were as cold as his younger brother's had been, even as a fever had raged in his upper body. And the sound and rhythm of his struggled breathing was a sound that Cridge had hoped to never hear again. The boy's soul was still in there, somewhere, but all Cridge could see was a physical body in the final stages of dying.

"The disease isn't yet as advanced in Eber and Grace."

Helmcken had offered the statement as consolation for the condition of Edward Scott. But Cridge couldn't ignore that it had been more than merely a diagnosis of Eber and Grace's present condition. It had implied a prediction.

He raised his eyes to meet those of his wife, Mary, seated across the small room on the edge of Eber's bed. He wanted to be able to offer her strength, but found himself desperate to find it in her eyes. Until two months earlier, they had been happily realizing their dream of raising a large family. The birth of Frederick had brought a sixth child into their home, in addition to Mary Bastian, a Nisqually orphan, and others who they would take into their home. But now Frederick was gone, and three more lay dying. The recent realization that a seventh child was growing in Mary's womb had come to the couple more as a cruel joke than a blessing.

The unexpected sound of a woman's tears drew all attention to the doorway. Alice Good arrived at the door, and once again, no words were required. Cridge instantly understood that the silent expression she conveyed to Helmcken on her tear-stained face was the same look his friend had given him just moments before, and he knew that Cecilia Helmcken was gone. It was a moment when any man in his position would step forward to comfort his friend with words of Christian faith. And as Edward Scott and Eber struggled for breath on either side of the room, he questioned whether it was a role he could possibly fulfill.

\* \* \*

"He doesn't look that sick."

Hubbs' dismissal of his son's illness angered Flora. She set a plate of shepherd's pie in front of him and returned to the iron stove to serve out her own dinner.

"He was deathly ill," she insisted, knowing he wouldn't believe her. "Was it not all over the Olympia area?"

Hubbs just grunted as he took his first bite.

"Did you hear about the Cridges? They lost four children. Four. Frederick, who I never even got to meet, Edward Scott, who was quite precocious, Eber, who had the sweetest disposition, and Grace, who was just a few months younger than Paul. My heart aches for them all. Could you imagine losing four children in a space of two months?"

She couldn't decide if Hubbs' second grunt suggested that he either couldn't imagine, or couldn't care to try. She took a seat across from him and took her first bites. It wasn't her best shepherd's pie. The potatoes she'd taken from the root cellar had a mealy consistency. She made a mental note to figure out how to increase the ventilation in the root cellar to better protect their harvests.

The small structure hadn't been constructed with a root cellar as its intended purpose, but as a jail cell, embedded into the hillside to reduce the number of walls through which a prisoner might escape. It had been a necessary addition to the farm immediately after their marriage, after Hubbs had been restored to his position of Magistrate and Justice of the Peace following Crosbie's departure from the island. The ventilation required for the health of a potato differed from the ventilation her husband had apparently decided was necessary for the health of a prisoner.

"Did you accomplish much in Olympia?" she asked, hoping to start the first conversation since his return that would cover anything other than illness or death.

"No way of knowing."

"There must be some way of knowing."

"There's no way of knowing."

"Perhaps if you spent more time here building a career that stands out, and less time trying to impress them by being there, they'd recognize you as the best representative for the area."

Hubbs slammed his fist on the table and rose from his seat. Flora jumped from the shock.

"This dinner tastes like shit. The least you could do after I've been gone is cook something decent."

"I had no idea you were coming back today, and the root cellar needs better ventilation to keep the potatoes from rotting."

"Then fix it."

Hubbs threw the back door open and stormed from the cabin. Flora watched him disappear across the field, stunned by his outburst. She ignored the tears that welled in her eyes, and turned back to her dinner in an effort to deny the realization that her husband had returned from a three-week absence and seemed less than pleased to be home. It was followed moments later by the realization that she shared the same emotion.

*** 

John Butts had hoped that his cell would be empty once he returned from his day of work, so that he could spend the rest of the afternoon enjoying a well-deserved nap, rather than having to listen to the stories his new cellmate was sure to go on about as soon as he had a captive audience. But the chances of having any time alone in his cell had been quashed by Capt. Jemmy Jones' pathetic escape attempt the week before. Liberties had been withdrawn, and Jones had been confined to his cell for all but a few minutes each afternoon.

Jones was standing in the open doorway of their cell as Butts arrived.

"You're back sooner'n expected," Jones began the moment Butts set foot inside their small cell. "Chain gang done?"

"One of the Chinamen crushed his foot with a massive stone, so we had to end early."

Butts realized that there was far too much glee in the tone of his voice. He hoped Jones recognized that the glee was purely a result of the early end to the workday, and had nothing to do with the injured prisoner's foot.

"And if you don't mind, I've been relishing the idea of a lengthy nap before dinner."

"How can ya sleep when there's so much t'be done?"

"What could there possibly be for us to do?"

"Ya see, Butts, that's what's different with us. This here's me first time in gaol. You've been here two, three dozen times?"

"I don't see any point in counting."

"Ya know Judge Pemberton's countin' each one."

"They put me in here for drinking a bottle of port."

"That ya stole afore ya drank. They put me here 'cause I canna pay back some of me creditors. Does that make a lick o' sense? Lock me up and take away me boat so I canna make any money to pay 'em all? Dunna make no sense to me."

Butts sighed as he heard sounds in the hallway that informed him that his chance to fall asleep in silence had just evaporated for good while his cellmate had droned on. The hallway between the cells and the front entrance was being swabbed clean. It meant that the hallway would be occupied by at least two guards overseeing the two prisoners carrying out the task because of the need to guard the open entrance door while the prisoners swabbed around it. And it meant noise right outside the cell until the hallway was spotless. His anger over the lost opportunity for a nap caused him to lash out.

"Well, if it don't make sense for you to be here, then perhaps you can do a better job escaping next time. Using mattress stuffing as fake hair wasn't remotely believable from twenty feet away. No one sleeps with their hat on. And the contours of your pillows under the blanket –"

Commotion in the hallway stopped Butts' lecture on the finer techniques of prison escape. He opened his eyes and looked up. Jones was gone. The commotion had escalated to yelling and scuffling, and then a gunshot, and all of it was disappearing into the distance. Butts jumped to his feet and peered into the hallway just as the door to the front room slammed shut. The guards were gone. Jones was gone. And he'd accomplished it without taking any of Butts' advice.

* * *

Flora pulled her shawl close to shield herself from the chilly breeze, and then took one last look back inside the small cabin before Lucinda followed behind her and shut the door. The emaciated body of twelve year-old Henry Myers, Jr., was laid out on a simple bed in the middle of the room.

His parents had brought their ailing son across the strait from their home on Lopez Island in the hope that the closest nursing care might save their son from scarlet fever. Stephen Boyce had found them an abandoned cabin a short distance from their farm, and Lucinda and Flora had tended to the boy in his last days.

Flora felt Lucinda take her hand and squeeze it supportively as they started back to the Boyce farm.

"I remember when I decided to be a nurse," Flora

began. "It was the idea of helping the old and the sick leave in less pain, balanced by bringing children into this world and ensuring the good health of the children and their mothers. I wasn't blind to the idea that I'd watch children die. But to see it like that ... what that disease did to that poor boy ..."

"It's never easy," Lucinda replied. "And sometimes I fear the only reason it's not as difficult as it once was is I've become numb to so much of what we do."

The two women walked in silence, allowing the gentle sounds of the evening to slowly replace the brutal images that remained dominant in their minds.

"I hear your man is back."

Flora heard hesitation in Lucinda's statement, and wondered if the hesitation was because of the events of the afternoon, or if she had intended something more personal in her question.

"He is. It's so wonderful to have him home."

"I'm so glad to hear that."

It wasn't until she looked over and saw Lucinda's forced smile that she realized that both of them had been lying, and that both of them knew it. Flora walked several paces in silence.

"Do you ever feel as though Stephen's changed since you married him?" she asked, concerned that the question might be taken as prying.

"Isn't that the goal of every wife?" Lucinda replied with a grin that quickly faded. "Husbands change, Flora. We all change. It's one reason marriage can be a struggle."

"Shouldn't we change together? Or shouldn't I at least know why he's changing in case there's something I can do differently?"

"You think it's your fault?"

"I don't know. That would make it easier. Then, at least, I could try to stop doing whatever I'm doing wrong."

Lucinda stopped in the path and turned to face Flora.

"If he's changed in ways that aren't for the better, then I doubt you had a thing to do with it. You know you can turn to me any time for help."

"Of course I know. You've been so generous to me as a teacher and a mentor —"

"I don't mean nursing advice, Flora. I mean help, with anything."

Lucinda nodded to confirm her point and then continued along the path to the Boyce farm. Flora hesitated for a moment, unnerved by the idea that there might be a reason that would lead her to seek help beyond mere advice from her friend, and far more unnerved by the feeling that they both already knew what it might be.

\* \* \*

## IDEAS ABOUT WOMEN.

Love in a woman's life is a history; in a man's an episode …

*The Vancouver Times*, March 8, 1865, p. 3.

\* \* \*

The first sensation Charles Wren noticed as he slowly regained consciousness was a terrible pain in his wrists and shoulders, followed by a feeling that his arms were being pulled from their sockets. A sudden sharp and unbearable pain across his back shocked him out of his stupor. He was hanging by his wrists. He was hanging from a tree. He recognized the forest. His shirt was gone. He struggled, but it only made the metal cuffs cut deeper into the skin of his wrists. The terrible pain seared across his back once again, as he felt the weighted tips of several strands of leather cut into his bare skin. He cried out in pain only to discover that his cries were muffled by a rag stuffed in his mouth.

The whip cut into his back a third time, delivered with as much force as its holder could muster. And once again, Wren's screams were muffled.

"What's the matter, Charlie? We thought this was somethin' you like."

"Least when you're doin' it to one o' your Indian wives."

They were the voices of two of Wren's neighbors, A.J. Burge and Charles McDaniel. Wren could see a third neighbor, Charles Mitchell, watching from the side. Burge and McDaniel had arrived in the territory in 1859 followed by rumors of a murderous past during the Fraser River gold rush. Wren had been quick to make enemies of them both, particularly after an unpaid loan to Burge had led to a court case later that year.

Wren could remember leaving the farm that morning to ride into Steilacoom. He could remember passing Burge on the path near Gravelly Lake, and offering a curt greeting. But he could remember nothing more.

The whip cut across his back a fourth time with more force than the first three blows. Through the pain, he could feel warm trickles of blood tracing paths across the raised welts and cuts that criss-crossed his skin.

"This here's a warning to you," McDaniel continued. "Either you leave the Territory and never come back, or we'll kill you, that new wife of yours, and the girls from the other one. And you'll be the one we kill last."

The whip cut into his back a fifth time, and Wren bolted upright in bed, screaming.

It took him a moment to realize that it had been a nightmare. The usual nightmare. He could still feel the pain in his back, and the blood trickling down his torso. The scars across his back seemed to carry the pain as a memory. He jumped in shock at the feel of a hand, before realizing that it was the hand of his second wife, Mary.

"Was it the same —"

"Of course it was the same," he responded swiftly enough to put an end to the conversation.

Mary Wren was a decade younger than Wren's first wife, and her older sister, Elizabeth, but she shared so many similar traits. Some of them, like her inability to understand when not to attempt a conversation with him, were particularly annoying.

A year had passed since Burge and McDaniel had attacked Wren in the woods east of his farm. Once the men had left, Wren had managed to free himself by fraying the rope that held the handcuffs to the limb above his head. He'd dragged himself into Steilacoom where he pressed charges against the men. He'd claimed that his assaulters intended to scare him from Washington Territory so that they could jump his extensive land claims. And he'd used the bloodied wounds that cut deep into his back as evidence.

Burge and McDaniel were arrested the same day and remanded for trial. Both men admitted assaulting Wren, but insisted it had been retribution for his own rumored attacks upon women, including his two wives. And despite the physical evidence of the wounds across Wren's back, and the confessions of the attackers, the jury subsequently acquitted each of the men, finding the charges against them to be "frivolous" and "not supported by the testimony." The verdict had underscored for Wren that the residents of Pierce County were no longer willing to put up with his rumored cattle rustling, his loans that carried usurious interest rates, his aggressive foreclosure tactics, and other offenses more lengthy in rumor than fact. And it underscored that the county's justice system wouldn't protect him and his family from his enemies. Within days, Wren, Mary, their four daughters by Elizabeth, and a son by Mary, had left Washington Territory for the Ross farm on Vancouver Island.

Wren re-established himself as a butcher in Victoria, though he continued to make frequent trips to Washington Territory to oversee his continuing business interests, which included the rental of his farm and other lands to various tenants in order to protect them from claim jumpers. But whenever he did so, he ensured that he had a well-armed supporter with him at all times.

"I could make you some –"

"I don't want tea."

Wren climbed from their bed and walked to the door, anxious for the whiskey that would calm his nerves enough that he'd eventually be able to get back to sleep. He could feel Mary's eyes silently pleading with him as he left the room, fearful that he would increasingly turn to whiskey in ways that had destroyed the lives of her brothers. But as he did most nights that the nightmare returned, he ignored her plea and continued downstairs.

\* \* \*

A Jerseyman was lately arrested for flogging a woman, and excused the act by saying he was near-sighted and thought it was his wife.

*The Seattle Weekly Gazette*, April 10, 1865, p. 1.

\* \* \*

Flora squeezed the final drops of milk from the udder of the last dairy cow, then sat back and stretched her aching fingers.

"I'll be heading out in the morning."

She looked up to see Hubbs' tense silhouette in the doorway to the barn. His announcement came as a surprise only because he had been home for nearly two weeks without interruption, and because he usually told her of his departures at least a day or two in advance. This one felt sudden.

"Where to?"

"All over. Lime kiln business. May be gone a couple weeks."

She didn't believe him. Hubbs wasn't a major partner in the island's lime kiln, and it didn't make sense that he would have two weeks of business to handle for the kiln. She considered challenging him, but decided instead to hold her tongue. There was no reason to start a fight that would only make him happier to leave, particularly as she realized she wasn't upset that he was leaving. The pressure of running the farm alone had become easier to address than the pressure of his time spent at home. Most conversations turned into fights. He spent very little time with their son. And he rarely came to bed before she was asleep. He had imposed himself on her twice in the two weeks he'd been home, waking her from sleep each time, and reeking of whiskey.

"That sounds like interesting business," she replied, hoping her tone wouldn't be interpreted as a sly criticism that would launch a new argument. Instead, he silently turned and left.

Flora picked up the bucket of milk and poured its warm contents into a large vat with the rest of the late afternoon's production. Butter churning could wait until the morning after Hubbs was gone. She exited the barn and walked to a pump to rinse the bucket. The sun had disappeared over Mount Finlayson, leaving most of the farm in shadow. But the fields to the south were still dappled by the evening sun, and Mount Rainier glowed in the far distance across the strait. The land hadn't proven to be the most hospitable location for a farm, as she had suspected from her first visit six years before, but it was still a most beautiful location for a home.

As she gazed across their homestead, she wondered if perhaps it had been the land she had fallen in love with, rather than the man. The land had proven difficult. It had been isolating, and it had fought her efforts to tame it into a farm, an orchard, and a home. But it had also returned a sufficient bounty each harvest. Hubbs had only proven difficult and isolating.

As she pumped water into the bucket to rinse it of its residue, she found herself suddenly overcome by an acute sense of loneliness, though she insisted that it had to be a different emotion. Loneliness made no sense. Hubbs was still at home. She'd been getting used to his time away. And she always had her son for company. And yet she couldn't shake the feeling of being utterly alone. The emotion felt heavy, painful, and she realized that it came from an understanding that she might never again know the sort of relationship she had once had with her husband. His distance wasn't a mood. It wouldn't pass in time. The happiness she had once found in their marriage would only be a memory. And yet the marriage would go on. She would cook his meals, wash his laundry, run his farm, and raise his son. And she would do it while burdened by a deep sense of loneliness.

Flora finished rinsing the bucket and hung it to dry on the pump's handle, then turned back to the house to make dinner for her husband one more time before his departure.

# Chapter 17

"Boys, you stay in the parlor and play," Flora instructed Paul and his cousin, Walter Wren. "And be good."

"Yes, mama," Paul replied, before pushing his cousin to the ground. Flora, Mary, and their eldest brother, John, had each had boys born within a six-week period in 1862. Paul and Walter had become close friends and even closer competitors from their many family visits.

"It always surprises me to hear you describe this as a 'parlor' in such a tiny cabin," Mary remarked as she followed Flora into the kitchen.

Flora ignored the implicit criticism of the size of her home, pushed the kettle onto the front of the iron stove, and added a log onto the glowing embers.

"I brought you these." Mary dropped two newspapers onto the kitchen table. A *Daily British Colonist* and its new competitor, the *Vancouver Times*.

Flora reached for the two papers. They were always a connection to home, and not easy to obtain from the U.S. Army sutler, the closest mercantile shop. The papers it carried from Puget Sound rarely had the news from home that she craved. She opened the *Colonist* to its third page and scanned for familiar names. Though her interest in politics was slight, she typically turned first to the stories that described the proceedings in the Legislative Assembly. The previous election had returned Doctors Helmcken and Tolmie to the tiny body, along with Amor de Cosmos. The idea of the two family friends having to work closely with a man they so despised was fascinating to her. For years, De Cosmos had used the *Colonist* as a personal mouthpiece to attack both men, and the Company as a whole, and now he was a colleague in government. She would read the descriptions of the debates and imagine the personal disagreements that weren't discussed, that were left to the sidelines of official business, and yet which steered the direction of government business.

In the most recent papers, however, her attention had been grabbed first by the tales of Jemmy Jones, and his escape from the Victoria gaol. As if baiting authorities, Jones had sent frequent letters to the paper, describing his exploits. The tale of his escape from the Victoria gaol, and his subsequent disguise using women's clothing in order to pass undetected through town and reach a waiting boat, had been particularly entertaining for any reader who knew the sea captain and couldn't imagine a man of his countenance passing in public as a believable woman. More recent tales had concerned his theft of his own impounded vessel, the confusingly named *Jenny Jones*, and the efforts of Jones and his crew to evade arrest, locate a supply of coal for the steamer, and escape to Mexico.

"Oh, and before you get to the *Times*, I should tell you the news I didn't wanna mention, and what you're gonna read," Mary continued.

"You read these already?" Flora asked with more surprise in her voice than she realized would have been polite.

"When it's William, I don't have to read papers to know what's goin' on."

"What's he done now?"

"Sold whiskey to Indians. Pemberton got really angry this time. Six months hard labor if he can't come up with two hundred and fifty dollars, and there's no way he'll come up with that."

"I so wish he'd followed Francis' lead and taken up work on Charlie's farm."

"Well, those two brothers of ours aren't happy with all that."

Flora barely heard Mary's story about Francis' desire to return to Victoria. Her eye had fallen onto a particularly familiar word on the third page of the *Colonist*. Hubbs. Her husband's name appeared on the passenger list for the *Eliza Anderson*, arriving from various ports along Puget Sound. Perhaps he'd been to Port Townsend to visit his father. Perhaps to Olympia. Or Steilacoom. Every reader of the *Colonist* had as much information as she had about the whereabouts of her husband, including a complete lack of information as to when he would return home.

"Are you listening?"

"I'm sorry," Flora replied. "Something about seeing your husband's name in print that can distract you for a moment."

"My husband?"

"No, mine. Well, both, I suppose. Yours is just below mine, but as a consignee—I assume a shipment of beef. But mine's here on the passenger list."

"Oh." The disappointment in Mary's voice was evident. "He could get home when we're here? He won't like that."

"If he's not going to tell me when he'll be home, then he has no right to complain if you're here."

"That's bold of you."

"I think I'd rather you be here when he returns. He might be a touch more civil."

Mary reached across the table for Flora's hand.

"Maybe you don't give him reason enough to stay? Do you think about your own behavior?"

Flora pulled her hand back.

"And that's bold of you. I behave perfectly appropriately as a wife, thank you. I run this farm with only meager assistance. I'm raising our son without any interest from him."

"And after more'n five years, you still have only one son."

"As do you and Charlie. Are we really to sit here and compare our success as dutiful wives?"

"It isn't a competition," Mary replied, "but it's our duty to make them happy."

"And if they won't speak to us about the reasons they're not?"

"Of course they won't. They're men. My husband's upset 'cause we have to live in Victoria, and it hurts our marriage. He hasn't said so, but I know. There's nothing much I can do about it anyway. Your husband's away so much. You need to ask what makes him leave."

"You think I haven't been asking myself that every day?"

Flora stepped away from the table, relieved that the boiling kettle gave her an opportunity to turn away from her sister's lecture of the obvious. She had hoped that Mary and Walter's visit would be a distraction from her unhappiness. Instead, the first conversations were laying the blame for her martial strife at her own feet, or in her own bed. Flora filled the teapot with boiling water from the kettle and turned back to her sister with the only defense that seemed certain to distract her from the present topic.

"Tell me more about what William and Francis have been up to?"

Flora set the steeping teapot onto the table, sat across from her sister, and struggled to listen to the tales her sister wove, while discreetly scanning the rest of Page 3 of the *Colonist* in case it might reveal anything else about her husband's whereabouts.

\* \* \*

No questions. It was the simple strategy that Flora had decided to pursue when Hubbs returned. If he chose to share tales of his travels and business affairs, she would listen intently, laugh, smile, and express whatever other emotion seemed appropriate to encourage him. But she would ask him nothing. There was enough news of her own that she would be able to create the appearance of conversation without putting him on the spot. She would just have to be judicious about when to share her own tales and how much detail to include to avoid annoying him.

But as she hung wet laundry behind the kitchen just a few hours after he had returned home, she found herself feeling overly optimistic by his decision to join her outside and chop wood. He had seemed receptive to the news she first shared with him about the two Cowichan men she'd hired to plow the oat fields and plant seeds, several weeks later than usual because of inclement weather. She had learned years before that he would rarely challenge her on any news she'd share about the operations of the farm simply because he knew so little about how to manage a farm. But she had also learned that it would bother him intensely to learn something new about the farm's operations long after the event had occurred.

She waited until he finished swinging the axe before speaking up. "Oh, I forgot to mention earlier, two men from the telegraph survey came by."

"The what?"

"The telegraph survey. Deciding where the telegraph line'll go. Obviously, from here to Lopez is the shortest distance, so they want to run it across the north of the farm and along the wagon trail inland. They don't expect it'll go up for several months, but they're deciding on the route and putting up the poles."

Hubbs stopped chopping and stepped toward her with the axe dangling from his hand.

"Why the fuck were you even talking to them?"

Flora froze, stunned by his sudden change in mood.

"What was I supposed to do? Ignore them as they're surveying next to the house?"

Hubbs stepped closer, his reddened face inches from Flora's.

"You tell them you're my wife and don't have permission to speak to them. And you tell them to get the hell off my land until they've spoken to me."

Even if the odor of whiskey weren't so strong on his

breath, she was certain she could taste it in the spittle that landed on her lips. She told herself that he hadn't intentionally kept the axe in his hand as he challenged her, and told herself that he hadn't meant to be yelling in a threatening manner, but she wasn't certain she believed her own hopeful explanation.

"You're right," she answered. "I'll leave them be next time, if there is a next time."

She leaned down for a wet shirt and stretched it across the line, hopeful that a return to ordinary tasks would lessen Hubbs' anger.

Hubbs watched her without moving for a length of time that seemed far too long, as if he had intended to make it more uncomfortable for her. Then he turned back to the firewood, embedded the axe deep into the chopping block, and stormed off to the barn.

It was only as he disappeared into the barn that Flora realized she was trembling.

* * *

## MEDICAL

DIET V. DRUGS — Really some physicians, instead of taking care of the whole health and comfort, moral and physical, of their patients, seem to think of them only as being created to be sick and born to swallow drugs. What sort of homes should we have if Paterfamilias kept a vile cook, bought wine at auctions, and let the decorations and furniture spoil, but meanwhile kept a capital fire engine in the hall and a brigade of detectives in the butler's pantry? So is the physician who studies drugs and knows nothing of diet.—*Medical Times and Gazette.*

*Vancouver Times and Evening Express*, Thursday, May 18, 1865, p. 3.

* * *

"Right hand to partner, swing once and a half around."

Flora followed the dance caller's instructions and reached out to Hubbs with her right hand. He smiled as they took the first steps of the money musk. It had been more than half a year since they'd danced together at any community event, and it seemed a tonic for both of them to be back on the floor.

Flora had dreaded the event from the moment Hubbs had informed her that they would journey to Port Townsend for the Independence Ball on July 4, 1865, at his father's invitation. Hubbs Senior had always seemed to watch her closely whenever they would visit, as if still measuring her worth more than five years into her marriage to his son, and it made every visit a burden. The recent difficulties she had gone through with Hubbs exacerbated her fears for the trip. But as Hubbs took her hand and led her in the dance, she allowed her fears to fade.

Depending upon the date one chose to mark the end of the Civil War, it had been over for a matter of weeks, or at most, months. Some men still wore black armbands in memory of President Lincoln, while a few women still dressed in black more than two-and-a-half months after news of his assassination had reached the northwest. The manner in which people had displayed their views of Lincoln's death had served as a visual reminder of the political differences among the area's residents. Most Americans had worn an armband or other sign of mourning in the initial weeks, while those who made no public display of mourning had generally been known for their southern sympathies during the war. There were even some who weren't afraid to express their support for the deeds of Booth. The Civil War might have ended, but it did nothing to end the political differences on San Juan Island, in Port Townsend, or across the nation. It remained fresh enough in everyone's minds that the Independence Ball was less a celebration of eighty-nine years of independence than a wary and somber recognition that the country had entered a new and uncertain era.

As the dance came to an end, Hubbs took Flora's arm and guided her across the floor to where Hubbs Senior and his wife, Maggie, stood in conversation with a man who struck Flora as familiar. She knew she should remember his name, but could only recall that when she'd first heard the name a few years before, she had thought to herself that it was the sort of name no one forgets after hearing it once. Hubbs Senior beckoned them over as they approached.

"Son, you remember Selucius Garfielde."

"Of course, nice to see you again, and congratulations on your victory, sir."

"Thank you, son."

Hubbs Senior turned to Flora.

"Mr. Garfielde is a fellow attorney here in Port Townsend, and he ran Mr. Denny's successful campaign for Territorial delegate in Congress."

"Oh, of course" Flora replied, remembering that she had met Garfielde at a dinner thrown at the Hubbs' Port Townsend residence several years earlier. "I do recall we met some years back. And congratulations."

"Thank you, ma'am. Mr. Denny'll be a fine representative for the Territory."

Flora wondered whether the relationship between Senior and Garfielde was as genial as it appeared given their political differences. The new territorial delegate, Arthur Denny, was a Republican and a longtime friend of Lincoln's. Hubbs Senior had been a Democrat, including a stint in California as a state Senator and statewide School Superintendant in the 1850's.

"I followed stories about the campaign with interest," Flora continued, "since your opponent, Mr. Tilton, has quite the history in Victoria. His court case there to recover his escaped slave a few years back was in all the newspapers. I would think the mere fact that he was the Democratic candidate would make one wonder if the end of the war has had any impact at all on the Territory's politics."

"Well, if that don't beat all? An Indian wife who reads

the newspapers." Garfielde laughed heartily at his own comment. "What'll be next?"

"I'm perfectly well-educated, Mr. Garfielde. I've been reading newspapers since –"

Flora's effort to reclaim her dignity was cut short by a sudden pain in her arm as Hubbs squeezed it with a violent intensity that caused her statement of protest to fade into a strangled expression of pain. She could see from the looks of all involved that they were aware of the reason for her inability to complete the sentence, and that none of them would say a word to acknowledge it.

"Paul," Maggie interjected. "Do your poor mother the pleasure of the next dance?"

Hubbs' grip on Flora's arm relaxed. Maggie was only a year older than her stepson, and seemed to find humor in describing herself as his "mother." The description had troubled Hubbs in the first years of their relationship, but he had relaxed into the absurdity of the concept.

"Of course, Maggie. It'd be my pleasure."

Hubbs reached out for Maggie's arm and escorted her to the dance floor without a word or glance in Flora's direction.

"You were saying, Mrs. Hubbs? About the newspapers?"

Flora looked over at Garfielde. The smile on his face showed far too much amusement for her situation. She no longer cared if he thought of her as educated or ignorant.

"If you'll excuse me, gentlemen."

She turned and hurried across the room, having lost all interest in the ball, the next dance, or the celebration of Independence Day.

\* \* \*

Barely a word was spoken between Flora and her husband for the rest of the evening. She walked home from the ball next to Maggie, silently, while Hubbs and his father walked in front of them, engaged in a discussion about the growing town of Port Townsend. It was a conversation they continued after they arrived home and shared a drink in the parlor, while ignoring their respective wives. It was behavior that seemed to trouble Maggie, but Flora accepted the silent treatment as a temporary respite from having to deal with her husband's anger.

But as she entered the bedroom where they would sleep that night, and as Hubbs shut the door behind them, her nervousness intensified. They would have to speak about what had happened. Hubbs wouldn't care for her opinion, but he wouldn't end the day without ensuring that she knew his views. Flora started to remove her dress, leaving it to Hubbs to decide when he'd be ready to speak to her again. She had barely opened half the buttons down her bodice when he stepped close. She could feel the anger in his tense posture.

"When we're at events like that you smile, you nod your head when I speak, and you make short, polite statements."

"Did you really think you were marrying that sort of woman?"

"I married a wife. That's what wives do. Did you hear Maggie talking about politics?"

"Of course not. I doubt she'd even be capable of it."

Flora regretted the insult of her mother-in-law before the words even left her lips, before Hubbs' hand connected forcefully with the side of her head, and before she collapsed to the hardwood floor.

She reached up to her face, stunned, expecting to find blood on her hand. But her hand came away clean. It was only her second thought to look up to see if Hubbs was about to strike again. He stood over her but made no move.

"Garfielde is one of the most important men in the territory. He has power. He controls jobs, nominations, appointments. And those'll go to men whose wives don't challenge him in public or make a fool of him in front of his colleagues."

A voice in Flora's mind composed questions that she might ask. Was her husband now a Republican? Was he committed to restarting his political career in this time of upheaval? Did he care what a lawyer in Port Townsend thought of his wife's ability to read newspapers? And was it really Garfielde who'd been made the fool at the ball?

But a stronger voice in her head insisted on silence. It wasn't a night she would look back on as the moment when her husband's political career took an unexpected turn. Nor was it a night she'd remember for its dances or conversation. Instead, she would remember it as the night when her husband struck her for the first time. When he drove her to the floor with his fist for defending herself against a man who spoke of her dismissively as Hubbs' "Indian wife." When he forced her to remain silent instead of defending her honor. And when he stood over her in the guest bedroom, making no effort to help her back to her feet. It was a night she would never forget.

\* \* \*

Judge Pemberton looked down at his docket and sighed.

"Calling the next matter for sentencing, *Regina v. Butts.*"

John Butts stepped forward and expressed a practiced look of penitence that Pemberton had faced far too many times before.

"Mr. Butts, when I released you two weeks ago on your own recognizance, it was so you could seek the means to leave the colony rather than face more time in the city gaol. And yet, here you are."

"Yes, Judge, I am mightily disappointed to still be present in the colony. I tried every means I could think of—only legal ones, of course—to raise the funds it would take to leave across the Sound, or return to my beloved family in Sydney. But I was simply unable to raise the necessary amounts."

Pemberton stared at the tragic young man and pondered the options for sentencing. Butts' crimes had never been serious, and he had never harmed another person in any significant manner. And yet, the sheer frequency of his crimes since his dismissal as town crier and bell-ringer for the city was unlike anyone else in the colony. Theft of minor goods that he resold to others. Minor physical or verbal assault. Theft of alcohol, though the charges had been dropped on one occasion because he had drunk the evidence. The latest charges weren't even for theft, but for helping the thief of a bed and its bedding to sell the stolen items to another.

Many of Butts' infractions over the years hadn't even been crimes, but had been mere misbehavior that had received substantial attention. He had angered the town's more respectable residents when he'd spiked the tea at a meeting of the ladies' temperance society. And he'd scandalized others by starting his own church for the sole purpose of obtaining a weekly collection from its congregation of Songhees and Cowichans to fund a Sunday evening's whiskey. There had also been his business of soliciting payment from merchants to clean the garbage from a particular street, which he would then deposit on the next street, after which he would approach the merchants on that street for payment to clean up their garbage, followed by a repetition of the act until he ran out of streets.

The most notorious criminal charges, which seemed to have instigated his downfall, were when he'd been charged in January of 1860 with, in the words of the *Colonist*, "one of the most abominable crimes" of sodomy, committed on the "rather good looking youth," William Williams. The paper's article on the charges against Butts had appeared to suggest that the crime was understandable, given the victim's attractive countenance, even if it was abominable. And though the case was tried before a jury, it ended in an acquittal thanks to witnesses who contested some of Williams' testimony, and Butts' spirited speech in his own defense espousing the theory that, though the act with Williams wasn't quite denied, the charges stemmed from a conspiracy to blackmail him of his property. Despite the acquittal, the nature of the charges, and the testimony of Dr. Helmcken diagnosing syphilis in both men, had contributed to Butts' transformation from celebrity to pariah throughout the community.

His most memorable escapade in the minds of many had been his claim, while imprisoned in the gaol on one of his many convictions for minor theft, that he had become paralyzed and had lost all use of his legs. Gaol officials had doubted his claim, but Butts had dragged himself about in such a pitiful manner that he was lodged in the Royal Hospital. Doubts prevailed, however, particularly given the manner with which Butts seemed to enjoy his ongoing care, leading hospital officials to adopt a thoroughly untested treatment for his paralysis. One morning, Butts was placed in a chair on the front veranda, naked, and then eighteen buckets of ice-cold seawater were poured onto him from the balcony above to determine if he had sufficient use of his legs. With the first round of buckets, Butts remained in place, cursing loudly, as he did with the second round. Finally, during the third round of icy water, he jumped from his chair and swore roundly at the officials, only to then promptly drop to the grass and feign a return of his paralysis. His departure from the hospital was swift, furthered by threats from his doctors that future treatments for his paralysis would include buckets of scalding water and a red-hot iron stove.

But the fascination that so many in the city had shown over the years with the man's immense and unique character had faded into exhaustion, and it was an exhaustion that Pemberton shared. He had hoped that Butts' promise of two weeks earlier to leave abroad would rid the colony of the young vagabond. Instead, he had returned for sentencing.

"Very well, then, Mr. Butts. I hereby sentence you to three months hard labor."

"Thank you, Judge."

Pemberton watched as Butts was led from the courtroom, certain that the sentence he had just handed down would do nothing to induce more appropriate behavior. He had given the young man room and board for a three-month sentence—though he'd likely be released in less than half that time—and Butts was the only man in the courtroom who appeared relatively pleased with the outcome. At least, Pemberton hoped, he had also given himself a respite from having to address the next inevitable charges to be laid against the young man for at least a few months.

\* \* \*

Hubbs dipped his paddle into the heavy waves and pushed his canoe toward the gravel beach of Decatur Island. A wisp of smoke drifting from the slanted roof of his small cabin told him that the girl was waiting.

He stepped into the shallow water and pulled the canoe past the line of high tide, then paused and took in his surroundings. He had built the tiny cabin on a small, isolated bay on the north side of the island. There were no signs of human habitation in any direction. Just trees, ocean, distant mountains, eagles, seals, whales. It was everything his San Juan claim had seemed to be so many years before. Isolation from society. From the demands of being a father and a husband. And from the expectations of being the son of Paul Kinsey Hubbs, Sr. He felt no need to drink when he was on Decatur Island.

He reached down into the canoe for his small bag and the salmon he'd purchased from an Indian family camped on a beach on Lopez Island. Something tumbled from his bag and clattered against the hull. Hubbs bent down and picked up a wooden alphabet block, one of his son's toys. It was a toy he associated most with frustration, having frequently stepped on some of the blocks while navigating their home in the dark. Paul had six of the wooden cubes, and Hubbs had yet to see the boy use them to construct a single word. He started to put the block into his bag, then reconsidered and tossed it instead into the lapping waves. He watched it bob in the water, considering for a moment whether to rescue it, then turned and trekked across the gravel to the small cabin.

\* \* \*

"*How long they will continue to peaceably enjoy a joint occupancy depends entirely upon the affection and respect each shows to the other.*" The words had circled through Flora's thoughts since she'd read them earlier that morning, when she had turned to her Bible for comfort and had found a copy of the wedding announcement she had pressed inside for safekeeping.

The words had been written almost six years earlier, yet she found them to be eerily prescient as she gazed into the small mirror on her bureau and surveyed the remains of a bruise that had colored her left cheek for days. She wondered if the author of her wedding announcement had intended to congratulate the couple on their marriage by offering such hesitation for its future. And if perhaps she should have taken heed rather than pride from the treatment of her wedding as a news story rather than an ordinary announcement. Most wedding announcements appeared as a brief notice on Page 3 of the local papers, if anywhere at all in the publication. Flora's wedding had been announced as a news story on Page 2 of both the *Victoria Gazette* and *New Westminster Times*. Nearly six years later, it felt as though her marriage had been held up that much higher so that more people could view its potential for mockery.

*"May the question of their boundary line never again be misunderstood, so as to call for the arbitration of our countries' courts."*

Flora dipped a cloth into a basin of cold water and gently pressed it against her cheek, wondering if anyone reading the announcement at the time of her marriage had thought it strange that it had concluded with a reference to the potential termination of the marriage.

Hubbs hadn't been home for three days, but he had left in a rage. In recent months, arguments had become their most common form of communication, usually over minor distractions. A cold dinner. The state of their finances. The chores that remained to be done. And if he had already been drinking, the arguments often ended with a raised hand. His behavior drove them apart, and Flora found it increasingly difficult to share any measure of intimacy with him, especially as he began to simply take what he needed without any intimacy at all. Sexual activity had come to her in the early years of their marriage as a joyful discovery, but now felt only as an act of her husband's anger and domination, and she found herself praying after each occasion that a child wouldn't be produced from such an encounter.

She patted her face dry and walked into the small parlor, where she found solace from the sight of Paul playing on the floor with toy wooden animals. A year earlier, it had bothered her that the boy reminded her far more of her brothers and nephews than of Hubbs or his father. She had wanted their son to mature in the image of his father without the burden of her darker features. But now she found greater comfort in seeing her son as more of a Ross and Mainville than a Hubbs.

Flora sat on the rough plank floor and ran a hand through the boy's hair.

"Are you playing a game?"

"I'm milking the cow." Paul held up the small wooden cow that Francis had carved for the boy. If it hadn't been for the large black spot that Francis had painted across the back, it could have served as nearly any four-legged animal commonly found in a barn. There was only a hint of an udder for milk, no tail, and the faintest suggestion of ears. But the black spot was all Paul seemed to need to make him understand that he was playing with a toy cow.

Flora hoped the boy's willingness to find play from the daily chores was a sign that he might take to the actual task of milking their dairy cows each morning and evening without much complaint. At least at first, she imagined, he might welcome the task as a sign that he was growing into a man. After that, it wouldn't be long before he'd rebel each morning in an effort to cling to his status as a small boy with only play on his agenda.

"Come on, I'll make you some porridge for breakfast." Flora rose, took Paul's tiny hand in her own, and walked to the kitchen at the back.

She stoked the fire in the wood stove and set a kettle to boil for breakfast, thinking ahead to what they would eat for supper that evening. She wondered if there was any point in cooking enough dinner to feed the three of them, just in case Hubbs might return home, and decided to cook only for herself and her son. She was offended by how much food had gone to waste over the years, as if every spoiled meal had served to ridicule her for each night Hubbs had remained absent.

Flora wasn't the underlying cause of the strife. And there was little she could do to ensure that future conflicts wouldn't arise. She was fairly certain of both conclusions. But logic did little to ease the anxieties that returned each time her husband crossed the threshold.

# *Chapter 18*

Flora rose up on her toes and looked back across the pews in an effort to get a better view of the proceedings unfolding on the porch of Christ Church. Those who were unlucky enough to watch the consecration from outside might have had to deal with the cold, wintry weather. But at least they could hear the official pronouncements of the Bishop of Columbia and others in his entourage as they began the ceremony to consecrate the small church as Christ Church Cathedral.

Flora had been barely fourteen when she'd heard Reverend Cridge deliver his first sermon in the newly completed church, known then as the Victoria District Church. Now Cridge was merely one of eight Christ Church officials receiving the Bishop of Columbia and his entourage as they arrived to accept a consecration petition from the church's subscribers.

The change had been difficult for him. He'd never spoken openly about it around Flora, but she'd sensed from comments and expressions that he was both proud of the church's growth, and frustrated by the loss of independence he'd experienced when the Church of England appointed

Bishop Hills as his superior, rather than elevate the man who had given the church its foothold in the small colony. Cridge had never been one to use pomp and circumstance in his services, while Bishop Hills favored what Cridge considered excessive pageantry. He had made his views clear that such indulgences had little place in a society where members of the congregation were carving their lives from virgin forest. But he was now simply one reverend in a larger body. Flora hoped that he found consolation in the fact that Christ Church, rather than the newer congregation of St. John's on the hill, had been chosen as the cathedral for the diocese, and that Cridge himself would shortly be made Dean.

The consecration ceremony had provided a perfect excuse for an escape to Victoria for several days. Aside from time with family, it would give Flora the opportunity to shop for a Christmas present for Paul. There were no toys for sale on San Juan Island, and the boy had reached an age when the excitement of Christmas began to build the moment it was December, fuelled more by the stories of other children than his few memories of any prior holidays.

"How long d'they stay out there?" Alexander whispered in her ear.

"How should I know?" Flora replied to her brother. "This is probably the first consecration ceremony this side of Canada West. I'm not sure there's a standard agenda."

She was glad that she'd left her son with his cousins at the Ross farm. He would have been even more restless at the ceremony than his uncle, Alexander. And though left at the farm, he was anything but alone. The farmhouse had become crowded with women and children ever since her elder brother, John, had died two years earlier, and his widow, Genevieve, had moved to the farm with her children. Alexander was the sole man at the farm, but for the rare occasions when William wasn't incarcerated, and was both sober and willing to lend a hand. The farm had suffered from the resulting burden of too many mouths to feed, and too few hands to work the fields. And though Francis had written recently to announce that he'd shortly return to Victoria, it wasn't clear when he would arrive, or whether the years he'd spent working on their brother's farm had given him the maturity he needed to be a productive member of the family enterprise.

Flora gave up trying to follow the proceedings that were happening outside the church, and turned to look at the changes that the building had undergone over the years. The apse. The north aisle. The south aisle. It was far more substantial than it had been on the day of her marriage.

"Yesterday was our anniversary," she whispered to Alexander as she gazed about the nave.

"Whose anniversary?"

"My wedding anniversary. Six years ago, yesterday, I was married right over there."

"Any regrets?"

He had delivered the question with a slight mocking smile, but one that had clearly not been intended to cause harm. Flora opted to treat the question as rhetorical since her brother had no reason to assume that she'd have regrets. She had never opened up to Alexander about her marital difficulties, and wasn't sure if she ever would. He had never been married. He was a man. And he would shower her with advice based on societal expectations for the role of a dutiful wife.

"Shouldn't you be with your husband on your anniversary?" he added, confirming her expectation that his perspective would generate advice she wouldn't care to hear.

"Oh, look, here they come," she replied, nodding toward the back of the church to where a procession of officials had entered the nave, rescuing her from having to figure out a proper answer to Alexander's question.

"I said, shouldn't you've been with your —"

"Shh." She put a finger to her lips and nodded to the approaching procession with an expression of reprimand. She had come to Christ Church to honor a special day launching the building's future. She wasn't about to allow her brother to spoil the event by focusing on one of the more questionable days in its past.

\* \* \*

Flora closed the door to the stables of the Ross farm, picked up her packages, and then walked toward the farmhouse. Even after more than a year, it felt wrong to know that she was the legal owner of a portion of her mother's farm, along with some of her siblings. But it had been a necessary change in ownership to protect the farm from the man Isabella had married two years earlier.

Lucius O'Brien was an ambitious arrival in 1864 who had recognized an opportunity in Isabella's loneliness. He had charmed Isabella and she had allowed herself to believe his advances. Within weeks they were married, and within days he was turning against her children in an effort to secure control of her valuable property. O'Brien filed charges against Alexander, alleging assault, while O'Brien himself was charged by the Crown for horse theft and assisting desertion by three seamen. The charges against both men had increased the public scrutiny, and a dispute that should have been a private family affair became a community spectacle.

Flora, Mary, and their respective husbands, eventually filed a lawsuit against O'Brien alleging bigamy, as it was the sole legal option available to nullify the marriage given the lack of civil divorce laws in the colony. It was ultimately resolved in a settlement that saw O'Brien and Isabella divide the farm and deed it to the children. The settlement had protected the farm, but she knew it would never change her own perception of the land as her mother's homestead.

She approached the kitchen entrance of the farmhouse, pleased with how the morning had gone. The streets of Victoria had been crowded with residents preparing for the holidays, but she'd found a few gifts that were sure to please her son on Christmas morning. A new toy store's advertised promise that it was "Santa Claus Headquarters" had been accurate. She'd never seen such displays of beautiful toys and games, and was relieved that she had left Paul at home. Far better that they get through Christmas without having his expectations raised by such a sight.

She entered the kitchen and stopped in shock. Hubbs stood by the fireplace, conversing with Isabella and Alexander. She hadn't seen him in nearly a week and his arrival was entirely unexpected. She struggled to repress the fear that gripped her stomach and focus instead on understanding what might explain his presence at the family farm.

"Goodness, I had no idea you were coming over," she exclaimed, hoping that her voice had expressed pleasure at the sight of her husband, rather than consternation. She realized that she would need to greet him in front of her family in a manner that she hadn't done in months. She smiled, approached him, and kissed him on the cheek.

"I had some business here in Victoria, so I thought I'd stay for the night and we could go back together."

"How nice," she lied. "I found some wonderful Christmas gifts for a certain someone at a new toy store in town."

She nearly continued with a statement about the wonderful Christmas their son would be certain to have in two weeks, but decided to avoid making any predictions about the emotional nature of future family holidays.

"Your mother was just telling me about the new neighbors, and how Douglas still hasn't built a road out to here."

"Not a thing has been done," she agreed. "That dirt track is getting so pitted and uneven. I'm not sure I'd trust driving a wagon along there anymore."

"I'm going to write a letter to him this afternoon. That road was a promise from years ago, and it needs to be built."

"That's very generous of you," Flora replied, surprised by Hubbs' willingness to assist. She removed her heavy coat and warmed her hands by the fire.

"Not so much generous as wise. I'm the ultimate owner of much of this farm, and it's in my interest to ensure there's a proper road along the property."

Flora froze, troubled by the meaning behind his statement. She knew just enough about the laws of coverture from the O'Brien experience to know that he was right. The property might be in her name, but she was his property under British law, as was everything she owned.

He wasn't looking at her, but she could tell from his expression that he was toying with her. With the entire family. He had to know that the idea of a husband threatening to take the family farm from Isabella's children would tear the family apart, as it had done when that husband had been O'Brien. She could see from Alexander's expression that he was as surprised and troubled as she was, but he lacked an awareness of their marital circumstances to appreciate the game that Hubbs was playing. At least, she hoped it was a game.

"I'm sure the whole family will be grateful if you can get that sorted out for us."

It wasn't much of a retort. But the more she might challenge his authority as her husband, the more she would put her family's farm at risk.

"Well," she continued, "I'd like to go find my son and let him know that mommy's home."

She turned from the kitchen, anxious to escape before her anger might find expression in words she'd regret. She needed time to think. The law might give him power over her. Societal expectations might force certain public displays to avoid gossip. But there was nothing that would force her to feel any fidelity to a man who had intentionally replaced affection in their marriage with cruelty.

\* \* \*

Reverend Cridge gently rocked Rhoda in his arms, beckoning her to sleep. But every ragged breath or cough that she expelled filled him with dread. She might eventually fall asleep, but he questioned whether he would be able to do the same. Rhoda was six months old and had been a sickly child since her birth the previous July. Edward and Mary Cridge had looked to her birth as a form of salvation after the loss of four children. But with each successive illness that the child had somehow survived, her parents were left wondering if they would survive the constant reminder that her illnesses forced on them.

Ever since their family's tragedy, and the added burden of having had to preside over the funerals of so many other children while still mourning the loss of his own, Cridge had struggled to understand the meaning of such a personal loss, and to search for a path forward. The Christian lessons he had offered to so many of his flock over the years when faced with the struggles of human existence and inevitable loss had done little to ease his own pain. He remained steadfast in his commitment to his ministry. But the daily tasks involved in that commitment—the fundraising and meetings to organize the Royal Hospital, the hours spent visiting members of his congregation, and the time spent focused on earning enough money to feed his own brood—had deprived him of so much time that he could have spent with the children he'd lost. If he'd appreciated how truly fragile his own domestic happiness had been, would he have selfishly spent more time with his children at the expense of his congregation and community? If he could have, should he have? They were questions he couldn't clear from his mind, and the uncertainty over his answers furthered a sense of guilt that he had failed his own family.

Cridge softly sung "See, Gentle Patience Smile on Pain" to his daughter, a hymn he often sung to his surviving children as he put them to bed, partly because it had proven so effective at putting so many of his parishioners to sleep in the past, but mostly because it was a hymn that spoke to his own pain. *"See, gentle patience smile on pain, see, dying hope revive again; hope wipes the tear from sorrow's eye, while faith points upward to the sky."*

As with so many nights, the moment that Rhoda was finally still and asleep was accompanied by a brief moment of dread, until Cridge saw her tiny chest expand with a raspy breath. He carefully lay the young infant in her crib and started back to his own bed, wondering if he would ever be able to look upon his children without a fear that he might lose them all at any moment.

\* \* \*

HIGHWAY ROBBERY—As a Chinaman, a cook at the Lion Brewery Hotel, was proceeding yesterday evening toward the Oakland Hotel, he was attacked by three ruffians, one of whom seized him by the throat, another caught hold of his arms, while the third ransacked his pockets and emptied them. Seventeen dollars was obtained, but the rascals were not satisfied until they had made the Chinaman give up his hat and his boots, the latter a new pair which had been purchased the day previous. The proprietor of the Oakland Hotel sent the Chinaman with a note descriptive of the thieves to the police, so that in all probability we shall hear of their arrest today.

*The Daily British Colonist*, Monday, January 8, 1866, p. 2.

\* \* \*

Isabella pounded the oat stocks that lay across a sheet of canvas on the barn floor, discovering that each blow she struck to thresh the oats was also a therapeutic release of anger. Alexander had insisted that he could thresh the oats by himself at least until his younger brothers eventually rose for the day, but Isabella wasn't about to let him carry the burden alone. She had wasted enough energy trying to get Francis and William out of bed to assist their brother, on this and so many other days, and had finally concluded that her energy was better served helping Alexander in the barn.

It bothered her that she held so much anger inside of her, yet it felt comforting to release some of it with every blow of the stick against the pile of stocks. She couldn't decide if the anger was a product of her two youngest sons' years of irresponsible behavior, or of her own apparent failure to put an end to their antics. Francis had seemed to mend his ways somewhat while living in Washington Territory, but he'd fallen back into his old habits since returning to Victoria. William had never altered his behavior at all while Francis had been away, but had continued his life much as before, only without his brother's inebriated company. He had seemed determined to flaunt his misbehavior in front of, or at the expense of, Isabella. She had hoped and prayed that the years of separation from one another would have forced William and Francis to grow into responsible adults, but it had done nothing of the sort. William was twenty, and seemed only taller for the additional years.

Isabella pounded the stocks once more before deciding that she had sufficiently cleared them of their kernels. She reached for a fresh bundle and found satisfaction in the number of kernels that came free with the first blow. Without words, she and Alexander fell into a rhythm. She found it soothing. Almost musical. Hypnotic by its repetition. And then broken as faint but growing shouts outside the barn led to the realization that something momentous was happening. Isabella and Alexander stopped their work at the same time and looked toward the barn door as the yelling and footsteps approached with increasing volume and urgency. William dove into the doorway in his bare feet and underclothing as a constable from the Victoria police force tackled him against the barn door, sending both men to the ground. In an instant, there were two more constables in the pile, subduing William while he screamed and cursed.

Alexander started toward the officers, as if to intervene, but Isabella grabbed his arm. There was nothing to be done but watch. Whatever had brought this upon William was most likely deserved, and Alexander's intervention could only make it worse. The constables pulled William to his feet and marched him out of the barn. William looked back at his mother, his eyes pleading for assistance. Her heart ached as she watched him being pushed along, and she expected that Francis was facing a similar fate elsewhere on the property. But the emotion that Isabella felt strongest of all, as William's pleading eyes disappeared around the doorway of the barn, was an undeniable sense of relief.

\* \* \*

Flora held out a towel for Lucinda, who lifted the tiny newborn from the basin where she had washed it clean and then laid the infant onto the soft cotton. Flora swaddled the baby, then placed the child into the waiting arms of its mother, Jessie Firth.

It had never crossed her mind, when she had slept on the floor of Aleck and Anna's cabin just yards away, so many years before, that she might someday help deliver a baby in the bedroom of Charles Griffin's Bellevue cabin. But it was no longer Griffin's bedroom, and she was no longer a girl.

"Ten fingers, ten toes, a bonnie little girl," she announced before stepping back to defer to Lucinda. Flora had delivered a few babies on her own during the years when Lucinda and her family had lived in Victoria. But ever since Lucinda had returned to the island, Flora had deferred to the older woman's experience, in part because it was clear that nearly all women on the island about to give birth would choose Lucinda's experience over Flora's.

"Do you have a name in mind?" Lucinda asked.

"Elizabeth," Jesse replied. "But to us she be Betsy."

It had been an easy birth. Jessie's fifth child in eight years. She appeared far less drained from the experience than any other mother Flora had witnessed.

"I'll go outside and let Robert know," Flora offered.

She opened the door of the bedroom only to see two of the Firth children run past her skirts into the tiny room.

"Children, no, outside," Flora scolded. "Your mama's not ready for visitors."

"I can manage, Flora," Jessie replied, turning to her curious children. "This here's your new sister, Betsy."

The children stopped and stood quietly, contemplating the arrival of a sister, as Robert Firth entered, holding their youngest son, trailed by their fourth, and eventually by Flora's son, Paul.

"You seen your sister, boys. Out." Firth's commands were always addressed with an air of affectionate authority that brought instant compliance. Flora patted Paul on the head, directed him out the door with the rest of the children, and then shut the door behind them.

Firth sat on the bed next to his wife for a closer view of his new daughter. "She's lookin' jus' like the others," he offered in dry jest.

"She should. She been made the same way," Jessie replied.

Flora dipped a cloth in cold water and wiped it across Jessie's brow.

"It astounds me how you can have so much energy after childbirth."

Jessie smiled in gratitude, reached up with her free hand, and patted Flora on the cheek. It took Flora a few moments before realizing that Jessie's thumb was circling an area of her cheek where she had used makeup to cover the remains of a fading bruise. She pulled back suddenly, embarrassed and offended, but aware that Jessie's intentions hadn't been to mock or judge.

"Flora," Jessie began. It was a hesitant start to a question that didn't seem to have any direction.

"I'm fine," Flora insisted. She considered the story she had practiced on so many prior occasions about a clumsy dairy cow that had kicked her against the barn wall. It would be seen instantly as the lie that it was, and she couldn't bring herself to lie to such close friends.

"Lucinda and I, we need to talk wit' ya," Jessie continued.

"Jessie, you need to rest," Lucinda insisted.

"I've enough energy to talk. And Robert, too. He's the one who seen it himself."

Flora turned to Firth, but he hesitated. She found herself hoping that it had something to do with her brothers and the serious charges they were facing in the Victoria courts. Or perhaps something young Paul had said to one of their children. But she knew they were about to discuss the private affairs of her marriage.

"When Paul's away," Firth slowly began, "it's not for business, Flora. Not most times. I'm sorry, but he done put a cabin on Decatur, more a rookel of driftwood, and he keeps an Indian lass there."

"We didn't want you to be the only one who didn't know," Lucinda added.

"She's just a lass, maybe sixteen," Firth continued. "I went ashore, tried to talk to her. She dinnae speak much English, but calls herself his *klootchman*."

The only part of the news that truly came as a surprise was that it was all happening a short canoe trip from her home. From their home. That he'd been paddling less than an hour from the farm, around the south end of Lopez Island to Decatur Island. Somehow that made it worse, as if he couldn't have been bothered to go to any effort to hide his transgression. A mistress in Olympia would have been almost expected. Even a girl in Steilacoom or Port Townsend. But it stung to think that he'd built a cabin so close to his own home to house a girl who thought of herself as his "*klootchman*." Hearing it all stung far more than she would have thought possible after so many months of fights and bitterness. He hadn't betrayed their marriage for another woman who could regale him in intelligent conversation, or run a farm twice the size of their own. By betraying her with a girl, a girl of Indian blood, who would likely be pliable and submissive to his wants, he had let it be known precisely which flaws in his own wife required compensation from a mistress. He might still be married to a competent farm manager, and a loving mother of his child, but for his own personal needs he required a girl who offered the specific qualities that were lacking in his wife.

Flora looked up at their faces. It was clear that they cared for her, and that the news had been delivered entirely from a desire to help. But a part of her still resented the messengers. They'd mentioned that others on the island knew, suggesting it was a topic of local gossip, and likely had been for some time. But perhaps most egregious, they'd presented the information to her in an environment where she had no choice but to keep her emotions in check. She couldn't cry in front of Firth and his children, or in front of her own child. Hubbs' child. She would have to finish cleaning up from the birth, get young Paul home for dinner, and only then find a moment of privacy to allow herself to feel the news.

Lucinda stepped forward and touched Flora's arm, destroying every remaining hope Flora had that she might make it home before breaking down.

\* \* \*

"Three days, maybe four," Hubbs predicted, while folding his clean shirt and laying it into his bag. "New election law's been passed, lots of planning gonna be happening. Less than six months till the election."

Flora watched as he packed a small bag with his belongings and tossed his soiled shirt onto the bed for her to wash without so much as a glance in her direction. She felt tears threatening, and struggled to distract herself by analyzing the reasons for them. She actually wanted him to leave, and it appeared that he would do so in a matter of minutes. This time without anger. Without liquor. Without violence. They stood in a room where they had found so much laughter and made so much love. She could still see him hammering misshapen boards and beams to build the walls of their bedroom, so obviously proud of his efforts. She could still see the pride in his eyes as he'd welcomed a son into their lives on the same bed where they'd made him. She could even remember the love he had once shown on that bed, and she was certain it had been real. Had been.

Hubbs had been home for five days, and they'd been some of the easier days in recent months. Their fights had been few, but that had been primarily because she'd avoided most discussions entirely, while he'd spent much of his time out at the limestone quarry and kiln. There had been little time for conversations that could lead to arguments. She hadn't even found the energy to tell him about her brothers' arrest on charges of highway robbery.

Hubbs picked up his bag and walked out of the bedroom. Flora followed.

"Is it so necessary you be there for those discussions?" she asked, intent on seeing how far he would spin the yarn, and relieved that she was able to deliver the words without a crack in her voice. "Won't the people who decide these things have already decided if they want you to run again?"

"Out of sight, out of mind, Flora."

How true, she thought, expecting that she and their son were far from his mind as soon as he was around Lopez Island.

"I'll try to get home next Sunday, late. The boys want me over at the kiln on Monday to meet with some buyers."

"Don't come back."

The words burst from her lips with a force that surprised her, and for a moment she wondered if she'd only imagined them. But his expression told her that she had indeed spoken them aloud. She had little choice but to continue, though she wasn't sure if she could finish the thought.

"From this trip. From any trip. You're not going to Olympia. I doubt you've been there in months. You're going to Decatur. I know about her. Everyone on the island apparently knows. You and I seem to be the only ones who haven't had a discussion about it."

Flora took a step back, expecting him to lunge at her. But he was sober, and instead simply stood by the door, considering her words, appearing more angry for having to discuss the matter than guilty for his conduct. She was relieved that the discussion was happening in the morning and not in the evening after a few glasses of whiskey.

"She's just a girl. It isn't anything."

"It's everything. We made vows to each other."

She realized that a tear had accompanied the words only when the salty taste reached her lips, and she struggled to hold back any further tears that might show weakness.

"Everyone says vows. You have to."

"And that makes them meaningless to you?"

"I made them to a wife, and you haven't seemed like one for years. You're a business partner in a farm."

"I'm the wife you walk away from every time you leave."

"And your vows included a promise to obey. You've broken that vow since the day we were married. It's none of your concern what I do when I'm not here, or even when I am."

"If you're spending your days and nights with some girl in a cabin instead of raising your son and tending your farm, it's every bit my concern."

Hubbs stopped at the door, steps away from the loaded musket.

"This isn't a conversation we're gonna have."

"We're already having it."

"So what are you saying? You expect me to make some kind of choice?"

"You already made it. You can have the girl. You can't have me, or our son."

It was only at that moment that Flora understood that she, too, had made a choice. Hubbs smirked, and Flora considered it a positive sign. A sign that he knew he had to leave to preserve his façade of dignity. That he was more likely to attack her with words than fists. It was only as he wrenched the door open and walked out onto the rickety porch that she realized that his smirk had probably been for the recognition that he had already caused her pain without using his fists.

"Good-bye, Paul."

She heard finality in her own voice as his feet hit the ground, for she knew that his pride wouldn't permit him to consider a change of course.

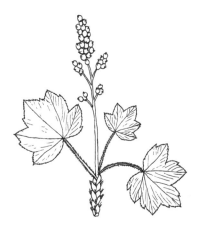

# Chapter 19

Flora gazed out the window of the steamer and craned her neck for a view of the distant southern shore of San Juan Island. She had been away only a few days in Nisqually, and she was confident that a neighbor she'd hired to watch over the animals would have kept the farm in proper running order, yet she was overcome with worry. Her brothers' trial was underway, and she had yet to arrive in Victoria. She silently willed the boat to increase its speed, hoping they would at least arrive before sentencing.

"I think you're missing an opportunity."

The words of her sister brought her back to the present.

"He strayed. You take him back. You get the moral high ground," Mary concluded.

Flora considered her sister's comment, then turned to gaze at her son who sat on the floor of the steamer playing with his cousin, Walter. He seemed far enough away to not hear most of the conversation, even if he was likely far too young to understand any of it. She took additional comfort from knowing that the rhythmic oscillations of the paddle wheeler's blades would keep most of their words from reaching him.

"If I do nothing when it's this open, this known across the island, nothing will change, and I continue to be the one publicly humiliated." Flora glanced around the passenger compartment, anxious to ensure that she had spoken softly enough to prevent other passengers from hearing. "And what's the point of moral high ground if it hasn't felt like a true marriage in years?"

"A true marriage?" Charles Wren exclaimed from his seat across from the two sisters, his bushy eyebrows raised. "And what's a true marriage supposed to feel like?"

"Like something God would sanction," Flora replied, hoping to end the conversation. She regretted having allowed Mary to raise the state of her marriage in front of Wren, and in a public setting.

Wren snorted, a response that offended Flora, not because of anything it suggested about her own marriage or his lack of faith, but because of what it suggested had been Wren's perspective on his marriages to two of her own sisters.

She turned away and gazed out the window as the steamer approached the southern shores of Vancouver Island, toward the Ross farm, Clover Point, and into Victoria harbor. After several hours seated on the thinly-padded benches of the *Eliza Anderson* while it had stopped at various ports along Puget Sound, Flora lacked any patience to receive a lecture on marriage, particularly when accompanied by the irony of being lectured by Wren.

It had been Mary's idea that Flora and her son spend a few days with their sister Catherine and her family, since Wren had business to attend to in the Nisqually area. Mary's four stepdaughters—Elizabeth's daughters—had stayed behind in Victoria to avoid missing school. The plan had been to return to Victoria in time for Francis and William's trial on charges of highway robbery on the 26th, but a mechanical problem with the steamer they'd intended to take back to Victoria meant having to wait for the departure of the *Eliza Anderson* on the 27th. Flora had expressed doubts from the start. About being away from her farm after her last encounter with Hubbs. About being away from Victoria in the days before the trial, even if a verdict of guilt was a foregone conclusion. And about being absent at a time when their mother needed their support.

Flora glanced over at Wren. She had never understood what Elizabeth had seen in the man, and was even less certain about what had attracted Mary to him, though she admitted that she herself had never been the best judge of a man's character or potential as a husband. Wren had money, but she doubted that money would have been Mary's primary attraction, particularly given the rumors that credited his minor wealth to a history of selling other peoples' livestock. She tried to not even consider the other rumors that circulated about Wren, especially the ones that included Elizabeth and Mary within their hateful words. She had tried to ask Mary about them in earlier years, before her own husband had ever laid a hand on her, but Mary had refused to have a discussion about the rumors, and had insisted only that her marriage was far more agreeable than any rumors would suggest.

As the steamer passed Clover Point and steered into Victoria harbor, Flora felt her fears return. Her brothers' lawyer had informed the family shortly after their arrest in January that the charge of highway robbery could result in the death penalty. There was always hope that Judge Pemberton, himself part of the society of families that built and ran the colony, and a neighbor with property just north of the Ross farm, would continue to grant her brothers a measure of clemency. But there was also the risk that Pemberton would feel mocked by her brothers' continuing misbehavior, as if they had taken each show of leniency as permission to carry on as before.

She knelt on the floor of the passenger compartment and gathered Paul's toys, then lifted him onto her lap as the *Eliza Anderson* rounded Ogden Point and entered the harbor. She wanted him to see Victoria harbor as they steamed toward the wharf, and remember the young city as it was during his infancy. The growing neighborhood of James Bay lay on the right, quickly filling with large homes of the town's wealthier inhabitants. To the left sat the remains of the Songhees reserve, decimated by the smallpox epidemic of 1862. The Royal Hospital stood beside it along the shore, already criticized for being too small less than six years after its opening. Immediately in front of them lay the cold winter waters of the harbor, a coldness that Flora had never forgotten from the trip to the Wren farm that she and Mary had made together so many years before.

Flora looked over at Mary and recognized a shared anxiety on her face.

"Perhaps we might yet arrive at the courthouse before it's over."

"We couldn't fix how they acted before," Mary replied. "We don't have any say now, so what good is it to worry?"

Flora nodded. It was a concept that she wasn't entirely ready to accept, but it had been the wisest advice her sister had offered all morning.

\* \* \*

Flora grasped her mother's hand and listened fearfully to the words that Judge Pemberton nearly spat from his lips.

"The defendants have been found guilty by a jury of their peers of highway robbery and larceny. There were facts alleged, and the manner in which the indictment was framed, that could have placed the defendants in the position of forfeiting their lives, for in addition to robbery from the person, there was personal violence offered, and the statute so provides such a punishment. The facts show that the Chinaman was violently struck on the head. The attack was brutal, and the only extenuation offered by the defendants is that it was a drunken frolic. This Court was anxious to consider well what might operate in favor of the prisoners, but could discover no such extenuation. However, the jury has recommended them to mercy, and though the Court cannot see sufficient ground for that recommendation—for a more brutal act, and one more deserving of suppression for the interests of the community this Court cannot conceive. Still, in deference to the jury, which it has always respected, this Court will pass a less severe sentence upon the defendants than it would otherwise have done. In the absence of a forfeiture of their lives, the prisoners were liable to fifteen years of penal servitude. But, upon the recommendation of the jury, and with the hope that a less severe sentence will act as a warning to others, this Court sentences the prisoners, Francis and William Ross, to five years of penal servitude. The prisoners are remanded to the Victoria gaol for their sentence."

The disparate emotions that were instantly expressed across the courtroom leaned more heavily toward relief, likely because those supporting the victim were unwilling to vocalize public distaste for the light sentence. Flora squeezed her mother's hand and shared a brief smile for the outcome. It was only when they rose from the benches and Reverend Cridge grasped her arm with a proclamation of the good Lord's mercy that she lost control of her emotions. Cridge pulled her close to comfort her tears.

"There, there, my dear. It could've been so much worse. Five years of servitude could ultimately be a blessing for them both."

Flora pulled back, embarrassed at her loss of control on Cridge's shoulder. Her tears were for so much more than her brothers. They were tears of relief for the preservation of her brothers' lives, that was certain. But they were also for the fear that she was about to disappoint Cridge when she would turn to him, as she'd have to, for marital advice. Fear that he would see her circumstances as proof that she'd failed as a wife. Cridge, unaware of the many reasons for the tears, consoled her as he had done for Isabella throughout the trial.

"And surely they won't be required to carry out the entire sentence. The gaol's far too small to hold every prisoner for the duration. We'll petition the authorities in good time."

Flora smiled at Cridge's innocence, wishing she could avoid disappointing him. "You've been so kind to be here for mother."

"As you have all been for Mary and I, my dear."

"Reverend ..." Flora started, but hesitated, struggling

to hold back more tears. "I wonder if I could have a moment of your time today. Not here. Somewhere private. And perhaps, if we could meet with Mr. McCreight as well ..."

McCreight had been the brothers' trial attorney and had been known as a skilled lawyer since his arrival six years earlier. Cridge's worried expression told Flora that his mind was already attempting to fill in the blanks, but she opted to say nothing that might confirm his fears until they could meet in private.

*  *  *

"From what I read in the papers, I know it's possible under English divorce law for a wife to seek a divorce from her husband, and that it's the law in British Columbia," Flora stated, looking across John Foster McCreight's paper-strewn desk in the hope that the young lawyer would agree with her. She turned to Reverend Cridge to gauge his reaction, but he seemed intent on ensuring that McCreight's views were spoken first.

"In England, most definitely," McCreight finally replied. "And as for British Columbia, the Matrimonial Causes Act was theoretically one of the received laws that went into force when the colony was founded, but I've yet to hear of Begbie recognizing it, or granting a single divorce. And even if he did, trying to predict how Begbie might apply any particular law is a fool's game. But here in this colony, the Assembly would have to adopt the act for it to take effect, and they haven't done so."

"Meaning I'm in the same position now as my mother was a few years back," Flora concluded.

"Well, in some regards, yes. Though I doubt you have the option of leveling bigamy charges at Mr. Hubbs in the manner Mr. O'Brien presented."

"He was married before me, but widowed," Flora explained, with slightly more regret for her predecessor's passing than she had expressed before. "But Mr. Firth would testify that this current girl claims to be his *klootchman*."

"But her claim that she's his *klootchman* didn't precede

your marriage," McCreight explained, "so it's nothing more than ordinary adultery."

Flora decided to ignore his implicit suggestion that adultery could exist in ordinary and non-ordinary forms.

"There are, however, some other options," he continued. "If you could establish residency in British Columbia for a sufficient period of time, Begbie might be willing to assert jurisdiction over your marriage and apply the English Divorce Act in your favor. But, of course, as a wife seeking a divorce under that law, you'd still need to prove far more than just adultery. Something such as bigamy or incest, or such other things I dare not mention."

"Or cruelty," Flora added, having read about the law's application in England.

"But cruelty is a fluid standard. One judge's idea of cruelty is another's idea of a spirited marriage. You might suppose Begbie would wish to favor your side of the dispute, if for no other reason than because he knows your family well. But he could just as easily decide, since he sits one pew away from your mother's at church when he's in town, that he needs to be overly critical of your case."

"But if my husband filed for divorce under the English Act and claimed I was the one who was unfaithful, that would be enough for divorce," Flora replied. "No need for him to show cruelty or bigamy."

"Yes, but you're not suggesting that –"

"Of course not. I'm merely pointing out the obvious discrepancy."

"Perhaps one alternative to establishing residency in British Columbia is to simply wait until union of the colonies is effective, and the law is uniform here and on the mainland."

"Which could be how long? Months? A year?" Flora inquired. "I've read the papers. It hardly seems to be a certainty."

"Yes, perhaps not an alternative," McCreight cautioned. "Consolidation of the court systems isn't likely to happen anytime soon. Maybe years. The other option, of course, is the courts of Washington Territory. Your husband is a U.S.

citizen—you are as well, now—and their new divorce laws are more liberal than even the English law in force on the mainland."

"Exceedingly liberal," she replied. "From what I recall, the court's conclusion that the husband and wife can no longer habitate together is enough for the divorce to be granted."

Flora noticed Cridge's look of surprise.

"My husband was in the Assembly when they passed the law," she explained, anticipating his question. "His father largely wrote it. Back then, he still spoke to me in tones other than anger, and I listened in kind, never imagining why it might be useful for me to know something about the law."

She turned back to McCreight. "But I imagine you're aware of my father-in-law, who bears the same name as my husband."

Flora stopped, confident that McCreight understood her point without further explanation. He would have been well aware of Hubbs Senior, his prominent legal practice, his time as President of the Territorial Legislative Council, and the fact that he could count most of the judges and attorneys in the region as being among his closest friends and political allies—at least, those who weren't his political enemies. A contested divorce in a Washington court would not appear to be a reasonable option.

"And even if I thought it possible to look to Washington Territory for a divorce," she continued, "the bigger concern is the family farm."

"Which is a legitimate concern," McCreight agreed. "While the English act might weaken the doctrine of coverture, your property remains his property unless and until you can pursue an action to try to recover it. And there's no telling how that might go in these Courts. I'm not familiar enough with the status of coverture under the laws of Washington Territory or how it would be applied to property here in the colony, but you might find a more favorable forum there to protect your share of the Ross farm, especially if you could get his consent to a stipulated termination of the marriage."

"A divorce from a court in Washington would be recognized here, where we were married?"

"It should be, although I dare say you'd likely be the first couple to find out."

Flora had hoped to hear more than a prospective response, but she'd come to understand from the family's past legal troubles that certainty in the law could never be guaranteed. She might well face a judge who'd been appointed in the early days of the colony when the qualifications to serve as a judge hadn't necessarily included past legal training.

"I suppose I could also simply pray that there's truth to the rumors of American annexation," Flora proposed only slightly in jest. "At least then I could take advantage of American divorce laws in a Victoria court without my father-in-law holding sway."

McCreight replied with a forced smile and a slight nod to acknowledge the attempt at humor. Rumors of a possible U.S. annexation of the colony had been rampant for years, back to the Fraser River gold rush of 1858. But they'd taken on a new character in recent months, driven partly by the expansionist views of William Seward, the U.S. Secretary of State. There was a fear across the colonies that the Union Army would be unlikely to disband following the conclusion of the Civil War, and might instead focus its attention on territories beyond its borders. It was a fear that was driving confederation negotiations in the eastern British colonies, and union negotiations in the two Pacific colonies.

Flora turned to Cridge, realizing that he had been silent throughout the legal discussion. His expression was an unreadable reflection of conflicted emotions, and Flora realized that inviting her minister to a discussion about divorce might not have been the wisest choice. Cridge offered a wan smile, as if recognizing that the time had come for his views to be included in the conversation.

"Which leaves one other option that is perhaps more in my bailiwick," he began.

"And the answer to that, Reverend, is no," Flora answered with a polite firmness, knowing exactly the option he would propose. "This isn't a marriage that can be reconciled by clerical advice or the efforts of the spouses. He's changed. Thoroughly changed. He's indifferent to our son, cruel to me, and entirely callous toward our marriage. He doesn't respect our vows because he has no respect for the idea of our marriage. And that doesn't even begin to address how unbearable daily life has been. There's nothing to reconcile."

"Even for young Paul?"

"Paul spends more time with Mr. Firth or Mr. Boyce than he does with his father. My desire to end this marriage is as much for Paul's sake as for my own."

"And yet you asked me to be here, and so I feel compelled to share my views so that you have a complete understanding of the implications of your decision. Divorce may now be legal in other colonies and territories, and perhaps soon, here, as well. But it will never be legal in the Church of England. A member of our congregation can be married once, and only once, absent the death of a spouse. If you return to Victoria as a divorced woman, I cannot promise you'll be welcomed back into our congregation. By me, of course, though perhaps not with demonstrative approval. But the judgment of our Lord is far more predictable than the judgment of his children. You are only twenty-four years old –"

"Twenty-three."

"Twenty-three. You have a child. You'll need income to raise him, and feed you both. Are you truly prepared to spend the entirety of your adult life without the security of a husband who will provide for you both?"

"That's a prospect I face whether or not I remain married to Paul. Our income is largely the result of my toils on the farm, and I need neither love nor provision from him. This isn't a decision to find a better husband, Reverend. I have to protect my son, and myself, from a man who threatens our security. I don't know how I'll accomplish this, but I have to find the means."

Flora hoped either man would have yet another option to consider, but they offered none.

"So, it seems my best approach is to wait for union—union of the colonies and eventually their courts—if and when that ever happens."

"And even then," McCreight cautioned, "you'll need a case far stronger than mere infidelity by a husband to ensure that a divorce will be granted. You said he's cruel to you." He hesitated. "Does he beat you?"

Flora hesitated, ashamed to make such an admission in front of Cridge.

"From time to time," she added quietly.

"Are there witnesses?" McCreight asked.

"To the bruises. Perhaps his father and stepmother to the sounds of a fight from the room next door. But only our son's witnessed the … his anger."

"Then in the meantime, as we wait for the possibility of colonial union, and as difficult as this might sound, I suggest you stay at the farm on San Juan as much as you can. Possession of the family home isn't much, but it at least shows you haven't deserted the marriage, and it may help you in any proceeding to establish rights to the farm here in Victoria if you've been the one operating the farm on San Juan. Ensure that you have witnesses to how you run the farm while he's absent. And most importantly, witnesses to his cruelty."

"How am I supposed to find those?"

"Keep a friend or two aware of events. And keep records. A journal. Notes. Anything."

"I've already told him to never come back. There might never be any more violence."

"That could be good for different reasons. We could perhaps build an argument for a petition on abandonment by him as a form of emotional cruelty."

Flora sat back, troubled by the advice. It struck her as sadly ironic that a political marriage of the two colonies was a necessary precondition to the dissolution of her own marriage. She had no control over the process, nor any certainty as to how many months it could take. But her motives made her one of the few residents of Vancouver Island who was convinced that union of the colonies was a

386

political development that couldn't possibly happen soon enough.

\* \* \*

# Excitement in Canada.

TORONTO, C.W., March 9—The popular rally under the call for volunteers exceeds thirty thousand troops. Over two thousand arrived here last night. The people are fully aroused and no man shirks his duty. The most exciting rumors prevail of Fenian intentions to invade Canada, and the Government has taken possession of the telegraph lines. Preparations have been made to send troops by rail to any point of danger at a moment's notice. St. Patrick's day is anticipated with intense apprehension, and loud calls are being made on President Johnson to interfere. The city papers of this morning give two columns of special despatches from all parts of Canada of the popular excitement and volunteering.

*The Daily British Colonist*, Thursday, March 15, 1866, p. 3.

\* \* \*

Flora stopped in her tracks. The front door was open. She had only been in the barn for a short time, and she was certain she'd closed the front door of the house as she'd left. Paul was still behind the house playing some game he'd invented with a pile of sticks, so he was unlikely to have been the one to have left the door open.

The idea of returning home to find a front door open was hardly out of the ordinary on the island. Local Indians didn't seem to recognize the concept of an expectation of privacy in one's home, and she had often entered her house to find one or more women in her kitchen waiting for her to return so that they could sell her the fish they'd caught or the plants they'd gathered. But attacks from northern Indians, though far less in number since smallpox had devastated villages along the coast, were still a concern for a woman and child spending most nights alone in an isolated farmhouse. She had always practiced two rules: know the location of her son, and know the location of the musket. Her son was playing behind the house. The musket was inside the open door. But she was less fearful of the possibility of an Indian attack, and far more troubled that the open door was a sign her husband had returned.

She entered the front parlor and listened. At first she heard nothing. She thought she detected the faint smell of whiskey, but that didn't provide her with any certainty as to who might have entered.

"Hello?"

Sounds of movement came from the bedroom. Hubbs appeared in the doorway. Even if she hadn't been able to smell the whiskey, she could see instantly in his eyes that he'd been drinking.

"Getting some stuff of mine."

"Fine." Flora stepped inside and crossed the room toward the kitchen, opting to give him a clear path to the door.

"I heard you went away," Hubbs began.

"Just for a few days."

"You think you can stay here?"

"As long as I'm your wife and the mother of your child."

Hubbs mulled over the concept, then turned back into the bedroom. Flora could hear him rummaging about, and she mentally ran through a list of all the things that were kept in the room, wondering if she had anything to protect other than her own body and their child. The knowledge that he'd been drinking in the morning, or perhaps all night, created far too high a risk of violence. Better to stand back quietly and allow him to carry out his intended tasks.

She had long ago reached the conclusion that the occupation of the island by Pickett's company of American troops had triggered Hubbs' downfall, though he continued to see it as the moment of his greatest glory. Immediately after the joint occupation had been determined, and after a petition by residents had restored Pickett as the commander of the American Camp in early 1860, Hubbs and Flora had been entertained on a regular basis by Pickett and his officers. It wasn't until Pickett's departure at the start of the Civil War that Hubbs began to struggle in his efforts to establish a career that could replace his position as deputy tax collector. He had seemed to be a man of such promise when they had first met. She wondered if that had simply been her own naïveté and inexperience, and whether disappointment combined with occasional bruises could satisfy the English Divorce Act's "cruelty" requirement.

Hubbs appeared in the doorway again, dropping a bag on the floor.

"This is my homestead. My house."

"And I'm your wife and Paul is your son, and as soon as you grant me a divorce, we'll leave and return to Victoria."

She questioned the wisdom of raising the issue when he'd been drinking, but more than a month of uncertainty drove her to search for a resolution. The smirk that had started to cross Hubbs' face as Flora pronounced herself as his wife was the same smirk that she'd seen far too often in the past year. It disappeared the moment he understood the direction of her statement.

"I'm not giving you a divorce."

"It would be far easier if you agreed."

"Why would I make it easy for you?"

"I meant for you. If you don't agree, I'll have to petition for one once the colonies are unified. The new English law means I can get a divorce because of adultery." She didn't mention the need for additional grounds, or the fear that a colonial divorce might leave him in control of much of the Ross farm. He already knew the latter point.

She could see anger build on his face, and for a moment she feared his reaction, although another bruise would also be an opportunity to reveal the extent of his cruelty to her friends and to gather witnesses for her case. Instead, Hubbs let out a deep sigh, reached for the bag he had dropped to the floor, and walked to the door.

"You're not getting a divorce."

He slammed the door as he left, though it rattled as much as slammed on its shaky hinges. Flora's immediate sense of relief at his peaceful departure was suddenly replaced by the realization that Paul was playing behind the house. She ran out the back door, fearful that Hubbs might have taken their son. For leverage. For spite. Her son was no longer behind the house. The sticks were just a pile.

Flora opened her mouth to call out for him, but then stopped, fearful that Hubbs might interpret a cry for "Paul" as a call for his return. She ran from the house, scanning in all directions. It was only seconds of panic, but lasted an eternity before Flora spotted her son chasing a hen that had escaped its enclosure, seemingly unaware that his father had even been at the house. Flora hurried to him, sending the hen into a panicked escape, then took his hand and led him back into the kitchen, locking the door behind them.

# *Chapter 20*

SUDDEN DEATH AT COWICHAN.—
Yesterday some persons on entering the
dwelling of Mr. Lucius Simon O'Brien,
formerly of Ross Bay, near Victoria, but
more recently a settler in Shawnigan, were
shocked at finding O'Brien dead on the sofa.
He had not been seen about for some little
time, and the suspicions of those around him
led to the discovery of his dead body as
described. There were no outward marks of
violence and death had apparently resulted
from natural causes. Mr. Morley, J.P., was
to hold an inquest on the remains yesterday.

*The Daily British Colonist*, Saturday, March 17, 1866,
p. 3.

\* \* \*

Flora stared at the short article about the discovery of
Lucius O'Brien's body, not believing that it could be true.
There were so many thoughts and emotions that should be

triggered by such news. But uppermost in her mind was relief that Francis and William were relatively secure in the Victoria gaol. At least it would prevent rumors from spreading about the cause of O'Brien's demise. She felt some guilt for her own lack of sadness over the passing of a man who'd briefly been her stepfather, but he had caused far too much bitterness in her family to allow her to feel any strong emotion, even after his death. But it being Sunday morning, and services at the schoolhouse on Portland Fair Hill having just concluded, Flora said a quick and silent prayer for his soul.

"Thank you for bringing this over," she said, handing the paper back to Stephen Boyce.

Boyce had returned that morning from a trip to Victoria, just in time for the services that local residents held each Sunday at the new schoolhouse. Although they lacked a cleric of their own, pastors from Victoria of various denominations would often travel to the island to minister to the residents. On all other Sundays, the men would take turns offering readings and informal sermons. It was an arrangement that required compromise, as no single service could accommodate the expectations or doctrinal needs of each attendee.

"Least I could do. I imagine your mother would know by now."

"I can't imagine news like this wouldn't have reached her far more quickly than it reached me. It'll be difficult for her, no matter how things turned out between them."

"Hopefully she'll be able to see it as an end to a bad period," Boyce suggested.

Flora looked over to where Paul was playing with other children in the tall grass in front of the schoolhouse. In so many ways, the community that was forming on the southern end of the island was an ideal place to raise her son. The population was growing. Many of her friends had children close to Paul's age. And the island had become a place where a family could ensure that their children were raised with a decent education, regardless of which country might ultimately obtain sovereignty.

Catherine McGeary approached and reached for Flora's hand. "Lucinda said he was by this week."

Flora nodded, not surprised that word had spread. "It lasted just a few minutes, but I suppose it went reasonably well. I asked him for a divorce, but he refused." Flora turned and walked slowly away from the church, beckoning Catherine to follow in order to avoid prying eyes and ears.

"Ya need 'im to agree?"

"It's the only way I won't lose everything—custody of Paul, much of my mother's farm. I need leverage, but how do you get leverage with a man who no longer cares about his own reputation?" Flora wondered aloud.

"It's funny how different he is from his pa," Catherine responded. "Though I only know 'bout him from reputation. Maybe they seem more 'like to ya?"

"Not at all. His father cares deeply about reputation. How can he not when he's one of the top attorneys in the …" Flora trailed off, realizing in an instant that her father-in-law might not be the formidable adversary she had supposed him to be, but that their interests might be more aligned than she'd ever imagined. It was an intimidating thought to consider, but it suddenly appeared logical that if she approached him with the proper strategy, Paul Hubbs Senior just might be a potential ally.

"What's that look on yer face?" Catherine asked.

"I dare say it's a little hope for the first time in a long while."

\* \* \*

Hubbs Senior studied Flora from across the table and pondered his next move.

"Maggie, dear," Hubbs Senior began, pushing his empty plate away from himself, "why don't you take the children outside and let them play in the yard? Flora and I need to discuss a little business as we digest our lunch."

He leaned back in his chair and smiled at Flora while he waited for his wife to take their two children and his grandson, Paul, outside to play. He felt confident that Flora's poorly disguised anxiety would only increase as they waited for Maggie to gain control of the three young children.

"Business?" Flora delivered it as an innocent question the moment they were alone, but Hubbs Senior was certain they both understood that she was playing a well-rehearsed part.

"You didn't travel here today just so I could see my grandchild. We both know this is about your marriage."

"I've wondered if he's been telling you everything."

"My son? He tells me nothing. What little I know is from rumor and the experience of watching the two of you together. Which is enough to know that you have reasons to come here to talk."

"I do."

"And?"

"We've been living apart for more than two months now."

"Because ..."

"There's a young Cowichan woman. A girl. He keeps her in a small cabin on Decatur Island. He's been spending more time there than in his own home, and all of San Juan seems to know it."

"And you can't accept that?"

"Six years ago we vowed to each other before God to forsake all others."

"For many men, a mistress is a necessary part of their marriage."

"I'm well aware that many men can't live by their sacred vows, but I doubt many of them make their wives as thoroughly miserable as your son's made me."

"Does he hit you?"

Flora hesitated, and Hubbs Senior realized that he hadn't needed to ask the question to know the answer.

"Didn't your own ears witness the answer to that question?"

"One fight doesn't suggest a habit."

"A fist is rarely raised only once. I came here to let you know that I intend to obtain a divorce. Unfortunately, a divorce in the colonies may take some time. Under English law, a wife has to allege more than infidelity just to be heard.

But, my lawyer will be able to present that case. There are witnesses to his cruelties. More than just you and Maggie."

"And yet you're here."

"Because I understand the laws of Washington Territory are less antiquated. I'm told it's enough to state that the two parties are incapable of continuing their marriage, so long as they're in agreement. There's no need to get into details we might both prefer to keep private."

"Ah. So you're here to blackmail me to ensure my son's escapades don't harm my own career."

"I'm here to do no such thing."

"Then ..."

"I'm here to ask for your assistance. As you pointed out, many men consider a mistress necessary to a marriage. I'm the one who'll be humiliated by public spectacle, the wife who drove her husband into the arms of a girl. A prompt divorce by agreement, without controversy, would be best for my reputation, but also in my husband's best interests, even if he can't see that yet. You know every lawyer in the territory, whereas I know only you. If I'm to get his agreement for a divorce, and make it happen without public spectacle, I can only do it with your assistance."

Hubbs Senior considered her explanation. Perhaps it wasn't technically blackmail if they could both agree that it would be in everyone's interest for the divorce to be consensual. Perhaps she wasn't aware of the efforts underway to convince him to run for Governor of the territory. Perhaps she didn't entirely appreciate the damage her allegations against his son could do if he were to agree to run. Perhaps it was innocent self-interest. The only certainty was that she was intent on using him, no matter how she might couch it as seeking his help for their mutual benefit.

"Obviously, I can't represent you."

"But you could refer me to someone who can."

Was she naïve enough to allow him to guide her to someone who could ensure that the terms of divorce would be favorable to his son, or did she have another card to play? He favored the latter and decided to address the issue head on.

"Why wouldn't I just recommend a close friend of mine who'd ensure you get nothing?"

"Because it won't make a difference. My terms are simple. I get sole custody of our son, and we each keep our respective properties; mine at Victoria, his on San Juan, and wherever else he might own property. That's it. I don't want alimony, and I doubt he wants custody. I can pay for my own lawyer. I don't want anything from him. No lawyer is going to convince me to fight for more, or accept any less. You could ensure I find a lawyer who'll respect our need for privacy, have the respect of whatever judge we appear before, convince your son that this is in his best interests, and ensure that this marriage can be put behind us all without becoming food for gossip. I won't file here unless he agrees to those terms. And if he doesn't, then I still have the option of petitioning for a colonial divorce."

Hubbs Senior smiled, pleased that he had read her properly. Had his son realized six years earlier that he was marrying a woman far cleverer than he was? It was a risk any man faces when marrying a wife who's still more of a girl, he had concluded months earlier from the lessons of his own present marriage. The husband might anticipate the woman she will become, and might presume that he'll have a say in that result, but she so often will grow into a wife who is far more of a challenge than a comfort. His son's anger at the prior Independence Ball suggested that he'd reached a similar realization about his own marriage.

"Have you ever met our neighbor, Mr. Dennison?"

"The Irish man?"

"The same. Excellent lawyer. And as of a few weeks ago, our new representative on the Legislative Council. I see a little of myself in him, if I may say so. Why don't you and I go pay Mr. Dennison a visit?"

Flora smiled her agreement. "I'm pleased we were able to have this conversation like two adults."

"Seems to me we've had this conversation more like two attorneys." Hubbs Senior rose from his chair, smiled politely, and gestured to the front door.

\* \* \*

Flora had journeyed to Port Townsend with her son in hopes of establishing a common interest with her father-in-law. She hadn't expected to be returning on the *Eliza Anderson* with her son asleep on the bench to her right, and her new attorney to her left.

She had discovered two days earlier that meeting with a prospective attorney in his home on a Saturday afternoon could prove to be a particularly advantageous way to obtain his services. Initially, Dennison had appeared wary of representing the daughter-in-law of his neighbor and mentor in a divorce proceeding against the mentor's son. But Mrs. Dennison had managed to insert herself into much of Flora's meeting on the pretense of acting as a good hostess, and had ended up being the most important ally Flora had found on the trip by helping to convince her husband to take the case. Flora didn't ask what might have passed between Mrs. Dennison and Hubbs in prior conversations, or if she had only come to know of Hubbs in passing. But Mrs. Dennison had seemed determined to ensure that Flora would have adequate representation, and Flora was grateful for her assistance, particularly given how intimidating she found Dennison to be.

Dennison was in his early forties, and carried himself with a stiff manner that was accentuated by his choice of clothing. His shirts had unusually high starched collars, which left Flora with the initial impression that his head was propped awkwardly in place by the starched fabric. It was only after a longer acquaintance that she concluded it was more likely that the cloth collars were held up by his rigid neck.

The first steamer back to Victoria had been scheduled to depart the following Tuesday, and Dennison was already planning to be on it so that he could meet with shipbuilding clients in Victoria who were pursuing a lawsuit in Franklin County. It was a fortunate coincidence, Flora had concluded. For it meant that she could arrange a meeting between McCreight and Dennison once they arrived in

Victoria, and it gave her and Dennison an opportunity to bond over a common individual.

"Jemmy Jones?" Flora exclaimed, still surprised by the frequency with which the errant sea captain appeared in her life. "You're involved in that case?"

"We go to trial against the bonding company at the next session of the District Court."

"And he's still at large?"

"Still in California, as far as anyone knows."

Dennison launched into the tale of Jemmy Jones with a self-satisfied smile. Flora could easily have recounted the story from her own knowledge, or assured him that she knew the story well, but decided it was best to let Dennison unravel the tale and fill some time on their journey. She had already concluded that he enjoyed hearing himself speak, a trait that seemed common in nearly all of the lawyers she'd met in her lifetime.

Dennison's clients were among the creditors owed money by Jones for the construction of the *Jenny Jones*, and their lawsuit against the Puget Sound bonding company arose from Jones' act to commandeer his boat out from under the watch of U.S. Marshalls after his escape from the Victoria gaol, and his subsequent escape with the *Jenny Jones* to Mexico. Whatever value the boat might have had if it could have been recovered was nearly lost when Jones' own crew had sabotaged the boat in Mexico as retaliation for Jones' inability, or refusal, to pay them for the journey. Jones then escaped to California where he remained at large.

Dennison droned on for nearly a half hour with far more detail than the story justified. Flora dutifully conveyed a sense of interest until she was certain that Dennison had finished, which he demonstrated by sitting back with a satisfied smile, pleased for having entertained his new client with such a tale.

"Well, being an attorney sounds far more interesting than I'd ever realized," she said, hoping her compliment didn't come across as cloying. "I have a Jemmy Jones story of my own, though hardly filled with the intrigue of yours. In many ways, it's a miracle I'm even here to tell it."

Dennison lifted an eyebrow in competitive concern as Flora launched into the tale of the capsized *Wild Pigeon* more than six years before. The journey to Victoria was, as Flora hoped it would turn out to be, the bonding experience that can develop when two people have the opportunity to share their respective tales about a common adversary, but neither feels that their story has been outdone by the other's. It was also the first time since the *Wild Pigeon* had capsized that Flora decided it might have turned out to be a particularly useful experience after all.

✳ ✳ ✳

Flora paused in the middle of Bastian Square and gazed at the police barracks that held the city's cramped gaol. There were so many buildings in Victoria that should have felt as familiar to her as the gaol had become. A theatre. A grocer. A favorite shop. But it was at the gaol where she had visited Francis and William so many times over the years that she found so much familiarity. She and Hubbs had visited his brother Charles each time he'd been imprisoned for various misdeeds. And she'd visited Alexander during his brief incarceration when Lucius O'Brien had charged him with assault in the midst of the family's marital drama. She wondered if there were any women in Victoria who had visited the gaol as often as she had, and concluded that only her own mother might hold such a distinction.

But this visit would be unlike all others. Francis and William had rarely remained in gaol on any prior offence for more than a few days or weeks at a time. On this visit, she would face her brothers barely a month into five-year sentences. It would be difficult to greet them, but it would be far more difficult to leave.

As Flora reached the barracks, the door opened and Helmcken emerged, nearly bumping into her.

"Dr. Helmcken."

"Flora, what a nice surprise. You are –"

"Passing through town, overnight. I trust my brothers are well and that they're not your reason for this visit?"

"As the official gaol surgeon, I can assure you that if irascibility is an indication of good health, then they are both perfectly healthy." Helmcken smiled. Flora took no offence at his description of her brothers. He had sewn up more than enough whiskey-related injuries— William and Francis' injuries, as well as those of their adversaries and victims—that he was entitled to comment.

"I do worry about them," Flora confided. "Five years is such a long time. And to be here, in the middle of the town, with life going on all around them, passing them by …"

"One might say life was passing them by already."

Flora nodded in agreement. Neither of her brothers appeared to have friends for any reason other than shared carousing. Neither was likely to be seen by any prospective bride as a viable groom. And neither had any occupation other than helping at family farms on those rare occasions when they managed to rise from their beds in time to be of any assistance. Perhaps working on a chain gang, watching life go on around them, would help them to realize how much of their lives they had wasted to the lure of whiskey.

Flora found herself searching Helmcken's face for the sparkle she had always seen in his eyes, a sparkle that had disappeared when Cecilia had died a year earlier, followed a few weeks later by the death of their newborn son. His eyes still expressed only sadness, but she told herself that the missing sparkle could be as much a product of visiting the gaol or having to control the Legislative Assembly in the midst of the colonial union debates as from anything else. She wondered if others ever looked into her eyes in search of the same sparkle, and if it had disappeared sometime over the past few years of marital strife.

"I apologize for raising a topic that suggests I've been listening to gossip," Helmcken began, hesitantly. "I'm sorry to hear of the difficulties you've had with Mr. Hubbs. And for the record," he added quickly, "it was in conversation with your mother that I learned of this, not from petty gossip on the street."

Her mother had meant no harm by sharing such details with a man so close to her family. But Flora hesitated in her response. It would be her first conversation about her marriage that wasn't with an attorney or minister, family member, or close friend on the island who had known the details of the infidelity before she had. She would need to decide how much to share. She wished to be free of her husband without the scandal, gossip, and newspaper articles that had accompanied her mother's separation from O'Brien. The gossip had been beyond their control, but so much of the press had come from the family's own public and petty disputes. She concluded that saying as little as possible even to family friends was the better approach, at least for the time being.

"Thank you. That's very kind. Well, I suppose I should go inside and visit with my poor brothers."

Helmcken held open the door to the barracks.

"And if you'll excuse me," he replied, "I must leave this bastion of troublemakers and preside over a far less restrained band of troublemakers, whose outrages go largely unpunished."

"You have an Assembly session?" Flora smiled, anticipating the direction of his humor.

Helmcken smiled and nodded as Flora entered the barracks. She paused by the door as the building's characteristic odor assaulted her nose. Dampness. Sweat. Human waste. Despite the frequency of her visits over the years, it was an aspect of the building with which she hadn't yet become accustomed. It struck her as a singular reason why the gaol's occupants might attempt to avoid return visits. And, as she stepped deeper into the building, she realized that it was an odor that would become far more familiar if she could obtain a divorce, return to Victoria, and visit her brothers with more regular frequency.

\* \* \*

# CANADA.

---

## MORE FENIAN EXCITEMENTS.

CHICAGO, April 5th.—The Canadians are again in great alarm. They have reliable reports that war vessels and convoys, including two schooners loaded with cannon, are fitting out at Chicago. There are rumors that an expedition under B. Doran Killian, consisting of three steamers, with 5,500 men, has sailed from New York for New Brunswick, and another report gives Bermuda as its destination. It is believed that General Sweeney designs an attack on Central Canada. An official proclamation from Colonel O'Mahony, announces the escape of James Stephens from Ireland, his arrival at Paris, and his speedy arrival in the United States to head the Fenians. Discussions are prevalent in the ranks of the brotherhood here.

*The Daily British Colonist*, Saturday, April 14, 1866, p. 3.

\* \* \*

Helmcken had often found the hard, wooden Speaker's chair to be uncomfortable, figuratively and literally. But having to preside over the fifteen-member colonial Assembly for over twenty-one hours without interruption, while Amor De Cosmos carried out a filibuster of a tax bill, made both concepts of discomfort seem far more obvious than ever before.

The bill had appeared innocuous enough, encouraging Sheriff's sales of property for unpaid taxes. But De Cosmos and a fellow legislator, Leonard McClure, found the bill antithetical to their efforts to secure a homestead exemption that would help struggling families keep their homes from the reach of creditors. If they could prevent the Assembly from voting until past noon the next day, then the bill would fail by its own terms. McClure had talked all night, spending sixteen hours on his feet, and De Cosmos was well into his fifth hour of speech with few signs of slowing down. Helmcken had made an effort earlier in the proceedings to listen to the words each man had said. Twenty-one hours later, all of his efforts were focused on trying to maintain the illusion of remaining awake without falling from his chair.

Since becoming a member of the Assembly, and leaving his role as publisher and editor of the *British Colonist*, De Cosmos' attacks on the men like Helmcken who had founded the colony had simply changed from print to speech. He had done much to turn the once amicable chamber into a frequent pit of angry debate, as well as provide a policy perspective that was distinct from the members who had a Company background.

Helmcken was no stranger to public attacks. He had become almost immune to them, whether the attacks were based on truth or lies. It was a necessary quality for any politician in the young colony, though Helmcken preferred to think of himself simply as a doctor fulfilling additional civic duties. There were still those who whispered behind his back that he'd been part of a government plot to further the smallpox epidemic of 1862 by withholding available vaccines from the Indian population, or by forcing visiting Indians to congregate on local reserves where the virus had spread, and then driving them back to their villages to carry the virus throughout the colonies. Some claimed it had been a policy of ineptitude, while others claimed it had been an intentional policy to erase Indian communities from desirable lands for arriving settlers.

Helmcken looked at his watch. It was nearly noon. Outside in the streets a celebration was underway in anticipation of a significant change about to arrive in the colony. In a matter of hours, at most, the transcontinental telegraph line from the Atlantic to Victoria would be completed, and the first signals of a new era would pass across the continent to the colony. It would launch an era of instant connection with the rest of the world. Of news that would be timely. Of reduced isolation. Helmcken had intended to be present to celebrate the milestone, but that prospect seemed increasingly unlikely as De Cosmos droned on about irrelevant matters.

Helmcken sat back in his chair and allowed his eyes to fall half-shut, knowing that just a little more time would permit the filibuster to succeed and, as a result, free him from his duties in the Speaker's chair. Just a little more time. And then, if he had the energy, he too would be able to mark Victoria's entry into a world of near-instant intercontinental communication.

\* \* \*

The Hubbs farm had never seen so much activity. But it had never before served as a location for history to unfold, and likely never would again. Nearly two-dozen of Flora's neighbors stood on the bluff above the beach and gazed across the narrow channel toward Lopez Island, to where the *H.M. Gunboat Forward* lay at anchor in the rushing current that passed through the channel, slowly lowering a thick telegraph cable into the water.

A month had passed since Flora had visited Hubbs Senior and hired Dennison as her attorney. Nearly two months had passed since she'd demanded a divorce from her husband. Yet she'd heard nothing. Patience was a word that she had repeated to herself with such frequency that she'd become tired of its sound. An urge to take action, any action, stirred inside her.

She leaned down and lifted young Paul into her arms, groaning at his weight and wondering how much longer she would be able to lift him.

"See the boat?" she asked him. "It's lowering a giant wire into the ocean, the last mile of a wire that stretches all the way from Victoria to the Atlantic Ocean. In a few more months, it'll go all the way across the ocean to Europe, halfway around the world. And as soon as they attach the end of that wire to that pole over there, people in Victoria will be able to send a message to people thousands of miles away in just a few hours or even minutes."

Paul stared out at the boat, not seeming to understand Flora's explanation, though she wasn't entirely certain that she understood it either. The technological concept was simple enough; an electrical charge was varied by the operator's keystrokes, and used to spell letters, words and sentences, much like a lantern on a ship would flash Morse code. But the implication, the idea that someone thousands of miles away could communicate with anyone in Victoria— with her, even—in a matter of minutes, hours, or at most a few days if wires were down, was far more difficult to comprehend.

Flora wanted to get the concept through to her son, but knew it was unlikely that a small boy not quite four years old would remember this day when he was older. She lowered Paul back onto the grass, took his hand in hers, and walked over to where Robert Firth was deep in discussion with William Fraser, whose son had purchased the old Lyman Cutlar claim several years earlier. Firth's older children were with him, but seemed far more intent on chasing one another through the tall spring grass than watching history in the making.

"You can see how the boat's strainin' 'gainst the anchors. The cable's dilderin' aboot under there like a leaf in a gussel," Fraser exclaimed.

"Maybe we dinnae kin what they do," Firth replied. "Maybe the wire's too heavy for the current?"

Flora smiled, noticing how each man spoke in a much thicker Scottish brogue whenever they were together. She had never been able to decide if they simply reinforced each other's linguistic habits, or if it was an unspoken competition between them to show which of them could maintain a stronger bond with their origins.

She looked over at the *Forward* and saw how the ship pulled against its anchors, as Fraser had described. It was fighting the strong current that flowed through the channel, as if the current was attempting to scuttle the *Forward's* efforts to bridge the final gap in the telegraph. The current flowed south as the tide went out, but was certain to be flowing north again in a few hours with equal ferocity.

"They've put down a few thousand miles of wire before getting here," Flora offered. "They must know what they're doing."

"A few thousand miles o' wire on land strung from pole to pole," Fraser replied. "A cable flutterin' in the winds hits air. A cable rollin' in the roost hits rocks n' shells n' such. Yer gonna have lots o' fowk comin' here over the years to repair this peedie bit o' wire."

Flora smiled, hopeful that she wouldn't be the one to witness the predicted repairs.

"At least if the Fenians invade, we winna wait months to hear what politicians back east think to do 'bout it all." Firth grinned at his own prediction, though the thought on Flora's mind was that another war seemed far more possible than his humor might suggest. Despite initial post-Civil War fears that the Union Army would look north, the fear of the moment was an invasion by the Fenians, a private army of Irish nationalists using the United States as a base. Their stated purpose was the bizarre plan to capture and hold British colonies for ransom, in exchange for a free Ireland. She wasn't concerned for San Juan Island. Any Fenian incursions would more likely be directed toward Victoria or New Westminster, rather than to a small island that might not even be a British possession once the boundary dispute was finalized. But the mere prospect of such actions by a foreign militia was troubling. All the more troubling because the U.S. government showed little interest in interfering with their efforts to launch such a campaign from U.S. soil.

"Maybe," Fraser answered. "But if there's another war, I dout it'll start wit' fellin' a swine. It'll be choppin' the wire."

Flora took Paul's hand and walked to where Lucinda and Catherine were watching events unfold, concerned that Paul might understand the talk of war more readily than the concept of a transcontinental telegraph wire.

"I just don't know who's gonna use it at such prices," Catherine insisted with a tone of disapproval.

"It's not for people like us," Lucinda replied. "It's for newspapers and the government."

"And rich people," Flora added.

Lucinda and Catherine both smiled a greeting, but Flora looked beyond their smile to a look in their eyes. It was a look that she'd seen in their eyes for several months. She'd presumed initially that it was a look of concern and sympathy, even pity, but had started to understand it more recently as fear that their own expectations of fidelity could be just as mistaken and as easily shattered as Flora's had been. They both wanted to be supportive, but it also seemed at times that they were afraid to broach the subject, as if her problems might be spread by merely acknowledging their existence. She concluded that it was best to simply get the matter out of the way so that it didn't hang unspoken in the air.

"Nothing new, by the way. Nothing from the lawyer. I presume it means they haven't talked him into anything, assuming they even know where he is."

"Apparently he's sleepin' out at the lime kiln these days, or down at Isaac's," Catherine offered hesitantly. "And, accordin' to the rumor," she continued, with far greater hesitation, "he's alone now."

Flora suppressed a smile as she realized that she had correctly interpreted the look of fear in their eyes, but had misunderstood the reason for it. She nodded as if their revelation was minor news and of no concern to her, but she knew she would rather have heard that he had the Indian girl with him. There was a time when she would have preferred to hear that he was alone, but ever since she'd emotionally let go of her marriage and found the courage to imagine a life beyond it, it had been comforting to believe that he had moved on as well. He wouldn't beg for her forgiveness or pressure her to stay just as she was determined to secure her freedom.

Flora turned back to gaze across the channel, pondering the irony of Catherine's words. All morning they had watched the completion of a telegraph line that would bring news of the world, and yet her own world was far more affected by the gossip of neighbors, reporting on events happening within a few miles from home.

She looked back at Catherine and forced a smile. "I'm

sorry to hear that," she said, knowing it was an answer that neither of her friends could possibly understand.

\* \* \*

Amor De Cosmos could barely stand after the conclusion of the filibuster, but he nevertheless found the energy to walk through the jubilant crowd gathered on Government Street to await the arrival of the first telegraph. Banners and flags decorated the street, and the competing odors of alcohol and urine were at every turn.

For a brief moment, De Cosmos wished he'd remained in the newspaper business. For years, he had published stories about events in Europe and the eastern states and colonies that had happened two or three months earlier; events that he had learned about only when a newspaper from the east coast or London had arrived by steamer. And he had published still more stories based on unsubstantiated rumors. For the past few months, local newspapers had contained stories sent to California or Washington Territory by telegraph, and on to Victoria by boat, shortening the lateness of the news by several weeks. But in the next edition of the *British Colonist*, readers were likely to find stories describing events that might have happened a day or two before. It was a new era for the colony, and a new era for journalists in the colony. A town that had for so long felt like an outpost at the edge of civilization would now be connected to the world, as if the thousands of miles separating it from the east coast had simply vanished. Perhaps, he wondered, it might be time to consider a return to the business of publishing a newspaper?

De Cosmos stumbled on something and looked down to discover the body of John Butts splayed across the wooden planks of the sidewalk. Butts seemed barely conscious, yet he struggled to proclaim a mumbled "hear ye" followed by something unintelligible that De Cosmos presumed was either a comment on the arrival of the telegraph, a plea for more whiskey, or something self-congratulatory that would have been a product of his own imagination.

De Cosmos realized that he felt sorry for Butts, and the emotion surprised him. Most Victoria residents had found it difficult to feel sympathy for Butts in recent years. Despite his official dismissal as town crier and bell-ringer several years before, Butts had often carried on the role at both public and private events, often without invitation, and demanding payment for a service that had never been requested. It was as though he could find no other identity, whether or not he might find other employment.

De Cosmos began to step over Butts, but stopped, realizing that what he had first believed was his own sympathy for Butts was more likely empathy. The mere idea of a town crier and bell-ringer was as much a relic of Victoria's past as a newspaper publisher who had published three month-old stories about European wars that might already be over. Butts' inebriation might suggest that he'd shown up to celebrate the arrival of the telegraph with the other Victoria residents who filled the streets, but De Cosmos felt more certain that Butts had been drinking to forget about his own increasing irrelevance.

\* \* \*

# THE LINE OPEN.

## COMMUNICATION WITH THE EAST.

### COMPLIMENTARY MESSAGES.

The 24th April, 1866, will be inscribed on the roll of time as an important era in the history of this colony. Ten years since Victoria, then a trading post of the Hudson Bay Company, rejoiced in communication once a year with the civilised world. Yesterday admitted her into the electric bond already girding the vast American

409

continent, and destined, ere the lapse of many months, to encircle the entire globe.

Shortly after two p.m. the gunboat *Forward* had successfully submerged the last mile and a half of cable between Lopez and San Juan Islands, and the fact of the completion of the line was immediately flashed to the Victoria office, where the intelligence was welcomed by a large concourse of persons, and flags of all nations were soon fluttering in the breeze. From the office in Zinn's building to a staff on the opposite side of Government street a line was attached from which were suspended the Union Jack and Star Spangled Banner, with the word 'Union' connecting the two, and on either side the Russian, Italian and other flags.

Some interruption on San Juan occurred, and directly communication was restored …

*The Daily British Colonist*, Wednesday, April 25, 1866, p. 3.

\* \* \*

The wire made no sound. Flora had been told that it might make a low hum, but she could hear nothing above the usual sounds of the wind, tree frogs and rushing currents. The wire simply hung between poles along the north side of the homestead, barely visible against the evening sky. There were bound to be messages passing back and forth at every moment in the rush of the first few hours of telegraph communication. Messages of congratulations. Messages announcing births, marriages, and deaths. Messages of a world that had seen itself shrink in an instant.

Just a few hours earlier, it had felt to Flora as though the farm was at the center of that world. All eyes on the southeastern point of San Juan Island, waiting for the first signal to burst through the last link in the completed line. But as night fell, with her neighbors no longer present, it was as if the world was passing the farm by. Passing her by. The messages were there, somehow contained in the wire as they passed, and she had some idea of the types of messages they might be. But that knowledge wasn't enough to make her feel as though she was still a part of the moment in history that played out across the thin black wire.

She wondered if Charles, her brother-in-law, was involved in the transmission of any of the messages. It had been just a few years ago that she and Hubbs had petitioned the colonial government to release the young man from prison for yet another of his many infractions, this time selling whiskey to local Indians. Now it appeared he was managing to maintain a steady job as agent at the Swinomish telegraph station, though she found it hard to imagine that he would ever settle into a life of such regular employment.

She had no idea what lay ahead for her. Indefinite separation? Divorce? A return to Victoria? Life with Hubbs had been perfectly miserable at times. But life as a divorced woman in a colony that didn't yet recognize the legal right to divorce? She worried most for her son. He might be teased by other children at school for being the son of a divorced woman. A divorced Indian woman. But however troubling it might be for him, it would be far better than growing up at Floraville.

She laughed to herself as the name crossed her mind. Floraville. It had been Hubbs' nickname for the farm in the early days of the marriage, when he had regularly addressed letters as being sent from Floraville, or in some cases, as if possessed by a desire to sound continental, Floravilla. She hadn't heard him use either name in a couple of years and she wasn't about to attempt to resurrect it. "The Hubbs farm" seemed a far better moniker for a place she found herself increasingly anxious to leave.

She had never expected that it would be easy to convince Hubbs to agree to a divorce, even if Hubbs Senior were part of the campaign. But she had found some comfort in the idea of presenting it to him as a choice between two women in his life. He might lose a wife, but he would keep a mistress. But if Catherine's news was accurate and the girl on Decatur really had returned to her family, then that was no longer an option, and divorce would likely come to him as the final step in a greater defeat.

Flora looked back up at the wire, knowing that its silence wasn't about to change, but unable to shake the idea that she should be able to hear something passing her by. Something to confirm for her that she wasn't sitting on the isolated point of a small, remote island, but rather on the axis of an intercontinental line of communication. But the wire offered no response. She rose from her chair and entered the farmhouse to check on Paul before going to bed for the night.

\* \* \*

"You dropped another one. Let me carry it."

Flora bent down and picked up another of her son's toy Union Army soldiers from the dirt path. They were a present from the Firths at the picnic that Flora and Paul had just attended. The ostensible purpose had been to celebrate the forty-seventh birthday of Queen Victoria, but the Firth's had made the event as much a celebration of Paul's fourth birthday, which was on the same day. And since the boy seemed unaware of Queen Victoria as anything more than a name spoken in a manner similar to God or the Governor, he appeared to feel justifiably at the center of attention. At least on this particular birthday, there were advantages in sharing it with a monarch.

Flora had been content to remain in the background of her son's celebration and have her own late-May birthday go almost unnoticed, finding it troubling to realize that she was about to become a separated and perhaps divorced mother while still in her mid-twenties. A single woman of twenty-four was an old maid in the eyes of many, with decreasing prospects. But a divorced woman of twenty-four, of mixed blood, raising a child? As a category, it was non-existent, as might be her prospects for any future marriage, regardless of whether any church might sanctify it.

"Can I carry all of them for you?" she asked Paul.

"No."

The boy was unwilling to intentionally allow any of the heavy lead soldiers to escape his grasp, though his small hands had dropped three of them in the first hundred yards of their journey home. Flora had decided earlier that it was easier to walk the short distance than saddle up a horse, and she was relieved to now be able to pick up the soldiers from the trail without having to dismount. She made an extra effort to watch each step and ensure that none of them were lost in the grass, even though she hadn't yet decided if she considered it appropriate to give Union Soldiers as a gift on Queen Victoria's birthday.

Flora dropped the tiny infantryman into a pocket of her dress that already held the other two she'd rescued, when she heard distant shouts from below the ridge, toward Griffin Bay. The commotion came from just above the old Company wharf and the scattered remains of the old village of San Juan. It was the same view Flora had once had of arriving U.S. troops, arriving British warships, and arriving boatloads of Victoria tourists who had journeyed to the island in the hope of glimpsing the outbreak of war.

Hubbs stood at the edge of a small group that had gathered on the old wagon road where it wound down the hill toward the bay. He didn't seem to notice Flora and Paul on the ridge above them, immersed as he was in a confrontation between Isaac Higgins and Captain Gray, the current commander of troops at the American Camp. Higgins had been attempting for some time to assert a claim on lands just west of the wharf, land homesteaded by Lucinda and her husband in previous years, and had recently gone to the trouble of building a fence across the old wagon road to further define his claim.

Captain Gray was clearly displeased with Higgins' efforts, a fact that was demonstrated by the actions of his subordinate, Brevet Captain Graves, and a handful of U.S. troops who busily tore apart the fence. Flora couldn't hear the words being shouted, but she could see Higgins' anger from his defiant stance. And she could tell that whatever Higgins' words had been, they'd made an impact, for Gray and Graves both tackled Higgins to the ground and began to beat him severely. Hubbs and the other men tried to leap forward to intervene but were held back by the troops, allowing the beating of Higgins to continue unabated.

Flora reached for Paul to guide him away from the ridge, but he struggled from her grip.

"No. Daddy."

She relented, realizing that she couldn't pull him away if his last view of the altercation would be a vision of his father confronting the troops while a family friend was beaten viciously by officers. He had to be able to fall asleep that night knowing that his father was safe.

Altercations of this type, between Gray or Graves, and nearly anyone else on the island, had become far too commonplace in recent months. The Royal Navy had established its post for the joint occupation on the Northwest side of the island, at Garrison Bay, which meant that they were too far from the settlers along the southern peninsula to be of assistance, or to moderate Gray's antics. Earlier in the year, Gray had banished one resident from the island without a hearing for reasons that remained unknown. The man had left on a mail steamer in the midst of a brutal winter storm to make arrangements for a new residence in Port Townsend before bringing his wife and infant son with him. But moments after the mail steamer had left port, one of Gray's sergeants expelled the man's wife and child from the cabin where they were staying, and threatened the man who owned the cabin that he, too, would be banished from the island and have all his property confiscated if he harbored the woman. The poor woman and her child likely would have perished in the storm if the mail steamer hadn't returned that evening to ride out the strong winds at the wharf, allowing the family to be reunited on the safety of the steamer before night settled in.

Most island residents had stories about Gray's reign on the southern end of the island. Flora already knew that

Hubbs and Gray were anything but friends, and this latest dust-up was only going to deepen their animosity. She wondered where she would fall in Gray's estimation, being Hubbs' separated wife. Banishment from the island no longer sounded fearful, but far better to resolve all her affairs and then leave on her own terms.

As Flora watched the altercation unfold, she found herself preoccupied by a thought that seemed inappropriate. Though it was from a distance, it was the first time she had seen her husband in more than two months. She felt no desire to be noticed by him, and wasn't about to run toward him. But seeing him made her realize how deeply anxious she had become to hear his views on the state of their marriage. Had Hubbs Senior contacted him? Had Dennison reached out? Had Hubbs given any consideration to the idea of ending their legal bond? For the first time she considered the idea of approaching him rather than waiting for him to approach her.

The beating of Higgins didn't last long. Gray and Graves stood over him for a moment, as if to mark the success of their efforts, then they turned and walked toward the American camp. The soldiers waited until their officers were a safe distance away, then turned back to their task of dismantling Higgins' fence, while Hubbs and the others tended to Higgins.

Flora knelt beside Paul and tried to find the words to explain to him that his father was safe, but the thought that ran through her mind was the realization that the bond between father and son—as it ran from the son to the father—was far more than she had ever believed it could be. Explaining to him that his father was safe would be relatively easy. How would she ever explain to the boy that his father felt no such bond toward him?

*Chapter 21*

# EXCITING NEWS!

## BY CALIFORNIA STATE TELEGRAPH.

### CANADA.

CHICAGO, June 1—The Fenians invaded Canada last night, crossing the Niagara river four miles below Buffalo (at Black Rock, about 1500 strong, and were to-day intrenching themselves to resist attack. They are commanded by Col. H. R. Stagg and Col. O'Neil, the latter from Nashville, Tennessee. The troops are composed of volunteers from the west and southwest. The crossing was effected by steam tugs and canal boats. Great excitement prevails in Buffalo and in Canada West. Reports indicate a movement by Fenians from

Rochester, Buffalo, and other land posts on a large scale to join the forces in Canada. Reports also indicate that large bodies of Fenians are at St. Albans and all points along the St. Lawrence River, threatening similar invasion. Reinforcements are moving from Boston, New York, and the Eastern States to assist Gen. Sweeny. This Fenian army of invasion is under the auspices of Roberts, and is in defiance of the organizer Stephens, whose counsels they reject.

Despatches from Toronto represent active military preparations being made to punish the invaders. ...

*The Daily British Colonist*, Friday, June 8, 1866, p. 3.

\* \* \*

Flora kissed her son on the forehead, left him in the care of her mother, and then strode across the churchyard in search of Reverend Cridge. She told herself that the stares she felt were her imagination, rather than precursors to gossip that would follow in her wake. Each time she would look up, feeling eyes upon her, she was met with a smile and a friendly greeting. But she had learned years before that gossip follows the morning service as certainly as death follows life. It was simply a matter of how quickly and how vicious. At least on this morning, most conversation seemed preoccupied with the fears of a Fenian invasion that, so far, had been limited to the eastern colonies.

The isolation of the farm might have proven safer than Victoria, but Flora had found it to be emotionally stifling. No answers from Hubbs. No news from Dennison. There was a risk each time she left the farm, whether for a few hours or a few days, that she could return to find that Hubbs had asserted a hold on the house. But she'd decided that if he was determined to take back their home, far better that it happen when she was absent. And so she'd concluded that a few days in Victoria were necessary, for her own sanity, for her son's boundless energy, and for an opportunity to make some inquiries about future nursing positions.

She and Paul had found passage on a small sloop carrying freight between the island and Victoria, and had been surprised to find the *H.M.S. Alert* guarding the mouth of Victoria harbor, with guns out and a launch circling nearby with a howitzer at the ready. Every boat entering or leaving the harbor was inspected, and it was then that Flora had learned that Fenian forces had invaded Canada West from several locations in upstate New York. Most of the rumors that filled Victoria were outlandish, but they flourished, nevertheless. Banks were rumored to have stored their gold on Royal Navy warships. A schooner filled with partying Australians was fired upon by a warship that took their kangaroo flag as a Fenian symbol. And a brothel even got involved in civilian defense by building a homemade cannon and installing it in the street. Flora concluded that the outlandish nature of the rumors was an indication that people weren't so much fearful as they were entertained by the possibility of having a brigade of unorganized Fenians landing on their shores and quickly populating the saloons and brothels.

The rumor mill reminded Flora of the San Juan affair of seven years earlier. Rumors had run amuck and taken anxieties along with them. Yet she found that most people would insist, with the benefit of hindsight, that a peaceful joint occupation had always been inevitable. Surely now, the entire Fenian affair was more hysteria than actual threat, at least for the colonies on the western side of the continent.

And yet, with so much to occupy conversation that morning, she feared that her own marital situation was being discussed around her. Every comment spoken to her had been friendly and polite, but also hesitant, as if the speaker wanted to signal that they'd heard about her marriage, and that they were thrilled to now have the ability to participate in the rumors by sharing a firsthand account of her demeanor.

She had no doubt that the gossip had continued in all the years she'd been away, with a continually evolving source of subjects to satiate its appetite. The marriage of Agnes Douglas to Arthur Bushby might not have involved much scandal, but Alice Douglas' elopement with Charles Good, her father's private secretary, had no doubt fueled gossip for months of Sunday services. John Butts' lengthy fall from grace had evolved from gossip to public reprobation. The criminal escapades of her brothers, and her mother's problematic marriage, had no doubt filled the gaps in between. Now, it was her turn. She wondered if she could find it in herself to look past the stares, the sideways glances, and the occasional remarks. All of them, she assured herself, would pale in comparison to any of the confrontations with her husband that she'd already survived.

She had come with an agenda that made it feel as though seven years of her life had evaporated. She could see that Cridge was attempting to make his way toward her, but she had to wait for several minutes as he patiently allowed other congregants to update him on mundane details of their lives—mundane, at least, from Flora's perspective, as she waited with far more important concerns of her own. She was reassured by Cridge's smile, as he finally broke free, that her own unburdening wouldn't be met with a similar effort to escape.

"Flora, my dear, so pleased you could join us today. It is just for today?"

"It is, yes. I'm returning in the morning."

Cridge discreetly guided Flora to the side of the lawn, farther from the prying eyes and ears of the congregation.

"And are there any developments?"

"I've hired an attorney in Port Townsend, and I thought I'd convinced my father-in-law that it's in his interest to pressure my husband to come to an agreement. But I've heard nothing."

"He'll come around. There's no benefit to him other than spite, and that will fade in time."

"The District Court doesn't sit in Port Townsend until September. So as much as I wish to resolve this immediately, it'll take several more months even if he comes around to the idea tomorrow."

"And then you would return home?"

"I'd like to still think of it as home. But I'm as uncertain as you are about the welcome I'll receive. I fear a judgment of divorce will lead to far more judgment from others."

Cridge smiled. "If you can accept that they mean well, beneath the gossip, then perhaps it won't feel like judgment."

"I can't begin to tell you how strange it feels to be coming to you here, all these years later, but I need to ask for your help once again to serve the community as a nurse. The concern you expressed a few months back, about providing for my son ... I know I dismissed the need for a husband, but I also know that confidence won't put bread on the table. The family farm can't seem to turn a profit, which has more to do with the lands than Alexander's efforts. If I do return, and I expect I will, I'm going to have to work as a nurse, and I'm just hoping that you —"

"I will do everything I can to help you find positions. There are certainly more nurses in town than there were, and the Sisters are providing their services for free, in the hope of a future donation to the convent, of course. But many still do come to me for referrals. You know that you'll always be the first name I suggest."

Flora hadn't expected a different answer, and she scolded herself for having allowed herself to fear anything other than his full support. But as supportive as Cridge had been to her, he hadn't always shown himself to be the most forgiving of others. He might stand by the side of a convicted murderer on the gallows, counseling the condemned wretch in his final moments, and then refuse to provide a Christian burial for a young sailor whose night of drunken and ultimately fatal misbehavior had struck Cridge as too offensive for his Christian sensibilities. Her quest for a divorce couldn't possibly sit well with him, no matter how supportive his comments had been. And so she responded in the only way that made sense to her. She thanked him for his continued assistance, complimented him on a pleasant and meaningful service, and promised that she would rejoin the congregation on a permanent basis as soon as she could arrange it. And then, firmly ignoring every gaze in her direction, she returned across the church grounds to retrieve her son and begin the journey back to San Juan Island.

* * *

She pulled the half-full bucket of blood out from under the steer's carcass and slid an empty bucket in its place, careful to not lose a single drop. Robert Firth had generously donated two hours of his time to kill the steer and hang the carcass from a rafter in the barn. The blood that Flora had caught dripping from the steer's neck, with some barley, oats, and a little milk, would make an excellent black pudding; a dish her son would most certainly refuse to touch now that he understood its ingredients.

The distance to the house wasn't far, but Flora found it a challenge to carry the heavy bucket without spilling the contents. She cursed the discovery that the kitchen door was closed, and wondered if she could yell loud enough to wake her son from his nap. She opted instead to carefully set the bucket onto the stoop and open the door herself.

"Flora."

He said it just as Flora grabbed the bucket to step over the threshold. The surprise at hearing her husband's voice made her involuntarily lurch, just enough to send a visually striking amount of the steer's blood sloshing from the bucket onto her hands, arms and the front of her dress.

Flora screamed as the blood soaked through, then looked up to see Hubbs, stopped in his tracks. For a moment they both stared in silence and shock at the sight of Flora, drenched in blood. Then they broke into laughter. Flora knew that she should be mortified by the mess, and troubled by the sudden appearance of Hubbs, but the realization that she might appear to her separated husband as both terrifying and ridiculous seemed hilarious. To both of them.

Hubbs hurried forward, took the bucket from Flora, and carried it into the kitchen where he carefully set it onto the butcher's block.

"I presume that's bovine."

"The steer with the bum leg."

"I'm sorry. I shouldn't have called out like that. I didn't see what you were carrying."

The word 'sorry' was the only part that Flora heard. It wasn't a word she was used to hearing in their conversations. Not a word that had ever seemed to fall from his lips with so little effort.

As the last vestiges of their shared laughter faded, Flora felt as though she had stepped back in time for just a moment; back to when she'd lived with a certainty that her husband viewed their marriage through the same eyes as she, and back to when humor had occupied a greater role in their communications than disappointment or rage. But as the blood in the bucket settled to stillness, and as the blood soaking through her dress began to feel cold and heavy, Flora's willingness to laugh faded into a reminder of the troubles that still lay unresolved between them.

"Is there … is there something you need? From the house?" Flora hoped his visit might have such a simple explanation. A shirt he still hadn't taken with him. A tool from the barn. Or perhaps a resolution to their marriage.

Hubbs hesitated, then pulled out a chair and slowly sat. "I was just heading around the point. Felt like saying hello."

Flora had learned over the years how he spoke when he was holding something back. An overly friendly yet hesitant tone, with a slight elevation of his voice, was usually a sign that he was building up to something planned and uncomfortable. He seemed to realize the direction of her thinking and made the decision to drop the pretense.

"I want to come back."

"Come back?"

"Here. To the farm."

Flora hesitated, afraid of providing the wrong response, or potentially misunderstanding his meaning. Perhaps he only wanted possession of the farm.

"I want to come back to you," he added.

It was one of her worst fears, and yet a part of her found

relief in his words. She'd never wanted to accept that he no longer loved her, or that he no longer wanted her. She hated him for breaking their marital vows, and especially for the mistreatment, but she also knew that she hadn't stopped loving him. Not entirely. She just couldn't remain married to him. She'd been aware for months that her feelings for him, for their marriage, were confused and complicated. But it wasn't until he spoke out loud a desire to return that she truly appreciated the conflict she'd been holding inside.

"Did you hear me?"

"I heard you."

The silence hung in the air, and Flora prayed that Paul wouldn't awaken and come into the kitchen, curious to learn what the earlier laughter and screaming had been about.

"The girl, she's gone back home. I'm spending most of my time with friends or out at the kiln. I guess I realized how much I miss being here. How much I miss being here with you. And Paul. We used to have a good marriage. I know we did. I want that again."

Flora listened to the words, each of them seemingly causing him pain to push from his lips. He had never been particularly accomplished at sharing his emotions, or even acknowledging having emotions, and far worse at offering apologies. But he was trying. She remained silent, certain that her silence would force him to say more.

"My father thinks I should just give up the goose and let you have a divorce. But he doesn't know anything about marriage. He and Maggie are barely speaking these days. I want to come back, Flora. I want to make this our home again."

Flora replayed his words in her mind, listening to everything he had said, as if there had to be a secret meaning locked away, certain to be uncovered if she focused on the words. He wanted to return. He wanted to be with her. He wanted the marriage they used to have. But the most telling word was the one word he didn't say. The word he had found so easy and natural to say after causing steer's blood to drench the front of her dress, but had proven incapable of saying after causing the destruction of their marriage.

"I think you should go before Paul wakes up from his nap."

Flora realized that delivering her response while clad in a blood-soaked dress had likely helped to underscore the seriousness of her words. Hubbs didn't show any of the anger of past visits. There was none of the rage that had simmered just beneath the surface. Instead, his eyes showed disappointment. Hurt. Flora didn't want to be hurtful, but she couldn't believe that any hurt showing in his eyes could compare to the hurt he'd caused her. The bruises had faded, but their cause was likely unchanged. And though the Cowichan girl on Decatur might be gone, she would be replaced in a matter of time.

Hubbs rose slowly from his chair, then turned and walked out of the house without a word.

\* \* \*

## The Union Bill.

Our readers will find the bill for the Union of the Colonies of Vancouver Island and British Columbia in our columns this morning. It is short, but explicit enough to convince all that British Columbia will get everything and Vancouver Island nothing— the natural result of the unconditional Union resolutions.

*The Daily British Colonist and Victoria Chronicle,* Friday, August 3, 1866, p. 2.

\* \* \*

"If you eat your oatmeal, I'll make some eggs. But oatmeal first."

Flora pushed the bowl back in front of Paul, then rose from the kitchen table, intending to head to the chicken coop for morning eggs. She froze at the sound of the opening and closing of the front door. It had been locked, she was certain of that, which meant that Hubbs was standing in the front parlor. Their last encounter hadn't ended badly, but there was no telling how her rejection of his advances might have played out in his mind. Especially if they had been filtered through whiskey.

"Stay here and eat your breakfast," she quietly instructed Paul. She struggled to calm the tension she could feel in her belly, then slowly walked into the main room. Hubbs stood at the front window, his back to her, gazing outside. The family musket by the door was far too close to where he stood for her comfort.

"Hello, Paul." He would have heard her footsteps, but she felt the need to start the conversation.

Hubbs turned. He seemed upset, but sober. She waited silently to allow him to launch into whatever speech he had prepared.

"So, if I agree to this, you'll leave the farm?"

"Yes. Paul and I would leave the farm for Victoria."

Flora recognized that she needed to lay out her terms, in case Hubbs' father hadn't explained them as she intended.

"It's a simple agreement, really. You keep this farm, and whatever else you have in Washington. I keep my share of the Ross farm. I have custody of Paul. I assume that –"

"I'm not looking to raise him. He's your burden."

Flora winced, hoping Paul hadn't heard his father, but knowing that he must have. All those times when she'd feared that Hubbs would take their son, use him as a pawn, that she might never see him again, and he'd never given his son so much as a thought. She chided herself for having expected any other attitude from a man who had another child living in a Haida community, who he hadn't seen in a decade.

"He's no burden to me," she replied with a hint of defiance. "I expect no support for his expenses, or mine. We pay our own attorneys. A simple agreement, and there's no need for a discussion of our reasons in any of the court papers, beyond whatever the lawyers tell us we have to say to satisfy the judge."

Hubbs looked up with a piercing stare. She tried to comprehend his emotions, but they seemed muddled. It was as if he were trying to understand at once everything that had gone wrong in their marriage over the years. As if one simple answer would explain it all. As if only now had the time arrived to try to understand his mistakes. Or hers. The intensity of his eyes felt painful, but Flora knew she had to hold his gaze.

"Fine." Hubbs turned for the door with a suddenness that caused Flora to jump. He was gone before she'd fully recovered from the shock, shock that was replaced by several sudden yet brief tears of relief.

* * *

Francis Ross lifted one end of the plank and waited for John Butts to pick up the back end, then started across the James Bay Bridge to where the remainder of the gaol's chain gang was at work repairing the structure.

They were watched the entire journey by both a bored gaol guard who trailed behind them, and the slightly less bored occupants of four carriages that sat on the north end of the bridge, waiting for the rotted plank to be replaced so that they could continue across the muddy bay. It would have been much faster to circle around the east side of the small bay rather than wait for repairs to be completed. But it was clear to Francis that they each preferred the option of obtaining their morning entertainment from watching the chain gang at work.

Francis recognized some of the observers. A few nodded a polite greeting, while most looked away in embarrassment as soon as he caught their eye. One man who appeared vaguely familiar smirked as Francis passed by, as if he couldn't be happier than to see Francis at work on the chain gang as a deserved punishment for some past misdeed Francis was unlikely to remember.

Francis and Butts were halfway to the section of the bridge where William and two Chinamen—whose names Francis had never attempted to learn—were still prying the last of the rotted plank free, when Francis felt the back end of the plank fall to the deck. The reverberation that coursed through the wood nearly caused him to drop the front end of the plank. Francis turned to see Butts making no effort to reach down and retrieve his dropped end of the plank, and he realized that Butts had dropped his end on purpose. The gaol guard stepped closer to Butts.

"Go on, pick it up."

Butts didn't budge. The Superintendent of the gaol, who'd been overseeing the efforts of William and the Chinamen, strode over to Butts and glared at him.

"What's the matter, are you sick?" he demanded.

"Yes, I'm sick! I'm sick of you, sick of the country—sick of everything—I'm driven to desperation. I'm a rebel, not a bridgeworker!" Butts exclaimed with inflated outrage.

Francis sighed, having long ago tired of Butts' relentless need for attention, and he feared that he would share the punishment for this latest outburst simply because he was the man at the other end of the plank.

"John, you'd better get to work," the Superintendent replied.

"Work?" Butts responded. "You can bet your life I'm not gonna work. I'm a gentleman, sir, in my own country, and I won't work here. You can't play that on me. I'll rebel. I'll join the Fenians, and make you walk off in fear whenever you hear the name of John Charles Butt."

Francis groaned at the realization that he had to hold up his end of the plank for as long as the altercation with Butts might take. If he gave in to the exhaustion he was feeling in his arms and lowered his end onto the deck, it might be seen as an act of support for Butts' campaign.

He pondered whether he had made a mistake that morning by dodging his turn to attend to the insane inmates. There were four of them in the gaol—three white men and a Chinaman—none of whom were criminals. They were kept in the gaol only because the colony had no better place to keep them. Tending to their needs had become the daily task of an inmate, usually one who was too ill or injured to work on the chain gang. It was a task that Francis often fulfilled due to various recurring illnesses, but he had successfully argued that morning that he could be put to better use outdoors, only to question the decision as his arms ached from the weight of the plank.

He glanced over at the smirking gentleman he'd noticed earlier. The smirk had widened into a grin as the man understood the predicament Francis faced. Francis turned back to watch the Superintendent's continuing argument with Butts, hoping that Butts would be dragged off to solitary confinement quickly enough that someone else could pick up the other end of the plank before Francis' arms gave way entirely. But he also knew, as was the case with all of Butts' efforts to draw attention to himself, that Butts would make the moment last for as long as he possibly could.

\* \* \*

FATE OF A REBEL.—John Butts, for his act of rebellion in refusing to do duty in the chain gang, has been sentenced to a bread-and-water diet with solitary confinement thrown in by way of lunch. John could be heard yesterday within the jail precincts, singing a hymn and the national anthem alternately in the most penitent tones.

*The Daily British Colonist and Victoria Chronicle,* Monday, August 13, 1866, p. 2.

\* \* \*

"*Flora Hubbs, Plaintiff, vs. Paul K. Hubbs, Jr., Defendant.*" The title on the complaint that Dennison had prepared struck Flora as far more adversarial than she'd expected. Despite months of uncertainty, hurt, anger, and finally reluctant agreement, the characterization of her husband as a defendant seemed almost unfair.

There was so much that could have been said about the reasons for her divorce petition. The reference instead to simply *"an incompatibility of disposition, temper and habits"* appeared almost innocuous. She read through the remaining terms of the complaint, struggling at times with Dennison's penmanship on the attached pages of lined paper. She expected that a few statements might trouble Hubbs, such as her allegation that a continuation of their marriage *"would render her life miserable in the extreme."* But Dennison had insisted that the complaint contain one allegation that the marriage had deteriorated to an intolerable state, even though the divorce itself was relatively amicable. As an attachment to the petition, Dennison had prepared a stipulation to be signed by Flora and Hubbs, detailing their agreement over property, custody, and alimony issues. The stipulation already bore her husband's signature.

She took the pen that Dennison offered her, dipped the point in ink, and carefully signed her name, first to the final page of the complaint, then to the verification, and finally to the stipulation. She had barely lifted the pen from the papers when Dennison pulled the documents out from under her, notarized the verification, and set the documents on a corner of his desk to dry.

"I'll get this filed with the Court this afternoon. Oh, and there's one minor change—a request. He asks that you stay on the farm until the end of the harvest."

Flora smiled at her own surprise. Of course he would ask that of her. He had never worked a farm in his life and would have no idea how to harvest the oats, potatoes, and other crops that would need an experienced eye in the coming weeks. Flora chided herself for not foreseeing the request. But though it changed her plans somewhat, it could also solve other matters of concern.

"What about the income from the harvest?"

"Garfielde proposed an even split."

"Fine. End of harvest, but no longer—wait, Garfielde? Selucius Garfielde is his attorney?"

Flora realized that she should have expected the possibility that Garfielde would be Hubbs' counsel. Other than Hubbs Senior, Dennison and Garfielde, there were only two other attorneys in Port Townsend, and they were

Dennison and Garfielde's respective partners. "Competitor" was a relative term among lawyers in Port Townsend.

"I take it you know him?"

"In a manner of speaking. I'll just say he finds it highly entertaining that a woman with Indian blood might know how to read a newspaper."

"Well, I consider it a positive development that your husband retained Garfielde."

"Why? I thought he was quite powerful these days?"

"In politics, most certainly. But in the courtroom of Justice McFadden, who was a staunch supporter of the man beaten by Garfielde's candidate, Garfielde starts with a disadvantage."

"As do I if we're in front of a judge who supported pro-slavery candidates," Flora protested.

"Fair point, but I think he'll allow his political differences to affect him more than any personal prejudices he might otherwise direct towards you."

"So, what should I do until the hearing on Friday?"

It was only a few days, but she felt her presence in Port Townsend might seem unwelcome once the complaint was filed.

"There's nothing in particular you need to do. Just be at the courthouse Friday morning before ten o'clock. McFadden tends to be a stickler for starting on time, and I've no idea where we'll be listed on the docket."

Flora rose from her chair and hesitated. "Will he be there?"

"He's required to be, just as you are, so he better be. He's been in town over the past few days. He was a witness last week at the Higgins trial against those army Captains, so you should prepare yourself for the prospect of facing him at any time."

Flora had heard about the Higgins trial. Someone was finally holding Captain Gray and Brevet Captain Graves to account for their abusive tenure commanding the U.S. troops on the island. The officers had followed up their earlier attack on Higgins by banishing him from the island, perhaps not realizing that forcing him to live in Port

Townsend would make it easier for him to find the support of civil authorities for his grievances. Flora could just as easily have been a witness to the events of the Queen's birthday, but she was relieved that no one had asked her.

"Would you like me to try to find out if he's staying in town until the hearing?" Dennison asked.

"As long as the query doesn't reach him. I'd rather he not know that I'm nervous about encountering him on the street." Flora smiled her thanks and started for the door.

"Flora, wait –" Dennison interjected. "Does that mean you're not staying with Mr. and Mrs. Hubbs?"

"Goodness, no. I thought that might seem a little awkward, to say the least, particularly if he's already staying there. I'll be at the Washington Hotel."

"You most certainly will not. A married woman alone at the Washington Hotel? They have a saloon. You'll stay with us."

"I couldn't. That's so kind of you to offer, but –"

"It's not an offer, it's an attorney's instruction to his client. Justice McFadden wouldn't think highly of a plaintiff seeking a divorce if she were staying alone at the Washington Hotel. And more importantly, Mrs. Dennison would have my head if she found out I allowed you to do so."

Flora smiled, more in relief than thanks, realizing that even though Mrs. Dennison did not yet know it, she had once again proven to be Flora's greatest ally in Port Townsend.

\* \* \*

"That rat bastard."

The angry gasp that sprang from Susan Dennison's lips, just inches from Flora's left ear, informed Flora that her hostess had been reading over her shoulder.

"Susan!"

Dennison appeared truly embarrassed by his wife's outburst.

"Have you seen this? Did you see what he says?"

"I've read the entire pleading."

"To say she didn't perform faithfully as his wife. The nerve."

"He doesn't actually say she didn't. He just refuses to admit or deny the allegation."

"Which is as good as saying she didn't." Susan turned to Flora. "You're better off without him, dear. I know I said that from the start, but this shows I was right. Better off without him, you are."

Hubbs' Answer to Flora's divorce Complaint was short and, for the most part, non-controversial. It was simple enough that Flora had little trouble understanding it, at least where the handwriting was clear. But she shared Susan Dennison's reaction to her husband's refusal to either admit or deny the second paragraph of the Complaint. The paragraph had stated merely that, at all times during their marriage, Flora had "*performed her duties faithfully, and conducted herself with propriety.*" Dennison had described it as little more than background information. Their expectation had been that Hubbs would merely admit the innocuous paragraph, as he had admitted all of the other paragraphs in the Complaint, even the statement that her life would be "*miserable in the extreme*" if she remained married to him. At least he didn't deny the second paragraph, but his refusal to admit it felt like a slap in the face. Susan's reaction only exacerbated the feeling.

"The thing to keep in mind," Dennison explained, taking back his copy of the Answer, "is that he consents to the relief, as expected. Tomorrow should be a very brief hearing."

"Maybe I should be there, too," Susan added, turning to leave the parlor for the kitchen. "To give him a piece of my mind."

"You most certainly will not, my dear."

Flora had no doubt that Susan Dennison would speak her mind if given the chance. But instead Flora would face Hubbs in court without Susan Dennison at her side—though with her husband's legal assistance as a far less entertaining substitute. Flora's last two encounters with Hubbs had been easier than she'd imagined they might be, but she sensed from his Answer that he might act in a petty manner.

"Now, I'm going to have a glass of sherry," Dennison announced, crossing the room to a side table. "May I interest you in a glass? It might help you sleep tonight."

"No, thank you. I don't drink," Flora replied.

"None?"

"It seems whenever something terrible happens in my life, or in the lives of those I care about, it's because somebody was drinking far too much and far too often."

"Hmm," Dennison replied, pouring a small measure into his glass, "you're making me wonder if I shouldn't just stick to tea this evening."

"Gracious, no," Flora answered, with a smile. "If it appears you're drinking too much, I'll be sure to let you know. Though I've a feeling your wife would tell you long before I would."

Flora watched Dennison sip his drink while her mind roamed to the prospect of facing her husband in court. She would be at the side of her lawyer, and Hubbs would have to be on his best behavior. There seemed to be no valid reason to be fearful. And yet her fears for how it might proceed generated a stronger desire for a glass of sherry than she'd ever felt before.

\* \* \*

JOHN BUTTS.—This unfortunate fellow-creature, who stands charged with stealing property (*200 Evening Telegraphs*) that the smallest coin in the realm would be too high a price to pay for, was brought before Mr. Pemberton yesterday for sentence. Inspector Welch stated that the pilot of the *Josie McNear* had promised to secure a berth for Butts in a vessel bound for Australia. Butts, who seemed very penitent, and wept freely, said that he felt he had disgraced his father, mother, brothers and sisters, and would gladly leave this country for his distant home. The Magistrate spoke kindly to the "erring one," and besought him to mend his ways, before he became too hardened in vice. The unfortunate man was remanded until the return of the *Josie McNear* and left the Court. Much sympathy is expressed for Butts, in view of the lightness of the offence with which he is charged.

*The Daily British Colonist and Victoria Chronicle*, Friday, September 14, 1866, p. 3.

\* \* \*

Flora followed Dennison to the counsel's table and took the seat that her lawyer pulled out for her.

"Mrs. Hubbs, how very nice to see you again." Selucius Garfielde approached with a formal smile.

"Mr. Garfielde, it's a pleasure," she replied, with less of a smile.

Garfielde took his seat at the next table, and focused on the papers in front of him.

"The next matter is, *Hubbs v. Hubbs*," Justice McFadden announced from the bench. "Appearances?"

Dennison stood. "Good morning, your Honor. B.F. Dennison for the Plaintiff, Mrs. Flora Amelia Hubbs, who is here with me this morning."

"Good morning, your Honor, Selucius Garfielde for the Defendant, Mr. Paul Kinsey Hubbs, Junior."

Flora looked behind her. There was still no sign of her husband, though her father-in-law sat on a bench near the back.

"I see we have a stipulation here between the parties." McFadden looked over his glasses at Garfielde. "Paul Hubbs Junior? Not Senior?"

"It's the son, Mr. Hubbs, Junior, your Honor."

McFadden grunted and suppressed a slight smirk, as if having expected Flora's father-in-law to be the one obtaining a divorce, not the son. Mrs. Dennison had insisted to Flora over the previous two days that she wasn't the type who would ever share such gossip, but nevertheless had dropped more than enough hints to suggest that loud arguments had become a regular event at the Hubbs household in Port Townsend. Hubbs Senior had just announced to colleagues a few days earlier that he, Maggie, and the two youngest children, would move back to California by the end of the year once he was able to wrap up his legal practice. Flora wondered if they were hoping that the warmer climate would produce a warmer marriage, or if perhaps Hubbs Senior had concluded that California's divorce laws would be more advantageous to him than the newer law he had helped draft in Washington Territory.

Flora looked back a second time to gauge the reaction of Hubbs Senior to McFadden's smirk. He was looking down at papers in his hands, preparing—or at least wanting to appear that he was preparing—for one of the next cases that he would argue. He'd been polite to Flora that morning when they'd arrived, but otherwise appeared anxious to keep a distance from her proceedings.

"Is your client present, counsel?"

"He is, your honor. I believe he's waiting outside. I just sent my colleague to fetch him before you called the case."

Footsteps on the staircase announced an arrival, and moments later Hubbs entered the courtroom and joined Garfielde at the counsel's table.

"And you are Paul Kinsey Hubbs, Junior?"

"Yes, your honor."

Hubbs made only a cursory glance in Flora's direction and then slumped into the chair next to Garfielde. He seemed sober and resigned to the proceedings, if not emotionally defeated. Perhaps she had misjudged what the marriage had meant to him? She had seen him through political defeats, career collapses, public ridicule and emotional downfalls, but had never before seen him without the energy that he had always seemed unable to fully contain; the determined urge to fight that stirred inside and had always propelled him into each successive effort to prove his worth. She found it difficult to imagine that the man slouched by Garfielde's side had once faced down boats arriving in Griffin Bay in order to assert U.S. tax laws, had arrested criminals and housed them in the tiny jail he'd constructed at the farm while serving as Justice of the Peace, or served his constituents in the territorial assembly. It seemed just as difficult to imagine him as the man who had once shared laughter with her, made love late at night, and welcomed their child into the world. Or as the man who had struck her repeatedly the previous year over incidents and issues that were too minor to even recall.

She turned back to face McFadden. He seemed to be studying the two parties, looking from Hubbs to Flora, and back again, before issuing a sigh that expressed more judgment than any official order he might enter.

"Is there anything else I need to know that isn't in the papers?"

Dennison deferred to Garfielde, who addressed the judge. "Everything is in the papers, your Honor. The only change to their agreement is the timing of Mrs. Hubbs' departure from the family farm, at my client's request, which needn't be in the papers."

"Very well. The relief is granted. A decree will be issued later today dissolving the marriage. Next item on the calendar ..."

Flora heard nothing more that was said in court that morning. She turned to face Hubbs, but he was already halfway to the stairs. She felt as though she were moving in a dream as she rose and followed Dennison past the benches to the back of the courtroom, briefly nodding without eye contact at the man who had instantly become her former father-in-law. It was only after they had emerged from the building, and after she was able to confirm that Hubbs wasn't waiting for her on the street, that she realized Dennison was speaking to her.

"I'm sorry, you said ..."

"The decree. He said it will be issued today, but I doubt Mr. Seavey will have written out a copy for you to have until Monday. In case you didn't notice, that was the Clerk's own divorce case that was heard immediately before yours. I imagine he'll devote the rest of the day to writing out his own decree before he turns his attention to yours. You're not in a hurry to leave town, are you?"

"I suppose not. My son is staying with my sister, and I told her I didn't know when I'd be back. But I can't possibly impose."

"Mrs. Dennison has already insisted you stay for the weekend. And you can't possibly be imposing," he added, with a grin, "since it ensures that Susan and I have a perfect excuse to turn down a dinner invitation to the home of our neighbors, the Hubbs."

"Thank you, that ..."

Flora burst into tears before she could complete the thought. The suddenness and intensity of her own sobs stunned and embarrassed her. The proceeding had gone well. It was behind her. But she was overcome with a mix of emotions. Relief more than sadness. Gratitude. And fear. Dennison stood awkwardly, offering nothing more than an uncomfortable smile that eased only as Flora regained control of her emotions.

"I'm sorry ... I don't know what came over me ..."

"It's perfectly understandable, I'm sure. To lose your marriage, your husband."

"Yes," she replied. "It is an overwhelming relief."

Dennison smiled in apparent confusion at Flora's response.

"Well, then, shall we return home for a light meal?"

Flora nodded and accompanied Dennison along the street, struggling to comprehend the idea that, with so little fanfare, and absent only James Seavey's initial attention to the drafting of his own divorce decree, she had just become a divorced woman.

\* \* \*

*Flora Hubbs*
*v.*
*Paul K. Hubbs, Jr.*
Decree

Held Sept. 14th, 1866
J. Seavey,
Clerk

This cause being called B.F. Dennison appeared as counsel for the Plaintiff, and S. Garfielde as counsel for the Defendant.

And the Plaintiff having produced proof in support of the Complaint, the Court finds therefrom that the facts alleged in the Complaint as grounds for a divorce are true.

Whereupon it is adjudged and decreed by the Court that the marriage existing between the Plaintiff and Defendant be and the same is hereby dissolved, and the parties forever released therefrom.

And it appearing from the evidence that the Plaintiff, Flora Hubbs, is a suitable and proper person to have the custody of the minor child named Paul Kinsey Hubbs, now about four years of age, it is further adjudged and decreed that the said Flora Hubbs have the future care, custody and education of said minor child until he shall have arrived at the age of majority upon this condition, however, that the defendant shall not be chargeable in any manner with the expense of maintaining and educating said minor child. And further that no alimony be allowed to Plaintiff, and that each party pay their own counsel fees and expense of this suit.

Territory of Washington
County of Jefferson
Filed September 14, 1866

\* \* \*

Francis Ross glanced up from his meager breakfast to see John Butts standing at the door of his and William's cell.

Butts' wrists and ankles were locked in fetters, and a guard stood immediately behind him. It wasn't a surprise. Francis and William had heard Butts work his way along the cells for ten minutes, making his final speeches of farewell to each of his fellow inmates.

"Francis, William, a small gift, a token of my affection for you both."

The chains rattled as Butts lifted his arms as much as the restraints would allow and handed each of the brothers a copy of the *Evening Telegraph*. Francis wondered if these copies, too, had been stolen.

"Don't make the mistakes John Charles Butt made. You boys are too young to be cast aside into the rubbish pit of society."

Francis braced himself for the speech, knowing that it could go on for some time. Butts might have been a frequent guest in the gaol alongside the brothers, but he'd rarely stayed long. The idea that he was calling them "boys" when he was barely a year older than Francis, and was telling two brothers facing five-year sentences to not follow his example, struck Francis as a thoroughly ludicrous farewell address. But then, ludicrous was what most of Victoria had come to expect from John Butts.

"When I was your age, William, back in California, I was tempted by the devil's brew. You bet your life. Tempted, but I kept to the straight and narrow. It's this town, it gripped my body, possessed my soul. My downfall. Nearly the death of John Butt. When you get out, if they send you away, it won't be a curse. It'll be a gracious blessing."

"So they're sending you back to Australia, John?" Francis asked.

"China," the guard behind him replied. "The other boat changed plans. Couldn't find another leavin' to Australia soon, so he's off to China."

Butts shrugged. "Maybe I can be a washee man among the Celestials, hmm? When you next hear of John Butt, I'll have carved out a new reputation in the land of pig-tails and chow chow." Butts grinned and turned to leave.

"John," William interjected, pushing past Francis. "Why

Butt? Your name is Butts. Why do you keep calling yourself Butt?"

Butts hesitated for a moment, purely for practiced comic timing. "Because as soon as I arrived here and got my job as the government's town crier, I realized the colony already had more butts than it needed."

Butts winked and then shuffled along the corridor, singing "God Save the Queen" at the top of his lungs.

\* \* \*

"Dr. Tolmie! Dr. Tolmie!" Flora pushed through the small crowd on the Port Townsend dock until she reached Tolmie, who was about to step aboard the *Eliza Anderson*.

"Flora. What a treat. How nice to see you."

"Are you finished with everything in Oregon?" she asked.

Flora had known from the papers and church gossip that Tolmie had spent much of the summer in Portland, at proceedings before a British and American Joint Commission to address the Company's monetary claims against the U.S. government for losses incurred during the Indian Wars of 1855 and 1856.

"An advantage of age and seniority is the ability to leave an underling in charge of a tedious affair," he replied with a smile.

"May I join you onboard?" Flora asked.

"I'd be deeply offended if you did anything else."

Tolmie gestured for Flora to precede him onto the boat. Flora chose a seat on the starboard side, as she usually did, to ensure the best views of her family's farm, but this time with the comfort of knowing that her divorce wouldn't endanger her ownership of the land. The starboard side also brought with it a more distant view of the Hubbs farm, and the entire southern shore of San Juan Island, though she imagined that she might be too deep in conversation to notice that portion of the journey's views.

Flora had travelled across the strait many times over the years on the *Eliza Anderson*, yet it still struck her as odd to travel on a boat named after a girl she'd known since childhood. She often wondered if Eliza ever looked upon her namesake with the same sense of silliness that Flora looked upon the "Floraville" moniker Hubbs had given to their farm. At least Flora didn't have to put up with hearing public comments about how her own namesake was slow, uncomfortable, rickety, expensive, and whatever other insults might be hurled at the *Eliza Anderson*.

Tolmie took his seat next to Flora. "I'm afraid I've been rather out of touch with matters at home for most of the summer, though not entirely ignorant. But I hesitate to ask your reason for being in Port Townsend ..."

"The hearing was Friday," Flora replied, realizing that she was smiling more than she should be for such a declaration. "And I am no longer a married woman."

Tolmie exhaled loudly, expressing the seriousness of such a proclamation. Several heads turned, having overheard either her announcement or simply Tolmie's reaction. She realized that he likely had no experience responding to an announcement of divorce, especially when made by a woman he'd known since she'd been an infant, and had counseled as she'd considered the prospect of a doomed marriage.

"I expect you're wondering," Flora continued, "if you should have expressed more doubt about him seven years ago."

"I was thinking no such thing. I had no idea he'd turn out to be the husband he was."

"But you didn't like him."

"There are a great many men I haven't liked when they were unmarried, who turned into reasonably tolerable men once they had wives to teach them a thing or two. He was on the other side of a serious conflict and I was concerned about you carrying the surname of the instigator of the whole affair. Victoria can be a rather cruel small town."

"I may be about to learn all over again just how cruel it can be when this boat arrives at the harbor with the divorced Mrs. Hubbs among its passengers."

"There will be some who will look upon you with

judgment, but many who don't have access to the courts of Washington Territory who'll look upon you with envy."

Flora laughed, immediately thinking of several marriages that she imagined were as unhappy as her own had been, but were without recourse under the colony's present laws.

"I realize you're not carrying out medical duties anymore," she began, "but just in case anyone should ask you, I'll be continuing my nursing work once I get back—after finishing the harvest, that is."

"That's very good to hear. And yes, your name will always be suggested for such work with the highest regard."

Flora smiled her thanks, pleased to have had the opportunity to plant the seed. She remembered the unwillingness Aleck Mcdonald had shown to the idea of hiring a nurse from the Songhees village, and she imagined that a divorced "Indian" woman might be looked upon with even greater uncertainty by much of Victoria.

"Well, no turning back now," Flora commented as the paddle wheels grumbled in their initial rotations, struggling to push the vessel from the dock to begin the journey across the strait. She sensed Tolmie watching her, measuring her emotions, but refused to let herself show whatever anxiety she'd revealed in five short words. Instead, she offered her old friend a smile, which sufficed only until she realized that its forced nature had simply confirmed any impression of anxiety that her words had only suggested.

\* \* \*

Flora stepped from the gangplank onto the wharf in Victoria harbor and allowed her anxieties to fade. It felt as every other arrival had felt. Home. Familiar ground.

"My goodness, what do we have here?" Tolmie exclaimed with a mixture of curiosity and concern as he stepped onto the wharf behind her.

Flora looked up to see a motley crowd approaching the docks, and her anxiety returned. It was difficult to tell if the few dozen people in the approaching crowd were angry or jubilant, although inebriated seemed to be a common description for most. It was also difficult to tell their destination, and for a moment Flora feared that they were heading toward the *Eliza Anderson*, determined to prevent the landing of a scandalously divorced Indian woman. She noticed several officers in uniform in the midst of the crowd—a few police constables, and what appeared to be guards from the city gaol—uniforms that Flora had come to recognize far too easily, thanks to her brothers. But she found it no less intimidating to realize that constables and gaolors were at the core of the approaching crowd.

"It's Butts." Tolmie was the first to see him. He was still in chains, weeping as he was led down to the docks by the gaol guards, along with two other prisoners similarly shackled. Across from the *Eliza Anderson* sat the sailing ship *Rodoma*, and it was toward the *Rodoma* that the guards were pushing Butts and the two others.

Flora turned to Tolmie. "It said in the papers last week that he'd been banished. Back to Australia, it said."

A dockworker securing the *Eliza Anderson* to the pier overheard Flora. "He's off to China, ma'am, all for pinchin' *Telegraph* newspapers. God help the Chinamen."

Flora watched the crowd that trailed behind the gaol guards. It was an odd mix. Some appeared as though they were there to pass sentence on Butts and whoever the other two unfortunate men were, caught up in a mob mentality of anger and judgment, while others were more jubilant and appeared to be following along for a last glimpse of an old friend. Butts seemed oblivious to it all, lost in tears that were either an act to ensure he was the center of attention, or legitimate because it would be his final opportunity to be the center of attention.

Flora and Tolmie watched as the guards led Butts and the two other prisoners onboard the *Rodoma* and removed their chains. Butts immediately stopped crying, stood as tall as his burly frame would allow, and looked out at the crowd.

"My friends, I have only one final question for you all. Why am I like a message sent through the Atlantic Cable?" Even as he asked the question, it was obvious to the onlookers that it was a set-up for a punch line that he had been planning for days. Several in the crowd turned away, uninterested in furthering his self-glorification in the midst of his moment of exile.

"Because I am dispatched across the ocean by the *Telegraph*."

Flora was one of the few people at the wharf who laughed at his farewell pronouncement. She had always felt a mild admiration for Butts' sense of humor in the face of adversity, even if the adversity he'd faced in his life had been predominantly a factor of his inability to resist opportunities for petty theft. As much as she wished for her brothers to avoid a similar life of transgression, she would have considered it an improvement in their lot if they could adopt the odd humor that Butts had shown about his own misadventures.

None of Butts' crimes had been remarkably serious. Stolen geese. Stolen newspapers. Stolen whiskey. The sodomy charge had been defeated at trial, even though the act it suggested was hardly unexpected to anyone who knew Butts. And many of his crimes had seemed committed solely to secure a period of rest and regular meals in the town's gaol, or, when he feigned paralysis, in the Royal Hospital. And for that, he'd been banished across the ocean. Perhaps it was a fate that would someday await her youngest brothers, each having already experienced a period of temporary exile.

"I'll be getting a carriage back to the farm. May I drop you at the Wren residence?" Tolmie inquired.

"Thank you, that's very kind." Flora smiled. She recognized the imposition it might cause to have Tolmie drop her at the residence of his former legal adversary, but appreciated the ride nonetheless. She picked up her bag, then turned for a final look at the *Rodoma*. Butts was being led along the deck, but he paused and turned in Flora's direction as if he felt her gaze. Their eyes met for a brief moment, and he smiled. They hadn't shared many conversations of great length over the years. When she'd been younger and he'd first arrived in the colony, she'd been intimidated by his garrulous personality, but had been fascinated by his stories of acting on the San Francisco stage, or his role in the McGowan trial—even if his stories were highly embellished by his own imagination. In more recent years, since her marriage to Hubbs, and since Butts' departure from the Christ Church congregation, she'd had few opportunities to speak to him.

His smile lasted only a few seconds, and then he was pushed toward the stairs to the deck below. Flora instantly feared that she hadn't smiled in return, but that her expression had shown only surprise rather a fond farewell.

Tolmie stopped, sensing Flora's hesitation to follow.

"Is everything all right?"

"John Butts. He smiled at me."

"I imagine he smiles at anyone who'll afford him the slightest amount of attention."

"It was more than that. It was ..." Flora decided it was best to refrain from completing the thought, certain she'd only make a fool of herself if she expressed the feeling that Butts had smiled out of recognition. Not so much recognition of someone he knew in passing, but recognition for a kindred spirit. A changing of the guard. Welcoming her back to a community that was exiling him at the very moment when she was poised to provide the gossipmongers with new fodder.

"Yes, I'm sure that's all it was," she replied, wishing she believed her own words.

Flora looked back for one more glance at the *Rodoma*, then turned and followed Tolmie along the pier.

# Chapter 22

NO NEWS. — Owing to the storm on Thursday, we are still without any telegraphic intelligence. A perfect hurricane, the operators say, prevailed on San Juan and Lopez Islands, and the line was prostrated in many places by falling trees of the largest size. The wires were repaired last evening to Fidalgo Island.

*The Daily British Colonist and Victoria Chronicle*, Saturday, November 17, 1866, p. 3.

\* \* \*

The bright sunlight that shone through the bedroom window came as a surprise. Flora had fallen asleep well after midnight, holding young Paul in her arms to calm his fears, while a powerful storm had howled across the fields and whistled through every crack in the walls for the third night in a row. She couldn't see the damage that had happened during the night, but she had heard the evidence. Snapping trees. Bellowing livestock. Branches and barn shingles hitting the house. And a wind that howled as fiercely as any she'd ever heard.

Flora jostled Paul. "Good morning, sunshine. Look. Storm's gone."

"Where'd it go?"

"Well, I suppose it blew over to the mainland."

"Why?"

"Because storms like to spread themselves out like that. Much more fun to cause destruction across the whole region, not just on one little island."

"Why?"

"Well, perhaps you should ask a storm next time we have one. Let's go see what happened outside."

Flora climbed from the bed, still dressed from the day before. She hardly looked her best having slept in her clothes. But there was little chance anyone would see her at their remote farm that morning, unless the telegraph repairmen were already in the area to fix the inevitable breaks in the line.

"Come on, we'll eat after we have a look around."

Flora entered the front parlor, relieved to see that all of the windows were intact, then opened the front door and walked outside with Paul trailing behind her, still half asleep. The air was brisk and fresh, and the sunlight shone across the fields with the low angle and amber hue of a late fall morning.

Debris littered the fields. Livestock had broken free and congregated by a depression that was a pond for the wetter months of the year, more interested in the chance for a drink than the potential to make a break for lasting freedom. The small orchard that had struggled to produce edible fruit ever since she and Hubbs had planted it in the first years of their marriage was nearly decimated. The two apple trees that Hubbs had brought with him on the day he'd proposed were both toppled at their base.

Flora thought of the privy, out of both need and concern, and looked over to see that it had been reduced to a pile of driftwood. The privacy of a bush would have to do.

The telegraph line was down north of the house, where

a thick branch had fallen. At least it was a visible break. Disruptions caused by breaks in the line under the channel to Lopez Island had become so common that a worker from the State Telegraph Company had informed her a few days earlier that the company would establish a cabin to house a lineworker across the channel, solely to address line failures with greater speed. It made her wonder if the Hubbs farm carried a curse that interfered with all forms of communication, whether across continents or within marriages.

"You survived."

Flora recognized Lucinda's booming voice in an instant, but was surprised to hear it all the same. She turned and saw Lucinda arriving on horseback from the narrow trail that snaked along the north side of the hill, through damp forest.

"Nothing that can't be fixed. Are you all fine?"

"We're more sheltered than you are here. Stephen can clean up what little needs to be done. I was more worried about you."

Flora pushed back an urge to cry. She would miss Lucinda and her mentorship, but most of all her friendship. She still had many old friends in Victoria, and would have the support of friends and family. But Lucinda's own brand was special, and Flora found herself feeling anger toward Hubbs for ruining so much more than her marriage.

"I could use some help getting everyone back into the barn."

"That shouldn't take too long. Then we can start on the rest of this mess."

"No need for that. Alexander should be done with harvest back home. I expect him any day to help us move back." She looked around at the debris strewn across the fields. The fallen trees. The shingles from the barn's roof.

"This is my former husband's mess to clean up."

\* \* \*

Reverend Cridge added up the advance subscriptions received for the hospital's fundraising efforts and entered

448

the total at the bottom of the column. It was still insufficient for their needs, and he wondered if there would ever be enough funding to operate the hospital free from the shadow of imminent closure. The town's new Amateur Dramatic Club had just voted that their first entertainment would be for the benefit of the hospital. It was a kind gesture, but unlikely to provide much assistance, and would be yet another fundraising venture that would force Cridge to accept funds from an undertaking of questionable moral propriety. He hoped the official ceremony the following day to solemnize the union of the Colonies of Vancouver Island and British Columbia would present opportunities to lobby legislators for additional funds, whether from government or their own generous pockets. But the mere thought of using the ceremonies for such a task exhausted him.

"Good night, father."

Cridge looked up from his papers to see Richard, now ten, dressed in his pajamas. Cridge suppressed the worries that had wrinkled his brow, and then offered a smile for his son before tousling his hair and wishing him a good night of sleep. Mary Cridge waited at the foot of the stairs until she heard the bedroom door close, then approached her husband.

"You're not going to find more money on the page just because you add up the numbers another three or four times," she said. "That's not how fundraising works. I should know."

Mary Cridge had been one of the primary supporters of the town's Female Infirmary, the women's modest equivalent to the Royal Hospital, and had shared as many troubles raising the needed funds for that institution as her husband was facing for his own. She had understood before she'd agreed to marry Cridge in 1854, and follow him to the rugged colony, that hers would be a life dedicated to helping others. But much like her husband, she had never conceived how much of her time would be spent raising money to pay for that help.

"We can only do as much as we can do," Cridge replied. "Is she asleep?"

Mary nodded. Rhoda had enjoyed several weeks of reasonably good health and had fallen asleep in her crib easily that night. Cridge reached for his wife's hand. They had shared so much loss and hardship over the previous two years, but their marriage had survived the pain, bringing them closer to one another, and closer to their surviving children. It was a closeness that had allowed Cridge to recover from the spiritual crisis he had felt earlier in the year and accept the strength that can come after moments of helplessness.

Mary placed his hand on her belly. It took Cridge a moment to understand, and he immediately felt, again, the terrifying mix of emotions of a parent who has experienced the loss of a child—of four of them—and must face the prospect of bringing another into the world. But it took only a moment for the conflicting emotions to sift themselves into order. He rose and kissed his wife.

\* \* \*

The ships of war fired a salute on the occasion—a funeral procession, with minute guns, would have been more appropriate to the sad melancholy event.

Inscription of Sir James Douglas, Former Governor of the separate colonies of Vancouver Island and British Columbia, in the diary of his daughter, Martha, remarking on the proclamation of union of the colonies.

\* \* \*

"Sweetie, come here for a moment. Sit with me." Flora took Paul's hand and guided him to a chair by the fire, then knelt on the floor in front of him. The decision she had made in the night seemed extreme, particularly in the light of day, and yet it resolved so many issues. A fresh start must be exactly that—fresh.

"This might be difficult to understand," she began, "but it's good news. Remember how I told you we're going to go live with Granny at the farm? And you'll see all your cousins more often?"

Paul nodded. Flora smiled, relieved that he had remembered that much.

"And, you know how sometimes, instead of calling you Paul, I call you sweetie or honey?"

He nodded again.

"Well, there's going to be a new name. I'm still going to call you sweetie and honey. But from now on, instead of calling you Paul, you're going to go by the name Charles."

It took him several seconds of reflection to come up with his simple and frequent response. "Why?"

"Because Charles was the name of your grandfather— my father. And he was a great man, and if you carry his name with you in life, then maybe you can be a great man like him, too. Charles Ross."

She wanted to make it easier for him to understand by explaining that she was trying to help him avoid the constant reminder that he was the son of a man whose name would be a burden in the British colony. A man he might barely remember in a few years' time. And a man who wanted nothing more to do with his son. The Hubbs and Ross names each carried their own history of scandal or judgment in the eyes of many Victoria residents, but the Ross name also carried advantages, as she'd learned from the many second chances her brothers had been given to reform.

"Or some people might call you Charlie, too."

"Like Walter's daddy?"

"Yes, just like Uncle Charlie in Victoria, and like Uncle Charlie at Nisqually. I know it might seem a little confusing at first, but it's part of our new life in Victoria. Charles Ross. Do you like the sound of that?"

He hesitated, then nodded. Flora wasn't sure if he was nodding because he liked the name, or because he could tell that she was hoping he'd nod.

"So, you're going to be Charles Ross from now on, and people will call me Mrs. Ross, not Mrs. Hubbs. We both